Praise for Whitley Strieber and

THE LAST VAMPIRE

"Whitley Strieber has done more than recapture the magic that made him a modern master of horror literature—he has surpassed himself. This is a wonderfully imaginative book, one that defies the reader to put it down."

—Peter Straub

"With a sensual ascent to an erotic crescendo, this vigorous sequel restores the vampire's power and mystique. Strieber's luxuriously soulless realm of the undead is disturbingly plausible."

—Katherine Ramsland

"Bloodkisses *supreme*. A deliriously meaty cultural anthropology, sickening and delicious."

—*Kirkus Reviews* (starred review)

"Offers a tour de force of mythmaking and emotionally intense action. . . . There's much here to admire, not least Strieber's expert modulation of tone and dialogue."

—*Publishers Weekly*

THE HUNGER

"Vivid, skillfully written."

—*The Washington Post*

"Fast paced . . . intriguing."

—*Publishers Weekly*

"Read this one with all the lights on."

—*Hudson Sun* (MA)

Also by Whitley Strieber

The Last Vampire

Whitley Strieber

POCKET STAR BOOKS

New York London Toronto Sydney Singapore

This book is a work of fiction. Names, characters, places and incidents are products of the author's imagination or are used fictitiously. Any resemblance to actual events or locales or persons living or dead is entirely coincidental.

 A Pocket Star Book published by
POCKET BOOKS, a division of Simon & Schuster, Inc.
1230 Avenue of the Americas, New York, NY 10020

Copyright © 2001 by Whitley Strieber

Originally published in hardcover in 2001 by Pocket Books

ISBN 13: 978-1-439-17329-9
ISBN 10: 1-439-17329-X

First Pocket Books paperback printing October 2002

10   9   8   7   6   5   4   3   2   1

POCKET STAR BOOKS and colophon are registered trademarks
of Simon & Schuster, Inc.

For information regarding special discounts for bulk purchases,
please contact Simon & Schuster Special Sales at 1-800-456-6798 or
business@simonandschuster.com

Cover art by Tom Hallman

Printed in the U.S.A.

To Michael Talbot,
of sacred memory,
author of
The Delicate Dependency and
The Holographic Universe

Acknowledgments

I would like to acknowledge the help of my editor, Mitchell Ivers; my agent, Sandra Martin; and my wife, Anne Strieber; all of whom have made essential contributions to the creation of this book.

And what rough beast, its hour come round at last,
Slouches toward Bethlehem to be born?

—*The Second Coming*, William Butler Yeats

"I am part of the justice of the earth."

—Miriam Blaylock, *The Hunger*

ONE

The Conclave

Everyone knew the sins of Miriam Blaylock.

Her crime, and it was an unforgivable one, was to enjoy human beings as friends and lovers, rather than to simply exploit them. She could kiss them and find it sweet, have sex with them and afterward sleep like a contented tiger. To her own kind, this was perversion, like a man with a sheep.

The fact that this prejudice was nonsense did not make what she was doing now any easier. She pressed herself back against the seat of the pedicab, instinctively keeping her face hidden, not only from man, but from her own kind. The *samlor* moved swiftly down the wet street, spattering through puddles left by the last storm. From the shadows of the passenger compartment, she watched a concealing fog rising from the moat that surrounded the ancient Thai city of Chiang Mai.

How could she ever do this impossible thing? How could she ever face her own kind?

Some theorized that she must have human blood in her family. The idea that there could be interbreeding was absurd, of course—nothing but an old husband's tale. She despised the narrowness of her kind, hated what, in recent centuries, their lives had become. They had once been princes, but now they lived behind walls, kept to the shadows, appeared in the human world only to hunt. They had opted out of man's technological society. They knew human breeding, but human technology was simply too intimidating for them.

Miriam owned a thriving nightclub in New York and had bookkeepers and assistants and bartenders, all humans. She had computers to run her accounts. She could access her stock portfolios using her PalmPilot, and she made money on the markets, plenty of it. She had a cell phone and GPS in her car. *They* didn't even have cars. Once the buggy no longer bounced along behind the horse, they had simply stopped riding. The same with sails. When ships lost their sails, her kind stopped traveling the world. And airplanes—well, some of them probably weren't yet aware that they existed.

The other rulers of the world were now just shadows hiding in dens, their numbers slowly declining due to accidents. They called themselves the Keepers, but what did that mean nowadays? Gone was the time when they were the secret masters of humankind, keeping man as man keeps cattle.

Truth be told, the Keepers were in general decline, but they were far too proud to realize it. Conclaves were held every hundred years, and at the last ones Miriam had seen a change—Keepers she had known a thousand years had followed her mother and father into death. Nobody had brought a child, nobody had courted.

Despite their failure, Miriam valued her kind. She valued herself. The Keepers were essential to the justice and meaning of the world. That was why she had come here, why she had tempted the humiliation and even the possible danger involved: she wanted to continue her species. Miriam wanted a baby.

The last of the four eggs that nature gave a Keeper woman would soon leave her body unless she found a man to fertilize it. For all that she had—riches, honor, power, and beauty—her essential meaning was unfulfilled without a baby. She was here for her last-chance child.

She gazed across the gleaming back of the *samlor* driver at the busy night streets of the bustling little city. How the world was changing. She had chosen a *samlor* out of love for the past, which she most certainly shared with the rest of her kind. She remembered Chiang Mai as a small community of wooden houses with *theps* carved on the pediments of their soaring, peaked roofs, and golden temple spires rising above lush stands of trees. Now, the narrow old streets resounded with the shrill clatter of *tuk-tuks*, which were so rapidly replacing the pedal-driven *samlor*. The traffic wasn't quite yet the hell on earth of Bangkok, but it was certainly going in that direction.

She longed to be home, in her beautiful house, surrounded by her beloved people, faithful Sarah and sweet young Leonore, just now learning her ways.

Just like the black, miserable dens of the other Keepers, her house was full of beautiful things. But hers were treasures of the heart, not the jade and silver and gold pieces her peers collected with total indifference, selling them later just because they'd become "antiques" among the humans. They didn't enjoy their priceless jade Buddhas or their Rembrandt drawings or their Egyptian gold. They just used them. She had a gold Buddha a thousand years old, before which she meditated, and twin Rembrandts of herself and her beloved mother. He had captured the sure gleam of their essence, she thought. She gazed often at her mother's wide, almost innocent eyes, at the subtle humor in her lips.

Over the millennia, Miriam had lost both parents and her husband. Her keepsakes of them were at the center of her life.

Rembrandt had known that there was something unusual about the two women who had commissioned him, a sense of independence and self-possession that human women in those days did not have. He had captured it in the proud, yet easy stance of the figures he had drawn, humming to himself as he made tiny pen strokes and smoked a long clay pipe. He had kissed Miriam's hand and said, "You are cold . . . so cold."

Not only did she enjoy human beings, she took pleasure in human things—painting and sculpture, writing and music. She had been an opera buff from the beginning of the genre. She had been at the opening night of a dozen great operas, had been transported by everyone from Adelina Patti to Maria Callas to Kiri Te Kanawa. She remembered the haunting voices of the *castrati* echoing in the palaces of the Old World.

The other Keepers looked upon humans as animals. Miriam thought that they had souls, that you could feel something leaving their bodies just as they died. It happened while you were all curled up around them, while you were comfortably absorbing their life. A sort of electric charge would seem to come out of them. Only after that would their eyes be totally empty.

They said it was the nervous system shorting out because of the fluid loss. Miriam hoped so. But what if the reality was that men had the souls, not us? If we were the brilliant animals, they the dim angels? That would be an irony, that an animal had created an angel.

When she meditated before her Buddha, she asked these questions: Why do we live so long? Is it because we have been denied a soul? If so, could I trade? And why, O God, if you are there, why are we cold . . . so cold?

The rest of her kind lived to eat. She ate to live. She spent heavily, just as her family always had. She consumed money without thought, like so much candy or caviar. Her club, the Veils, was the most exclusive in New York. In a strong month, and most of its months were very strong, drugs and liquor would bring in a half-million-dollar profit. There was no cover charge, of course. If you were important enough to enter the Veils at all, you certainly weren't the sort of person who would be expected to pay a cover.

Miriam had been the friend of kings for two thousand years. She had seen their generations rise and fall. She loved them in their pride and momentary lives. She loved their finest things, the jewels and whispering silks, the attention paid to the very rich.

When the wallets of her peers opened, you could practically hear creaking. She had fun; they had their careful customs and their dreary, conservative habits. She wanted meaning from life, they wanted only to keep breathing.

But now, for all their rejecting ways, she needed them. Her plan was to travel to all of the current conclaves, at once charming and, hopefully, seducing a man.

Deep in memory's mist, she'd had a baby. She still remembered the moment of conception as if it were yesterday. For women of her kind, conception was the most exquisite pleasure they could know. At the moment a man's semen fertilized one of your eggs, your whole body reacted with an unforgettable explosion of nerve-tingling delight. Even after all this time, part of her being remained focused on that stunning moment.

They always knew the sex of the baby within them, and she and Eumenes named their boy and fell in love with him from that first, joy-filled night. Then had come the pregnancy, a year of gestation . . . and the pain and the loss she'd felt as the silent, blue form of her dead infant was laid on her belly. Soon after, her beloved husband also died. Practically nothing could kill them—they never got sick, they couldn't. But he had weakened and wasted, and no one knew why. All her love, all her care, was not enough to save her dear Eumenes, not after he stopped eating.

He had grown as narrow and cold as a mummy, but his eyes had continued to glow . . . as if death had some special meaning, as if hunger had become for him a state of transcendence. She had begged him to eat, had tempted him, had tried, at the last, to force her own blood into his veins.

Was it grief that had killed him, or some greater despair? Like her, he respected the mind of man. Like her, he was unsure about whether or not humankind had ascended to a point that made it evil to prey on them.

Was it evil to be a Keeper? Was taking conscious prey murder? She thought that her husband had starved himself over these questions . . . and over the blue, hopeless baby he had so gently deposited upon her breast.

The dead may die to the world, but they do not die in the heart. Miriam's side of their love affair had continued on for whole cycles of years. But eventually his memory faded like the encaustic of his face that she'd had painted by Eratosthenes, that hurried little genius, in Alexandria.

Old Alexandria . . . redolent with the scents of myrrh and cardamom, whispering by night, singing by day. She remembered Cleopatra's hollow palace, and the Academia with its great library. She read all 123 of Sophocles' plays there, and she saw thirty of them performed. How many had survived? Seven, she thought, only seven.

Over all the intervening years, she had not been able to

find a man of her own kind to replace Eumenes. Part of the reason was that conclaves only happened once in a hundred years, and *they* did not court except during conclave. For somebody who lived for the moment, that kind of planning just did not work.

Now she was at the end of her choices. Either she would find someone or she would never, ever give another Keeper to the world.

Keeper children learned in school that humans were bred to appear similar to us on the surface so that Keepers could go among them more freely. In the beginning, they did not look at all similar and were not at all smart. They were little apes with lots of hair and huge teeth. We Keepers have always been as we are, beautiful beyond compare.

Miriam had drifted into the habit of taking human lovers because she was lonely and they were satisfying and the emotional commitment was not great. You found a cute male or a sweet, sensual female—the sex mattered not to Miriam, both had their charms—and you seduced, softly, gently, with the caressing eye and the slow hand. Then you put them to sleep with hypnosis and opened their veins and filled them full of your blood, and magic happened: They stayed young for years and years. You told them you'd made them immortal, and they followed you like foolish little puppies. Like the dear creature who now kept her home and business in New York, who warmed her bed and hunted with her . . . the dear creature, so lovely and brilliant and torn by her silly human conflicts. She had almost lost Sarah a few years ago, but had brought her back. The girl should be grateful and compliant, but that was not always the case. Sarah made mistakes. Sarah lived much too dangerously. She was haunted by what she had endured, and Miriam could not blame her. Indeed, she could hardly imagine what it would be like to lie in a coffin like that, slowly deteriorating but unable to die.

Sarah knew that one day the torment would certainly come again. She strove to save herself, using all of her considerable knowledge of medicine to attempt to defeat the process of aging that must slowly consume her, despite the fact that Miriam's blood now flowed in her veins.

To live, Sarah had to prey on man. She was even more tormented by this than Miriam's other lovers had been. Her Hippocratic oath haunted her, poor creature.

Miriam stopped herself. Best not go down that path again. She was always troubled by the tormented lives and horrible deaths of her lovers. The delicious little things were her guilt, her pain.

But not now, not on this nervous, excited night, the opening night of the Asian conclave. At least a proper lover would never die as the human ones did, pleading for deliverance even as their flesh became dust. But she would have to submit to him, obey him, live in his cold cell . . . at least, for a time.

Her body was her life—its rich senses, its wild desires, the way it felt when strong hands or sweet hands traveled her shivery skin.

There would be none of that in her future, not when she was part of one of *their* households, as she would be expected to be, at least for the duration of her pregnancy. Long, silent days, careful, creeping nights—that would be her life behind the walls of their world.

But that was how it had to be. She could almost feel that little body in her belly, could imagine hugging it after it came out, while it was still flushed and coal-hot. Only a newborn or a freshly fed Keeper was ever that warm.

The *samlor* glided along Moon Muang Road, heading for the Tapae Gate and the temple district beyond, moving through the murky, soaked night. How did the Asians stand this wretched climate? And yet, the heat was also nice. She enjoyed sweaty beds and long, druggy nights doing every decadent thing she could imagine.

The others shunned drugs. *They* said that they would rather die than become addicted for the thousands of years of their lives. She hadn't had that experience at all. Your blood protected you from all disease and weakness. *They* were just prejudiced against drugs, which were a human pleasure and therefore assumed to be trivial. But they had never done hash in ginger-scented Tangiers, or opium here in pillow-soft Chiang Mai, the last place in Asia where a good pipe of well-aged opium could be found. They had never smoked lying on silk beneath a hypnotic fan. When the nights were hot and the air was still, she was drawn back to the brilliant oblivion of the pipe. Drugs were less dangerous to enjoy here than in the States. No blustery, narrow-eyed policemen were apt to show up, waving guns and yelling. She'd had to race up too many walls to escape from those annoying creatures.

Well, all that was going to change. She was going to become a proper wife, and she certainly didn't need drugs for that. She wasn't addicted, so it wouldn't be a problem.

She could imagine her man, tall and silent, his face narrow, his skin as pale as a shadow. She could feel him, muscles like mean springs, long, curving fingers that could crush a human's bones or caress her plump breasts. She took a deep breath. These thoughts made her feel as if she were drowning and being rescued at the same time.

The wind rose, sweeping through the dark trees, sending

ripples shivering across the puddles that were like lakes in the street. Much lower now, the clouds raced and tumbled. Voices rose from a little market, two girls singing some popular song, oblivious to the *samlor* that whispered past and to the being within, who was carefully listening to the patter of their heartbeats from a thousand feet away.

Her interest in them told her that the hunger was rising within her. She felt it now, a faint gnawing in her belly, a hint of ice in her veins.

This was bad news. Most of her kind could detect their hunger coming for days, and they could prepare carefully to do a hunt. She'd never been able to prepare. One second she was fine, the next it was starting.

Buddha said it was good to live in the moment. In the Vedas, she'd read that there was only the moment. Her species had no holy books, just records of their possessions. Her mother had told her, "Humans have holy books because they've journeyed closer to God than we have."

She noticed that the smell of the *samlor* driver was washing over her, blown back by the breeze. She took a deep drag on her strong Thai cigarette, attempting to blot out the delicious scent.

It did not work. Okay, she thought, I'll go with it. She looked at the driver's sweating back. A thirty-second struggle and she'd be fed for another couple of weeks. The thing was, the hotel had written down her destination in Thai for him. He would not deviate from the route. She needed to get him to go down some darker side street. "Speak English?"

He did not respond. So she'd have to jump him right out here if she wanted him, and that would never do. You did your kills in private, and you destroyed all trace of the corpse. Even Miriam Blaylock followed those two essential rules.

The driver's skin rippled, his muscles surged. Mentally, she stripped him of his black shorts and T-shirt. She imagined laying him down upon a wonderful big bed, his penis like a cute little tree branch. She would kiss him all over and hold him closer and tighter, filling her mouth with his salt sweat and her nose with his every intimate smell. Her mouth would anesthetize his skin as the feeding began and in a few delightful moments, his blood would be sweeping down her throat.

She closed her eyes, arching her back and stretching, forcing his smell out of her nose with a rush of air. Think about opium, she told herself, not blood. Later, she would smoke to relieve this damned hunger. She needed to get back to familiar territory before she fed. It wasn't safe to do it in an unknown place.

Too bad her flight to Paris, where the European conclave was held, didn't leave until tomorrow evening.

This Asian conclave would end with dawn, and she'd have liked to have gone straight on to Europe. She could feed easily in Paris; she knew the city well. She'd hunted there recently—no more than fifty or so years ago, when it was swarming with Germans.

Of course, she might meet a man here in Chiang Mai. If she did, her new husband would attend to her need for prey during the pregnancy. If she wasn't leaving tomorrow, she'd be staying in Asia a long time.

If she was still alone after this conclave, she'd make her way along Samian Road, then cut into the welter of little streets that concealed a hole-in-the-wall she'd discovered called the Moonlight Bar. Down in the cellar a tiny old woman waited with pipes. Once, there had been thousands of opium dens in Asia. Now only Chiang Mai was left, with two or three small establishments.

At home, she kept her two-hundred-year-old opium in clay pots sealed with beeswax. Her ancient pipes delivered the vapor cool and easy, and Sarah was beautifully trained in the art of preparation and lighting.

She gazed up at the racing moon, thought of New York. It was about noon at home, so the cleaning crew would be at work in the club. Sarah and Leo would be asleep at home, probably in one another's arms . . . probably in Miriam's own bed, a curtained, canopied heaven made for Nellie Salter, cane-mistress to Sir Francis Bacon, and William Shakespeare's Dark Lady. She'd drunk too much before she died, had Nellie. She'd made Miriam positively giddy.

Maybe the thing to do would be to convince her husband to come back with her. Or, if that proved to be impossible, maybe she would break even that taboo, and bear the child without a male's protection.

Suddenly, a positively sumptuous girl appeared on the sidewalk, her features carved as if by a master, her skin as soft as mist.

"Speak English?" Miriam called to her. No answer. "*Parlez-vous français?*"

The girl hurried off, disappearing into a doorway. Miriam knew that she appeared enormous and intimidating to these people, an improbable apparition with ash-gray eyes and improbably elegant clothes.

Chanel sent her a *couturier* and staff each year, and she bought a new ensemble. Still, she was told it was all much too conservative.

It was true enough that her kind had trouble with fashion. Fifty years would pass in a blink, and suddenly you would find yourself wearing the last bustle in the world or the last top hat. That's why the few even slightly accurate stories about them so often portrayed them in antique clothes. Bram Stoker, she thought, must have known a little something about the real thing. How else could he have known to portray his Dracula as such a stodgy dresser?

An odor struck Miriam with the force of a slap. Involuntarily, she hissed. The driver's head snapped around, his eyes wide and white. The scent of human blood had invaded her nostrils, raw and still very much alive. Then she saw why: there was an accident ahead.

A powerful instinct urged her to leap out of the cab and suck the bodies dry while the life force was still there to consume. But this was another instinct that had to be stifled.

As they passed the site, she held her breath. She could not trust herself with the scent of raw blood, not when the hunger was spreading through her body. Her skin was already cooling, making her feel heavy and slow. She'd be as pale as ashes when she got to the conclave. They'd all think, *Look at her, she can't even feed herself.*

The moon burst out from behind furious clouds. Lightning flickered on the spire of Wat Chedi Luang. The temple spires here in Chiang Mai were so lovely and exotic. She was used to the canyons of Manhattan.

Again the smell of the driver reached her nostrils. This time her body started to prepare to eat, her muscles growing tight for the assault, her mouth swimming in the mucus that would anesthetize her prey.

She took a long, last drag on the cigarette. If you pulled their blood into your gut with sufficient strength, your feed ended with delicious dregs.

"Be sure and get the organ juice, dear," her mother would admonish her. "It makes for strong bones."

Mother Lamia was hard to remember and hard to forget.

When Miriam needed to fall out of love with a human, she would use her memory of what humans had done to her mother to help her along. It had come as a great surprise, the capture. When Keepers slept, their bodies reached a state near death. They were entirely helpless. So sleep was carried out in deep hiding, or—in those days—in great and protected palaces.

A man they had thought a friend had betrayed Lamia. He had been a faithful partner at cards, had been the Graf von Holbein. But it evolved that he was not a petty count but a powerful priest, and his name was not Holbein but Muenster, Father Deitrich Muenster.

Miriam had escaped across the roofs of the little town where they were living. She had not been able to take her comatose mother, nor to hide her. Miriam had expected to remove her from their prison either by bribery or by brute force.

But they had not tried her. They had not even imprisoned her. They had wasted no time. Mother Lamia had awakened already chained to her stake. She realized instantly what was happening. But all of her struggles and strength did not break the chains or topple the stake.

Mother Lamia had stood proud on the pyre they had made for her, her hair flaring sparks into the night. She had stood there for a long, long time, because Keepers could only die when their blood stopped completely.

They had laughed when she screamed, and when they realized that she was dying so unusually slowly, they were even more delighted. Mother had been burned for a witch in 1761, in a village near Dresden. She had been the most alive, the best person Miriam had ever known. She had a fabulous sense of humor. She loved to have adventures, and she loved to dance.

Mother introduced Miriam to music—sackbuts, violas . . . her beloved viola da gamba. Miriam had been taught to sing, to read and speak many human languages, so many that she'd lost count. The languages of the ancient world had been works of art, Sumerian and Egyptian and Zolor, among many others. They had been supplanted by Greek, with its sublime verbs, and Latin, which was too rigidly constructed—somehow crude. English was a practical tongue. Of the modern languages, Miriam thought that French and Mandarin Chinese stood out as being the most satisfying to speak.

Unfortunately, she had never learned Thai, so she was at a disadvantage here. "Will you hurry, you stupid creature," she growled at the driver in English. He sped up. Her tone needed no common language to make itself understood.

The spires of the temple district rose all around her now. The district bore an ancient enchantment, for it was sacred to her kind, too. Here in the deep eons they had met, ten thousand years ago, fifteen thousand . . . when the world had been their toy and man a mute race of cattle. Look at the pavements left by her kind, still perfect after all this time. Look at the foundations of Wat Phra Singh and Wat Chedi Chet Yot—no human engineer could fashion such precision in stone. Stars curse what had happened among her kind, to make them vagrants in their own world. Give me opium, let me smoke. Let me forget.

She touched the golden key that lay at the bottom of her new purse, the key that would let her into the sanctum in the cellar of the Moonlight Bar. The purse was a Gucci bought at the local night market for 2500 baht. It was a luxurious item and finely made. She didn't need another purse, but she loved to shop and she'd been unable to resist. Every Keeper loved exquisite leather, and calfskin was deliciously close to human . . . which was *very* taboo to wear outside the home. The prey might notice something—the remains of a tattoo or a human birthmark on your gloves or your pocketbook. Personally, she never wore leather from human skin. They might be prey, but they were sensitive, conscious beings and that had to be respected. But their skins tanned *très* softly, the flay off a smooth back or buttock.

The *samlor* driver hunched forward as if some deep instinct was drawing him away from her. The thought again crossed her mind to just jump him. She'd ride him like a little bullock. He would shriek and buck, and it would be a thrill.

His living scent stung the flower-sweet air. Then he turned the *samlor*, going down a narrow street. It was little more than a passageway, very quiet.

She shoved another cigarette into her mouth and lit it. Closer they came to the ancient temple of Wat Chiang Man, the *chedi* within it buttressed to the four corners of the world by four gilded elephants.

The *samlor* stopped. Beneath the *chedi*, in a cellar no human being had ever entered, was the ancient *ho trai* of the Asian clans, a place founded before Siddhārtha was Buddha, indeed before Siddhārtha was born. "Stay," Miriam said. "Wait."

An eye took her in. The slightest of nods. She knew that this temple had a reputation among the ghost-conscious Thai. He sat with his head bowed and his feet clicking his pedals.

Her heels clattering on the wet paving stones, she crossed the short distance to the temple, then entered the *chedi*. Here, it was suddenly quiet. There was a scent of sandalwood and smoke from the single guttering lantern that hung from a rafter, shining on the great Buddha that reclined in the center of the ornate chamber.

She paid respect to the Buddha, drawing her hands together and bowing. Had any of her peers seen her, they would have scorned her utterly.

She ran her fingers along the cunning mortise work, then tapped softly three times, causing the concealed mechanism to give way with a soft click. It was a little surprising, the way the mechanism felt. It was almost as if the lock were sprung. She thought she might have been able to open it just with a push. You'd never find this kind of carelessness in Europe or America.

She went down the steep, curving steps. She didn't need illumination, of course. Theirs was a nocturnal species . . . miserably enough in this electric era. How her father had moped when the humans had discovered electricity. "We should have kept it from them," he'd said.

Keeper men and women did not live together except during pregnancy and, to some extent, child-rearing. But the love between them could be great, and he had never recovered from the loss of his Lamia. "I find myself searching the world for her," he would say. He'd persisted in doing dangerous things—climbing mountains, dueling, and traveling, endlessly traveling. It was death he sought, when he sought the far hills.

Her father had died in the explosion of the Hindenburg in 1937—taken like his Lamia by fire. He saved human beings from the flames, and those he helped can be seen in the newsreel film scrambling from the windows as the ship descends. He comes out last, and his form disappears in the fire.

Over and over and over again, she watched that film,

longing for one more rolling murmur of his voice, one more touch from his kindly hand.

She stopped on the fourth step. There was sound down below, definitely. Good, the conclave was in session. For most of the Keepers down there, this would be the first contact in a century with any of their own kind. Lovers met in sweet battle, and mothers lived with their children. But for the most part, they were a species as solitary as the spider.

A little farther along, she stopped again. Something she was hearing below did not seem quite right. Her people didn't laugh. She'd never heard anybody laugh except her mother and herself. Not even her dad had done it.

She went a little farther—and then she saw something incredible. On the dark wall there was a figure drawn. Or no, it was painted—spray-painted. She had to raise her head to see the whole of it. When she did, she saw that it was a crudely sprayed painting of a human penis in full erection.

Graffiti?

Farther along yet, there were paper cartons from a restaurant, still smelling of pepper and garlic. Nobody ate human food. They had no way to digest it. Inside, they were not made like humans at all. Liquor, however, was a different story. They could get drunk, fortunately. The others disdained alcohol, of course, but Miriam enjoyed fine wines and adored every form of distilled liquor from Armagnac to Jim Beam.

She moved a few more steps down, getting past the odor of the cartons. Her nostrils sought scent ahead.

Then she stopped. Fear did not come easily to her kind, so she was not frightened by what she smelled, only confused. She smelled humans—the dense odor of men, the sweet-sharp scent of boys.

A shock went through her as powerful as one of the lightning bolts that had been tearing through the clouds. She saw, suddenly and with absolute clarity, that the reason for all the odd signs was that there were human beings in this secret place. She was so surprised that she uttered an involuntary cry. The sound shuddered the walls, the moaning, forsaken howl of a tiger at bay.

From below there came a rush of voices, then the wild flicker of flashlights. Footsteps pummeled the stairs, and suddenly two Occidental men and three Thai boys came racing past her, cursing and pulling on their clothes.

Behind them they left a greasy silence, interrupted after a few moments by the scuttle of roaches and the stealthy sniffing of rats. Treading as if her feet were touching sewage, Miriam descended into the sanctum. She growled low, striding about in the filth and ruins.

They must have moved the sanctuary. But why hadn't they told anybody? Keepers might be a solitary lot, but ancient custom dictated that everybody be informed of something so basic as this. Unless—was she really *that* shunned, that they would move a place of conclave and keep only her in the dark?

Surely not. They were far too conservative to alter an ancient convention. So maybe there had been an emergency. Maybe the sanctuary had been discovered and they'd had to move it suddenly.

That must be it. She hadn't gotten the message because there'd been no time.

But then she saw, lying in a corner beneath the ruins of a shattered bookcase, a familiar red shape. She caught her breath, because what she was seeing was impossible. Her skin grew taut, her muscles stirred—the predator sensed danger.

She picked up the red-leather book cover and held it in reverent, shaking hands. From the time their eyes came open, Keepers were taught that the Books of Names were sacred. By these books, a whole species knew itself, all who lived and had died, and all its works and days.

That red leather was unmistakable, as was the inscription in the beloved glyphs of their own tongue, glyphs that no human knew. *The Names of the Keepers and the Keepings*.

They called themselves Keepers because they kept herds. If the rest of the book had been here, there would have been descriptions of the various territories that belonged to the different Asian Keepers and who had the right to use which human herd.

She ran her fingers over the heavy leather. It had been cured from the skin of a human when they were still coarse, primitive creatures. These books were begun thirty thousand years ago—a long time, even in the world of the Keepers. But not all *that* long. Her great-great-grandfather, for example, had been able to imitate the cries of the Neanderthals. Buried in the Prime Keep in Egypt were careful wax paintings of the human figure going back to the beginning.

She crouched to the crumbled mass of paper, tried to smooth it, to somehow make it right. When she touched the pages, roaches sped away. She spread a crumpled page to see if any useful information remained.

The roaches had eaten the ink, what hadn't been smeared by the vile uses to which the paper had apparently been put. She laid the page down on the dirty floor, laid it down as she might lay to rest the body of a beloved friend.

She made another circuit of the chamber, looking into its recesses and crannies, but not a page remained.

She was face-to-face with what was without a doubt the

greatest astonishment of her life. Some of the richest and most ancient Keepers were Asian. There had been—oh, easily a hundred of them.

She slumped against a wall. Had man somehow done this, simple, weak little *man?*

Keepers could be hurt by man—witness her mother and father—but they couldn't be destroyed by man, not this way. They *owned* man!

She looked from empty wall to empty wall and fully grasped the fact that the Asian Keepers must have been destroyed. If even one was left alive, this book would be safe.

When she grasped this enormous reality, something so rare happened to Miriam that she lifted her long, tapering fingers to her cheeks in amazement.

Far below the crazy streets, in the fetid ruin of this holy place, a vampire wept.

TWO

Blood Nocturne

The *samlor* moved with what now felt like maddening slowness through the sighing showers of rain, down the empty streets, while Miriam listened to the tremble of her own heart and smelled the air for danger.

What odor did she seek? The acid stink of a dead Keeper, perhaps, or the oil of a policeman's gun?

How could a human policeman kill one of them? The idea was absurd.

Yet the book had been destroyed. No battle among the Keepers, no matter how violent, would have resulted in the destruction of a Book of Names. Keepers fought for love and herds, but only occasionally, and never *that* hard. Not even in their days in the sun.

Miriam longed now to spend the night beneath the whirling fan, sucking deeply on her pipe, but thousands of years of hunting brilliant and dangerous prey made her too wary now even to consider such repose.

"Airport," she'd told the *samlor* driver. She'd pulled the plastic curtain across the front of the cabin and sat in the stuffy interior smoking and watching the rain pelt the driver's back, trying not to dwell on the scent of his blood.

The ride to the airport was a long one, and toward the

end the creature had slowed to a slumped, struggling walk. If this had been another time, she would have whipped him.

She might be a rebel, but just now she felt an absolute, burning loyalty to her own kind. They had a right to life, just like any other creature. More of a right—this whole earth and every single creature living on it was their property, and much of it—including man—was their creation.

They had given man everything—his form, his mind, his life itself. It was the Keepers who had originally bred the crops that man had been taught to cultivate, the grains and the fruits of the land, and the dumb beasts that he had been given to eat.

Her own great-granduncle had given the northern herds the apple, breeding the plants carefully through a hundred generations, then planting them where human tribes would discover the apparently wild orchards. This had been done as a solution to a nutritional problem. Humans needed fruit or they became constipated. It was most unpleasant to feed on a constipated human.

The *samlor* came to a stop before the shambling Chiang Mai airport, which proved to be empty in the predawn. Flights, it seemed, did not begin early here. She certainly couldn't sit alone in the lobby, not and invite the curiosity of security guards by being the only passenger present.

Nearby there was an area of warehouses, lit only by a few overhead lights. As the driver walked down a ramp to an area where others of his kind slept beneath plastic sheets, she slipped into the shadows at the edge of the main terminal building. A few yards away there was a chain-link fence with a locked gate. She twisted the lock off and moved toward the nearest warehouse, slipping in through a side door.

The black interior smelled of cotton and turned out to be full of T-shirts intended for the western market. "Grateful Dead," "Adolf Hitler, European Tour 1939–1945," "I Am a Teenage Werewolf."

She knew a great deal about fear, as something that her prey experienced. It was interesting to watch, in an abstract sort of way. She never felt it herself unless she got careless or unlucky. After all, humans couldn't do anything to a Keeper. Being killed by man was regarded as a freak accident, about as likely as being caught in an avalanche. Or, that used to be the case. Since about the time of her mother's death, things had been changing. The Keepers had responded by becoming more and more wary and reclusive.

Keepers were ten times as strong; they could climb sheer walls and leap long distances. They were far more intelligent. But were they faster than a bullet or a warning cell-phone call? Had they the skill to outwit investigators armed with the tools of forensic science?

She had been surprised to see the shadow of man in that ruined holy place. But she realized, now, that she should not have been.

Given the destruction of the Asian Book of Names, she had to assume that there were human beings who knew of their Keepers and were efficient enough to have destroyed a whole conclave.

The question was, how much had they actually understood of that book? If man had learned to read Prime, the ancient Keeper language, then a terrible doom might be upon all the Keepers. That book not only contained records of the locations and property of all the Keepers in Asia, but also all of their familial and fiscal relationships to every other Keeper in the world. It told the locations and times of the other centennial conclaves that would be held this month.

Miriam had to warn her kind.

An hour after dawn, workers were coming to open the warehouse, and the airport was slowly returning to life. As Miriam went among the crowd in the terminal, she found herself coping with strange urges, ferocious urges. She wanted to grab a few of them and tear their heads off and drink their spouting necks with the savagery of the ancients.

Perhaps she *was* afraid. A predator experiences fear as an urge to attack. It was why her mother had roared and gnashed her teeth back when—but she didn't want to brood on that again, not now.

Her hunger was starting to actually make her bones ache, and her skin was turning whiter and whiter. The dry, corpse-like coldness that marked a hungry Keeper's skin was stealing her usual girlish flush.

"Bangkok," she said to the ticket clerk, producing a Visa card in the name of the traveling alias Sarah had set up for this trip. A French national called "Marie Tallman" had entered Thailand from the U.S. and would leave for Paris. Miriam Blaylock, a U.S. citizen, would return to New York.

She went to the surprisingly ornate first-class lounge. A hostess came up. Miriam ordered sour lemonade, then sat down and lit a cigarette. She contemplated what had become the problem of her hunger.

She'd ignored it for too long, and now she was going to have to feed before she left Thailand. Why hadn't she noticed this back in New York? She could have sent Sarah down to the Veils to bring back some wanderer. At home, she had reduced the hunt to a simple, safe procedure that delivered her prey right into her arms. Sarah found appropriate victims and lured them to the Veils. Miriam consumed them in a basement room built for the purpose, or she took them home and dined there.

She gave them a lovely time. They died in ecstasy.

She sucked a cigarette hard, blasted the smoke out of her nose. If she didn't feed soon, she would slow down, she would lose her edge. Then she'd have to find some weak human and do a thin feed. This would only stave the hunger off for a few days, no more. So there would be a second hunt in Paris, and more danger.

She ought to race straight back to New York and the hell with the rest of the Keepers. They probably wouldn't appreciate her efforts anyway.

But she couldn't, not when the greatest disaster she had ever known had befallen an entire continent. Of all the Keepers, how could it ever have been the Asians who would be attacked by man? Many of them were true ancients, more than ten thousand years old. Immensely wise, extraordinarily careful, not moving so much as an inch except to feed, they would stay in their black lairs, shadows with gleaming eyes and slow, slow breath, amusing themselves for months by gazing at a bit of intricately woven cloth or some subtly reflective gem.

When these Keepers walked among their herds, the humans would stir in their sleep, sighing with the sighing wind, clinging to one another without knowing why.

They had seen vast ages of man pass, empires rise and fall and be forgotten, thousands of human generations go to dust. More effectively than any other group in the world, the Asians had managed their herds, inducing migrations in order to evoke new strains, breeding their stock for beauty and intelligence and succulence. Humans called it famine and war and migration. Keepers called it stock management.

The more she thought about it, the more uneasy she

became. How much of the secret of their Keepers had the humans involved understood, and who were these creatures? How could cattle enjoying the riches and ease of the feedlot ever realize the truth about their lives? Especially when not one in a hundred thousand of them would ever come into contact with a Keeper. But human beings were not cattle, and it was a mistake to think so.

Somehow, they had used their clever little brains to discover a secret that was larger than they were. They had used their damned science. They never should have been given the wheel, let alone electricity and—God forbid—flight.

But they had been. They were fun to watch, damned things. Also, as their population had risen out of control, they themselves had taken their science to greater and greater heights, seeking to make more food, to move faster, to create room for more and more of themselves on the groaning planet.

She'd had a brush with human science herself back twenty or so years ago. It was hard to believe, now, just how much trouble dear Dr. Sarah Roberts had caused her back then. She'd taken samples of her own blood into a laboratory. She'd damned well discovered the secret of the Keepers, that smart little vixen.

Miriam had eaten her cohort and seduced her. She'd flooded Sarah's body with her own blood, but Sarah had fought the transformation. She had refused to eat, claiming that her medical oath was stronger than her love of life. So she had spent a little time among the undead, her soul trapped in her slowly decaying body.

Meanwhile, Miriam had read Sarah's scientific papers and gained new insights from them about the synergy between Keeper blood and human blood. She had managed to resuscitate Sarah.

In doing so, she had gained a complex and fascinating companion. Sarah had honor, and so could be trusted. But she did not like to feed. She considered it murder.

Miriam had lured Sarah into finding buried parts of herself that loved the soft skin and the considered touch of another woman. When they lay together, Miriam would draw her to climax again and again, with the pressure of the finger or the exploratory flutter of the tongue.

"Passengers for Thai Airways Flight Two-Twenty-three to Bangkok may now board through Gate Eleven."

She began to file toward the gate that led to the plane. Normally, she minded travel far less than other Keepers. For a woman of their kind, travel was limited to courtship during her four fertilities and, of course, attending the centennial conclaves.

Defying convention, Miriam had traveled all over the world. She had tasted it and enjoyed it and watched it change across time, had walked in the grand alleys of ancient Rome and the perfumed halls of the Sun King.

She had lived a long time in the cellars of the House of the Caesars on the Quirinal Hill, had heard mad Caligula screeching and fed on the blood of his slaves, who were fat from their constant stealing of his peacock breasts and zebra haunches, and were too numerous to be missed.

Despite all her journeying, she detested small spaces. During the eastern European crisis of the nineteenth century, when local humans had briefly learned to recognize their masters, Keepers in the Balkans had been forced to hide in graves. Miriam had gone there to see firsthand what had gone wrong. She ended up spending a week hiding in a coffin, an experience that still haunted her dreams. It had taken almost all of her strength to dig herself out of the grave.

Their use of this particular hiding place was how the legend that Keepers were somehow undead had begun.

It was some time before anybody understood why simple Transylvanian peasants had come to understand that they were property. Not until the publication of *Dracula* did the Keepers realize that out-of-date clothing could give you away in a world where fashions had begun to change more than once in a human generation. The Romans had worn togas for a thousand years. In the Middle Ages, fashion had changed perhaps twice in a century.

In the nineteenth century, it began to change every fifteen years or so. Isolated in the Carpathians, the Keepers who lived there had failed to notice that powdered wigs and buckle shoes had ceased to be worn by humans. The peasants soon realized that every time one of these bewigged oddities was seen in the night streets, somebody disappeared. Twenty-six Keepers died during the Balkan troubles, the largest number by far ever to be destroyed at one time by man.

But there had been sixty or more here in Asia. *Sixty*. What if they were captured, starving in prison, or being tracked like foxes? Or worse, already dead.

They *were* dead. She sensed this. There was something missing in the air . . . a sort of silence where there had been music.

She strode toward the far back of the fetid tube full of seats. The only place she would sit on most flights was the very last row. If something went wrong, her great strength might give her an edge, for she would be perfectly capable of ripping a hole in the fuselage in order to escape, if escape was possible. The impact of a jet slamming into the ground at four hundred miles an hour would reduce even a Keeper to pulp.

The damn plane was going to be full, she realized. The wretched creatures were just piling on, and her belly was churning. She had to feed, and soon. She had to do it in Bangkok, and never mind the urgency of the situation or the danger of just being in Asia.

The plane was an A-310 Airbus, a type that particularly troubled her because it was too easy to fly. Pilots got careless in this airplane. Worse, it had only two engines, and she knew from her hobby of reading technical manuals that one of them was not enough to keep it aloft forever.

The Thai were smoking and chattering and eating human fodder: bits of pork and mushroom and pepper wrapped in what looked like edible plastic. Various of her human lovers had tried to introduce her to the pleasures of sweets and such, but she had not been able to digest any of it. She watched human food evolve steadily for thousands of years—until recently, that is, when continued population pressure had caused an increase in quantity and a corresponding decline in quality.

Herd tending was not her specialty, so she wasn't particularly concerned with what the creatures ate. Her parents had been breeders and practiced the art of inducing particular humans to breed with each other, so that babies with preferred characteristics would be born.

Her father and mother had bred a new race among the Egyptians, seeking to make a smarter human. They had eventually caused the birth a brilliant child called Ham-abyra, who is known to history not by his Egyptian name, but by the Hebrew inversion, Abyra-ham. He had been cut out of the Egyptian herd and sent to found a new one in another part of North Africa.

The herd of Abyra-ham were great survivors because they were so clever, but their blood had a bitter aftertaste, unfortunately. You ate a Jew, her father always said, you remembered it for a week.

Originally, there had been good reasons for wanting

humans to be smart. The brighter they were, the better their survival skills, and the cheaper they were to manage. Also, the blood of the brilliant usually offered more complex, interesting bouquets. Keepers bred humans for blood the way humans bred grapes for wine.

The engines of the airplane began to whine. She hated to fly as much as or more than she had hated to sail, but she did it anyway, just as she'd always traveled. Her thirst for knowledge had made her take the spring galley from Rome to Alexandria to read in the library, and the summer galleon from Spain to Mexico to plumb the secrets of the Maya.

There was a problem, though. She'd often ended up eating every single soul on those slow old sailing ships. She never meant to do it, but it was just so tempting, all alone in close quarters with a gaggle of sweet-blooded humans for weeks and weeks. She'd do one and then another of them, starting with the low slaves and working her way up. She'd create the impression that they'd jumped or fallen overboard. Come a storm and she'd do five or six, gobbling them like bonbons.

Ships she took would arrive empty . . . except for one seriously overweight Keeper well hidden in the bilges. One of her most particularly self-indulgent trips had been aboard a Dutch East Indies spice trader. She'd consumed a crew of fifty and all six of their passengers in just two months. She was so packed with blood she feared that she must look like a big blue tick. She'd come into Surabaya at night on the ship's sailing dinghy. As for the ship, it had sailed on alone for years, still a legend among humans, the *Flying Dutchman*.

Shuddering, the jet rose into the air. Fog, touched golden by the sun, hung over the ancient Thai city below. Miriam gazed down at the temple district, at spires just visible through the billowing fog, and wondered.

The hunger was beginning to claw at her belly. Her muscles were tensing, instinctually getting ready for a kill. Her mouth was filling with the sour flavor of need. The scent of people swept through her with every breath.

She turned on the air nozzle above her head to full force, but there was no escaping the succulent odor of her fellow travelers, not packed into this tin can.

You certainly couldn't feed on a jet. If you stuffed the remnant down the toilet, it would be found later in the plane's holding tank. Remnants had to be completely destroyed—ground up and burned, usually. Humans had found just a very few of them over the generations, generally taken for mummies. In fact, she'd once wrapped a news hawker in tape and put him in a mummy case in the basement of the British Museum. That had been when—oh, a few hundred years ago. He was probably still there, her old hawker. It had been the *St. James's Gazette* that he'd been selling. Pretty good paper in its day.

Look at the humans around her, she thought, all happy and fluttery and unconcerned about the thirty-thousand-foot maw of death beneath their feet. How could anybody be as careless of their lives as humans were? They flew all the time; they raced around in automobiles; they went on roller coasters and fought wars. Miriam's theory was that humans did indeed have souls, and inwardly they knew it. That was why they came to her for sex, thrilled by the danger they sensed. They weren't really afraid of death, the humans. For them, it was nothing more than another thrill ride.

For the Keepers, death meant leaving the cosmos forever.

The plane leveled off. Miriam knew by its motion and sound exactly what it was doing at every moment of the flight. Actually, she could have flown it herself. She'd trained herself on her PC with a flight simulator, just in case some pilot died from the airline food or something. If some fool were to attempt to hijack the thing, she'd hypnotize him immediately and simply sit him right back down. They'd have to try to figure it out later.

Two shy children peeked at her over the seat ahead. They gazed steadily at the European, but it wasn't only curiosity in their eyes. She knew that the longer the flight, the more uneasy she would make her seatmates. The presence of a Keeper evoked instincts that humans, being so near the top of the food chain, were as unfamiliar with as she was with fear. What a human felt in the presence of a Keeper was what a mouse felt in the presence of a snake—a sort of horrible question.

They would grow unaccountably suspicious of her, be strangely drawn to her, grow sick in her presence, and if they slept, they would have nightmares about her, every single soul in this airplane.

The stewardess came, her smile fading as she laid eyes on Miriam. She had a cart full of boxed food and piles of plastic chopsticks. She stood close, handing food to the people jammed in the nearby seats.

Her blood had a soft, plain scent, like Beaujolais from an uninteresting year. Even so, it would be smooth and warm and wonderful as it went down. Miriam kept her eyes closed, barely breathing.

Never guessing that Miriam could see through her own eyelids, the stewardess took the opportunity to look long at the tall European in the old suit. Miriam worried that her makeup was too light. By now, her skin would be terrifying to a human. She'd appear as pale as a corpse. But she was also thirsty, so she had to interact with the girl, risk a moment of the creature's attention. "Excuse me."

The stewardess stopped. She organized her face into a carefully professional smile. "Yis," she said, uttering what was probably one of her few English words. *Yis. Nah. Okeh.*

"Water," Miriam said, pointing to a bottle with blue Thai writing on it.

The girl gave her the water and moved off nervously. The plane shuddered, the tone of the engines changing. Miriam fumbled with her water bottle. She knew that the sounds weren't abnormal, but they still made her uneasy.

Again, the plane shuddered. It was heading down, definitely. Surely there wasn't a situation. The engines were fine; she could hear that. But what if they were having control problems?

She took in breath, prepared to tighten the muscles that might be needed if she had to tear her way out of a crumpled fuselage.

But no, the plane *was* landing. Or more accurately, beginning its descent. She fumbled her itinerary out of her purse. Yes, the flight was forty minutes, and running exactly on schedule.

The flaps went down, making a terrific racket. Her startle reflex made her suck her water bottle so hard that it became involved with her teeth, and she accidentally shredded it. Water gushed down her front. Wiping her breast, she stuffed the ruined bottle down into the space between the seats.

She sat facing straight ahead, ignoring her accident. They didn't notice, anyway. They were too preoccupied with their snacks.

The plane was so thick with the smell of human blood that she would have liked to have gone into some sort of feeding frenzy like a shark. Total indulgence.

She'd never been on an airplane while this hungry before,

and she resolved never to do it again. She should have eaten that *samlor* driver. She closed her eyes. Time passed, one minute, then another. She found herself inhaling the smell of her seatmate. He was a plump little thing, just popping with sweet blood. *Délicieux*. The odor of his skin was lively. This was a tasty morsel, sitting here. She sucked in more scent.

She began to imagine how she'd take him. She'd pretend to be one of those European whores who did such a lively trade in Asia. They'd get off the plane together, and then— well, sooner or later the moment always presented itself.

She could get a very nice feed out of this creature. He had noticed her glances and was scanning her. She could smell the spicy scent of his interest.

"Lovely flight," she said.

"Oh, yes," he answered. His English was good, which was a nice convenience.

She gave him a smile, very slight, a bit arch.

He squirmed in his seat, his eyes flickering between her folded hands and her face. Male victims always felt as if the strange woman who had taken notice of them was the most beautiful, most desirable creature on earth. Females found her personable and engaging. They never knew that they'd been bred to react this way to interest from their Keepers.

He crossed and uncrossed his legs, tossed his head, then leaned a little forward. "You spending some time in Bangkok?"

So, he was available for consumption. She considered. She might miss her flight to Paris, and the rest of the world had to be warned about what had happened here, and at all speed. But by the moon and the stars, she was *so hungry!*

"Perhaps," she said softly.

His smile widened to reveal a gold-capped tooth. She glanced down at his fingers, at the shimmering of his wedding ring. There would be a complication right there—a disappearing husband.

He followed her glance, shrugged.

Her gut hummed.

The pitch of the engines changed again. She evaluated the sound, concluded that all was still normal.

She lifted her fingers, poised them above the back of his hand. To touch him now was an ancient act of possession, by which the Keepers had claimed their prey from time immemorial.

She lowered the cool tips of her fingers until they came into contact with his skin. "I'm staying in Bangkok for a few days." She laughed, a musical trill. "At the Royal Orchid," she added, drawing the name of the hotel from somewhere in her memory. She knew only that it was a very fine place.

"As it happens, I'm staying at the Royal Orchid, also, miss." He smiled from ear to ear.

She hoped they had a room. She had no reservation. Doubtless he didn't, either.

A moment later the plane hit the runway, then went jolting along the much-patched tarmac. Despite Miriam's grim worries, it slowed steadily. Still, she was tense, waiting for the damned thing to get off the runway. For an unspeakably long moment, it hesitated. Were the pilots lost? Had the surface traffic controllers made some stupid mistake?

She pictured a 747 landing on top of them, its entire flight crew dead asleep. Years ago, two Keepers had been killed in a catastrophic runway accident in the Canary Islands. But the engines revved up again and the plane moved forward. A few twists and turns and it came to a halt. The seat-belt chime rang.

Immediately, Miriam's mind focused on her victim. Now

she must ignore him a bit, play the coquette, the Occidental woman who was just a little indifferent to the Oriental man.

As they filed out of the plane, she stayed behind him, evaluating moment by moment every subtle change in his manner. A musty smell flowed from between his legs, a sharper odor of sweat billowed off his skin.

There was something just a little odd in these odors. He should have smelled far more of sex and less of . . . well, it seemed that he was afraid. Probably, it was because they'd been in proximity too long. You wanted to move quickly when you hunted, not sit cheek-by-jowl with the prey for an hour before proceeding.

In the airport, they were hit by the wall of filthy air that enclosed and defined life in Bangkok.

No matter his perversion, here the wanderer could find satisfaction. The Thai had originally been bred by luxury-loving Keepers, and they preserved the remarkable zest for pleasure that had been bred into them. But then, every herd in the world bore the mark of its Keepers. You could see the stark love of order and the obsessiveness of the northern Keepers in the Germanic peoples they had created, and the passion and subtlety of the southern Europeans in the French, the Spanish, and the Italians. She loved the wild mix of the Americas, never knowing exactly what to expect from that mongrel herd.

As Miriam and her victim moved out into the main hall of the airport, she laid her hand on his shoulder, the second time she had touched him. Each time she did it, she felt more of a sense of possession.

She felt not the rippling whisper of desire in his muscles, but the tense vibration of fear. This was going to take a great deal of care and attention. This man must be very sensitive indeed to feel as he did now. Perhaps she should turn back.

He plunged into the chaotic cab rank, a mass of bills in his fist, and they were soon in a taxi.

She disliked being driven by others in motorized vehicles, and this driver was typical of these wild folk. In addition, he would certainly remember a run with a Thai man and a European woman.

Her victim sat rigidly, gripping the handhold above his door. When he offered her a cigarette, she did not like what she saw in his eyes. Did not like, did not quite understand. Their instinct was to be drawn to the predator, to be fascinated.

She let him light her cigarette, inhaled deeply. Cigarettes didn't matter to Keepers. Their immune systems swept cancer cells away like crumbs.

An impulse told her to give his cheek a sudden kiss. "Asia," she whispered, "Asia is such a mystery."

"I'm in outsourcing technology. No mystery there."

"Your accent isn't Thai."

"My father was a diplomat. I grew up in London and then Burma."

She remembered the days of the British in Burma, when they used to grow opium poppies on huge Crown estates. They had looked upon their laborers in much the same way that Keepers looked on humans. You could go out into those opium plantations and chew seed and take one picker after another, like an ape gobbling fruit. And then you could engage in the social life of the planters with their whites and their billiard rooms and their gin and tonics. Sometimes, you could even take one of them, for there were still tigers in Burma then and the corpse could be left suitably mauled.

Sweet nostalgia.

They arrived at the Royal Orchid, the cab at sea in an ocean of limousines. She went forward into the broad, echoing lobby. Women stared in open amazement as the fabulous clothes strode toward the check-in desk.

"I'd like a suite please." She presented her—or rather, Marie Tallman's—Visa card. The clerk ran it and gave her a keycard, his polite glance moving toward the next customer in line.

She had made no effort as yet to seduce her victim away from his uneasiness. He needed more subtle handling, and she had to accept that this might not be a successful hunt. She'd be damn mad if it failed, though, and the long journey to Paris would be hell.

She held out her hand to her victim. As sweetly, as innocently as she could, she smiled at him. He looked down at her hand. In it was a keycard. "Twenty-five-oh-seven," she said.

When they were alone in the lift, he finally smiled up at her. His odor had not really changed, though. He was not happy to be here. He was acting.

She kissed him on the forehead. Now that she was committed to what was probably a very foolish kill, she decided that she might as well enjoy herself thoroughly. She would take him slowly and drain him to the very last drop. She gave him a stern look. "How much am I worth to you?"

"How much do you want?"

"A thousand dollars."

His eyes widened, he reared back as if astonished. The lift came to a stop on the twenty-fifth floor. "Two hundred, miss. H.K. dollar."

They got out. She would not bargain all that hard, but also she must not raise his suspicions. "Three hundred, U.S." she said as they walked down the wide hallway.

"Five hundred, H.K."

"It isn't enough to cover my expenses, handsome."

"You'll do twenty men before the night's out."

She slid her keycard into the lock. Here she was, as magnificent a beauty as the earth might know, and this greedy little roach actually believed that she was going to give herself to him for the equivalent of about sixty U.S. dollars. He'd been afraid of her price, that was all. Wretched thing.

Sunlight poured in from the wall of windows that faced the door. There was a couch upholstered in yellow chintz and a huge vase of exotic flowers on the coffee table.

Far below, the wide Chao Phraya River shimmered in sunlight that shafted down between great banks of clouds. Tiny river taxis and long-tails wove the river with their wakes. Up the bank, she could see the spires of distant temples, Wat Phrathukhongka and, just visible along the Klong Phadung, Wat Trimitr, the temple of the Golden Buddha. Farther away, awash in glowing air pollution, were the graceful tile roofs of the Grand Palace and the pencil-narrow spire of Wat Po.

The two of them gazed in silence, both awed for different reasons. He no doubt thought it glorious; she was horrified and fascinated, as always, when she saw how vast were the works of man.

She sat down on the bed, drew her prey down beside her. Too bad she had to eat and run. Normally, she would have gone into the sleep that followed feeding, but this time she'd have to load herself up with amphetamines and do her sleeping on the plane. She'd book a first-class seat for this twelve-hour journey, no matter that the seats were in the most dangerous part of the plane. Still, the idea of entering helpless sleep amid a mass of humans was not pleasant.

She caressed her victim. He stirred, his clothes rustling. A moment passed, another. He had become still in the way human beings did when they were subconsciously aware of danger.

They were sitting on the foot of the bed. She took his chin in her hand and turned his face to hers. She looked into his eyes, looked deep.

What did the gleam in those human eyes mean? She always wondered that, right before she fed.

"Kiss me," she said to the creature. He smiled a drawn smile, then lifted his face to hers, his lips going slack, his eyelids fluttering down. She laid her lips upon his, careful to keep the anatomy of her mouth concealed. Their tongues met, and she felt his muscles stiffen a little as he detected that hers was as rough as a cat's. If he bolted, she would be ready. She was ten times stronger than the strongest human being, ten times faster.

A cat worries its prey because pain flushes muscles with hormones that season the meat. This was true also of her kind, and some of them were casually cruel to their victims.

Stroking his head and purring, she laid him against the pillows and opened up his pants with her deft hands. She took his member out, smiled, then kissed it.

Then she stood before him. She removed her blue silk jacket, twirled, then unbuttoned her blouse. He watched with steady concentration, a slight smile on his face.

Instinct made her sway into the death dance, her arms undulating, her hips moving gracefully. Each time she twirled, her body became tighter and harder, more and more ready. As she danced, she threw off her clothes.

She stood before him naked, like a wound spring, her hands ready to grab him. There was in his eye a sort of curiosity, for she was very pale indeed, as pale as a ghost and as slick as glass, more like a statue than a being of flesh and blood.

He would soon discover that she was also cold, very cold. She sat down beside him and kissed him. But something was not right. As she had kissed him, he had returned himself to his pants.

No matter, she was sexually excited now herself. That was part of her reality and what made her so very different from the others of her kind: humans excited her. She liked their bodies, the way they tasted and smelled, the way they looked, the curves of the females, the pert rods of the men. Perhaps this was because she had discovered that she was capable of taking them to states of pleasure that Keepers could not reach with one another. Sex between species could be a stunning aphrodisiac, if executed with skill.

She lay down upon her little man, snuggled him into her. He seemed to be struggling with himself, fighting an inner battle. She reached into his pants, to see if she could resolve the conflict for him. A few deft strokes, and he was ready.

The human male was not blessed with a large penis, and it probably felt strangely lost in her vagina. He would also be noticing the cold. In fact, she could hear him making little exclamations in his throat. He was becoming aware that something was wrong.

"There, baby," she cooed, "little baby boy, all is well."

He started heaving. He wanted out from under her. She was, of course, far heavier than she had appeared. She tightened her vaginal muscles, over which she had exquisite control. When she began undulating them, he yelped with surprised pleasure. He'd probably never felt anything like it before, not even in Asia.

Her mouth was pressed against his neck, her mucus flooding his skin with anesthetic. Her sharp teeth parted the skin so easily that he probably felt nothing at all. There was a bit of resistance from the wall of the vein. She made love furiously as she exhaled, made herself ready for the ferocious sucking motion that would consume his life.

His muscles worked, he twisted and turned. He would be feeling both the pain of penetration and the pleasure of sex. He grimaced, his eyes shut tight.

She stayed like that for a while, making love at first fast and then slow, bringing him close, letting him relax. She left her mouth wide open to the wound, letting the blood tick past, tasting it just a little, enjoying herself.

When he began to really squirm, trying to reduce what must be by now a quite noticeable pain deep in his throat, she pinned his arms to his sides and enclosed his legs in her own. Her strength was so great that it felt to her human lovers as if they were being encased in iron, or so they had always told her.

The penis, on the other hand, would feel as if it were being massaged by thousands of tiny, careful fingers. One man described it as the most divine sensation he had ever known. He begged her for it, even while he was dying.

She worked him to the edge twice more. His body was a roaring furnace; his blood was singing. She was deep in him, her drinking beginning to kill him. It was now, at this moment, that she was sure that she felt his soul.

She sucked massively and fast, the sound of it roaring through the silent, sunny room. He did not even have a chance to cry out. As he died, the pumping of his loins became disorganized, then stopped.

The blood came into her like living fire, like a flower opening in her gut. Then came the bittersweet flavor that followed the blood, that meant that the organs had also given up their fluids.

She got off him, sat on the bedside and lit one of his cigarettes. Taking a long drag, she enjoyed the sensation of absorbing his life. The males and females felt quite different. After consuming a woman, you had a ferocious sort of an energy in you. You felt as if you could tear the world in half. A man left the flavor of his strength. You got a heady, hard-edged high from testosterone.

She got up and strode to the window. The healthier they were, the more you got from them, and this creature had been very healthy. Her face got hot, her body flushed warm and pink.

She went over to the mirror and touched the reflection of her face. She had been a woman before; now she was a girl, fresh as dew, her eyes sparkling and innocent.

Still enjoying the taste of blood that lingered in her mouth, she rifled through the man's clothing. She'd get his money, then dispose of the remnant and go straight to the airport. She could still make her Paris flight. The European clan was not as big as the Asian, but it was wise and ancient, not like the adventurous Americans. Europe had fixed the Transylvania situation by transforming true vampire lore into myths and stories. Europe would know what to do.

She drew a fat brown wallet out of his hip pocket and tossed it open. Poor wife, smiling so desperately, will you miss this man or feel relief that he has gone? And here were children—damn!

She was furious with herself for looking at the pictures. She never looked at the damn pictures! She held the weathered print of the kids, wondering how old they were, poor little things. She stuffed it back into the wallet, pressing it deep into one of the pockets.

It was then that she noticed a rather strange card. At first, she thought that it might be a Thai driving permit, but when she looked more closely, she found that it was very far from that.

Lying in her hand was an identification card. She stared at it, reading it carefully. It was in French, English, and Chinese, not Thai at all.

The sunken husk lying on that bed over there, now nothing but forty pounds of bones and drum-tight skin lost in a pile of sheets, was no innocent Thai businessman. Lying there were the remains of Kiew Narawat, police inspector with Interpol.

Her breath came short, her skin grew hot and dry. She felt dizzy, her bowels threatened to let go. She threw on her clothes, settled her wig on her head, and applied a smear of lipstick to reduce the glow of her fire-red lips. Going deep into her purse, she pulled out three yellow-and-black bennies and threw them down her gullet. Sleep would drag at her now, but she must not let it come, not until she was in her plane in her seat and covered with a blanket.

Forgetting the remnant lying on the bed in full view, forgetting everything except escape at any and all cost, Miriam Blaylock made a mistake of spectacular proportions, one that she had not made in three thousand years upon the earth. Indeed, it was a mistake so rare that it could bring a Keeper the penalty of confiscation of property.

So distressed was she by the events of the past few hours—the discovery of the disaster in Chiang Mai, and now this horrible discovery, so loaded with dreadful implications—that she left the remnant where it lay.

There was only one thought in her mind: Get out of here. She hurried into her clothes, barely even stopping to see if she had left any of her possessions behind, and took a taxi straight to the airport.

THREE

Hunter of Hunters

When Paul Ward had first realized what the confused Interpol e-mail was about, he'd felt as if the entire Petronas Towers complex were about to topple into the streets of Kuala Lumpur. But the towers were fine. Only his program had collapsed.

Jesus God, he screamed silently, they were like roaches. He had cleared them out of the whole continent, sanitized it. And now, instead of cleaning out his office in Kuala, preparing for departure to the States and the start of the endgame against them, he was racing through the streets of Bangkok in this clanking old embassy Caddy.

Paul Ward was dealing with one smart breed of animal. How smart, he had just plain not understood, not until now.

He pressed himself against the seat of the limo, instinctively keeping his face in shadow. It was always possible that they knew him, he thought, that they would recognize him. He watched the people thronging the streets and wondered if Bangkok, or any city, would look the same if its inhabitants knew that predators a thousand times more dangerous than the tiger or the shark might be walking just behind them.

The damned thing of it was, he'd even run his traditional victory celebration, with all the traditional goodies, stolen in all the innovative ways that his crew could come up with. There had been a couple of cases of Veuve Clicquot borrowed from the Sûreté outpost in Ho Chi Minh City, a couple of cases of beluga borrowed from the KGB in New Delhi, and a whole bunch of dancing girls who came to the crinkle of the dollar—counterfeits made in Myanmar and borrowed from Pakistani intelligence by the redoubtable Joe P. Lo, who could steal venom from a cobra.

They'd been saying good-bye to the General East Asia Pest Control Company. Good-bye and good riddance to their ironically named front organization. This had been a miserable, exacting, assignment, and an extremely dangerous one. Will Kennert, Addie St. John, Lee Hong Quo, Al Sanchez—these were just a few who'd died fighting the vampires.

If he hadn't needed to be totally and completely centered for the task ahead, he would have told the driver to stop at a bar. He'd go in and suck sacred Stolichnaya like a Russki at the nipple of his still. He'd get a massage that lasted all night. Masseuses in relays. Every sin he could think of and—thanks to being in good old Bang-yer-cock—some he probably couldn't.

"Goddamnit!" he suddenly said aloud.

"Sir!"

The driver didn't know that he talked to himself. Why would he? People didn't know Paul Ward, not even embassy people. They weren't supposed to. "Sorry, son."

The flight from Kuala had exhausted him—just sitting in that damn seat, waiting through what seemed an eternity. He'd tried the phone, but it hadn't worked. The Gulf of Thailand was still an empty corner of the world. He hated empty places, dark places. He hated small places even more. Recurring nightmare: he comes awake, starts to sit up in bed, and *wham*, his forehead hits something with such force that he sees stars. Then he realizes that the air is heavy with his own breath and he can't sit up without braining himself. He knows, then, that he is in a coffin.

He knew a CIA guy called Richie Jones, who'd run afoul of the Khmer Rouge and been buried alive. Somebody who'd been in that prison compound had reported that you could hear him screaming for about half an hour. From Ohio State to a lonely hole in the jungles of Cambo. Had Mr. President ever been told about Richie? Had Mr. Director of Central Intelligence known or cared? Weep a tear for the Buckeye state, for it has lost a son.

To die the way covert ops died in the field, damn hard and damn alone—Jesus God, pass the bottle. And to do what he and his crew were doing, to live the way they were living, chasing these monsters in the sewage and the filth of some of the world's most terrible cities, getting yourself eaten if you weren't careful—Jesus God, pass the bottle again.

He was tired. They were all tired. It had been a hard operation, soaked in the blood of fine men and women. And what a death. It'd be better to be buried alive by a bunch of twelve-year-old Khmers with AK-47s and dead eyes, than to be stung in the neck by one of those filthy things.

Long before he'd been forced to come back, Asia had been a place he wanted to put behind him. Vietnam, Laos, Cambodia, 1971 to 1973. In those days, life had less value than dirt out here, especially American life, and most especially the life of a clean-cut CIA virgin with a buzz haircut and wire-framed glasses. He had made it through the Parrot's Beak massacre when Danny Moore had been pulled apart between two backfiring tractors. He had lived through six weeks in a bamboo cell with nothing but roaches and rats for food, while Betty Chang was methodically raped to death and George Moorhouse starved. He had survived because he was too ugly to rape and so cussed that he could crack rats and drink 'em, blood, guts, and all.

He fumbled in the little cabinet that was supposed to be stocked with booze. "Got any vodka in this thing?"

"No, sir."

Of course not. A CIA officer didn't rate booze in his car. This was the U.S. Government. The foreign service kid driving this thing outranked him by a damn country mile. The kid and the limo had appeared at the airport only because there hadn't been time to find a conveyance shitty enough for a CIA field officer. Had he been from State, there would have been booze and ice both.

"The goddamn bastards."

"Sir?"

"Nothing."

Paul wished they'd sent a girl driver. He wanted the scent of a woman in this car. He wanted, he thought, what all men want. He wanted deliverance.

He closed his eyes. Instantly, he saw an old and hated vision, the prairie grass dancing in the moonlight. He opened them again. He could not go there, no. Better to stay with the wartime memories or the memories of sterilizing those filthy dens with acid. How in hell was it that these things looked so much like people? How had they evolved? Had God gone nuts?

The prairie grass dancing in the moonlight, his curtains billowing with moon wind, and in the distance, the most beautiful voice singing: that was the beginning of a life woven from nightmares.

Paul slapped his breast pocket. Pillbox in position. He'd take two tonight, maybe three. Black sleep, please.

"Shit," he said softly, and then, "Shit!" louder.

"Sir?"

This kid would chatter that he'd had to drive a muttering old crazy man to the Royal Orchid Hotel, and then he'd try to find out just who this VIP third class was.

He would not find out.

The State Department could not tell anyone about Paul Ward because they could not tell anyone about the vampire project. If they did that, they would also have to explain that humans are not at the top of the food chain, that we are prey, legitimate prey, just as nature intended. What is worse, they'd have to explain that the predator is damn clever and has evolved some very remarkable camouflage. The predator, you see, looks just like you. Except that his skin is as pale the light of an October moon, and he will sing to you and dance for you, and comfort you in his arms while he kills you. As far as looks are concerned, you can't tell the difference between a vampire and your postman or your doctor, or your own damn brother.

No involved division of any involved government had questioned the secrecy of this operation.

He stared balefully at the back of a stopped truck. Was it parked, or what?

"Can't you hurry?"

"Sir, this is Bangkok."

"Mind if I drive?"

"You want to drive, sir?"

"I need to get there before dark, for Chrissakes."

"Look at the street!"

"Son, excuse me, but get me there now!"

The car shot forward, slamming up onto the sidewalk. An enraged pedestrian hammered the window as they smashed through a food cart.

"You damn fool! That was that guy's rice bowl!"

"You told me to!"

"I didn't tell you to hurt people." Above all things in the world, Paul hated to hurt. He would put a fly out the window rather than swat it. He would watch quietly as a mosquito gorged on his blood, then brush it off when he thought it was getting greedy.

Ironic, in a man who had killed so much. When he slept at night, his legions of dead would steal near: the kids who'd died in the dark corners of Vietnam, the victims of the vampires, the crew members who had not returned. They would call to him; they would stroke him with their cool hands; they would beg him to return them their lives.

He would wake up awash in sweat and choking with terror and regret. He would go to the brutal light of the bathroom as to an altar afire with candles, and gulp the pills of oblivion. Black sleep.

Asia had made him love certain very bad things, chief among them opium. Better than hash, better than grass, better than coke or any of the new designer drugs, far better than the brute high you got off horse. Opium was a deep pleasure, something wonderful that connected earth and soul. It made you feel at peace with the eternal world. He loved the mechanisms of an opium high: the long pipes, the sweet vapor, even the tickly lice in the greasy old sheets of today's few real opium dens.

Paul Ward had sunk deep and sinned hard. Why not, my friends? Tomorrow we die.

Well, that was what they'd thought back in the seventies, listening to Kissinger on Armed Forces Radio. It had seemed hard then, before he knew about vampires, but it had really been easy.

The Jungle Jamboree. No way could you do opium then. He who tripped died.

Still true now, at least for him and his crew. Killing vampires was horribly dangerous. They were quick, so quick that they could throw a knife at nearly the speed of a bullet.

They could not be killed with normal gunfire. You could empty the biggest, most evil weapon in your arsenal right into one of the damn things and it would just stare at you with its deceptively calm eyes, waiting for your bullets to run out. You had to destroy the head.

If you cut them open after they'd fed, they would gush blood like exploded ticks.

The Book of Names had identified twenty-six vampires in Asia. He and his crew had burned out or poisoned or dismembered twenty-four vampires in Asia, and found the remains of two ruined lairs, creatures that had lost their lives on their own.

Accidents happened even to vampires. They weren't perfect. Statistically, if you live long enough, you will meet with some sort of accident. That was their disease—statistics.

That's why vampires did not travel. They were highly territorial and obsessed with accidents. So the trick was to kill them all in a given area as quickly as you could, then move on before the others realized that they were gone.

Paul's next target was going to be Europe. There were many references to Paris in the Book of Names. He'd been looking forward to working out of Paris. Not that he disliked Kuala, but he could use a little less humidity and a little more familiar beauty around him. The Musée Marmottan with its magnificent collection of Monet water lilies was a favorite. He considered Monet to be one of the most evolved of all human beings, on a par with the D. T. Suzukis and Foucaults of the world. From those paintings, a man could obtain the true balm of peace. The light that shone in from the garden at the Marmottan, that light was holy.

"God help me!" he cried out loud.

"Yessir!"

"Please, son, be quiet. And stop running people down."

"I didn't run anybody down. I just got around that truck."

"You need to go back there later. Give that guy some dough for his cart."

"Sir?"

"Without the cart, he and his wife will starve. Their children become prostitutes. Do you understand that?"

"Sir, I hardly think—"

"Do you understand that?"

"Sir, yes, sir!"

Could this be a marine out of uniform? No, look at the hair. Foreign service all the way. He was just yanking Paul's chain with his military lip. He'd be sneering later with his State Department buddies about the old CIA asshole he'd driven around.

With his cart wrecked, that fruit vendor might as well open his veins, and Paul knew this kid would *not* go back, he would not give the guy the twenty bucks it would take to put his life back together again.

Funnily enough, Paul was in his work because he liked people. He'd seen the CIA take such incredible shit over the years and save so many damn lives. The Company could not defend herself, not without giving away secrets she was bound to keep. So she just took it. He'd seen the effects of all the Company bashing in his own life. There'd been a time when the merest hint of a Company connection brought women swarming like darling honeybees. Not anymore.

The car swung around another corner, and the Royal Orchid Hotel finally appeared down the smog-hazed street.

What the hell was he about to find? This would be the first actual victim they had ever had a chance to study. The vampires were obsessive about destroying remains. Except, apparently, this time.

Still, there was something very bad about all this. He could smell it, but he couldn't quite see it. A place is wrapped up, finished. Then, suddenly, it ain't finished.

Okay, think. Think it out, Paul: All of a sudden, they leave evidence in a hotel. The hotel is on a continent that has just been sterilized of their presence.

It was not like them to taunt you. They were too shy, too careful for that. Their lives were incredibly precious to them, because this life was all they had, at least in Paul's opinion. In his opinion, nature had given them immortal lives—potentially, if they were very damn careful—but they had not been given souls. They were damn animals and they knew it.

So if this wasn't a declaration or a taunt, then it must be something else. The thing was, when the National Security Administration had cracked the language in the Book of Names, the whole vampire world had been opened up to Paul and his crew. He returned to the States to become head of a whole new division that would be devoted to eradicating the menace. There were to be units operating on every continent, using the methods that Paul and his group had evolved.

One of the reasons that he was racing back to the States so soon after completing his work in Asia was to deal with a stupid but potentially serious problem: The director of the CIA had been asking legal questions. Specifically, were these creatures to be regarded as animal or human? If they were human, then they were committing crimes, not killing prey.

Declaring that the creatures were human meant that a whole different approach would be necessary. There would have to be due process and trials and prison sentences, and the vampire would like nothing better than this type of leverage. The vampire was powerful and quick and so damn smart. It could get away from prison.

They were almost unkillable. Something about their blood gave them extraordinary powers of recovery. You had to blow that head apart, then burn the creatures to ash, to be absolutely certain they were dead. Then the lair had to be washed in acid.

How could you ever call anything that lived in a filthy hole like a vampire lair human?

But he couldn't stop the wheels of the bureaucracy from turning as they turned. "What is this bunch of agents doing out in Asia killing people?" "Who are these 'vampires,' a terrorist group? A secret society? What in hell is going on here?"

Some Thai were passing the car, banging gongs and chanting. Funerals made Paul physically ill. He had to drown out that sound, and *not* with a Thai radio station because the Asians, God love 'em, had not figured music out yet, not in any way whatsoever. "Are there any CDs in this car?"

"Destiny's Child, Santana, Johnny Mathis. Some kind of opera."

"Put in the opera, turn it up to full volume."

"Yes, sir." The boy sounded crestfallen. Which one would the kid have preferred? Destiny's Child, no doubt.

"Full volume! I want my ears to bleed! You got any cigars?" Paul was a creature of appetites. Fine wines, lots of them. The best vodka in the world, lots of it. The strongest opium, the most exotic, the sweetest, the most delicious of whatever the world had to offer. One of his great regrets was the failure of either the Company to assassinate Castro or, better, of the U.S. to just come to terms with him. The loss of the Cuban cigar had been a blow.

Well, good god damn, that was *Callas!*

"Louder!"

"It's as loud as it gets!"

He reached forward, turned the knob all the way up.

Oh, God, *Lakmé.* Oh, God, the "Bell Song." That she had lived, this goddess Maria Callas, was proof that human beings were of interest to the good Lord. Nothing so fabulous could have come about by accident. "Hey, kid!"

No answer.

"KID!"

"Yessir!"

"That *goddess* is called Maria Callas. You ever worshipped a woman?"

"Sir?"

"It is a very special pleasure, I assure you. To worship something so gentle, so soft, so willing as a good woman."

"Okay."

He'd worshipped at the altar of the female all of his life. Three marriages, six mistresses, and whores enough to populate a small army were testament to that fact. Jesus, but she could sing. "Death, be not proud!"

"Yessir!"

"Do you fear death?"

"Yessir!"

"The goddamn Pathet Lao stuck an electric cattle prod up my ass and left it on so long steam came outa my nose. You know what I told them?"

"Name, rank, and serial number?"

"I told them, if they filled out the forms, they could get

Visa cards from the Thai Farmer's Bank. The deal was, let me go and I would help them fill out those forms. When they got their credit cards, that was the end of that Pathet Lao cell. Who wants to run around in the jungle covered with leeches when you could be sipping a Singapore Sling at the Poontang Hilton, am I right?"

"I guess so, sir."

He could see the kid's eyes rolling in the rearview mirror. Well, let 'em roll.

Let the DCIA and the president whine about whether or not the damn vampires had human rights or whatever. Paul decided that he'd like to *taste* vampire. Probably like—not chicken, no, they'd taste like something else. Snake maybe, except he'd eaten snake in Cambo, and it *did* taste like chicken. They made dynamite snake curry in Kuala backstreets. Little pieces of sour asp meat marinated with asafetida and fried in ghee. Oh, that is good.

They reached the hotel at long living last. It was a pretty place, luxurious. What was a vampire doing in a place like this? Vampires didn't go to hotels. They didn't sleep in beds. They were *animals*, God for damn it! The thing must have been crawling around in the ducts or something.

The problem he was here to solve was twofold: First, he had to get a line on the whereabouts of this animal. Second, he had to contain the curiosity of the local cops, who had a corpse on their hands they could not understand at all. They also wanted to know why an Interpol officer was operating in their country without their knowledge. Of course, the problem there was that he was on CIA's payroll.

Kiew Narawat was a precise, solemn man from Sri Lanka, an excellent operative and a profound friend of the United States. But Narawat wasn't a member of Paul's team, just a garden variety asset who had been detailed to observe any nocturnal comings and goings at a certain temple in Chiang Mai.

Paul went into the hotel.

If they hadn't messed up the corpse somehow, that would be one good outcome from this tragedy. Not only would there be a useful forensic and medical yield, the condition of the body would help him make his case that the vampire killings should not be declared crimes. "This was the act of an animal," he could hear himself saying. "This man was not murdered, he was fed upon."

If they could just get a little more vampire DNA, that would be it. The discovery of the vampires had taken place in 1989, when the Japanese government had asked for help with a very strange murder. They had the attack on videotape from a traffic control point. It was three in the morning and the streets were empty.

An old man was struggling along the sidewalk. He was the only person in the area. Then this strange creature came loping along, and grabbed the man. It had put its mouth on his neck and suddenly the entire body had withered, disappearing into its own clothing. The creature had stuffed it into a satchel and walked off.

The man was unattached, very poor, and normally wouldn't have been missed even in that very careful country. But the police made an effort, because what they had seen was so disturbing. They identified the old man. They went to the spot where the crime had taken place and took careful samples of everything. A hair had appeared in the debris they vacuumed up from the sidewalk that was not human, and not from a known animal.

It had taken years for the mystery to percolate into CIA's

pot. Paul got it because he was an old Asia hand and had his own father's mysterious death in his file. The way the old man looked after his blood had apparently been sucked out of him and the way Paul's dad had looked when he'd been discovered had been strangely similar.

They gave it to him because they thought he'd be interested. Well, he wasn't. And damn them for dredging up his father's memory like that.

Nothing more was done, not until 1998, when a crime reporter, Ellen Wunderling, had disappeared in New York while innocently doing research for a Halloween spoof about vampires. She had delved too deep into the gothic underground, an eerie, subtly murderous subculture that would be an ideal place for real vampires to conceal themselves. He'd begun his own investigation of the disappearance, but then came Tokyo and an opportunity to take immediate and direct action. He had been finding and killing vampires ever since.

Paul got into the elevator. He hated riding elevators. It opened on a wide corridor, with rooms open here and there. The management had cleared the whole floor. In front of one of the open rooms, a small crowd of Thai police, medical personnel, and plainclothes officers came and went.

The instant Paul entered the room, the smell hit him. What was it? A human odor, maybe. But so strange—salty, dry, distressingly organic. He looked down at the yellow flowered sheet with the angular lump under it.

"Thailand will expect extradition of the perpetrator, if he is found elsewhere, Mr. Ward," the colonel inspector said in his heavy, careful English.

Paul grunted, wishing that the man could be made to go away.

Kiew Narawat had been ordered to report if he saw anybody enter the temple. So why had he ended up in this room like this, instead? Paul took the sheet and pulled it back.

He actually had to stifle a scream. This was the most spectacularly destroyed human body he had seen in his adult life. But not in his whole life, and that was what made it so terrible for him.

He was twelve again. He was awakened by a sound like the last water getting sucked down an eager drain.

The sleepy-eyed boy looked out the window, gazing into the glowing dark. The prairie grass was dancing in the moonlight, and there was a dark figure moving through the field with a burden of some kind on its shoulder.

Paulie stared. Who was that out there? But Big Boy wasn't barking and Big Boy was a hair-trigger watchdog.

The figure disappeared off into the woods. Tomorrow, Paulie would get Dad and go down there, see what had happened.

And then came the terror of the next morning and of the haunted life of Paul Ward: Where's Dad? he had asked his mom. I don't know honey, she had said. When is he coming back? I don't know! I don't know!

Flash forward four years: Paul is walking along the stream beside their pear orchard when he sees something strange down among the roots of a tree. Again, Big Boy notices nothing.

Now, Paul knows why. He knows that they secrete a blocking pheromone that makes it impossible for animals to pick up their scent. The remains of their victims are covered with it.

When he saw the skeleton of his father in a casement of dry and disintegrating skin just like this, he had run back to the house screaming in terrified agony, Big Boy gamboling beside him.

The dental records had been definitive. It was Dad. But Dr. Ford, their local medical examiner, could not figure out what had happened to him. The state police couldn't figure it out. The FBI finally issued a report: death by misadventure unknown.

Little Paulie had become obsessed with secrets. What had killed Daddy? An animal? Space aliens? Nobody knew. Daddy had been strong and big and good, so why had he ended up like that down in the roots of a tree?

Some years later, Paul had awakened to see a woman standing at the foot of his bed, a woman dressed all in black, with golden hair and an angelic face. She looked at him out of sweet eyes, eyes that made the heart melt. But when he sat up, when he called out to her, she faded like a dream.

"The woman in here with him was French," the policeman said, breaking Paul's reverie. "We have determined that her name was Marie Tallman. She took the Air France flight to Paris. She will be detained there when she gets off the plane."

"It was a female?" Paul responded. "You're sure?"

"A woman, yes," the Thai said, his voice gone sharp with surprise at Paul's odd use of the word "it." But Paul couldn't help himself. Paul hated these animals whether God had made them or not, and he was damned if he would dignify them with personal pronouns.

"Under no circumstances is she to be detained."

"Excuse me, but that is a violation of our sovereignty. I am sorry."

Paul really noticed the officer for the first time. "Ask the French to photograph her and follow her. But *not* to detain her."

The Thai smiled. Paul could only hope that they would cooperate. He could not push the matter further, not and risk an inquiry to the embassy about the nature of his activities. The Thai were hair-trigger friends. They did not like CIA operations taking place on their soil without their knowledge.

At high levels in the government, he was golden. But these cops were strictly low-level, and they didn't know one damn thing about Paul's secret brief and his secret powers.

He gazed down at the remains, almost willing them to speak. But they said nothing. The face was stretched so tight against the skull that it looked like something you might buy for Halloween.

"Turn him over," he said. "I want to look at the back."

Two of the cops obliged. Paul knew that the vampires used human skin for articles of clothing—gloves and such—because you found such things in their lairs. He'd thought maybe the back of this man would be as neatly skinned as his own father's had been.

He'd held some of those gloves and purses in his hands for a long, long time. He'd wondered which of the creatures had worn garments made from his dad. Whenever he and his crew found these things, they collected them with reverence and they blessed them and they cremated them and made a little ritual of scattering the ashes.

Melodramatic? You could say so. Sentimental. Sure. But his crew were united on two things: Any human remains they located would be respected, and no vampire would be left alive. Scorched-earth policy. Absolute.

Think if they had to read Miranda warnings. Think if the vampires were allowed legal defense, say, in India, where the prisons leaked and it could take years before a case came to trial? What if they claimed murder as their natural right, and proved that they were created by God to prey upon the human being? Presumably, laws would then have to be written allowing them to take a certain number of humans as prey each year, much as we allow ourselves to take whales.

And what about the endangered-species acts in various countries, most especially Europe and the U.S.? If the vampire was declared an endangered species—and it was conceivable, given their comparative rarity—then Paul and his crew would be out of business altogether. Governments would end up in the business of encouraging the vampire to breed and protecting its habitat—the ghetto, the teeming slum, the homeless shelter.

A man with glasses approached Paul. "We understand that you will be able to inform us of the manner of death."

"Death by misadventure."

"Excuse me?"

"The man had a bad adventure, obviously. So that's the conclusion—death by misadventure."

"You are coming all the way from KL to tell us this—this nothing?"

"The corpse is U.S. property," Paul said. "I'm going to remove it to the States." He needed it. He needed any trace of nonhuman DNA he could find. The hair from Tokyo wasn't enough. But two samples—that would end the human-animal controversy.

"Now, wait," the colonel inspector said, "now—"

"It's a done deal." He pulled the fax he'd gotten from the Thai foreign office before he left KL. He unfolded it. " 'You will deliver the remains to Mr. Paul Ward of the United States Embassy.' That is what it says."

The man nodded, reading the letter. Then his eyes met

Paul's. His eyes pleaded. "Please tell me in confidence what has happened."

"He met with a misadventure."

You rarely saw anger in the Thai. They were a reserved and very polite people. But the inspector's eyes grew hard and small, and Paul knew that there was fury seething within him. Thailand had never been colonized for a reason. The Thai might be polite, but they would fight for their independence quite literally to the last man. No deals. "I would like to know, then, if I may, whether or not we are likely to see any more such murders."

Paul gestured toward the yellow, sticklike corpse. "I'm a scientist. I'm trying to figure it out."

"Is it, then, a disease?"

"No, no, he was killed. You can count on that."

The room was full of police and forensics experts. Bangkok was not happy with this bizarre situation. Interpol was not happy, and asking all sorts of questions about who the hell had been running around with forged ID of that quality in his wallet, while at the same time pretending to Thailand that they knew who the guy was. Lots of secret handshakes being traded all around.

Somebody was going to have to tell the widow and her three kids, too, and Paul suspected that he would be elected.

"I am Dr. Ramanujan," a compact man said, jostling up, gesturing with his sterile gloves. "What has done this? Do you know what has done this, because I do not know?"

Paul hated to lie, and he did not lie now. He kept his secret and revealed it at the same time. "A killer did it, using a very special and unusual method of fluid extraction."

"And where are the body fluids? The blood, for example?"

"The fluids are gone."

"Gone?"

"We will not find the fluids."

Ramanujan grinned, shaking his head. "Riddles, sir, riddles instead of answers."

They bagged the body for him and delivered all their forensic gleanings in a series of plastic pouches, each neatly labeled in Thai and English.

On the way down, the colonel inspector said, "Would you care to have a drink with me?"

Paul would have loved a drink right now. Twenty drinks. But he had an urgent mission halfway around the world. As fast as humanly possible, he and his crew had to follow "Marie Tallman" to Paris. And not on tomorrow's flights, either.

"I'll take a raincheck. I need to get to Paris as quickly as possible."

"There are no more flights from Bangkok to Paris today."

"There's one."

"I know the schedules very well, I am sorry."

"This is off the schedule."

"The American embassy has its own flights?"

Paul thought of the cramped USAF Falcon Jet that would carry them to gay Paree. "Just this one."

"Then that's good for you."

He wondered. He had the sense that Paris was going to be a ferocious confrontation. For the first time, they would be facing vampires who expected them.

The question was stark: Without the advantage of surprise, did he and his people—his brave people—have any chance at all?

FOUR

The Castle of the White Queen

Miriam had been moving effortlessly through human society since before mankind had invented the arch, and she considered herself entirely capable of handling their customs, from the letters testament of the Imperial Roman Curia to the passports of the American Department of State. So she was surprised when the customs officer said, "Please come this way, Madame Tallman."

She stared at him so hard that he blinked and took an involuntary step back. Shaking his head, he glanced again at her passport, then up to her face. "Come, please."

"Is there something wrong?"

"You will talk to the prefect."

The prefect? That sounded ominous. As Miriam followed along behind the customs official, she considered that they must have found the body. They had traced Marie Tallman; it was that simple.

As she walked, she felt somebody fall in behind her. She could smell the gun the man was carrying, just as she could smell the polish on his brass and the wax on his shoes. She knew he was a policeman, in full uniform. His breath was young and steady, powerful. He was also quite close to her, alert for any attempt at escape.

They thought, therefore, that she would be aware of why she was being detained. Ahead of her, the customs officer had hunched his shoulders. He feared that she might attempt to harm him.

These men did not think that they had apprehended some poor soul caught up in a fiasco of identity confusion. They believed that they were escorting a criminal who knew very well that she was in serious trouble.

These thoughts passed through Miriam's mind in a flash. The next instant, she was looking for a means of escape. She was a master of the human being, smarter, stronger, and quicker. It would be nothing for her to overpower both of these men. The gun was a trivial problem. Before his hand had even started to reach for it, both creatures could be knocked senseless.

The problem was the surroundings. There were other people going up and down the hallway. The customs area they had just left teemed with dozens more. The offices, most of which had glass walls, were also full of people.

So Miriam kept walking, hoping that she would be in a private situation for the few seconds she needed, before they locked her away. They would lock her away; she had no doubt of it.

It had been extraordinarily foolish to abandon that remnant. It was drilled into them from childhood: Never let man see the results of your feeding. Humans are cattle, but they are bright cattle and they must not be made aware of their true situation. The entire species could, in effect, stampede.

As appeared to be happening—in effect. There simply wasn't anything left to think. The Asians had already been swept away in the onslaught, and now she had endangered herself in a foolish, heedless moment of panic, and possibly many others of her kind as well. Because of what she had done, she was in the process of being captured by human beings. A Keeper!

They came to a door. The customs officer said, "Enter, please." She could feel the young policeman's breath on her neck. There was no more time. She had to act, and no matter the crowd.

She stepped away from the door and into the center of the corridor. This left the two men facing each other, their eyes widening in surprise at the speed of her movement. To them, she would have seemed to temporarily disappear. Keepers had bred humans to be slow, for convenience. That way they could be outrun, outjumped, and outmaneuvered. Prey should be easy to herd.

Before the two men could turn to face her, she had slipped her hands behind their heads and pressed them together sharply. They dropped like sacks.

A secretary rushed out of an office two doors down. She looked at Miriam. She could not associate a young girl in an elegant suit with two unconscious men. "What has happened?"

"Gas," Miriam cried. "The corridor is full of gas!" She turned and went striding on toward the emergency exit at the far end. A moment later, a horn started hooting. The terrified secretary had pulled the fire alarm and then rushed out into the customs area shouting, "Gas!" as she ran.

Opening the emergency exit, Miriam looked about for a way back into the main part of the terminal. Once out of the customs area, she would be able to go into Paris. She'd have to get Sarah to work up a new identity and FedEx her the passport. She certainly could not use the Tallman identity, and dared not risk her own.

Others were coming out behind her, so she climbed some concrete steps, then went down a long, empty passageway. Behind her, a man shouted that she was going the wrong way. She noticed his American-sounding voice, then glimpsed a narrow, dark figure starting to run toward her. She did not look back again.

She soon found herself in a bustling staging area for the assembly of airline meals. There were shelves full of little trays and plastic cutlery, and a wall lined with institutional refrigerators. Workers stood at tables putting the meals together on trays. Others covered them with plastic wrap. Others still packed them in steel shelves, ready to be wheeled out to the waiting planes.

There were aluminum double doors at the far end of the room. Striding with the confidence of a person who belonged exactly where she was, Miriam went to these doors.

Behind her there was a cry, *"Halte!"*

Miriam ran. She ran as hard and as fast as she could, speeding along the corridor and into a locker room. This was where the various workers changed into their uniforms.

"Halte Halte!"

A new man had burst into the room at the far end. Her throat tightened; she felt a sudden surge of rage. The reason was that this creature had appeared ahead of her. They knew exactly where she was. They must be using radios to surround her. She looked around for doors other than the ones she and the gendarme had entered.

She slipped through one, found herself in a shower room. The door had nothing but a handle lock, which she twisted. At once, he began to shake it violently from the other side.

She threw open a window. There was a drop of about three stories to an area of tarmac crowded with baggage lorries. As the door burst open behind her, she went to the window and jumped.

Her teeth clashed together and her ankles shot pain up her legs from the impact. The palms of her hands burned when they slapped against the pavement. Immediately, she rolled under the overhang of the building, making herself impossible to see from above.

The shock had damaged the heel of one of her shoes. She struggled away, moving among the speeding baggage lorries. Stopping for a moment, she pulled off her shoes. The heel was not usable.

This dim, booming space was extremely alien. She'd never been inside a factory, never seen the raw side of human engineering and architecture. She'd preferred to live her life in an older, more familiar aesthetic. Her home in Manhattan was a hundred and fifteen years old; she stayed almost exclusively in old, familiar hotels when she traveled. She could handle the human world, but she'd never seen a place like this before, never imagined that the hidden parts of the human world were this mechanical.

Ahead of her she saw a passageway. The floor was dark and marked by white and yellow lines. The passage curved up and to the right. This appeared to lead away from the customs enclosure, so she began walking along it. It was lighted by fluorescent tubes, some of them flickering and some completely out. The effect was eerie, and made more so by a high-pitched whining sound coming from ahead. She stopped to listen and tried to place this sound, but she could not.

The farther into the passage she went, the louder it

became. She stopped again. It would rise and fall, then rise again. Then it almost faded entirely. She resumed walking, passing the endless, black-scuffed walls, moving beneath the flickering lights.

The sound screamed out right in her face, and her entire field of vision was filled with glaring lights. A horn began sounding.

There was no room to lie down, the oncoming machine was too low. She looked up—and there, where the lights were, she could grab hold. She leaped, missed by inches. The machine got closer, the lights growing as big as saucers, the glare blinding her and pinning her like the stunned animal that she was. The horn blared and blared. She crouched.

Like most animals', the backs of a Keeper's eyes were reflective. When she looked directly into those lights, the driver would have seen a flare as if from the eyes of a deer or a tiger. Human night vision had been bred away. Better that they sleep at night, giving the Keepers time to tend herd and feed.

There were only seconds left now. The machine would tear her to shreds. She would die from that—actually die. It was an oblivion that had haunted her all her life. She did not think that Keepers persisted in the memory of nature. She did not want to cease to be.

She sprang up from her crouching position and reached toward the light fixtures. She grabbed the edge and drew herself up, hooking one leg along the lip of the long fixture and pressing the rest of her body against the ceiling.

With a hot blast of air the machine went shrieking past, not an inch below her breast. It seemed to take forever, and she soon felt her fingers and toes slipping. She was going to fall onto the roof of the thing.

And then it was gone, and she fell instead to the floor, which she knew now was really a subterranean road. Would another machine come? Of course. Would the driver have radioed her position back to her pursuers? Of course.

She knew, now, that she was in an extremely serious situation. Man had changed. Man was now effective and efficient. She remembered the Paris of fifty years ago, a compact, intricate city traveled by tiny automobiles and herds of bicycles. Only the Métropolitain sped the way this thing had. But it had been on rails.

Ahead, the screaming sound had started again. Another of the machines was coming. She saw, perhaps two hundred yards farther on, a ladder inset into the wall. It led to a service hatch of some kind.

The machine was coming, getting louder. There was a wind blowing in her face, getting steadily harder. This must be a subway system that served just the airport. But how could that be? Paris had a compact airfield, as she recalled, albeit a busy one.

It had grown huge, that was the answer, and she was thinking that maybe her brothers and sisters were at least somewhat right. Maybe she needed to stick closer to home, too, because this situation was getting out of hand, *way* out of hand. She sprinted, moving easily twice as fast as the fastest human runner—but what did that matter in a world where the machines hurtled along at phenomenal velocity? Even the strength of a Keeper was nothing against fifty tons of speeding steel.

As she reached the ladder, the lights of the train appeared. Immediately, the horn started blaring. Worse, a screaming sound began and the train started to slow dramatically. This time, the driver had seen her and put on his brakes. The last thing she needed was a confrontation in this damned tunnel. That would be the end. She'd be trapped then.

She bolted up the ladder, only to find that the steel hatch was battened down tight. Her great strength enabled her to push it until it bent and popped open.

The train came to a stop about ten feet from her. It stood there, invisible behind its lights, its horn honking and honking. Back where she had come from, voices rose, people shouting in French not to move . . . French, and also that one American voice.

She clambered up through the hatch. Now she was in an access tunnel, and not far away there was a door. She didn't think it would make any sense to go along this tunnel, even though it was obviously meant for pedestrians and not trains. Tunnels were damned traps. She went through the door.

Light flared in her face; a roar assailed her. She staggered, and a voice said, *"Pardon."* She had stumbled into a man in a taxi queue. He reached out, took her waist. *"Madame?"* he said, his voice rising in question.

"Sorry," she babbled in English, then, in French, *"Pardon, je suis confuse."*

He looked her up and down. The other people in the queue were staring.

"I have broken my shoe," she added, smiling weakly. Then she crept to the back of the line. She had escaped the horrors of the police and the dangers of the maze. Somehow, she had reached the outside world.

She must get a hotel room, she thought, then seek out Martin Soule. He had been a friend of her mother's back in the days of powdered wigs. She'd seen him fifty years ago. Martin was very ancient and wise, very careful. He was also stylish, powerful and daring. Like Miriam, he was a wine enthusiast, and had even desensitized himself to some of their fodder, because it was so difficult to move in French society without eating. Once, he'd made her laugh by drinking the blood of an enormous fish. But then his preparation of it according to human cooking principles had revolted her. She still remembered the ghastly odor of the hot, dense flesh when it came steaming out of the poacher.

She was still well back in the queue when she noticed the policeman with a radio to his lips, staring at her as he talked. Her heart sank. At home, she dealt easily with the police. The police were her friends. She had the Sixth Precinct, where her club was located, well paid off. But she could not pay these cops off.

The policeman came striding toward the queue. He had his hand on the butt of his pistol. She thought to run, but there were two more of them coming from the opposite direction. Her only choice was to leap out into traffic and trust to her speed and dexterity to get through the cars that shot past just beyond the taxi stand. But even that would lead only to a wall.

When she realized that there was no escape, she let out an involuntary growl that made the woman standing ahead of her whip round, her face pale, her eyes practically popping out. Miriam's whole instinct now was to kill. Had she not applied her powerful will, she might have torn the creature's throat out.

Quelling her damned instincts, she forced a smile onto her face. She'd play her last card—give them her emergency Cheryl Blackmore driver's license and claim to have lost her passport. Maybe before they discovered that Cheryl Blackmore was a long-dead resident of Nebraska and most certainly did not rate a passport, she would have found some means of escape.

The three policemen arrived—and began chatting together. They were laughing, completely at their ease, taking no notice whatsoever of her. They'd been talking on their radios merely to arrange their coffee break.

Now, she thought, laughing to herself, there was the old mankind, the gentle, sloppy, genial humanity that the Keepers had so carefully bred.

As she slipped into her taxi, she was filled with a sort of glee. It was delicious to have escaped, delicious and lovely and joyous. And damn, damn lucky.

Her mouth began to dry out, her muscles to relax. The waves of hate stopped crashing in her heart. The taxi moved up a long ramp into the sunlight, and Miriam relaxed back against the seat.

"*Votre destination, madame?*"

"The Ritz," she said. She'd take a huge suite. The Ritz would mean silk sheets like the ones at home, and a long call to Sarah to say how lonely she was and how far away she felt . . . and to tell her to get that new passport over here fast.

In the cab, she pressed her shoe together as best she could, rearranged her hair, freshened her face, and tried to smooth the wrinkles in her suit. Her suitcase was gone forever, of course, and so she would have to buy new clothes, and there would be no time for proper tailoring at Chanel. That would make Sarah happy. They were both extremely fashionable, of course, but Sarah thought Miriam much too conservative.

So much of the Paris whizzing past was unfamiliar. The huge roads, the endless blocks of buildings that had grown like monstrous cliffs beyond the Périphérique distressed and confused her.

It was remade, entirely remade, and in just these few years! But then the taxi swung off the flying roadway and went down into territory that was, thankfully, more familiar. They were on the Rue de Vaugirard, where Philippe Vendôme had lived. She'd been fascinated by his alchemical studies, had stayed with him a few years while she was recovering from the grief of her mother's destruction. She'd adored him, with his wonderful, sophisticated manner and his passable skill at whist. Miriam loved games, but finding humans who could be effective opponents was not easy.

She had given Philippe of her blood, and turned back the years for him. He had become a searcher after the secrets of the Keepers. Useless, that, in the early eighteenth century. But he had been a pleasant companion, her entire pleasure for a while, until she'd met Lord Hadley's son John.

"Philippe," she murmured, thinking of that lovely house of his. In 1956 it had been something of a ruin. She had walked silent halls where she had laughed and loved with him, and reflected on the brief lives of men. Now she could only glimpse it, the once-proud estate little more than a front on a huge building. The street the taxi bounced along had been laid over part of the elegant park. Here, she and he had come and fed his swans.

Now they went underground, into a roaring tunnel full of autos and lorries, speeding along at a deadly clip. And here, quite suddenly, was the Champs Élysées. They had come by a new high-speed route.

It was all so familiar and all so dear. She remembered it from fifty years ago, even a hundred—the same marvelous width, the same trees, the same grand ambiance. Yes, this was just as it had been since Louis Philippe had commissioned Haussmann to reconstruct the intricate, ancient spaghetti-bowl that had been the Paris of the last age.

They were soon passing along the Rue St. Honoré, lined

with luscious shops, in the windows of which she glimpsed the strangely simple clothing of this era, clothing that increasingly emphasized anything that was male about the female. The ideal form for human women was becoming that of the boy. She preferred elegance.

Then, here was the Place Vendôme. The Ritz was *exact*. Lovely and beloved! She had first come to this place on a rainswept evening back before the motor. What trip had that been? Perhaps 1900, when she and John Blaylock had come here in search of the luxury that was just then gaining the hotel its grand reputation.

Getting down from the taxi—or up, actually, out of this tiny modern sardine tin—she found herself face-to-face with a doorman in the hotel's familiar green livery, even his coat reminiscent of more gentle days.

She went into the lobby, passing across the thick carpet to reception. No face was familiar, of course. Fifty years and all the humans would have changed. They came and went like so much foam on a restless wave. Well, at least she had Sarah free and clear for another century, perhaps two . . . unless, of course, the dear found some clever scientific way to last longer. Sarah knew the ugly secret of her own artificial longevity. Such knowledge would have driven a lesser human mad, but Sarah was often at her test tubes, poor thing.

"I'm afraid I have no reservation," Miriam said to the clerk, who managed to appear affable and also a little concerned at the same time. A blink of his eyes as she approached had told her that he knew exactly how old her suit was. She was travel-weary and hobbling from the broken shoe. Altogether, she could not look to him as if she belonged here. She dared not throw the names of fifty years ago around to impress him, either. Coming from what appeared to be a girl of twenty-five dressed in her grandmother's old clothes, such an attempt to impress would instead seem like the babbling of a madwoman.

"I am so sorry," he began.

"I would like a suite. I prefer the fourth floor front, if you don't mind." These were among the best rooms in the hotel, and the only ones she would even consider using.

He asked for her credit card. She gave him Sarah's Visa. It annoyed Sarah for her to use this card, but there was at present no choice. Using her own card was a serious risk, and Marie Tallman was retired forever. She waited while he made a phone call.

"I'm sorry, madame, this is declined."

Must be crowding its credit limit, she thought. Just like Sarah to have a card like this. Too bad she didn't have a copy of Sarah's American Express card, but the only one of those in her possession was her own.

"Perhaps it's defective, madame. If you have another—"

She turned and faced the doors. She had no desire to push this, even to remain here for another minute. She had to call Sarah. She started to open her cell phone, then hesitated. The call would not be secure.

"Is there a public telephone?"

"But of course, madame." He directed her to a call box. She took out her AT&T card, which was in Sarah's name, and dialed the call straight through to their emergency number. This only rang if it was absolutely urgent, so she could be sure that Sarah would pick up right away.

She did not pick up. It was five hours earlier in New York, making it eight o'clock in the morning. Sarah would be home, surely. She tried the other number, the regular one. Only the answering machine came on.

She tried the club. No answer there, not at this hour. Damn the woman, where was she when she was needed?

Maybe she'd fed. Maybe she was in Sleep. Yes, that was it. Of course, that must be it . . . must be. She put the phone down.

She thought matters over. She was effectively broke. But she was never broke; she'd had scads of money, always.

Perhaps she could try another hotel, some lesser place. There must be some credit left on the Visa card. Then she thought—how could she get into any hotel, this one included, without giving them a passport? The answer was that she couldn't, and the smaller and sleazier the hotel, the more obsessive it would be about identification. The Tallman passport needed to be burned; that's all it was good for.

She saw that she was still in mortal danger. They would have a description of her, and she hadn't even a change of clothes. They'd be searching the hotels, of course. It was logical.

She had to go to the Castle of the White Queen. Fifty years ago, Martin had been there. Maybe he still was, and maybe he could help her. Of course he could. He'd been a more worldly sort than Lamia, or even Miriam herself.

She began walking, soon coming into the Place de l'Opéra. She headed for the Métro. On the way, she stopped at a small *bureau de change* and turned her Thai baht into euros. She got forty of them. As well, she had two hundred U.S. dollars in cash. Not much, not much at all. But she never traveled with cash; she didn't need to. Being limitlessly wealthy made her sudden poverty especially difficult. She didn't know how to function.

She went down the steps into the clanging world of the Métro. She remembered it from her last visit, but she'd only used it once, and that was to get around a traffic accident when she'd been hurrying to the opera. There was difficulty with the change booth, then confusion about which *direction* she wanted. The hurrying crowds made it no easier. But, in the end, she found herself primly seated in a car going in the correct direction.

The Castle of the White Queen had been built on land that the Keepers had reserved for themselves from time immemorial. It was on the Rue des Gobelins, and parts of it had been rented to the Gobelins family and fitted out by them as a tannery. At night, after Gobelins and his people went home; the hides tanned there were not necessarily bovine. The Keepers lived in the upper reaches of the building.

Locally, there were many legends about why it was called the Castle of the White Queen. Some said that Blanche de Castille had built it, others that it had belonged to Blanche de Navarre. The real builder was Miriam's dear mother, who had been known among her peers as the White Queen, for her grandeur, her splendid pallor, and the fact that their family had come out of the white sands of the North African desert.

The scent of man that filled the Métro did not make Miriam's jaws spread, let alone fill. As troubling as all this was, at least she was full, and very satisfactorily so. That had been a healthy little thing she'd eaten. She could easily bear this swim in a sea of food.

An accordionist began to play, and Miriam closed her eyes to listen. Certain things about Paris were almost timeless, it seemed. When she and her mother had been here, the humans had been making similar music, but with different instruments. The music was rougher and wilder then, but they were wilder also, the humans, in times past.

In those days, feeding in a place like Paris had been so easy that some Keepers had overfed, gorging until they bled out through their pores, and their orifices ran with the blood of their victims. The human population had been a seething, helpless, ignorant mass, living in the streets, under the bridges, anywhere there was a bit of shelter. The old cities had been full of nameless, aimless wanderers who could be plucked up like fruits fallen to the ground.

She missed Gobelins and left the Métro at d'Italie instead. Coming up to the street, she looked around her. She experienced a sense of satisfaction: things were really unchanged here.

She quickened her step, eager to get a sight of the castle. If the Keepers had been driven off—well, she'd deal with that problem when she had to.

Ahead was the tiny Rue des Gobelins, hardly an alleyway running off the much wider avenue. She turned into it— and stopped, staring struck with wonder. The Castle of the White Queen was *exact,* just like the Ritz. Worn, but so precisely the same that she thought it must still be in the hands of Keepers.

Until this moment, she had not realized how afraid she had actually been. She needed her kind now. And she needed, also, to warn them. In the hurly-burly of the past few hours, she had all but lost sight of why she was here and not back in New York.

Ironic indeed that the strongest, most intelligent species on the planet, the very pinnacle of the food chain, was in the same predicament as the frog and the gorilla.

It had crept up on them so easily, the result of a long series of what had, at the time, seemed like brilliant breeding maneuvers.

Back thirty thousand years ago, they had almost lost the entire human stock to a plague. They'd rotted where they stood, the poor things. It had been determined that overeager breeding had been the culprit. Generations of them had been bred for their nutritional value, which meant an imbalance of red over white blood cells. The result? They'd become prone to all sorts of diseases.

To ensure that they would survive and still remain the delicious food source that they'd been made to be, the Keepers had decided in conclave to increase the human population. To accomplish this, sexual seasonality had been bred out of the species entirely. This had been done by breeding for high levels of sexual hormones. As a result, the creatures had bloomed into bizarre sexual parodies of normal animals. Their genitals had moved to the front of their bodies, the penises and mammaries becoming huge. Their body hair had disappeared. They had become sexually obsessed, the females much more retiring than other mammals, and the males far more aggressive.

She moved toward the old castle. The last time she had entered this portal, it had been hand-in-hand with her mom. The building had been new then, smelling of beeswax and freshly hewn stone. Inside, the great rooms had glowed with candlelight. Lovely bedchambers had been built high in the structure, behind small windows so that Keepers could linger over their kills, and the cries of pleasure and anguish could not be heard from the streets below.

Just under that garret there, behind the little, arched window was a sumptuous chamber where a Keeper could make sport with his kill for as long as he cared to, flushing it with fear again and again, then calming it and delivering bursts of incapacitating pleasure to it. This would bring the flavor of its blood to an incredibly delicious richness, sweet and sour, reflecting the secret harmonies that sounded between agony and ecstasy.

She had not fed like that in a very long time. Mother Lamia always did. Sometimes her feedings would last for days. But Miriam's human lovers had not cared for it and had felt awful for the victims when she did it.

Sarah, for example, could only bear to see Miriam do the quickest of kills. She herself struggled to live without killing, taking her nourishment from blood bank goop and pleading with Miriam for frequent transfusions that left both of them dizzy and bitchy.

Miriam went to the door. The way she felt now, she'd like to take a big, blood-packed human straight up to that chamber. Full or not, she'd spend a couple of days on it, using all of mother's old techniques.

They were the Keepers, not the kept. No matter how brilliant, how numerous, or how violent, mankind remained first and foremost, their damned *property!*

She pushed at the door. Locked. She shook it three times, making the very precise movements that were designed to dislodge the tumblers, in the event you had no key. Keepers did not have private property. All belonged to all.

It opened. She stepped in, treading softly in the footsteps of her lost past. A profound silence fell, a Keeper silence. Overhead, the great beams that had been so rich a brown in mother's day now were glowing black, as if they had turned into iron. The tanning vats were empty.

She went across the echoing floor of the factory to the narrow stair. Mother had hauled their victims up these very treads, Miriam following along to watch and learn.

How silent it was here, more silent than any human place.

This was still a lair, oh, yes. But where was its inhabitant? Would he not be at least a little curious about the stealthy noises down below, the unmistakable sounds of another Keeper entering the sanctum?

"Hello," she said, her voice uttering the sibilant, infinitely subtle sound of Prime for the first time in many a long year.

He was much smaller than she remembered, and as dirty as a coal-scuttle, a creature that had not bathed since the French court had filled its tubs with milk. His eyes were tiny and narrow, and he had the pinched face of a bat. He came forward wearing the tattered remains of a hundred-year-old frock coat, otherwise as naked as at his ancient birth. He was hungry, hissing hungry, as shadowy and insubstantial as a ghost.

A wound opened in his ghastly face, bright red and dripping. He uttered a sound, horribly eager, and she realized that he thought her human. She was so radically different looking from other Keepers that he believed her one of the kept.

His skeletal hands snatched her wrists, enclosed them in a Keeper's iron grip. Then his eyes met hers. The bright glow of eagerness flickered, faded. He had realized his mistake.

He dropped his hands to his sides, then slumped at her feet. "*M'aidez,*" he whispered, not in Prime but in French.

As she looked down at this filthy, groveling, helpless creature, she stuffed her fist in her mouth. But he was not deceived. He knew that he revolted her. Because he laughed, bitterly, angrily, laughed to cover her screams.

FIVE

The Skylights of Paris

Paul had missed the traveler by ten seconds. He'd glimpsed the creature—tall, wearing normal clothes (an old-fashioned-looking woman's suit), a blond spray of hair, that was all he'd seen.

Rain roared against the skylight; thunder echoed across the roofs of Paris. He shouted into the phone, "Your people lost her. You and the French."

He listened to Sam Mazur's whining, complicated reply. He was CIA station chief at the U.S. embassy. Cupping his hand over the mouthpiece, Paul whispered to Becky Driver, "That's a paper cup. I said *bucket*."

"A paper cup is what we have."

Sam continued whining away about how the French had not cooperated and were not going to cooperate, that unless they knew chapter and verse exactly what the operation was about, it would absolutely not unfold on French soil.

"Tell me this, Sam. I'm curious. Why the hardening of the heart? I mean, the French don't like U.S. intelligence. But we aren't the enemy. They've always recognized that in the past."

"Cold War's over, my friend. Europe is sick of us, and France is sickest of all. They hate the way we and the Brits use the Echelon system to spy on them electronically. U.S.

intelligence has had it here, man. Time to pack up our silencers and go home."

The paper cup into which the entire thunderstorm appeared to be dripping had filled up. "Becky, do you think you could empty this? These are Burmese shoes. I can't risk getting them wet."

She cast her big brown eyes down toward his feet. "You got those in Myanmar?"

"Had them made. I'm suspicious that there's cardboard involved."

"They look like funeral shoes."

"What the hell are 'funeral shoes'?"

"The kind guys wear to funerals. Shiny, black, and from about 1974."

Charlie Frater snickered. Paul glared at them both. He'd brought dumpy, bespeckled Charlie and lithe, lovely Becky because they were the most ferocious close-in workers he had. Charlie was one of those people who just did not stop, not ever. He walked into danger like a priest walking into his church. The wonder of it was he looked like a guy who lived behind a desk deep in some civil service nowhere.

Becky, on the other hand, fancied herself a lady spy from the movies. She cultivated the effect with her dark, flowing hair and her long coats. She was only twenty-three, but she was the most cheerful and fearless warrior he had. And quick. So breathtakingly quick.

Not a man on the team hadn't thought about Becky, probably dreamed about her. Paul had. But she kept to herself emotionally. Paul didn't pry.

The rest of the team would assemble in the States. Paul's highest priority was to eradicate the vampires there, always had been. Asia had been done first because it was available.

Now he had to stop this traveler, lest she get to the U.S. and organize opposition. He had to stop her here.

He returned to Sam. "Bottom line is this: We lost that damn thing and it is now running around Paris telling all of its fuckin' friends that somebody's onto them. I regard that as your fault. I'm sorry."

"May I hang up?"

"You may not."

" 'Cause I have something to do. Important. Secret."

"Tell me, does a ritual chewing out *always* make you need to take a dump?"

"Yes, it does."

Paul carefully replaced the receiver in the cradle.

Becky and Charlie were staring at him.

"What?"

"What do you mean, what? What the hell did he say?"

"He's a CIA bureaucrat. He said nothing."

The skylight was now leaking in five places. As night fell, the immense skyscraper across the street began to light up. Whatever slight sense of privacy the room might have afforded was gone. Worse, there was no way to curtain off the skylight. At least two thousand office workers could look directly down into what was supposed to be a secret CIA safe house.

Paul stared up at the office building. "Let's put together some dance numbers," he said.

Charlie, who was, for some reason, practicing rolling cigarettes with a little machine, responded. "Stick a hat up there and maybe they'll throw change."

"Goddamnit, how are we gonna use this sty? Do either of you have a room that has a little privacy for us to work in, at least?"

"They're way too small, boss," Becky responded.

"Bullshit. We can manage."

"More than one person in my cell and the zipper gets stuck."

Paul thought, *sounds like fun*. He said, "Goddamnit!"

"Is this the cheapest hotel in Paris?" Charlie asked.

"Our employer is not in the habit of billeting its personnel in the cheapest anything. The *Sans Douche* is the cheapest inconveniently located piece-of-shit hotel in Paris. It's conceivable, although just barely, that there exists another hotel with a marginally lower price. But it will not be as bad as the dear ol' S.D. Would you care for some cat hair?" He slapped the bed, which was making him break out. "I've got plenty more than I need."

"What we need is a plan of action," Becky said, stating what was painfully obvious.

"What we need is a way to prevent the minister of the interior from calling in the ambassador and asking him why there are CIA personnel in Paris searching for the goddamn Bride of Dracula!"

"There was no Bride of Dracula, boss."

"There damn well *was* a Bride of Dracula."

"No, I don't believe there was, actually." Becky clicked the keys on her laptop a few times. "Nope. No *Bride of Dracula*, says the Internet Movie Database."

"Take a letter. Steven Spielberg: 'Stevie! Have I got an idea for you. It's Dracula, except she's a woman!' Ladies and gentlemen, I will now retire."

"Thing is, boss, how're we gonna find her?"

"To fuck around with the French or not to fuck around with the French, that is the question."

Charlie began to shuffle along beneath the skylight. "The

problem is, we need to get this done." He started singing, and that was terribly sad. " 'Cause she's spreadin' the news, she's doin' it today, 'cause she wants to be a part of it—"

"Don't they test for people like you anymore, Charles? I mean, when we signed on, the first thing they gave us was a test to see if we were assholes. In my generation."

"Cold War's over, boss. They're putting the old assholes out to pasture, not hiring new ones."

The phone rang. It was Sam, back again for more punishment.

"Hey, bro." They'd been in Cambodia together, in Laos. Paul Ward and Sam Mazur were allies of the blood and soul.

"Tell me something. Where's a good place to get sick on the food in—where are we, again, Beck?"

"Montparnasse."

"Montpissoir."

"There's thousands of restaurants out there."

"Good."

"Very."

"Cheap."

"Not very."

"McDonald's?"

"What're you doing in Montparnasse, anyway?"

"We're billeted in one of the shitty little hotels."

"God, you're low. You're so low that it worries me even talking to you. I have ambition. I want to be a big-timer back at Langley. Got my sights set on the Lesotho/Chad/Botswana desk. Can't swing something like that if people realize I'm tangled up with a liability like you."

"The French said Mrs. Tallman was believed to have taken a taxi into the city. They give you any details?"

"Well, actually, yes."

Paul tried not to hope, but did.

"The taxi is believed to have been French."

Had he not hated the vampires so much and been so obsessed with them, he would have been ready with a comeback. All he could do was plead. "I need French cooperation, Sam. You gotta get it."

"Whatever this is, they think it's some kind of crazy American bullshit, or maybe we're trying to make assholes outa them or whatever. What's that noise, anyway?"

"The rain."

"Really!"

"Really."

" 'Cause it's beautiful here."

"Oh, shut up. Something's bothering me, and lemme tell you what it is."

"I'm all ears."

"Well, this should look to the French like an Interpol operation. So why are they being so damn shirty?"

"Because they know it isn't."

"And why would they know that?"

"Because Interpol told them."

"Clever boys. Okay, Sam—and guys, both of you listen up. Because I do have a suggestion. I think that we ought to detail a fluent French speaker to liaise with the police on the pretext that we have a missing national—"

"All hell will break loose."

"No, listen to me. Tell them it's a matter of the heart. We just need to search around a bit—very discreetly—because this lady has run away from home, and it's politically sensitive. The French will buy this. It's the kind of thing they understand."

"The French will buy. They will not understand. They'll

want the name, rank, and serial number; then they'll tell you whether she's d.o.a. or not. That'll be the extent of their cooperation."

"What we need—look, Charlie, quit fucking with that— what is that?"

"A cigarette maker I bought in Bangyercock. It's neat."

"Bangkok, you sexist bitch," Becky said.

"Put the toy away. What we need—are you still there, Sam?"

"Patiently waiting."

"What we need, and I am talking about right now, the next few minutes, is we need to find the vampires she has come to see. We've lost her. No description except what looked like a Chanel suit circa about 1975 and real blond hair that was probably a damn wig. With no cooperation from the locals, we gotta shift gears. We use the same basic technique we've been using since Tokyo."

"Which is?"

"We cull police records for patterns of disappearance. My guess is that they'll cluster around the lairs, just like every- where else we've been. Here in Paris, we'll be able to get good maps—sewer lines, wire conduits, building plans, drainage pipes, all of it. It'll be easier than Singapore. A hell of a lot easier than Shanghai."

"Boss?"

"Yeah, Beck?"

"Ask him, who keeps crime records here? Is there a miss- ing persons bureau?"

Paul found a button on the phone next to a grill that was hidden on the side. When he pressed the button, he discov- ered that he had a decent speakerphone.

"Sam? You're on speaker."

"Hey."

Becky asked her question again.

"Prefecture of Police, Hall of Records," Sam replied. "There are going to be ordinary murders and disappearances mixed in," he continued.

"Meaning?"

"You're gonna have to read the description of each crime to find out if it started as a disappearance. You read French?"

"I read French," Charlie said.

"Sam," Becky asked, "when is a missing person declared dead in this country? If there's no presumption of foul play, say."

"Nine years."

"Are those records held separately?"

"I don't truthfully know. We'll need to ask the French."

"Shit," Becky said carefully.

"What if we tell them it's a historical survey," Paul suggested. "Becky's a student from Harvard. She's got a powerful daddy, and the embassy's been asked to help her do research for her thesis."

"That'll work," Sam said. "I can have her in the Hall of Records within the week."

"Tomorrow, Sam, first thing."

"There's bureaucracy, man. This is France."

"Do it, Sam."

"Is this stuff computerized?" Becky asked.

"You'll be looking at everything from the best databases you ever saw in your life to big black books that weigh forty pounds and make you sneeze."

It was agreed that they'd meet at a bar called Le Lapin Robuste on Rue du Sommerard tomorrow at noon. By then Sam would know exactly how the records were organized.

From there, they'd go to the Prefecture of Police, which was nearby, and see how far they could get.

As soon as the conference call ended, Charlie and Becky began looking through a Paris Zagat's guide for a restaurant for dinner. Paul watched them. He felt once again the awful, frantic feeling that had been coming over him from time to time ever since he'd seen the grotesque remains of poor Kiew Narawat.

For a while, the knowledge that vampires were real had depressed the hell out of him. He'd tried to find some special meaning in the fact that it had happened to his father, but all he'd found was special hate.

There was something ghastly about discovering that you weren't at the top of the food chain. It was like discovering that you had a hidden and fatal disease. You were left feeling horribly out of control. It entered your dreams . . . it was a cancer of the mind.

"Uncle Paul," Becky said, "since there's nothing we can do tonight, could me and Charlie please, oh please, take you out to some cheap-jack hole-in-the-wall for some onion soup and wine?"

That snapped the twig that had been about to snap ever since he'd lost track of the damn vampire. He looked at them—two kids made arrogant by too many easy victories.

"Do you think we've won? Is that why you're so damn smug, with your goddamn toys—" He swept the cigarette making machine out of Charlie's hands. Charlie, who was wound tight by training and had a hair trigger, just barely managed to restrain himself, stopping his flying fist with a sudden jerk of effort. Paul looked at him. "Do it," he said with an easy smile that he did not feel, "and I'll lay you out."

"Paul?"

"And as for you—" He grabbed her purse, which had been on the floor beside a chair. He held it up to the desk lamp. "What the fuck is this made out of?" He knew damn well. They all had this stuff—purses and wallets and belts, God only knew what else. The skin of the vampire was more delicate even than calfskin . . . probably than human, for that matter.

He emptied the purse on the desk and stuffed the damn thing into the trash can. "If they saw this skin, God only knows what they'd do."

"I'm not exactly planning to take it with me into some fucking lair. I'm not *that* stupid."

"Don't you understand? Even yet?" He looked from one surprised face to the other. "No. You don't. So you listen up, children, and you listen close. Something has changed. Big time. We've been dealing with something that's very old and very slow to react, and so far it's been easy. Like killing big bugs. You surprised 'em all, didn't you? Token resistance— gnashing teeth, hissing. It was fun! It got to be, anyway. The professionals. Fuck! Fuck us, we're assholes."

"Not me," Charlie said. His face was burning up. His eyes were beads. He was not trained to take abuse, and he did not take it well.

"Not you, little boy. Little, innocent boy. Lemme see your wallet."

"What the hell for?"

"Lemme see the goddamn thing!"

Charlie held it out. "They use human skin," he muttered.

Paul emptied it and threw it away with the purse. "Belts, shoes, anything?"

"That stuff is valuable!"

"If they see you with their goddamn *skins* in your hands, they're gonna know exactly who you are."

"They are not going to see us."

"Listen to me. One of them has gone up to the fifth floor of a hotel, killed one of your peers, and then flown from Bangkok to Paris on a god-for-damned *airplane!* I've seen it and it looked like some damn lady. *Very* human! So they don't all spend all their time hiding in lairs, do they? We're up against something new! Something we know not one damn thing about! They may be as old as damn Methuselah and they may be slow to respond, but they've taken a blow to the gut, and they are now responding! So you better watch your backs, because they are strong and they are smart and *now they know!*"

In the silence that followed, he became acutely aware of the humming of the little electric clock that stood on the table beside the bed. Charlie went to the window. Becky sat staring at her hands. Then she looked up. He saw tears gleaming in the edges of her eyes. He saw, also, that they were not tears of pain or embarrassment, but tears of rage. That was good. He liked that. Let her burn.

Dad was calling him from the back porch, "Paulie, Paulie let's make ice cream!" Dad smelled of the raw earth that was his livelihood. He smelled of the leaves of summer.

After Dad had disappeared, Paulie had walked on his knees all the way down the pasture road to the river and all the way back. He had done that while begging God that if Dad was found, he would never stop praying forever.

Mom had worked the farm until her bones stuck out, and been scared all the time, because if she did not get her crop in, she said, this family was gonna hit the road. There was no bank in North Carolina, and probably not anywhere, that would give her a crop loan.

"What're we supposed to do?" Becky asked.

"Your jobs!"

"I mean right now, Paul. Right this goddamn *second*, Paul! Because I don't see one damn thing we can do. We got a vague description of a woman who apparently looks nothing—not one thing—like the creatures we've been killing. I mean, I wouldn't make a damn handbag outa some *lady*. I saw little, shriveled monsters coated with dirt. I didn't see anything that looked even remotely like a tall, blond woman."

"We've known about these creatures for just a few years. They've been around for centuries and centuries. They've had a lotta time to think up a lotta things—"

"Not my point. My point is, you're having a goddamn hissy fit because Charlie and I—who happen to have been risking our lives in a filthy, horrible, and completely thankless job for three hellish years—wanted to sneak a couple of hours of downtime when there wasn't another goddamn thing we *could* do!" She folded her arms. "Explain yourself."

"Simple. I'm a field supervisor and you're not."

"So, what do we do, boss? Right now?" Charlie was trying to put his smashed cigarette machine back together.

"Whatever you damn well please. Go to Tour d'Argent and blow a month's pay. Moulin Rouge. The Slow Bar. Paint the goddamn town red, that's what Paris is for."

"I just want a good bouillabaisse."

"I'd like a nice *steak frites*."

Charlie and Becky went out into the rain. Paul listened to it hammering the damn skylight for about five minutes. And he began to think that maybe he should've gone with them. Maybe he could find a liquor store open somewhere; who the hell knew? He'd buy himself a quart of Stoli and toast himself into a stupor. Do him a world of good to wake up tomorrow with a hangover.

He went down in the tiny elevator, jammed his hat over his head, and set out into what might as well become an all night bar crawl. Maybe he'd even break up the tedium with a few fights. He loved to use his fists, always had. Just loved it. Probably be pretty easy to pick a fight with a frog. Hopefully, he'd find somebody with good enough moves to make it fun. Guys who liked to fight, they could spot each other in a bar. There were signals—some heavyset asshole glares at you for no damn reason, that's an invitation. Practiced bar fighters lived in their own secret world, and he was very much part of it. Nothing like beating the shit out of each other to make a couple of guys friends for life.

He set out along the Boulevard Montparnasse. There were lots of theaters, more than he remembered from when he was last here. Too bad it was night; he could have slipped over to the Orangerie and seen some fuckin' Monets.

Maybe the thing to do was go to a movie and brush up on his French. But there were also lots of bars. He went into one. Fulla damn tourists, wouldn't you know. Nervous Arabs sipping glasses of wine; Americans loudly demanding martinis.

There were a few Frenchies at the bar huddling over drinks or coffee. He slid up and managed, with some effort, to get a Stoli.

It was small and overpriced, but it worked okay, so he ordered another. He wondered if the whores around here were as overpriced as the liquor. He'd been spoiled by the Asians, who worked their asses off for a few bucks, massaging, blowing, sucking, fucking, combing, tickling, licking, and then handing you off to the social director for another round with a fresh face.

He said to nobody in particular, "You know why the predator is always smarter than the prey?"

Nobody answered.

"He has to be. The prey lives by work—crop the grass, till the field, whatever. The predator lives by his wits. That's why the gazelle hardly ever sees the lion. It's why the damn deer doesn't see us." He paused, then raised his glass. The barkeep did him. He knocked it back.

He'd come in here to fight, let's face it. But he was damn forty-eight years old; what was he gonna do? Also, you couldn't insult people who didn't understand your goddamn lingo.

He left. Rain hit him in the face. Striding along, he wished to God he had something to do that mattered. Why hadn't anybody taken a picture of the woman? Why hadn't they confiscated the damn passport? You couldn't even dragnet for her!

He was going so fast that he was practically running. The rain came down in sheets, in torrents. He watched the droplets sailing through the streetlights out of a low, rushing sky. He realized that he was running because he was scared. How must it feel to be eaten alive that way? They were parasites. Big, filthy suckerfish.

How *the fuck* had she eluded them? You don't sneak past customs when they have you caught. You can't! But she had.

Intelligence, of course. She was brilliant, obviously. So what did that mean? How many steps ahead was she? Ten? Fifty? A thousand? "Goddamnit!"

Then he thought, what if she knows about me? He couldn't see how, but he didn't have any two hundred and fifty IQ, either. She could be three feet away right now and he would have no way of knowing.

He found a little shop where they had some wine stuck in the window along with the displays of Orange Crush and Evian water. There was what looked like it might be a nice muscatel for about nine bucks. He shelled out and took it home under his arm.

Back in the hotel, he realized that he had no corkscrew. So he busted the neck and lay back on the bed drinking out of the jagged hole and staring up at the office building. All those dark windows and not a single human figure anywhere.

It wasn't muscatel, not by a long shot, but the wine did him okay, especially on top of the vodka. Maybe toward dawn he slept, and maybe not.

He awoke to gray, sad light and music coming up from the street—some kind of wild Arabic tune. The office building towered like a monster ghost above his skylight. He got up, wanted a cigarette, and went through the goddamn motions with the goddamn gum. He chewed it brutally, stuffed in another piece, and bore down until his jaws hummed.

He'd been rough on the kids last night. But that was nothing new. They'd gotten their frogs' legs anyway. Thing was, he loved his kids. He wanted them to get their fucking frogs' legs whenever they could.

The phone went *brrt-brrt brrt-brrt*. Neat sound, he thought.

"Yeah?"

"We got three places, boss. Three *arrondissements*."

"Beck?"

"Yeah, boss."

"Where are you?"

"Prefecture of Police Department of Records."

"Am I wrong, or is it six-fifteen in the morning?"

"Shit, they're gonna be opening this place up in an hour. We gotta get moving."

"But how the hell did you get in there? That's what I want to know."

"They got a lotta skylights in this town."

SIX

Martin Soule

Miriam had done her screaming and her weeping, and now sat in a little café seeking with increasing urgency for a victim for Martin. She had called Sarah again and again, and still had not gotten an answer. But she could not let this problem, as disturbing as it was becoming, intrude on her urgent mission. She did not know exactly what had happened to Martin, except that he was starving, and it was the most horrible thing she had ever seen.

Patience was essential on the hunt, no matter whether you were in a hurry or not. The trouble was, you could not easily imagine the prey to be dangerous, and in an emergency like this, your instincts screamed at you to just grab one, drag it off by the hair, and give it to the poor sufferer immediately.

She forced herself to sit still, to appear seductive. The waiter was admiring her and so were some of the male customers. But nobody moved, nobody *did* anything.

She sucked in warm smoke from her cigarette, drew it deep into her lungs, then blew it out with a carefully manufactured seductive pout. At least they had reasonably good cigarettes here. This Gitanes reminded her of a Bon-Ton. American cigarettes were awful now.

Why were these stupid men ignoring her? Had customs

changed so much? When she had last taken a victim in Europe, everything had been different. There had been an immediate flirting response, a quick seduction. That had happened on a quiet day in Clichy, in a little bar full of bums and Americans.

She was contacting men's eyes, but they wouldn't take it farther. She did not intend to let Martin starve, or any Keeper she could help, for that matter. As to why this had happened to him, she did not yet know. She could well imagine, though—something awful that had to do with human oppression of the Keeper. She sucked the cigarette hard, blew out a furious stream of smoke.

The temptation was growing ever stronger to just go off down the street and do what instinct urged. To some Keepers, the finest of all meals came from a sudden, spontaneous impulse to just snatch a victim, tear it open, and drink. That was her instinct, always. She'd been drawn to America in the first place by the easy, rambling life it offered her kind. She'd guzzled her way across the wild frontier. You could go a few miles on horseback and pluck your fruit along the trail without the slightest worry. People disappeared out there all the time.

She'd finished her cigarette and was just starting another when she realized that a young male was heading her way. She said in French, "Can you help me? May I have a light?"

He moved past her toward the loo. Could this be a homosexual bar? No. Clearly not. Owning a club in New York as she did, she could tell the sexual orientation of a place at a glance.

From the bar, another man said, "You speak the French of Voltaire, lady. All those 'thees' and 'thous.' " He raised his voice, mocking her, " 'Cans't thou render me assistance? Mays't I take a flame?' We call it a 'match,' now. New word! Where are you from?"

"The past," she snapped. She got to her feet. To hell with the French, if they were no longer interested in a pretty girl.

"Oh, mademoiselle, please, I am just making conversation! Don't be so quick. You must be an American. You learned your French in school. Well, you had an old teacher. Damned old, I'd say! But that can't be held against you."

He was plump. The back of his hands revealed the telltale blue streaks that suggested that the drinking veins would be nice and big. The flow of the carotid would be delightfully powerful.

She gave him a slow, careful smile, the kind that made the males pant. She had practiced smiling for years, and she considered herself an artiste. As soon as she showed her rows of perfectly believable but entirely artificial human teeth, he came to her table.

Finally. She responded with practiced indifference. Smile too eagerly, and he would back off . . . at least, that used to be their way.

"You are not telling me to go?"

She shrugged.

In a lower voice, he asked, "Is this going to cost me?"

"A little." Meaning everything you value the most—your breath, your blood, your very life.

"Then you're for real—a whore staking out the rear table in a café. It's so—I don't know—*charmant*. So 'old Paris!' And that language and the ancient suit. You *are* from the past. Look, I don't mean to spoil the effect, but I have only a couple hundred francs."

"How sad."

"Do you take credit cards?"

How could he ask something so profoundly stupid? A whore who took credit cards, indeed. She sucked in smoke, let it drift slowly out.

"I wish you wouldn't do that."

"Excuse me, my sir?"

"I gave it up. Bad for the chest." He tapped his breast, expanded his lungs, let the breath out. "Bet you couldn't manage that."

She could hold her breath for an hour. Keepers could drown, but it was not an easy death. For them, in fact, there were no easy deaths. The very body, every bone and sinew, was fanatically devoted to life. Man had the immortal soul, not his Keepers. Man could afford to die. Keepers had to stay alive forever, if possible.

Miriam put out her cigarette.

"You have the loveliest hands," he said, watching her.

She lifted a hand, bending her wrist delicately. When he kissed it, somebody over at the bar went, "Oh, my."

"Be quiet, you fucking gorilla!" the victim roared. "Never mind him, he has the manners of an animal."

She lowered her hand, touching his with the tips of her fingers: possession. "Good sir, I cannot stop with you the day long."

"Your French is advancing. Now you sound like somebody from about 1896."

"I have a pleasant room, and two hundred francs will be a good price."

She strolled with him down the Rue de Bobbilo, then crossed the Place d'Italie into the Avenue des Gobelins. It was raining, and she leaned in toward him to be under his umbrella. As they crossed the street, she stumbled against him. He glanced at her out of the corner of his eye, frowning slightly.

It had been a costly slip: he'd noticed her weight. Keepers had dense bones and muscles like rock. Inch for inch, they were twice as heavy as the prey.

The smallest slip would sometimes be all it took to spook a victim. Like most predators, Keepers were successful only about a third of the time. The myth of the vampire as a creeping, unstoppable supernatural force was just that, a myth.

They were passing a small hotel. He started in.

"No, not here."

"Where the hell is it, then? This is the only hotel around here."

"Just a little farther, good sir."

His pace slowed. She could feel him glancing at her again. Archaic language, excessive weight for her shape and size—he was not understanding, and that was making him nervous. She had to brush up on her damn French. Back in 1956, nobody had commented. But then, she hadn't fed here, either, only gone to Chanel for a thorough reoutfitting. She'd spent thousands. They would never have commented on her French.

She gave him a carefully rehearsed look—eyebrows raised, gray eyes gleaming—that was meant to disarm him with a combination of girlish sweetness and womanly experience. This look had worked since she had first developed it, back in the days when one's only mirror was a pond.

He went, "hmpf," like a slightly shocked horse. Then he grew silent. His tread became determined, even dogged.

She had him, by heaven! That was a wonderfully effective look. It had set the hook along the Via Appia and Watling Street, in Ur and Athens, in Venezia and ancient Granada.

"This isn't—oh, Christ—what the hell do you want to go in here for?"

"You'll see."

"Not for two hundred francs I won't. A blanket on the floor of an old wreck like this rates no more than fifty, sweetheart. No way you're gonna cheat Jean-Jacques. No damn way at all."

If she accepted his offer, he'd decide that she was probably diseased and that would be that. She had to waste time bargaining.

"Upstairs is very nice. You must pay a hundred and fifty."

"The hell—"

"But only when I conduct you to the chamber, and if you are pleased." She lowered her eyes.

"If I ain't pleased?"

"Then I am desolated. I will do it for your fifty, and fulfill your pleasure, for one hour of the clock."

"Now we're back to the ancien régime. Your French is fascinating." He looked up at Mother Lamia's old palace, the gray limestone, the sharp peak of the roof, the tiny windows in the tower. She knew what he was thinking: *Dare I go in there with such a strange woman?*

"I have my domicile within. It isn't as it appears."

He smirked, but followed her through the door into the cavernous space. He stopped, looked up into the high shadows. "My God, what a place!"

"Come with me." She moved deeper within, toward the stairs at the back of the enormous, dark room.

"That stairway's a deathtrap!"

She thought, *Don't make it hard, not when I am so frantic!* She said, "But, my sir, this is the way to my chamber." She moved toward the stairs, swinging her hips.

" 'My sir!' 'My chamber!' you're weird, and I'm not going up there with you no matter how pretty you are. Anyway, you probably taste like a damn ashtray, you smoke so much."

Then the damn thing turned and strode toward the door. She sucked in her breath, turned also.

It had moved fast. It put its hand in the ring, started pulling it. She leaped with all her might across the space between them. At the last instant, it saw her, raised a hand. For the split of a second, their eyes met. She fisted the crown of its head, doing it in precisely the right place and with the exact force necessary to knock the thing senseless. It dropped with a sodden thud.

"Martin," she said. "My dear, look what I've brought you."

He'd been watching from behind one of the old tanning vats. He came out, moving with the slow, dragging gait of a very weak Keeper. He smelled like dry, old flesh and rotted blood. His eyes were glimmers inside their sunken sockets.

She watched him lay his long gray form upon the cushioning body of his prey, watched him stretch like a lounging panther. Some of the old Martin could be seen in those easy movements, his grace, even a little of his power.

He laid his jaws on the neck, in the traditional spot. Keepers sometimes took their food from under the leg, or even, if they were particularly hungry and had really strong suction, from the main artery itself, which could be reached by a ferocious penetration of the small of the back.

It was decadent and cruel to take the blood from a small vein, but this was done as well. The victim knew, then, for it would remain conscious for most of the feeding. Awful, mad fun that was. Children did it, and Miriam could remember a few Egyptians she'd tormented that way, when she was still a little slip of a thing. She and that boy Sothis, the son of

Amma, had experimented with all sorts of ghastly and peculiar ways of consuming their prey. Playing the role of child prostitutes in the seedy backstreets of Thebes, they'd often sucked their customers dry right through their erect penises, leaving nothing but a skeleton tented by skin ready for the tanner. Children can be so awful.

Martin's body began to undulate. His esophageal peristalsis was quite strong. The prey woke up and shouted out something, "Oh, shit," or some such thing. He began to toss and turn, and Martin, who was far from a normal weight and strength, started to slip off.

He needed all the nutrition he could get, so she most certainly could not kill the prey to prevent it struggling. Dead blood made a poor meal.

The thing heaved. There was a pop and a gooey, declining hiss. Martin's suction had broken. It heaved again, and this time he slid completely off. The creature sat up. Its neck was red, but there was no blood flowing. Miriam had the awful thought that Martin might be too weak to feed.

"What in the name of God is this?" The creature looked down at Martin, who was sliding across the floor, looking very much like a great beetle. "What in the name of *God!*" It scrambled to its feet.

Martin grabbed an ankle. The creature shrieked, its eyes practically popping out of its head. It kicked him away.

"Jesus in heaven, what's the matter with that guy?"

This creature was surprisingly self-possessed. Miriam did not like this. She stepped forward, grabbed one of its wrists.

It kicked upward with its knee, directing the blow expertly toward her forearm. That was well done; that would have shattered a human bone. She didn't know what she had here. Stars forbid it was another damn cop.

Its free fist came plunging straight toward her face. She caught it, stopping its forward motion so suddenly that the animal's jaws snapped with the shock. She began to squeeze the wrists. It writhed and kicked again, this time getting her right in the midriff. Her muscles were far too hard for the blow to be painful, but it pushed her off her feet, forcing her to let go her grip. Instantly the creature recoiled from her.

"What are you?" it shrieked. "Aliens?"

That again. That was a recent bit of human myth that the Keepers ought to start using. They hadn't been aliens to the earth for fifty thousand years.

Martin had risen to a sitting position, was ineffectually dusting his tattered waistcoat. When she looked back to the human, it was already starting to make once again for the outside door. With a quick leap, she put herself in its way.

"God in heaven! That's three meters!" It showed its teeth, displayed the palms of its hands. "Look, we can work this out. I'm a family man. I can't go to Pluto or whatever it is you want."

Pluto was the human name for Nisu, the farthest of the planets. Beyond that was only Niburu, the wanderer.

"Child, you must give up your life. You cannot escape us."

That would get the mind racing, the blood speeding.

"Don't be absurd. That would be murder! And look at you; why, you're just a baby in your mother's old clothes! You mustn't do something so terrible. You'll regret it forever, *child*."

Behind him, Martin had come to his feet. He began to stagger toward the victim, his shoulders slumped, his jaw gaping. The sound of his shuffling caused the creature to turn around. And now a moment occurred that did not happen often: a human being saw a Keeper naked of disguise, as he really looked.

It drew in its breath. Then silence. Then a burst of wild, panicked shrieking. But it stood rooted, mesmerized for the same reason that the mouse is mesmerized by the snake.

The deepest unconscious of the human being, the depth of the soul, knew the truth. It bore an imprint of that face from the days when Keepers kept them in cages. They had been pure animals then, without any conscious mind. So the terror they had felt had been imprinted on the unconscious and passed from generation to generation as raw instinct.

Too bad that the free-range human had made so much nicer a meal than the caged variety. Inevitably, they'd begun to run them in packs, then in herds, letting them make their own cities, have their own history. Inevitably, the Keepers had taken to living in the cities, and what fun *that* had been. Still would be, if they hadn't all gone into hiding.

It was so unnecessary. Miriam had probably done a thousand kills in New York City since the creation of its police department, and she hadn't had a bit of trouble there. In fact, she'd had almost no trouble at all, not until this last little lapse.

There'd been the Ellen Wunderling affair, when Sarah had panicked and eaten a reporter who had gotten too close to Miriam. But that had blown over.

The truth was, it was not hard to get away with killing humans if you were just a little careful, and the other Keepers should not have become so fearful. Caution was appropriate, of course. But this business of hiding in holes the way they were doing—they were nothing now but parasites. She was the last of her kind, the last true Keeper, the last vampire.

Well, she had to rehabilitate them, starting with Martin. She would feed him and nurse him back to his grandeur, teach him to live in the modern world. She'd teach them all. Then she'd have a beautiful baby, and he would be a prince among them and lead them back into the sunlight.

The creature began to move away, but Miriam was quicker. She embraced it from behind.

It let out a terrific bellow and began to fling its head back and forth, attempting to slam its skull into her forehead. It connected, too. The blow mattered not, wouldn't even leave a bruise.

She tightened her grip. The creature struggled to draw her hands away. She could feel the ribs start to compress. The carefully orchestrated attempt to break her grip degenerated into hammering. Finally, the breath whooshed out.

Martin's jaw opened, and he fell against the prey. It wriggled, flounced, shook its head wildly. Martin fell away, then regained his balance. Miriam crushed out the last of the breath. Martin locked his jaw against the neck once again. The creature's legs, which had been kicking wildly, now began to slow down. Miriam squeezed tighter. She smelled hot urine, heard it sluicing out.

Martin's suction finally took, and the creature's body weight began to decline, slowly at first, then more noticeably. Martin, by contrast, began to flush red through his curtain of dirt. She felt the life go out of the human. The body became limp. A moment later, Martin let go.

"There's more," she said.

He slumped. "I cannot." He found a chair, fell into it. At least he wasn't crawling anymore. That was an improvement.

The blood and fluids that were left had to be taken. The remnant could not be left to rot. She carried it across the room and sat also, on the foot of the stairs. She laid the body out on her lap, bent down and sucked it until there was nothing left to take, just the dry, cream-colored skin tight across the bones.

"Is there acid in any of the vats?"

He shook his head. "That's all finished. No more tannery."

Too bad. It had been a great convenience in the old days, because the remnants could simply be dissolved. It had been Mom's charming idea to let the tanners come in.

"What do you do?"

He looked at her. "Miriam—it is you, isn't it?"

"Yes, Martin."

"I haven't eaten in a year."

Her mouth opened, but she did not speak, could not. She'd heard of Keepers going hungry for six months, even more—but how could he ever have survived this? How could he still live?

"Martin—"

"I begged for death, many times. But it did not come. Would not come." He smiled a little. "I was turning into one of those . . . those things that *you* make."

He was referring to her humans, to what happened to them when her blood in their veins stopped keeping them young. Keepers might not communicate with each other much, but it seemed that everybody knew of Miriam and her humans.

"It's nothing like that. You would have died in the end."

He nodded. "No doubt." He raised his eyes to hers. She looked deep into the burning, black pools. Martin was thousands of years older than she.

"We are coming to our end, Miriam," he said.

"We aren't!"

He nodded slowly, not as if he was agreeing with her, but more as if he was humoring her. "You need to find a way to destroy that," he said. "They'll miss that man soon, and they're bound to come here searching."

"Why here? We've always been safe here. This is my mother's house."

"The City of Paris owns this structure. There are plans to make it part of the Musée des Gobelins, starting next year." He made a dismissive gesture with his hands, a gesture that expressed vast defeat, vast sorrow. "They'll clear all this rubbish out."

"Martin, you were thriving just—well, just a few years ago."

His face, which had filled out and now bore a smeared, filthy resemblance to the narrow-lipped elegance she remembered from the past, opened into a smile. The smile quickly turned bitter and ugly. "During the war, the Resistance built a secret headquarters in the Denfert-Rochereau ossuary. They heard us, deeper down, in the old labyrinth."

This had been the traditional shelter of the Paris vampires, a honeycomb of tunnels that wound beneath the city, from which its stone had been quarried since the time of the Romans.

"They noticed us. They thought that we were spies working for the Germans, and they pursued us."

"But . . . how?"

"With sound! They have those little tins full of carbon black—"

"Microphones."

"Yes, those things. They put them about, and our voices were conducted to their ears through them."

"But they can't hear our speech."

"Ah, Prime is such a trial, isn't it? So complex, so many words needed for the simplest expression." He shook his head. "We spoke French, which requires the central register of tones."

"You're speaking Prime now."

"Am I? Yes, I am. How lovely. I'll try to keep it up. Anyway, they did not really do anything at first. They were perplexed. But you know the French, they are a careful and patient lot. They did not give up on the strange stories collected by the Resistance, of a band of *hommes sauvages* living in the catacombs. When you were last here, we knew nothing of this. But they were working, you see. Always watching, always working. There began to be deputations from the Service Sociale going through the catacombs calling, 'come out, come out, we are here to help you.' Then a stupid fool, that idiot Emeus—"

"He and I grew up together. He was with the Thebes gang, me and Sothis out of Amma, Tayna of Tothen, that crowd."

"Tothen now calls himself Monsieur Gamon. He is here. The others, the wind has taken."

"Tayna was in Shanghai, living as a Mr. Lee." Destroyed, now, Miriam supposed. She did not say it.

"Emeus ate one of the damned Service Sociale people. The hell that resulted has not stopped."

So humans knew, also, here in France. "How much do they understand?"

"I don't know what they know. How they find us. Only that I could not safely feed these years past." He gave her a look that she had never seen from a Keeper before, almost of despair. It made her most uneasy to see such a weak and human expression in the eyes of one of her own kind.

"Why did you have to stop? What exactly did they do?"

"They came! I had just fed—in the Twelfth, coming up out of the labyrinth. The usual method."

"When you say 'They came,' what do you mean?"

"I had chosen a very nice one, smelled great, skin tone

said it was first class all the way. I took it into a—oh, some little covered place, a toilet, as I recall. I ate it and put the remnant in my little case that I carry, and suddenly—there they were, the police! Running after me. Coming in autos. Jumping out of doorways. It was phenomenal. I only escaped by leaping a wall, then to the sewers."

She pulled out her cigarettes, lit one. How tired she suddenly felt. She sensed that more had happened to him than he had as yet said, and she wanted to hear it all.

"Go on, Martin."

"You look so beautiful."

She thought, *I don't want to bear the child of a weak creature like this. I need the strongest blood now.* She said, "But you haven't finished your story."

"Miriam, I have been captured."

The words vibrated into Miriam's shocked silence.

"They examined me, Miriam. They opened my jaw, they weighed me, they extracted fluids!"

"But you escaped?"

"They tried to make me think I had. It was a silly business, though—unlocked doors and such. I knew they had let me go."

She could feel her heat beginning to rise. Her blood was flowing faster. If he had been let go, then there was danger here.

"What happened next?"

"I waited months—a full season of moons. Then I took something—a rat of a thing, half-starved, living under a bridge in the trackless neighborhoods beyond the Périphérique. I had not even opened a vein before they were there, falling on me from the roadway above, rushing up in automobiles—it was horrifying. I ran. All I could do."

"But you must have been terribly hungry."

"I tried again a few days later. This time I took the RER to the outskirts, to an area where live the brown ones that they call *ratons*. Again, I singled one out, cut it out of a little herd in a cinema, then started to have my dinner."

"They appeared again."

"Dozens of them! All around! This time I barely escaped. I came back here. I have remained within these walls ever since."

"But, Martin, how could you have not eaten for—what— at least a year? It's impossible."

" 'Nothing is impossible when you must,' that is the motto of my family. Miriam, I have drunk the feral cats, the mice, the rats. I have eaten the very flies that are spit by the air!"

No wonder he stank so. A Keeper could not live on such blood, or could barely live. She did not want to pity one of her own kind, especially not one she remembered with such respect. He had been a charming lover in his day. She remembered him in the flashing brocades of the last age, a powdered wig upon his head and a gold-knobbed stick in his hand. He knew the fashions of the age; he dallied with duchesses and played cards at the table of the king. Among the Keepers, he was known as an expert on the ways of man.

"You and I have always been kindred souls, Martin."

"I have thought of you often, child. You still live among them?"

"I have a club in New York that is quite *façonnable*. And a human lover called Sarah."

"That business of yours."

"A human to serve you is most useful." Or could be, if only she would answer the damned phone.

"I don't even know the names of those who pursue me."

They had left him alone for these years, interrupting him only when he was—according to their idea—about to "murder" one of their own. There could only be one reason why he had been left like this: He was bait, and the house was a trap.

They must even now be rushing to this place. For they had undoubtedly bugged the entire building. God only knew, maybe there were even cameras. They could make cameras the size of a fingertip, microphones no bigger than specs of dust. Sarah used such things in the club's security system.

"We have to leave here," she said.

"But I—where?"

She stood up. "Is there any fuel?"

"What sort of fuel?"

"To make a fire! Chemicals! Petrol!"

He gestured toward some steel drums.

She went to them, ripped off the soft metal cover. It was some sort of chemical, but it didn't smell flammable. Another was the same stuff.

But a third stank gloriously of the esters of earth-oil. It had been sent through their great retorts until it was a volatile. "This makes the auto go," she said.

"I know what petrol is."

She threw the barrel into the middle of the room. "Is the hidden route the same?" Every Keep had one, usually more than one. There were escapes for fire, escapes for attack, escapes for everything.

"The same."

The petrol had finished gushing out, and now stood in a puddle on the floor. Miriam took the empty drum and rolled it back and forth over the remnant until it was nothing but a sack of powdered bone. Then she tossed it into the petrol, making sure that it was thoroughly soaked.

At that moment, she heard a sound, the creak of pressure being applied against the door. She took Martin's shoulders, leaned against his ear. "They're just outside," she said. "About to burst in the door and all the windows at once."

His lips twisted back in an ugly rictus. He really, really despised them, this hunted creature. Taking his still ice-cold hand, she led him to the far wall, where once the waste from the tannery had poured into the little river Bievre, long since covered over. She counted one, two, three stones up from the floor. Now she pressed the one that was under her hand.

A brutal shaft of sunlight shattered the darkness. The doorway was a white blaze filled with darting shadows. Martin screamed, the shuddering ululation of a Keeper in absolute fury. So rarely had she heard it that Miriam screamed, too, throwing back her head and howling to the rafters.

"Essence!"

The human cry stopped her. They came out across the great room. They had nets, nets and guns. She felt tears of anger streaming down her cheeks. She was almost immobilized, such was her rage at being threatened by them. She did not let herself succumb to these feelings, though. No, she must not. Instead, she drew a book of matches from her pocket.

"Madame, si'l vous plaît!"

Lady, please, indeed! She struck one and lit the others and threw the whole flaming book. Instantly, fire roared up everywhere. The men began to shriek. They leaped and jerked in the flames, as her mother had leaped and twisted in her pyre.

Miriam pressed the stone that would open their route into the sewers of Paris.

Nothing happened.

SEVEN

Deathtrap

Paul called Becky's cell phone for the fifth time in an hour. Her recording came back for the fifth time in an hour. He'd already requested that Communications in Langley track both officers, but their cell phones were off or the signals were blocked, so the GPS system could not find them. Just for the hell of it, he tried Charlie again, also. Same shit.

It was now ten A.M. By his estimation they were two hours overdue, maybe more. He thrust another stick of gum in his mouth and chomped on it. Thank God he hated French cigarettes.

The cell phone rang. He grabbed for it. "Ward here."

"Paul, this is Justin."

What in hell was Justin Turk calling him for now? It was five A.M. in Virginia. "Yeah?"

"I'm getting back to you."

"Look, man, I gotta have more support personnel."

"Shit."

"One of the damn creatures escaped from my net. I've followed it to Paris and lost it. I need more people and more equipment real fast."

"How fast is real fast?"

"Yesterday would've been good. I need at least five more field ops."

"I can't just put people in this thing. You know the kind of problems we're having. The discussions."

"I'm losing a vampire. One that *travels*, for Chrissakes!"

"It takes weeks to clear people for you. A whole new background check, all kinds of shit. Even when I don't have the director on my ass. Which I obviously do."

"At least authorize the people I've still got in Kuala to follow me."

"That's a no-go."

"Come on, man, help me, here."

"This whole operation is under study. Until I have fresh orders, you're all frozen in place."

That sure was shitty news. "I need those people, man. This thing is going south fast."

"I'll work on it."

"Don't sound so convincing."

The conversation ended there, with muttered good-byes. Justin was a sort of a friend. That is to say, he'd be there for Paul as long as Paul wasn't a liability.

One thing was quite clear: There would be no new people, not with international human rights questions beginning to hang over the operation.

He saw somebody getting dropped down a shaft, and that somebody was him.

He hammered Becky's number into his cell phone, then Charlie's. Same results as before. "I'm in trouble," he muttered to himself.

Still, it was possible that the kids were okay. He just wished that they'd followed procedure with this break-in. There would be a hell of a stink if the French found out that

CIA personnel had invaded the records office of their security service. He'd be recalled, of course. He'd have to explain what he was doing in France, and why he'd gotten here by commandeering an Air Force general's private jet.

He sat and stared up at the blank, sunlit wall of the office tower and listened to the water drip in the sink. He looked at his watch. "Ten-fifty," he muttered to himself. "Damn and *god* damn."

And he decided to use the time well. A situation like this could burst into flames at any second. He was as prepared as he could be for the Sûreté and the White House. What he needed to do was to get ready for the really hard ones—the vampires. And there was actually something he could do right now, something damn useful.

Becky had mentioned two areas of Paris: the Ninth and Thirteenth Arrondissements. He opened his laptop and went to the CIA's database. The site didn't offer any magical insights into the workings of the world, just some very good information and lots of detail. You could find practically anybody here, and at his level of clearance, he could input requests for Echelon searches on keywords of concern to any operation approved for the system. Echelon would then look for those keywords amid the billions of phone conversations, e-mails, radio transmissions, and faxes that it monitored.

Problem was, you had to be damn specific to get anything useful. What words might the traveler use on the telephone— what special, unique words? He didn't know who she might call or where she might go, or even if Paris was her final destination.

The CIA database also had a wealth of maps, better ones than could be bought in any store, including maps of Paris that had been drawn by the German military during World

War II. Originally intended to be used in house-to-house warfare, they included detailed floor plans and plans of the sewer system that offered information down to which tunnels and pipes were big enough to admit a man.

The Germans had done this for most of the large cities in Europe. Many of the maps were outmoded, of course, and many like Paul had knowledge that the disastrous bombing of the Chinese embassy during the Kosovo conflict in 1999 had been caused by reliance on an improperly updated Werhmacht street plan of Belgrade. Since then, all maps in the CIA database been clearly marked with the last year of update.

He saw that the Ninth Arrondissement had not been touched since 1944. The map legends and street names were still in German, which wasn't very reassuring. By contrast, the Thirteenth had been revised by the French in 1998, and there were annotations that it had been updated yearly since.

He settled down to stare at the screen. He had to memorize every street, every sewer pipe, every building plan.

The vampire would know its world down to the tiniest corner. It would be able to pick every lock, use every shadow, climb all the walls and cross all the roofs. It would use the sewer system like a railroad. It would be able to navigate the ductwork, the window ledges, the eaves.

Paul hadn't believed how smart and capable the vampire was, at least not at first. He hadn't believed it when he first saw one staring back at him with dark, still eyes, looking small and helpless. There had been a slight smile on its face, a drifting little smile that communicated a sort of casual amusement. Jack Dodge said, "Hey," and stepped toward it— and a knife shot out and sliced Jack's head from his body like a blossom from a stem.

Paul could still hear the sounds: the rip of Jack's skin, the crackle of his bones, then the *shuss* of the fountain of blood that pumped out of the stump.

Those sounds came to Paul in his sleep, in the whine of the jets he took through the night, in the whispering of the wind in the ancient cities where he worked.

The creatures drifted through the cracks and corners of their world, leading him on an infinitely careful chase. They played a kind of chess with him, appearing here and there, slipping away, only to reappear somewhere else.

His pursuit of them had taught him how brilliant they were. They always stayed ahead of him. His only useful weapons were surprise and technology. Brilliance and speed were their tools, but they had no technology. They had been neatly outclassed by a computer database and infrared sight.

The death of the vampire was appalling. It haunted Paul, and he knew it haunted his people. The vampire fought harder for its life than it was possible for a human being to imagine. They hid like rats, because their lives were just so damn precious to them. When you saw their death struggles, you could almost, at moments, sympathize. The vampire died hard. "Real hard," he said aloud.

He sat staring at the map of the Thirteenth Arrondissement's sewer system. There had been structural changes made as recently as a year ago. He tracked his finger along a tunnel that had been blocked up. Probably something to do with containing old waste from the tanneries and dye factories that used to be in the area.

No doubt that was why this map was so carefully kept up. The French had a problem with contaminated water and soils in the area, and they were cleaning it up.

The hotel phone rang. He grabbed it instantly.

"Two of your people were caught in the Department of Records of the Prefecture of Police at six-thirty this morning." It was Sam Mazur at the embassy.

"Oh, Christ."

"The French had them on video from the second they climbed down into the damn room, Paul! Come on, this is amateur night, here!"

"Are they being—"

"They're being released under diplomatic immunity. But the frogs are gonna take 'em straight to the airport and put 'em on the first plane to Washington. They're totally, completely, and thoroughly blown. I'll tell you another thing— the reason that they got to stay so long in that very secure facility was so that the Sûreté could record every damn keystroke they made as they hacked their way into the database. They know how they did it, what they found—everything."

"I'm on my way."

He didn't know the Métro well, but he did know that it was the fastest way around Paris in midday traffic. He got in the train at Montparnasse. It moved off at what seemed to him to be a maddeningly leisurely pace. His mind clicked methodically from possibility to possibility as he tried to devise a new way of saving Becky and Charlie and his whole operation.

In less than fifteen minutes he was trotting up the steps into the Place de la Concorde.

The American embassy was beautiful and very well guarded. It was also quiet, unlike many of its counterparts around the world. The crowds of visa seekers and unhappy citizens reporting lost passports were at the consulate a few blocks away. His own diplomatic passport got him straight past the French guards and the marines.

He entered through a metal detector, declaring and checking the gun that his false Interpol ID allowed him to carry. Well, *false* was maybe too strong a word. The Interpol papers his team used were the result of an accommodation between the CIA and the international police agency.

Sam's office was halfway down a wide corridor that looked as if it belonged in a palace. As indeed, it did. This building had been one before it became the U.S. embassy. He went in, and the atmosphere changed at once. Here there were computer screens and filing cabinets and a dropped ceiling. The outer office blazed with fluorescent light.

"I'm Paul Ward," he said to a receptionist who, to his surprise, turned out to be French. What a local national was doing working in a clearance-required job he did not know. Times had changed.

Sam sat at a steel desk. His venetian blinds were firmly shut on what was probably a view of an air shaft. The rumble of air-conditioning equipment shook the floor, but this office, itself, was not air-conditioned. It was just near the equipment.

"Paul, you old asshole, I thought you'd be arrested on your way here."

"What about my people?"

"Business class on Air France. Not too bad."

Until they reached Langley. This was not over, no way, not for any of them. It was a major screwup, and it was going to take a lot of time to fix it. If that was even possible. The White House had started asking its damn questions at just the wrong time.

"Are they in the air yet?"

"They're being signed out of the hoosegow as we speak.

The Frenchies don't like people getting into their secure areas, *especially* not us."

"Sam, you're gonna hate me for this. But you gotta find a way to keep my people in country. I need them urgently, right now."

He shook his head. "It's over. So over."

"Call in favors. Do anything."

"Nothin' I can do. They're toast."

"Then I need an immediate appointment with the ambassador."

Sam blinked. "You're kidding. You'd bring the politicos in on something like this? A jerk like you couldn't possibly have a congressional sugar daddy."

Paul tried using what he hoped might be a trump card. "It's terrorism, Sam. I'm in the middle of a heavy operation that involves France only because we happened to follow an international terrorist onto French soil. If we lose this woman, innocent people are gonna die."

Sam picked up the phone. "You don't need the ambassador." He spoke in rapid-fire French. Paul couldn't follow it precisely, but he could tell that he was going up the ladder to somebody very senior somewhere, and this senior individual was being asked for urgent and immediate intervention.

Sam hung up. "The chief of the Division of Internal Security of the Sûreté will see us in ten minutes."

This time they had an embassy Citroën with a driver, so it was a lot easier to get around. "You're out there in the middle of nowhere without any support staff, the three of you," Sam said. "Bound to be a problem, an operation that's being run that far outside of guidelines, that thinly staffed."

"We're effective. That's the bottom line."

"I don't want to intrude, Paul. But I gotta tell you, you

look like hell. In fact, I'd give road kill a better rating. Whatever it is you're doing that you're so effective at, it's taking you apart."

He and Sam had learned to strangle people with piano wire and plant microphones under the skin of pet cats together. They'd been in Cambodia together, where none of their training applied and nothing they did worked. They had fought the silent war together when it really was a war.

"It's just another shitty op, my friend. You look great, by the by. Tennised, golfed, and swum."

"Also pokered every Tuesday night with the Brits. It's a good life here, as long as you don't get yourself in the kind of trouble your two goons are in."

If only the French customs agents hadn't made such a mess of things at de Gaulle. If only he hadn't had to screen the operation through Interpol. The way he saw it, they should have disabled the creature with a shot as soon as it reached customs, then dropped it in a vat of sulfuric acid, or cremated it. Instead, they took it to an airport brig. It escaped before they even got it in the cell. Of course it did.

"I wish I could tell you what it is I'm doing," Paul said. "It'd be a lot easier if every damn security officer and cop on the planet knew. But there would be huge problems. It'd be the most unpredictable goddamn thing you could imagine."

"Well, that explains that. You gonna get yourself wasted, old buddy, on this thing. Your politics are all used up, way I hear it."

They pulled up in front of the long, impressively French Victorian building that housed the Sûreté. Paul expected a lot of bureaucracy and a long wait, but they were soon in a very quiet, very ornate office facing an extremely fastidious midget.

"I am Colonel Bocage," he said.

"Where's Henri-Georges?" Sam asked.

"You will interview with me."

Paul said in French, *"J'voudrais mon peuple, monsieur. Tout de suite."*

Colonel Bocage laughed. "Mr. Mazur, this is the man in charge, that you promised us to meet?"

Sam nodded. "I made that promise to Henri-Georges Bordelon."

"And he transmitted it to me."

"I need my people," Paul said. "We're saving lives."

"You speak French. You should think in French. It's more civilized ..."

"I can't think in French."

"... because we have so many ways of expressing concepts of good and evil." He smiled again, and Paul thought he looked, for a moment, like a very hard man. "Mr. Mazur, could you step out for a moment? I am sorry."

This wasn't the usual drill when you went to beg to keep your spies in place. But Paul was in no position to ask what was going on. When Sam had left, the colonel went to his window, which looked out over a lovely park. There was a difference between being a high official in the Sûreté and a lowly intelligence officer like Sam.

Colonel Bocage closed a manila folder he'd been appearing to review. It was only a pose, a tension builder. Paul had done it himself a thousand times, to a thousand nervous supplicants in ten different countries. "So," the colonel said at last, "you are here investigating *les sauvages*. Tell me, what do you Americans call them?"

Paul Ward had not had the sensation of his heart skipping a beat since the moment he had looked upon his father's remains. No matter how violent or how dangerous his situation, he always remained icy calm . . . until this second. His heart was skipping a whole lot of beats. He parted his lips, but nothing came out.

The colonel raised an eyebrow and with it one corner of his mouth. "I am your counterpart," he said, "your French counterpart."

Paul wiped his face clean of expression. Tell him nothing.

"You are surprised, I see," Colonel Bocage said. "Genuinely surprised. Tell me, how long have the Americans been working on this?"

Paul reminded himself never to play poker with Colonel Bocage. "A few years," he said dryly.

"My friend, we have been struggling with this problem for fifty years."

"We cleared Asia."

"Cleared?"

"We killed them, all of them."

"Except for Mrs. Tallman."

"Except for her."

"*Elle est une sauvage, aussi?*"

"You call them savages?"

"To keep the record clean. We know what they are. But you come from Asia, where we know you have been working very hard. Why not start in America, where the lives are more important to you?"

"Our first solid lead was in Tokyo."

At that moment, Charlie and Becky were brought in.

"Ah," Colonel Bocage said, "your colleagues. Now, please, we shall all sit together."

"You guys okay?"

"Fine," Becky said. She looked wonderful when she was

angry—her eyes full of sparks, her cheeks flushed, her lips set in a line that was at once grim and somehow suggestive.

Beside her, Charlie played with the damn cigarette machine. His style under this kind of pressure was sullen defiance.

There was a silence. Paul was trying to remember if he had ever felt quite this embarrassed and uncomfortable before. He decided that the answer was no.

"This matter has the very highest level of secrecy attached to it in France," Bocage said. "Government does not care to inform the population of such matters." He paused. "You have concluded the same."

"All governments that we've been to have concluded the same."

"Given that we cannot protect our people, there seems little choice but to hide this until matters are resolved."

Bocage rested his eyes on Becky, so frankly that she looked away. Paul was fascinated. Becky was the very essence of self-possession, and Becky did not look away.

"You obtained what you needed, I trust," he said to her.

"Yes."

He strolled over to his desk. "We used a computer spying program to watch your keystrokes," he said, his voice rippling with self-satisfaction. There were few things more pleasant in the life of an intelligence agent than getting the drop on a colleague from a friendly country. Paul knew, he'd done it. "If you'd like a copy of your work—" He held a file folder toward Becky and Charlie. "In the interest of friendly cooperation."

"It'd be friendlier," Paul said, "if you shared something with us that we didn't already have."

"With pleasure, Mr. Ward," he said. Then his mouth

snapped closed, as if he had caught himself in a moment of indiscretion.

Paul saw that the man's carefully relaxed appearance was concealing a state of extraordinary emotional tension. Paul's experience as a wartime interrogator told him that this man was about to address something that he considered extremely terrible.

"Go ahead, Colonel," Charlie said, no doubt reading the same signs.

"We have had one of these creatures under observation in a house in—"

"Let us tell you that," Becky said. "Thirteenth Arrondissement. Rue des Gobelins."

"Very good. Do you know which house? Or exactly what has happened there?" The colonel was sweating now.

"Tell us," Paul said. He decided that the colonel was a man who habitually exploded in the face of his own staff, but in this situation had to contain the energy.

"We have had *une sauvage* trapped in a house in the Rue des Gobelins for over a year. It hasn't eaten for twelve months, but it still lives."

"So why not go in? If you got the thing trapped, kill it."

"We were hoping that it would attract some response from its peers—curiosity, compassion, something that would draw them to it. But it did not, and now—well, it's too late."

Something had gone terribly wrong, which explained the ominous lowering of the colonel's voice.

"What's the trouble, Colonel?"

"The house is at this moment burning to the ground. In it, there are two vampires that we know of." He stopped again. He rubbed his cheek, as if hunting for stubble. "There are six of my own people."

"God save them," Paul said. He knew, now, why the map of the Thirteenth Arrondissement was so up-to-date, and also why the sewer system had been altered. They had cut off access from the vampire's lair. Exactly the approach Paul would have taken.

"But I do have some good news for you. This 'Mrs. Tallman' of yours was in the house."

"That's goddamn good news, Colonel!" Maybe she hadn't had time to spread her warning. Maybe now she would never have time. "Do you know how long she's been there?"

"She appeared yesterday afternoon at about six. That we know."

"Yesterday afternoon?"

He nodded. "The taxi brought her from a hotel."

"It's possible that she didn't reach any of the others."

"It is. But they are aware that something is wrong, the Paris vampires."

Paul had assumed that there would be resistance if they realized they were under attack.

"Only very recently," the colonel continued, "have we been able to deal with them. Only since we understood the difficulties involved in—the difficulties with the blood—"

"How do you kill 'em?"

"We shoot them to incapacitate them with a gun that has been especially designed for the purpose, then we burn them to ash."

"That'll work."

He bared his teeth, sucked in air with a hiss. Paul thought, *This is one tough bastard. I like this guy.* Bocage stuck out his jaw. "We made many kills over the years. But the numbers, they still went up. Slowly, but always *up!* My God!"

"It's been hard for us, too."

"We would shoot them in the chest, then bury them. They would come out, but carefully, so we would not notice the disturbance to the grave. We thought we were eradicating them, but we were accomplishing nothing. Eventually, even we could see that the pattern of killing went on. But we could not track it because they come up out of mines under the city. All sorts of places. No pattern, you see."

"What about the Ninth and the Thirteenth," Becky asked.

"We eventually tracked one of the creatures back to the Thirteenth. To Nineteen Rue des Gobelins, to be precise. The only one in Paris living aboveground. The rest of them—dear God, those mines are a horrible place." He fell silent for a moment. "We have a seventy percent casualty rate down there."

Paul said nothing. Of the seven people who had started with him, he'd lost four. He and Justin had thought over fifty percent was monstrous.

The telephone rang. Colonel Bocage went around his desk and answered it. He spoke in French at some length, then put it down abruptly. He stood, silent. Paul knew what had happened without even asking.

"Another casualty report. The whole team that entered Nineteen Rue Gobelins was lost. Six men."

"Shit!" Charlie said.

In the distance, a church bell sounded.

"There is good news. Of one *sauvage*, bones were found. They are being taken out to be burned."

"And the other one?"

"Mrs. Tallman was reduced to ash."

"Then we're done," Becky said. "Back home to find out if my fiancé remembers my name."

"We are going to attempt to isolate and sterilize the mines," Bocage said with that carefully practiced mildness of his. "We're short six essential personnel. It'll take us months to find and train replacements." He raised his eyebrows. "I think that our two countries have some secrets to share."

Langley would be as nervous about this as an old maiden aunt about a slumber party. There were protocols to create, careful integration procedures so that the secrecy laws of both countries could be followed during the operation. He ought to go back and make a full report up supervisory channels. On the other hand, he could just stuff the whole damn process straight up Langley's ass, and do it without telling them.

"May I take it that you're on board," Colonel Bocage asked.

He didn't even need to look at Becky and Charlie. Their answer would be the same as his. "You bet."

EIGHT

Flicker of Fire

If she did not have blood immediately—absolutely fresh blood—she would die. Where she lay, trapped, helpless, and in agony, there could be no blood. Here in this dank place, with pain radiating through her body as if an army with burning coals for heels were marching up and down her, Miriam saw that she was coming to the final edge of life.

She had ended up here for one reason only: She had been surprised by the disaster in Chiang Mai and running like a desperate rat ever since. No planning, no forethought, simply a wild race across the world.

The humans had blocked the escape tunnel with concrete and reinforced it with bars of iron. She'd taken to the stairs, running up to the top of the house, to the ancient rooms where Lamia had lived. The old brocades still hung on the walls, rotting and falling though they were. And there was the bed she had used, where Miriam had cuddled with her, and where they had so happily shared kills. But the flames had come, marching like soldiers, and Miriam had been forced to the roof. She'd looked from the edges of the house; the streets had been filled with dozens of police and firemen. She could not climb down the wall into that, not in broad daylight. She could not jump to another building, not quite.

She'd found a way, though. She always found a way. She had climbed down inside the chimney, down into the hearths in the basement, below the level of the fire. As she crawled out, covered with ash, the floor above had begun to cave in. Fire had swept over her, fire and the agony of fire.

There had been a tiny space at the back of the fireplace, where they had pushed the ashes. She'd pulled bricks out and made her way into a brick pipe not more than eighteen inches in diameter, forcing her body into the space until her joints ground.

She lay with her eyes closed, willing herself not to cry out with the agony of it. If she opened her eyes, all she saw was wet, moldering brick a few bare inches above her face. The whole time she was struggling through the crack, she'd heard Martin screaming and screaming. The only thing the food she'd brought him had done was give him enough energy to die slowly.

They were gaining control over the fire, and above her she could now hear human voices. Water cascaded down.

She heard a sound, very distinct, and very different from the water, or the popping of Martin's hot bones. This sound she heard was breathing—*snick snick, snick snick*—quick breathing, very light.

A rat was coming along the tunnel she was in, interested, no doubt, in the scent of raw, bleeding flesh. Or perhaps it was a devotee of cooked food. A French rat might be expected to be a sophisticate.

This rat represented a chance—a small one, admittedly, but its presence changed the odds from nonexistent to . . . well, a little bit better than nothing.

Here, little one, come here, little fruit. "The closer they are genetically to man, the better they are for you. The rats, the apes, the cows, all may be consumed to benefit." So had said the Master Tutomon, her childhood tutor, with his lessons in geometry and languages and survival.

The rat hesitated. She could not see it, but the sound of its breathing and the patter of its feet were clear. It was on her left side, just parallel with her foot. To encourage it to come closer to her hand, she began to wriggle her fingers.

She needed to open her eyes, and she prepared herself as best she could. The space might be entirely dark by now, and that would be better. The light was much less, but she saw the bricks, so close that they were blurred to her vision. An involuntary gasp came out of her. The rat scuttled away.

She raised her head until it was pressed against the top of the pipe, then looked along her arm. The creature came back. She could just see its interested little face as it went *snick-snick, snick-snick* against her fingertips.

She stretched her arm, opening her fingers, letting the rat venture closer to the center of the trap. But it came no closer.

The indifferent trickle of water that had been slipping around her body was becoming a steady stream. If this pipe backed up, they would notice. They would send a crew down to unblock it. They would drag her out, even if it tore her to pieces. There would be no mercy. There was never any mercy; that had become quite apparent.

Now, the rat was returning. The rat, in fact, was very close to her fingers. Her exquisite nerves communicated the sensation as it sniffed their tips. Finally, it decided to stop sniffing and try a bite of the cool, still flesh that had drawn its curiosity. Instantly, it was in Miriam's hand. It was wriggling and screaming its rat screams—*ree-ree-ree*. She sucked in her breath and moved her arm, drawing the creature closer to her mouth. She had to drag it against her naked breast, and as she did its needlelike teeth slashed the pale skin.

Then the creature was at her mouth. She bit off the shrieking head and drank the body dry, crumbling the remains, which were no more substantial than a little leaf.

The blood of the rat tasted surprisingly good. She could feel it spilling through her. It was going to be useful. But would it be enough for the task that lay ahead?

To continue the motion that her exhaustion had stopped, she had to work her arms over her head and press hard against the edges with her feet. In time, her bones would compress a little more, and she would move a few inches. However, if the pipe got any more narrow, she could be trapped.

Now that she was moving again, the water was sluicing around her, bringing with it bits of spent coal and ash. She pushed, felt more pressure, waited. Nothing.

If she was trapped—her heart began going faster. Harder she pushed, harder and harder. Still nothing. She felt her tongue swelling from the effort. Her bones ground and creaked. Her tongue began to push past the rows of cartilage that filled her mouth, that provided the seal when she sucked blood.

Still nothing, nothing, *nothing!* And then—worse— louder voices. Yes, the humans were in the basement, speaking about the slowness of the drain. They must unclog it, of course. They would find within it this strange, distorted being that would slowly return to its previous form, and they would know another secret of the Keepers, that vampires' bones that were not brittle like their own, but pliant.

How would they kill her? Burn her until she was ash, as they had done to her mother? Hammer a stake into her heart until her blood stopped, then let her die over however long it took in a coffin—years, or even whole cycles of years? Or explode her head and dissolve her in acid?

There was a sound, and immediately a dagger of pain shot

straight up her spine. The next instant, she slid along the pipe a substantial distance. She could have howled with the sheer joy of it, the wonderful sensation of release from the terrible compression.

The water she had been stopping came behind her, a gushing torrent that swept her down a wider sluiceway. Where she was now, there was considerably more light. It was coming from slits near the ceiling, that appeared at regular intervals. The space was high enough to stand up in, and she could peer through these slits.

She rose to a sitting position. She was exhausted. A rat was not worth much to her body, and she soon must feed again. She needed a human being.

She drew herself up and up, fighting the great blasts of pain from her tormented body. Finally, she was crouching. To see out, she would have to straighten herself, and she could not until her bones had spread again. She forced herself to try, to hasten the process as much as she could. Agony ran up and down her spine, causing her toes to curl and her lips to twist back. She hissed with it, she stifled the screams that tried to burst out of her throat.

Minutes passed. The water, which had been gushing past her knees, subsided to a milder flow. Its acrid stench was replaced by a surprising odor—the scent of a fresh spring. Her kind needed a lot of water and loved fresh water. She was smelling a clean, limestone spring beneath the streets of Paris, in the very sewer. She turned herself toward it and began slowly placing one foot in front of another, walking toward the source. Now she could see that the arched space widened. To her left and right there were muddy banks. In the water, there swam tiny fish, sweeping along before her like little schools of pale starlight.

This wonderful, entirely unexpected place must be the ancient River Bièvre. The rumbling overhead was a street. And indeed, when she finally managed to peer out one of the slits, she saw passing tires. As she moved along, the water became better and better. No sewage here at all, just the stream still dancing in its ancient bed of stones.

She began to look for a spring. There was certainly one nearby. She could smell its wonderful, stony freshness. Ten steps along, twenty, and she found it, its water bubbling cheerfully out of the ground. Above it, somebody in the long-ago had made a little grotto and set a cross, which now stood encrusted with rust. She lay herself down in the water and let it flow over her, let it kiss her wounds with its clean coldness.

The pain grew somewhat less. The cold was helping to heal the burns, the clean water to reduce the need of her blood to ward off infection. If the process was to speed up to a normal rate, though, she had to have food.

She lay in the pouring spring, twisting and turning slowly, allowing the water to clean every part of her, to sweep away the ashen skin and the burned flesh, and the debris that had collected in the wounds. The thick stink of it all washed away with it, leaving behind only the smell of the water and the smell of her.

Finally, when those two odors had not changed for a long time, she rose from the stream. She began moving along the riverbank, a naked, burned creature, svelte and, she supposed, pale. She was looking for a manhole, some means of getting up into the city again, to the food supply that swarmed in its streets.

What she found instead was a door. It was steel and set high up in the wall, at the top of a series of iron rungs. The door was half the normal height and had a lever rather than a handle.

She climbed the rungs, pulled the lever, which dropped down with a thud. She drew the door open and found herself looking into a dark room full of humming machinery.

She climbed into the room. In contrast with the wet cold that had surrounded her for hours, it was warm and dry. It felt fiercely hot, although she knew that this was only the effect of the sudden change.

Her nostrils had been seared, but her sense of smell seemed unimpaired. She smelled machine oil, the fumes of burning, and the scent of lots of electricity. This was a furnace room. She knew boilers and furnaces well. She had special uses for them. This one reminded her of the Ehler that she had in her house, a good, hot system with an ample firebox.

Beyond the furnace, she saw stairs. She mounted them, stopping at the top to listen and catch her breath. She laid her ear against the door that was there. On the other side, she heard the tap of footsteps. They moved slowly about, *tip-tap, tip-tap,* pausing here and there, then moving on. Suddenly a voice began to speak, using English. It spoke about the manufacture of tapestries.

This work had been going on when she was last here. Across the street from her mother's house there had been a manufactory of tapestry. So it was still in operation, but there were also observers now, people from the English-speaking world being taken on tours of the works.

She turned the handle of the door. Locked. This was of little consequence. They had not learned the art of the lock, the humans. Shaking it a few times, she dislodged the tumblers. She knew exactly what she sought: a female creature of about her own size, preferably alone.

The tour group consisted of about twenty people being led about among the tapestries, which hung on large looms.

She stepped out onto the gloomy area before the door, then slipped behind the nearest loom. On the other side, the weaver worked, stepping on her treadle and sliding thread through her beater.

Beneath the smock, the girl wore dark clothing of some sort; Miriam could not see exactly what it was. The casual dress of the modern age. She peered at the creature. It was intent on its work. She listened to the talk of the guide. The tourists drifted closer. In another moment, they would see this person, observe her working at her loom.

Miriam stepped into the girl's view. She didn't notice, such was her concentration. Miriam moved closer. Now, the girl stopped working and glanced her way, then looked harder. Her mouth dropped open. She looked the naked apparition up and down. An expression of pity crossed her face, mixing with horror as she realized that the woman she was seeing was severely burned.

Miriam stepped toward her. She swayed as if falling, causing the girl to instinctively move forward to help her. Miriam enclosed her in her arms and drew her behind the loom, then opened her mouth against the neck and pulled the fluids in fairly easily, requiring two great gulps to finish the process.

Her whole flesh seemed to leap with joy; it was as if she were going to fly up to the sky. She fought against crying out, such was the pleasure. Her body from the top of her head to the tips of her toes filled with an electric tickling as her newly refreshed blood raced to repair her wounds.

The shuddering, tickling sensations were so overwhelming that she was dropped like a stone to her knees. She pitched forward, gasping, her body deliciously racked with a sensation very like climax. Again it came, again and again, and the voices came closer, and the tip-tapping of the shoes.

She grabbed the remnant, invisible in its heap of clothes, and pulled it behind the loom. As she untangled the dry, emaciated remains from the clothing, she heard a ripple of laughter. The tour guide had said something that amused her audience. The click of other looms went on. Quickly, quickly, Miriam put the clothes on—black jeans, a black turtleneck, shoes that fit her, unfortunately, quite badly. Then the blue smock. No hat, and that was not good because her hair would take time to regrow. She needed a wig, but that could not be had here. She stood up.

"Noelle?"

It was the guide, curious about why she was not at her loom. They would know each other perfectly, of course.

"Noelle, what are you doing? Why are you back there?"

She could not speak. She had no idea what Noelle's voice sounded like. If the woman came around the loom, she would see something impossible—a skeleton covered with skin, and standing over it, a hairless and eyebrowless creature, its skin flushed bright pink. The burns were probably still very much in evidence as well, making her the stars knew only how grotesque. She picked up the remnant and crushed it. The cracking, splintering sounds were appalling.

"Noelle!"

"I'm fixing it!"

"Who is that?"

"It's me, please."

The guide began her spiel again, but her uneasy tone told Miriam that she was not satisfied with what she had heard, just unable to understand what was going on. She'd send a guard around in a moment, almost certainly.

Staying behind the looms, trying to avoid being glimpsed by the workers or the tour group, she went quickly back to the door. She slipped through and down into the basement. She went to the furnace and opened the grate, stuffing the remnant inside. Never again would she be so foolish as to leave one of these little calling cards behind. In this new world of aggressive, smart human beings, one more mistake like that would be her last.

She looked around for a doorway to the outside, saw one marked *Sortie,* with a red light above it. She went out, finding herself in an alleyway. In one direction, there was a blank wall, in the other, an entrance into a rather quiet street. It was early evening now, and the shadows were growing long.

She immediately noticed a curious flickering effect against the walls and roofs of the street ahead. Each time the flickering got brighter, there would be an accompanying roar.

She moved forward cautiously, knowing that she had to go out into that street in order to escape. The closer she got to the opening of the alley, the brighter the flickering became, the louder the roaring. Now she could also hear crackling and smell a smell of burning petrol. The flickering reflected against her black clothing. She held out her hands, looking down at them, at the orange light dancing on them. Then she stepped forward and immediately looked to the left, toward the source of the light.

The first thing she saw was the gutted ruin of her mother's house. The Castle of the White Queen was streaked with soot, its every window black and dark, its roof collapsed into the shell of the building.

Before it there were dozens of police and fire vehicles and milling gendarmes. The light was not coming from their vehicles, though, it was coming from a bonfire in the middle of the street, which was being fed by men with flamethrowers. At the mouth of the Rue des Gobelins a high barrier had been erected. No member of the public could see over it. She did not think that she could easily get around. In fact, going out into the street would cause an immediate reaction, given all the police and the care with which they were preventing sight of this place.

In the center of the fire, she saw black bones and bones glowing red. It was Martin, of course. Obviously, the humans knew enough about the Keepers to take extreme care that they were really dead. A gendarme glanced at her, made a clear gesture: *stop there, come no closer*. His glance lingered for a moment, then he turned away.

The ring of people around the bones were different from the gendarmes. They were dressed casually; they looked brutal. Nearer, stood a small knot of others whom she took to be the supervisors. These people around the fire, making sure that the very bones of their quarry were reduced to ash, were the killers of the Keepers.

It was possible, if she listened intently, to make out snatches of conversation—a gendarme muttering about overtime, one of the murderers saying something about the temperature of the fire. Then the voice of a tall supervisor boomed out. "Fine ash," it said, "then hose down the street."

That was to be the fate of her kind, then, to be reduced to ash and sent down the sewer.

Silence fell. More orders were given and one of the *pompes* was started up. Soon, water was pouring from its hoses and sluicing along the street. She watched it come toward her feet, watched as it reached the drain. It carried floating bits of burned material and chips of bone. A button came tumbling and bobbing along, and she saw that it was her own button, from the suit she'd had to leave behind in order to squeeze down the pipe that had saved her.

"Excusez-moi, mademoiselle."

One of the gendarmes was coming toward her. He smiled slightly, then took her arm, but quite gently. "I will conduct you out." He drew her forward. He blinked, seeing her bald head.

"What has happened?" she asked, trying to deflect his concern.

"Vagrants set fire to the White Palace. There were deaths."

"Why were they burning the bodies?"

He shook his head. "It's what the authorities said. Who knows why."

She let the gendarme conduct her along. His body was loose, his breathing soft, his expression indifferent. Obviously he knew nothing of the Keepers and only assumed that she was a rather unusual looking woman. Her eyes were on the men who knew.

Closer she came to them, marching beside her policeman. They were engaged in intent conversation. She passed just behind the two supervisors. Then she saw one, a female, suddenly turn and face her. The creature was beautiful, with swaying blond hair. But its eyes, almost black, appeared as hard as chips of obsidian. "Excuse me," it said in American-accented English.

As instinct prepared Miriam to fight, her body became tight beneath the restricting clothes. There were still many burned and injured areas, especially in her limbs, and the pain tormented her like the persistent hacking of slow, dull blades.

The creature followed her a few steps. *"Pardonnez-moi,"* it said, now in French. This creature was concerned and it was curious. It was not sure, though, of what to do. So it could not be certain of what she was.

Then the gendarme was letting her out onto the street. He asked her if she felt well enough to keep on. Instead of answering, she slipped into and quickly through the sparse crowd of onlookers. She did not look back, did not want to delay another moment her escape from the deathtrap.

Now that she had fed, her body wanted to sleep. She knew that it would be the deep, deep sleep of her kind, and that she had to find a place in which to lie safely for the helpless hours it would bring. But she could not afford it. She had an urgent mission to perform. The French Keepers must be warned, their Book of Names protected.

She walked quickly along the busy Avenue des Gobelins. She would go to a hotel somewhere, using the credit cards in this woman's pocketbook. Or no, there was a better idea. She would go to the woman's flat. It was a risk, of course, but she had the keys and the driving license with the address.

A little farther down the street, she saw a taxi at a stand. She hailed it with the same sort of casual gesture she had seen others using. She would also update her language as best she could. Any fool would remember a passenger who spoke like Voltaire.

As she got into the taxi, she opened the pocketbook. Noelle Halff, 13 Rue Léon Maurice de Nordmann. "Treize Rue L. M. Nordmann," she muttered, slurring her words like a modern Parisian.

The driver made a strange sort of a face, then drove on. He rounded the corner into Boulevard Arago, and then they were there. It had been idiotic to take a taxi. The place was barely a quarter of a mile away. "I injured my foot," she said as he stopped in front of a lovely artist's atelier.

"Too bad," he responded as he took her money. She seemed to have done perfectly well. He hadn't noticed anything about her. Perhaps baldness was not unknown among women in Paris. Some *outré* fashion, perhaps.

She went through the bag, looking for keys, soon finding a set. There were four of them, and rather than tumble the lock, she found the correct one. She let herself in, then turned the timer that lit the foyer. As it hummed through its few minutes, she located the next key and entered the atelier itself.

The room was furnished with another Gobelins loom and more tapestries, medieval reproductions that the woman must have been selling in the tourist market.

"Hello," she said. There was no answer. She went across the studio to its small kitchen, and beyond it into an equally tiny *salle de bains* and *toilette*. For sleep, a *couchette* had been installed at one end of the studio.

She searched the *salle de bains*, looking for makeup, but also trying to determine if more than one person lived here. The results were ambiguous. There was a man's razor, also two toothbrushes.

Somebody moved. She glimpsed in the shadows a strange, dark creature. She reeled back out of the tiny room, raising her arms, preparing to defend herself.

But nobody came leaping after her. The only sound was her own breathing, that and a trickle of water from the toilet.

She turned on the light and saw in the mirror a Miriam Blaylock so profoundly changed that she'd thought herself a stranger. The head was bald, the face sunken, the eyes black sockets. She raised a finger to her cheek, felt the skin. It ought to be pink and soft right now, glowing with the life she had just consumed. But it revealed another surprise. She was not sallow, but covered with fine gray ash. The outer layer of her skin seemed to have been carbonized, at least on her face.

She splashed some water on it, then dried it with a serviette. It came up muddy white. The sink was full of gray. She stripped off her clothes and looked down at herself. She had sustained tremendous damage, more than she had realized. There were great rifts in her skin, filled with raw, angry flesh. Her hips were scraped almost to the bone. In one place, she could see actually see some bone.

She drew a bath, watching as the wonderful, steaming water gushed into the big tub. When she sat in it, the ash clinging to her body soon turned the water dark gray, tinged pink with the blood of her wounds.

Soon her whole body was tickling as her blood raced to repair the damage. She closed her eyes. How lovely. How much she needed to sleep. So easy it would be, so warm was the water.

No! No, she had to find stimulants—coffee, pills, any-thing—and she had to locate the woman's passport, call an airline, and buy a ticket to New York, go to the mines, warn the other Keepers.

She rose from the tub and threw open the medicine chest. There were three bottles of pills—vitamins, an herbal rem-edy for colds, nothing of any use. The poor young creature had been healthy and clean of even simple drugs. Miriam could not avoid a sense of waste when she destroyed a vital, young life like this. The girl had been not unlike her Sarah.

She had given up telephoning Sarah. All that mattered now was getting home. She was afraid that the disaster had already crossed the Atlantic and that was why Sarah couldn't respond. Would she find her beautiful home in Manhattan a ruin, just like the Castle of the White Queen, and Sarah's very bones burned to ashes? There was no way to know that. It was not given to her.

She peered into the mirror. Actually, her face wasn't so bad. A little makeup here, a little there, a bit of lip gloss, and she would be a girl again. She would be—

She stopped. Like the fall of evening or a black cloak dropping over her, a shroud, a sorrow so great fell upon her heart that it inspired not the usual gnashing anger, but a deep questioning of her own value as a creature, and indeed of the worth of the Keepers as a species upon the earth.

Look around you, she thought, at the complex life that had been unfolding in this atelier, at the wonders in the looms, their colors glowing in the faint light that came in from the street. Look at the book beside the bed, thumbed, earmarked, a book of poems with which Noelle Halff had put herself to sleep at night. *Les Fleurs du Mal*—"The Flowers of Evil." Miriam knew the poems, appreciated them as well.

The girl might not have any pills in her cabinet, but she kept lip gloss and other cosmetics of the very highest quality. Miriam started to make up her face, to return to it an approximation of the endless youth that lay beneath her wounds.

She felt the weight of sleep urging at her brain, at her exhausted muscles, increasing the weight of her bones. She tossed her head, her eyes gleaming with a kind of fury. Even without drugs, she would not sleep. She could not, must not.

For she knew without question, if she lay down in this atelier—if she slept—they would certainly catch her.

NINE

Lady of the Knife

The lower condyles of human femurs lined the walls, joint-end out. Above them were stacked skulls. Paul had known about the Denfert-Rochereau ossuary, but only vaguely, as the sort of grotesque that tourists of a certain kind—fans of horror movies, say—might visit. For ten francs you could spend as much time as you wanted to with the bones of seven million Parisians.

"What's that smell?" Becky asked.

"Maybe there's a fresh corpse."

"Thank you, Charles."

"No bodies were ever buried here. Just skeletons," Colonel Bocage said.

Still, there was a certain smell, and smells were important to this work. Paul inhaled carefully. They all knew the fetors of the vampire—the sour, dry odor of their unwashed skin and the appalling stink of their latrines. Their waste was dead human plasma.

Colonel Bocage and Lieutenants Raynard and Des Roches walked ahead. The two lieutenants had interesting histories. Raynard was not French but Algerian. He had been a Foreign Legionnaire. Des Roches, a solemn-looking man with a quick sense of humor and what looked to Paul like a whole lot of physical power, had been a GIGN officer. The Groupe d'Intervention de la Gendarmerie Nationale was France's elite terrorist intervention unit. These were the guys who stormed planes being held by madmen. These were also the guys who were sent in when the government didn't want prisoners, only bodies.

Because of the catastrophe that had just occurred, these were the last two men Bocage had. Signing people on was just as difficult for him as it was for Paul. They had to be excellent, they had to be clearable to a high level, and it was just damn hard to find people like that.

As they moved forward, everybody was quiet. The French were grieving over the decimation of their team, and everybody was well aware of how this hole had chewed up people in the past. Theirs was brutal, extremely dangerous work. Vampires died, but it cost. God, it cost.

They were passing rows and rows of bones, an incredible sight. They were still in the ossuary itself.

"No teeth," Charlie observed, "no lower jaws."

Des Roches said, "The teeth were sold to button makers to help finance the ossuary."

"Was that legal?"

"Perhaps, at the time," Colonel Bocage replied, "although not politically correct, I am embarrassed to say. But old France—it was not politically correct."

"Madame de Pompadour," Becky said, pointing to a sign.

"Who was?" Charlie asked.

"She was the executive secretary of King Louis XV," Raynard said.

"And the mistress," Bocage added, "of course."

"How'd she end up down here?"

"After the revolution, the bones of aristocrats were no longer held sacred." The tone of Raynard's voice suggested that he did not entirely approve of the revolution. Like many men engaged in extremely difficult military pursuits, he was ultraconservative.

"Stop, please." Des Roches consulted his PalmPilot, which contained a map not only of the ossuary, but of the entire system of mines beneath the streets of Paris. The mines were more extensive even than the legendary Paris sewer system. The map, provided by the Inspectorate General of Quarries, covered the two hundred plus miles of tunnels and shafts that were interconnected. This was estimated to be roughly three-quarters of the total. The rest of it, among the most ancient of the shafts, were either completely detached from the main body, or connected only by openings too small for a human to enter.

Given the danger of entering the tunnels, ground-based radars and sonars had been used to complete the maps, so they were not nearly as accurate as the hunters would have liked. Paul had spent the night with Charlie and Becky studying them. Each had committed a section of the complex to memory. They had quizzed one another on twists and turns, blind alleys and unexpected crossings, until dawn.

They reached a dead end in the ossuary, which was blocked by a gate and marked with a sign, *Entrée Interdite.* Over the past hundred years, the Prefecture of Police had recorded sixty disappearances from the ossuary. It wasn't many, but the points at which these people had last been seen were all closest to this particular connection with the abandoned labyrinth of mines. It was here that Bocage's teams had entered in the past.

"Regard," Bocage said, "beyond this point, we must assume that we are, at all times, in peril of our lives."

Raynard opened an aluminum case that he carried. He distributed lightweight Kevlar body armor. "Remember that they are experts with knives. They can throw a knife almost with the speed of a bullet, because of the arm strength."

Paul remembered the Sinha Vampire. It had killed Len Carter with a knife thrown so hard it went completely through his body and struck Becky, who was standing ten feet behind him. She'd taken thirty stitches in her neck. Had she not been turned slightly away from him at that instant, her carotid artery would have been severed.

Bocage gave out pistols, weapons unlike anything Paul had seen before. "This pistol will fire five of the fifteen special rounds that it carries with a single pull of the trigger. There is no sight because laser sights are useless. They see it and they are too fast. The bullets are designed to fracture into millions of tiny bits of shrapnel. A burst will pulverize everything in a five-meter square. Remember please, to assume that the creature, no matter how badly damaged it appears, is only stunned. Do not get near the mouth, and bind the hands immediately with your plastic cuffs. Is this clear?"

They all knew the drill by heart. But they all listened as if they'd never heard it before in their lives. A professional never ignores a chance to get an edge. Maybe hearing it again just now would speed up reaction time by a hundredth of a second. Maybe that would save a life.

Miriam paid her ten francs and passed through the entrance to the catacombs. She'd spent an hour at the Galeries-Lafayette buying casual clothes and a wig, so the person who came into this place did not appear much like the one who had passed the Castle of the White Queen yesterday evening. All that remained of her ordeal were angry red areas on various parts of her body. Her right hip was still somewhat stiff, as well. But this gum-chewing teenager with black, close-cut hair bore almost no resemblance to the pallid, sunken horror of twelve hours ago. She was soft, her pale eyes sparkling with the eager innocence of eighteen or twenty sheltered years. Any man would want to protect her, even to cherish her. The little gold cross around her neck suggested religiosity. A man, managing somehow to penetrate the mysteries of this sweet child, would not be surprised to hear her murmur, "But I'm a virgin."

Moving as swiftly and carefully as a cat, she descended the spiral stair that led into the crypt. The touristic map she had gotten with her ticket covered only the ossuary itself, but she knew the ancient signs that would indicate the route from the public area to the lairs and, above all, to the Keep where would be stored the Book of Names and whatever other things the French Keepers owned collectively.

Her intention was to warn the other Keepers if she could, but without fail to take their Book of Names with her. She could not risk leaving it here, no matter how they felt about that. If they resisted, she would fight.

There were two sightseers at the foot of the stairs. She shifted her body language, becoming a casual girl, a little nervous. The tourists were German, plump and smelling of their recent lunch of ham. The man had ugly, narrow veins. She loved the woman's carotid. A charming nibble, she would be.

She sniffed the faint wind coming out of the corridor. None of the lovely, infinitely subtle scents of other Keepers. Each Keeper had his own particular scent, mixed of skin and the dust of ages. Miriam longed to smell the skin of a robust male Keeper just after he had fed, when he was warm and moist, his muscles like flowing iron, his odor overlaid by the creamy, intricate scent of fresh human blood.

The rankness of the couple was strong, mixed with the

rather sandy, musty odor of the bones. Again, she inhaled, flaring her nostrils. Yes, there were other human beings within, also, all stinking of their foods and perfumes and the orifices they had secretly neglected. She smelled the damp biscuit odor of little boys, the soft cheese fragrance of girl children, and a bit of an older woman's perfume. A class of mixed sex between the ages of six and ten was a short distance ahead, with their female teacher, who was thirty, no younger, and healthy. Miriam tested the air for new odors, filtering out those she had already identified. Some sort of exotic foodstuff came to her, spices of the East mixed with the odors of skin and spent cigarettes—a couple from Asia.

She entered the corridor. Her glance at the map had left her with a memory of precisely the number of steps she would have to go in every passage in the ossuary. In childhood, every Keeper was trained to use measured gaits, so she knew exactly how many inches she traversed with every step she took, no matter how fast her stride.

The entrance to the ossuary was marked by a group of thick, square columns painted white with black borders. She passed them, entering the earliest of the crypts. The most recent bones, quite naturally, were deepest. By human terms, they were ancient, but she remembered Paris perfectly clearly when there had been no catacomb full of bones and gawking tourists. In those days, the Keepers had the entire system of mines to themselves. One could ascend by an unknown stair into the street, take a victim down, and enjoy it at leisure, then have a nice sleep in the safety of the depths. The Paris Keepers had a pleasant life then.

She moved forward cautiously, seeking a certain spot that led from the ossuary into the deep shafts. There were other entrances, but this one was what you took if you knew what you were doing. Anyone coming down another tunnel would be assumed to be human.

The entrance was signaled, she knew, by a great cross. It would not be difficult to find. But to know its true meaning—that would be very difficult indeed . . . if you weren't a Keeper. When she was certain that she was alone, she sprinted along the galleries. Here was Madame du Pompadour—that hideous old crank who reeked of sour milk and had somehow captured the heart of one of the later Louises, a prancing unwise fellow who blew farts and stank horribly himself from a fungal infection of the skin. Madame de Pompadour, indeed. Her real name was Jeanne Poisson—Jenny Fish. Well, so much for that marble tomb of hers. This was far more appropriate. Philippe Vendôme had made fervid, ratlike love to her, hadn't he? Miriam recalled watching some sort of entertainment like that.

She'd been down here in the early eighteenth century with—which one—was it Lollie? Yes, poor Lollia, she'd been on her last legs then, frantically trying on powdered wigs and loading her face with leaded creams. No use, any of it.

Now another turn—and there was the great cross. But would the entrance still be behind it? Had the French found it and walled it up, also? She looked at the cross, refocusing her vision so that the glyphs that were invisible to the human eye stood out clearly. There was a word to utter in Prime, according to the instructions, that would open the wall. It would also alert the Keepers inside that she was there. She was instructed, as well, to append her name. She drew a deep breath, expanded her lungs, and released the call. It vibrated against the stone, its echo fluttering off down the corridors. Now, the instructions told her, press thrice the upper corner of the left tine of the cross.

The hidden door swung inward. Beyond was absolute dark. From within there came the odor of many lairs.

"*Halte!*" Everybody froze. "Do not move," Colonel Bocage said. "Listen."

It came again, a sound so deep that it was more a sensation than a noise.

"Could it be the Métro?" Becky asked. "Are we under a tunnel?"

Des Roches laid his arm around her neck, drew her close, uttered a breathy, almost-silent whisper. "That was a vampire."

The French were in some ways far advanced in their knowledge. Becky and Charlie and Paul had been down many a dark tunnel, but they had never had to face anything this elaborate.

The place stank of wet stone and the musk of bats. The group had stopped its march and was clustering together in a low gallery. Becky shone her light on a stone where graffiti had been carved. "*Merci à Dieu, m—*" and there it stopped, as if the carver had run out of strength or light or time. The letters were formed in an old script, perhaps from the last century or the one before.

"Listen—again," Charlie said.

It was eerie, that sound—so deep that you wouldn't notice it unless you were trained to. Paul had heard it echoing off the walls of the night in Beijing, in Osaka, in Bangkok. As a boy, he had heard it mixing with the sullen hoot of the owl and the barking of the fox.

After some moments, there was no sound but their breathing and the busy scuttle of rats. The roar of the great city above them was a bare whisper. Water dripped, echoing as if somewhere deeper there might be a hidden pool or even a small lake.

"Lights out," Paul said. "We go to light-amplification goggles." Their equipment packs rattled as they put the night-vision goggles on.

You could see perhaps fifty feet. Beyond that was the haze of a darkness so deep not even the goggles could gather enough light to be of use.

"Do you wish to go to infrared," Bocage asked his men, his voice, in its softness, sounding curiously as if he'd meant to utter words of love.

"Let's do it," Raynard said. He and Des Roches clicked on the infrared floods.

A hand grabbed Paul's shoulder, the fingers digging in. Becky was staring down the long, sloping corridor.

There had been something there, most certainly. "Vampire," Bocage murmured.

Paul had seen what might have passed for a tall, elegant man, tall and very quick of step. The moment the infrared flood had turned on, it had gone.

The Keepers were calling to one another that human beings had penetrated the barrier. Their voices were calm, which made her throat turn sour and her mind race—*don't you understand, don't you realize even yet?*

She had the map of the ossuary, but there was no map of the labyrinth beyond. She had to go by scent and hearing and what little sight was available.

She had not moved ten steps before the darkness completely enclosed her. Now she had to walk blind, on faith only, trusting in her nose and ears for direction.

Behind her, she could hear the breathing of tourists in the

ossuary and their occasional murmured conversations. There was something about the place that kept them quiet, as if the spirits of the dead demanded it.

Along a low side tunnel that angled sharply down came a faint reddish-purple glow. For a moment she did not know what it was. But then she saw a Keeper, dressed all in black, standing not fifty feet away from her. His back was to her. He was watching the glow, which was bouncing, waxing and waning, as it slid along a far tunnel.

When his odor touched her nostrils—powerful, richly masculine—a thrill trembled through her. He stood tall. His absolute stillness made him seem so very noble.

She murmured low, in Prime, "I, Miriam out of Lamia, greet you." His back did not move. Then, very suddenly, he turned round.

He faced her now, the glow waxing and waning behind him. "I, Uriel from Enoch, now called Henri, greet you." He inclined his head.

She bowed deep at the waist, as was the formality for a Keeper entering from outside a given Keep. He came close to her and laid his long fingers under her chin and raised her.

"I come to present myself before the conclave," she added, still speaking in the measured, formal cadences of Prime.

He switched to French. "You want a kid, Miriam? Or a husband?"

"Both," she replied.

He smiled, then. "You still live in that house, I presume, with your wonderful little pets."

He did not sound too disapproving. Dared she hope? "Yes," she said carefully. She lowered her eyes to him, as manners required.

"How can you bear the smell?" His tone slapped her. He was as contemptuous of her as the rest.

She tried not to reveal her disappointment. But she raised her eyes. Damned if she would show respect to a man who had contempt for her. "What is that glow," she asked. It was getting distinctly brighter, so much so that she could now see the walls of this tunnel clearly, and even Henri's narrow, solemn face.

"It's trivial."

She dropped the manners and looked directly at him. Martin Soule had been in such terrible condition that he had presented no appeal. Henri, by contrast, was not hideous. He was dirty and poorly dressed, but his body was gorgeous. She could sense his strength, and the thought of being held in his arms was not without appeal.

He seemed indifferent to the light. "It's getting brighter."

He was looking at her with the attention a jeweler might pay a gem. "It's true, then," he said.

"What is true?"

"Your beauty is the greatest in the world." He reached toward her, a tentative, caressing touch. As his fingers shivered along the edge of her lips, she tasted of their flat salt. Desire flamed in her. She imagined herself lying beneath him, absolutely, wonderfully helpless as he came roaring into her like an inflamed lion. She would receive him, an open flower, an open wound. She would be a slave to him then, hold his cup and kneel before him. She would let herself be possessed, and in turn she would possess him.

The glow flared, and now she heard a steady tread of—she listened—twelve feet. They sounded to her like human feet. "That light—it's the humans, isn't it?"

"It's nothing. Ignore it."

"Is it human?"

He gazed at her. "You are a forward creature, just as they say."

"Humans are dangerous."

"Don't be absurd."

"You knew Martin Soule, of course."

He nodded. "He went to live in that house your mother so foolishly built."

"He died there."

"Did he?" His voice took on a note of question. "Why would he elect to do that?"

"They burned him! As they intend to burn us all!"

"I remember your mother's misfortune. But that should not—"

The lights appeared like ghostly eyes, six of them, all glaring straight down this tunnel. Henri was trapped in the purple glow. He turned to face it, smiling slightly. "Stop," he said in flawless modern French, "you have no business here."

Paul's breath whooshed out of him when he saw it. He'd never laid eyes on one like this, so large, so strong looking. In Asia, they'd been smaller, and they'd hidden at the back of their lairs.

"There are two," Bocage said laconically.

Then he saw, behind the towering male in its fusty suit from fifty years ago, a female. It drew back into the shadows, but it also had a human appearance . . . just like the traveler. Had he seen blond hair? He couldn't be sure. The creature had moved with the speed and grace of a panther.

"*Mon Dieu*," Des Roches said.

"You saw that female?"

"The face—it was . . . so strange."

Paul had not seen the face. But he didn't care about that now. It wasn't the traveler, the traveler was dead. He raised his gun and fired, and so did all the others.

The noise was shattering; a gust of wind blasted back into his face, as the narrow tunnel compressed the expanding air. The screaming thunder of it was accompanied by a dazzling flare of green light, and followed by hollow, zipping echoes as bullet fragments tore along the walls.

Silence. A distant howl, growing louder. Charlie tore off his night-vision equipment and went for his flashlight. He flicked the switch. The beam shone like a white laser into the murk of dust that now filled the tunnel.

"*Non!*" Bocage screamed.

There was a flicker in the air, no more. Out of the dust had come a knife, thrown with the vampire's bizarre force, moving so fast that it was only a flash of light.

The beam of the flashlight wavered, then went crazy, then dropped to the floor. It rolled toward the vampires, and in a second nothing could be seen but a dim yellow glow in the murk of dust. This glow was pointing straight at them, away from the vampires. So they were visible, but they could not see.

Charlie began to make a sound, one that was almost comically like the whistle of a toy train. It changed to gurgling and splashing and the clatter of a body in seizure. He fell back, his head striking the ground with a crack like a breaking egg.

Des Roches went down beside him. Becky, stifling a scream, pushed close. Her hands touched the knife as if it was blazing hot. She made little, choked sounds in her throat, awful sounds. Her fingers fluttered around the handle. The sounds had a sense of question in them, but it was a question that nobody could answer. There was no answer.

How do you extract a knife that is embedded up to its hilt in a man's face?

There was another blast, this one from Raynard's gun. Then Bocage fired twice more. Paul probably should have been terrified, but he felt the same calm, clear sense of inner control that always came to him at moments like this. His heart was sinking because of Charlie's death. But he did not stop fighting, not for an instant, no matter his breaking heart. He watched that dust, looking for shadowy movement.

Another knife appeared, headed straight for Becky. He saw it gliding as gently as a leaf on the sea, gliding toward her neck. He felt her hair under his hand, and then he pressed with lightning speed and she slammed flat, and the knife went clanging and clattering up the tunnel.

From off in the yellow gloom he heard a faint sound, an unmistakable sound: it could only have been a gasp of surprise.

Wild emotions sped through Miriam—horror to see a Keeper blown to pieces, fear that the next blast would kill her, and then, above all, amazement at what she had seen that man do, and amazement at how she felt about him.

That man—only a human—had moved as fast as a Keeper. She knew the human genome intimately. There was nothing in their makeup that could enable them to do this. Their physical limitations were bred into them. But not into this one, no indeed.

Then there was the way he affected her when he pulled off his ridiculous goggles and she saw his chiseled, complex face. Her body responded to this human as if he were a Keeper. This was not the attraction she felt normally to human prettiness, but powerful, shivering, blood-pounding desire. She wanted him not under her but over her; she sweated and lusted for him; she wanted him to possess her and fill her with a startling, frenetic hardness. Her body was begging her; it was pleading as if he were the strongest, finest male Keeper in the weave of the world.

She backed away, as horrified at these feelings as she was at the power of the weapons that were being raised against her.

She dashed to the end of the corridor, took a turning, another, then flattened herself against the wall. She listened—the ever-present dripping, the scuttle of rats, the deep fluttering of Keeper voices as they called back and forth, in mixtures of French and Prime, inquiring of one another: "What was it?" "Is there reason for concern?"

There were a lot of them here. They had indeed been assembling for their conclave. She knew, after seeing that man, that there would be no conclave. He was going to go through this labyrinth like the red shadow of death, like the hand of an angry god. None would survive him, not with his exploding bullets and his team and his eerie personal speed.

Off behind her, another blast of fire echoed, followed by the awful thudding of another Keeper body being ripped to pieces.

They were going to lose their battle. Therefore, she had to do what was necessary to protect the rest of the Keepers. She had to go to the heart of this Keep and secure their Book of Names. To find it, she must be careful to make certain that every step she took was downward. Turning here, there, she went farther and deeper. Soon the dripping was general, water was running in rivulets, and she was concerned that the center of the Keep might be awash.

Every few minutes, there would be an awful roar behind her, followed by a series of weaker explosions. The humans—led by that eerie, beautiful monster—were clearing out the Keepers, moving with careful method. For their part, the Keepers, who had no call of alarm and no real way to react to an assault like this, were responding piecemeal, although with growing anger and ferocity. One after another, they would attack the human group. Then would come the roaring of the guns, and the distant, liquid thuds of bodies being torn apart.

She was moving fast, head down, when she suddenly sensed a change around her. She was in a much larger space, and not only that, she could see a little.

This was not a manmade tunnel, but something very much more ancient. The precise lines of its walls, the low, graceful arch of its ceiling, suggested that a far more careful hand than human had been at work here. Stalagmites rose from the ground. It looked like a forest on an alien world.

"I am Miriam out of Lamia, come seeking entry to your conclave."

At first, there was silence. Then the light wavered and, with the softest of sounds, a shadow emerged. "I am Julia out of Helene who was Nef-ta-tu."

She had not seen Julia since the days of splendor, when their kind had ruled Egypt, walking as princes among their human herds.

Julia had been as sweet then as a roe, as tender as an apple from the bough. What came to Miriam was a dark creature, so crusted with eons of dirt that only her eyes seemed alive.

Julia had the Book of Names with her, tucked under her arm as casually as some novel. "There is a human band in these caves," she said, her voice mild.

"They are killing us."

She gave Miriam a careful look. "How is that?"

"With guns."

"We are faster than their hands. We can step out of the way before they pull the trigger. I've done it myself now and again."

"These guns leave you no place to go. They spread a mass of tiny bullets. Keepers up there are being torn apart. The humans are coming for that book." She smiled. "Let me take it."

"I will not. You're a pervert, Miriam. You're unclean."

"If they get your book, our whole world will be in danger."

"They will not get our book."

"They will be here in minutes. And they will get it."

"There have been three hundred conclaves in this place. My grandfather built it when the humans were covered with hair."

"May those days live in memory."

"They were sour. The new ones now are much sweeter."

Horribly close, there came the roar of gunfire. It was so close that the flash was faintly visible.

"We have to get out. We cannot waste another minute."

"What is a minute or a hundred years? You have fallen from your nobility, Miriam. Everybody says it. I remember you in linen, how tall you were, your limbs like gold."

"That memory is three thousand years old, Julia! This is now, and the humans are not armed with bronze daggers. Don't you understand that they're tearing the Keepers apart with their guns?"

"They will become lost. The labyrinth is more cunning than their minds can understand."

"That was true a hundred years ago. But now they have

sonar and digital maps and handheld locators. And they're trained to kill us. They have killed all of Asia, and they have their Book of Names."

"Asia is far away."

"It's an airplane flight! I was in Bangkok a few days ago."

"You have the restless soul of a human, always traipsing about."

Miriam heard human voices. They would be here in moments. "Do you not think it strange that you alone are here at the appointed time? Where are the others? Can you explain it?"

"Don't cross-question me. All will unfold in its course."

"Then why hasn't it? What's wrong?"

"What has changed to prevent the conclave? Nothing."

"Everything has changed."

"A few humans cannot change the course of the world."

Miriam saw the humans creeping among the shadows ahead, four of them.

"It's lit," the tall, powerful one said. He walked into the gray glow from the ancient batteries. Humans had found some of the Keepers' batteries in the Valley of the Euphrates some years ago. They were still trying to understand how the ancients could have had electricity.

"Lookit—a power line!"

Discreetly, Miriam drew Julia into a pool of shadow. The humans were now at the far end of the chamber, perhaps a hundred yards away.

"How do you work the lights?" she whispered to Julia.

"They're always on during conclave. That's the rule."

"Julia, there is no conclave. We're all being killed. Turn out the lights."

Julia broke away from her, strode out into the center of the chamber. For a moment, the humans froze. They drew closer together.

"Julia!"

"Miriam, they're only—"

There came clicking noises, ominous, echoing. Only seconds remained. "Julia, run!"

Julia turned to her. Her smile said that she found her friend of old times pitiful.

The tall human raised his weapon, followed by the others. Miriam watched his face, the careful sculpture of it, the hard fury of the eyes.

The guns blasted—and Miriam herself felt a hot slash of pain along her exposed hip. Just a few shots had filled the entire space with bullets—all this huge area!

Then she saw Julia, who still stood, who still held the all-important book. Julia, pouring blood, placed the book beside her on the ground. She sat then, a dark and bloody Venus beside a still-ringing stalagmite. Again the guns rang out, and this time her head went bouncing off her neck. On its face Miriam saw an expression of mild curiosity, nothing more than that.

"There's another one," a voice said. "Over there—that shadow behind the stalagmite. That's a vampire."

Miriam must not waste another instant. But the book—it was lying beside the torn ruins of Julia. It was only a few cubits away, but right in their line of fire.

It was deep brown, its cover an ancient, profoundly aged human skin. On its cover was the Keeper's ancient symbol of balanced nature and balanced rule, known to humans as the ankh. The humans looked toward it, too.

She had to reach it, she had to get it. But first, she must

turn off these damn lights. The copper wires were set on insulators a few feet above her head. She knew that these batteries were very, very different from what the humans had, that they drew their energy from the earth itself, and they were powerful.

To kill the lights, she had to stand up in full view, reach overhead, and yank a wire loose. The electricity would jolt her. If she wasn't fast enough, or could not let go of the power line, she would be burned inside—an injury that would take weeks to mend. In moments they would be upon her, though, and she would end up in their sights.

She was well up behind one of the stalagmites, but they nevertheless fired, all together, the roar of their guns causing the chamber to resound like the interior of a bell. She felt no injury.

The leader said, "Spread out," in a resonant, icy voice.

They came closer to her, led by their monster. His face was so determined, so truly terrible in the hate that was written across it, that she was compelled to think that his emotions were almost full-circle. This human loathed the Keepers so much that he nearly loved them. She would not forget this.

"We need to angle off that wall," he said, "it's pressed itself against the back of the stalagmite."

He spoke with detachment. Well, she also was professional. She reached up to the humming wire. Her fingers paused, hesitating. But this was no act of ritual possession. She curled them, closing them on the wire.

There was a buzzing sound and a choked, sizzling cry, and the lights went out. "Shit," Bocage said.

Paul went down on his hands and knees. "The book," he whispered.

"Forget the damn book; get some light in here," Becky hissed.

"Get the goggles—" Des Roches said.

There was no time, and Paul knew it. "Cover me," he said as he moved off toward the book.

"How?" Bocage asked.

He crawled two, three feet, then five, then ten. He could hear them putting on their goggles. They mustn't use the infrared floods. Vampires could see into the infrared.

Then he felt it. He felt the book's smooth surface and grasped it. But then he knew that other hands also had it, another hand was grasping it, too.

She was there, face-to-face with him, but he could see nothing. He could smell her, though—not the stink of the vampire but a scent unlike any he had ever smelled before, rich and complicated and sexy as hell.

When she growled—as vampires did—he thought that it was the gentlest and yet most lethal sound he had ever heard. She was stronger, he knew that, but he didn't intend to let go of that book. "I know you can understand me," he said.

There was only breathing in reply, breathing like the soft and edgy flutter of a swarm of butterflies. He thought, *She's scared, too—a vampire that knows how to be afraid.*

She yanked the book right out of his hands. Instantly, he dove at her, slammed into her, felt the book clatter to the ground. Again she growled, this time with a mixture of surprise and raw fury that made him think that he would shortly die.

He tried to get his fingers around her neck, to choke her, to try to close off that crucial blood flow.

He sensed somebody coming up from behind. Then

Becky was with him, grabbing at the creature's arms, trying to throw it off balance.

The vampire's neck felt like steel. He couldn't manage to throttle the creature, and his hands were strong. He struggled, getting closer, seeing the face before him, a glowing moon in the darkness, smelling the sweat of a woman and—perfume. Yes, it was perfumed, this one. What in damn hell was going on here.

"Get a light! A light!"

In the split of an instant, the vampire was gone. Des Roches and Bocage appeared. As Paul looked across the empty cave floor, a wave of rage and frustration swept through him. He'd lost the damn book! This meant years more work, hundreds of lives.

Then Becky's hand came into his, her cool hand. A flashlight glowed, and he saw in that glow her shining, triumphant eyes. She gave him the book.

"Goddamn," he said, "good god damn."

She moved toward him, her lips parting, her eyes steady and strong.

There was no time—not here, not now. "We can get it," he said, breaking away.

"It's gone," Bocage said.

Paul could not accept that. He turned; he went a few steps into the deadly blackness.

"Paul! Paul, no!"

He went on.

TEN

The Traveler

As he ran along a low, narrow corridor, he flashed his light from time to time, making sure that he hadn't passed any side entrances and that he wasn't about to hit a wall. He did not think about the fact that he was a man alone penetrating into a lair that was crawling with the creatures. That female—he had never encountered anything like that. It had been clean and perfumed. It had felt soft and smooth, if immensely strong. He had not seen the face, but he knew that there had been beauty, perhaps great beauty. Its scent still lingered: Arpège and womanhood. Its touch had inflamed him even as it had made his flesh crawl. He wanted to bathe, to get its smell off him . . . and he wanted never to bathe again.

Was it the traveler, still alive after all?

He knew that the safety of the book was everything, but he also had to kill this vampire. He had never wanted to kill a vampire so much, not in all the years he'd been at it. This thing could walk the streets without a problem. The idea of vampires that could function in the human world was horrifying.

He came to a T—blank wall ahead, a passage to the right sloping up, another to the left sloping down.

He stopped, shone his flashlight first in one direction and then the other. Far away he heard Becky. "Paul! *Paul!*"

He heard something in her voice that was tender. But she was a professional killer, for God's sake. What man could romance a woman like that?

"Paaaaul!"

Her fear for him was heartrending. But he could not answer, dared not. They would have to do their best to follow. Waiting for them to catch up would cost at least two minutes, and there were no minutes available at all just now.

He listened ahead, closing his eyes and cupping his hands behind his ears. The rising passage was silent. But not the descending—down there he heard all sorts of noises—murmurs, scuffling sounds, the low thutter of vampire calls.

He hesitated only long enough to make certain that his gun had a fresh clip and there were still more in the rucksack that Raynard had given him. Three more, to be exact.

It was a lovely gun, the way it tore the things apart. His hand on its comforting butt, he stepped into the downward passage. The descent was steep. Soon, his flashlight was revealing carved inscriptions in Latin here and there on the walls. This tunnel must be very old indeed. The Arénes de Lutèce, where the Romans had held bearbaiting contests, could not be far overhead. Maybe they had quarried the stone for it here. But he did not think so. There was something too perfect about the way these walls were made. As old as it all appeared, every line was dead straight.

He was in a vampire place, something made by them in some uncountably ancient time. When this place was made, mankind must have been—well, maybe still living in caves.

What did it mean?

If they had been advanced enough to make this, they must have ruled the world then, in the deep long ago. The implications for human life were chilling. Anything could be true—they could even have bred us the same way that we breed cattle.

Fear kept rising, and he kept pushing it down. But what if he couldn't win? What if they had reserves of power that he had never imagined?

He tried to be philosophical. If he died here, he died here. At least he'd take some of them with him.

And then—was that somebody breathing?

He stopped, listened. No, it was nothing, just the wind in the halls, or far-off street noise. He started off again.

One of them appeared ahead of him, leaping, screaming, a blur of darkness and fury. He fired, then fired again and again, until it exploded along the corridor with a series of wet splats.

He flicked on his light. He'd expected to see a mass of carnage, a flowing river of blood. But there wasn't all that much blood. And then he saw a bit of fur, gray, and he realized that the light had played a trick on him. He'd shot at the looming shadow of a rat.

"Goddamnit!"

He went on, deeper still, closer to the murmuring, to the whispering movement.

Then he heard a totally unexpected sound. A voice. A child's voice. "Sir?" His heart started hammering—not only because the voice was there, but because it was behind him.

Dare he turn? Dare he?

"Sir?"

Boy or girl, he could not tell. It sounded about ten, perhaps a little older. His finger slipped around the trigger. He felt sick, he did not think he could do this. But he whirled round, dropping to the floor as he did, firing.

There was nobody.

They were tricking him. The rat had also been a trick, he realized. No rat would cast such a big shadow. Somehow, they'd done it. They were tricking him, in order to get him to use up his bullets. They were probably counting his shots.

He looked out into the darkness, could see nothing. He listened, could hear nothing. Only his own breathing disturbed the silence. He was a strong man; he had learned that over the years of his life. But he had also learned that all strength has its limits. He had seen the Khmer Rouge bury a man alive, and listened to that man go mad in his hole. Paul himself had wept with fear, thinking he would be next.

The vampires knew the human mind. They knew his mind. They knew his limits. And that was why, when he heard the creaking, coming slowly closer, it was so very hard not to use his light or fire his gun. It was so hard. But he could not, because he knew that no matter how sure he was, this, also, would be a wasted shot.

As quietly as was possible for a large man, he moved so that his back was pressed against the wall. To give his ears whatever tiny extra edge that might be gained, he closed his eyes. Even though there was no light, doing this would direct his brain a little more toward hearing than sight.

He stuffed the book into his pants and cupped his free hand behind his ear. He listened in one direction. There was the creaking, just over there. But it was not a living sound, and no closer. In the other direction, though, there was another sound, more complex, far harder to hear.

It was, he thought, a living sound. It was the sound of breath being drawn, in his opinion. He would have to lower his hand, grab his light and shine it, then instantly fire if something was there.

But what if it was that child? They had known that he would be unable to fire at a child. They had known that he would take the split of an instant to be certain. That would be *their* time.

It was a duel, and they had rigged it for him to lose the instant he disclosed his position. The only way to win would be to fire into the dark and risk a child . . . theirs, but still a child.

The breathing was close now. He would have to act and instantly. He did not go for his light. Instead, he reached out. He caught a sleeve. It was yanked away but he was fast; he'd always been damned fast. He found himself grasping a large, powerful, cold hand. The fingers closed around his wrist, closed and began to tighten.

There came laughter, soft and entirely relaxed. Foolishly so, he thought. He fired into the sound. In the flash, he saw a male face, powerful, dark, with a long, sharp nose and deep gleaming eyes.

There was a cry, deep, abruptly cut off.

Then he was deaf, as you always were deaf after that blast. When he could hear again, there was a high noise, the most terrible of noises, shaking the walls, echoing as it pealed again and again through the limestone chambers, the screaming of a woman in molten agony.

Now he used his light. It appeared, a female vampire, with beaded hair and a long dress on, dark blue silk, white collar, and the mouth fully open, a broad O filled with teeth. They had awful mouths, filthy and stinking of the blood in their guts, mouths that were made for sucking. They looked okay—a little thin-lipped was all—until they opened those wet, stinking maws of theirs. If you kissed a vampire, he thought, it might suck your insides right out of you.

The agony of grief was great for them, greater even than for a human being, as he had seen in Asia. She came maddened by it, her arms straight out ahead of her, her fingers long, lethal claws. He knew that she wanted to tear him to pieces. He knew that she wanted to feel his gristle break.

He pulled the trigger. In the flash, he saw her dress billow as if lifted by a funhouse blast. Her face folded in on itself, and her cry joined the cry of the gun and was gone.

Her body hit the wall behind her with a slapping thud, and she slid down a slide of her own thick, black blood.

They lay side by side, and he was amazed at what he saw. The male wore slacks and a black sweater, and a leather jacket so supple that Paul hardly dared touch it. The female beside him was equally passable.

These European vampires were not like the Asians, things that moved only in the shadows. These things could go anywhere they pleased, any time they pleased. But how modern were they? Was there anything to prevent them from getting on the phone, calling their friends in the States?

Of course there wasn't. Paul had to admit to himself that he'd been lucky in Asia. But that level of surprise was over now. The only thing he had on his side was speed.

Every single creature in this hole had to be killed, and it had to be done right now, today. Otherwise, there were going to be phone calls, God knew, maybe even e-mails, to vampires in America, in Africa—wherever they were as modern and technologically capable as he had to assume these creatures were.

Either he and his cohorts cleared the place out immediately or they lost any and all chance of surprising others.

A long shape like a gigantic spider came striding toward him from along the corridor, its shadow briefly visible in his light. He turned it out.

He listened to the steps, one, two, coming up the tunnel. He could hear its breathing now, slow, almost soulful, like a man in love. Closer it came, until it seemed as if it were directly before him. But tunnels deceive, and he knew that there was more time yet to wait. It seemed to slide along, as if it wore silken shoes or moved like a snake.

He held his gun straight out. He waited.

The footsteps stopped. The breathing became soft and low. Where was it? He was uncertain.

He turned on the light, and there were eyes glaring at him from three inches away. The face was sallow, gray, not a face from the world of the sun. He fired into the dark crystal hate in those eyes. The body took the whole force of the bullets and went sailing backward fifty feet, bouncing against the walls as it broke up. A leg went tumbling on down the steep incline into the dark.

The head was not severed. The eyes revealed shock, not death. He had to fire again, and he hated it, to waste a shot, but then there would be nothing further to worry about from this vampire.

He aimed, squeezed the trigger, felt the familiar satisfaction that came when they blew apart.

He went on down the passage. He was spattered with vampire blood, and he could smell its rankness. He could feel it in his shoes, slick between his toes. The blood could invade your body. If you had a cut, it could make you damned sick. He'd seen it, they all had—the fevers, the monstrous, weird hungers, the slow recovery.

As he went deeper, he felt his adult personality slipping

into its own past. The love of wine, the love of music, the long days spent in elegant places—all that was going. There remained only a hurt, furious little boy looking for the killer of his father.

On he went, deeper into the secret heart of the ancient nest, deeper still. He was below the meeting hall now, down where no human being would or could ever go, down in narrow corridors painted with glyphs, walls and ceilings and floors forged by the perfect hand of the vampire.

This was the great secret of the world, that places like this existed hidden and embedded in the planet, where terrible minds had orchestrated with terrible cunning the bloody history of mankind.

He knew, suddenly, that he was in a larger space. He knew, also, that there was a new smell here. When he turned on his light, and he would have to do that, he feared that he would find himself face to face with hundreds of them.

He put his thumb on the switch. He pressed.

At first, he did not understand what had appeared in the beam. The place was so large that his light faded before the room ended. There were long brown lines of round objects arrayed in two rows facing a narrow aisle, and it took him a long moment to understand that they were skulls tightly encased in their own skin. Some had hair, and it hung in tufts like something left on totems.

He thought that there might be a million skeletons here. No rat came for them, no maggot, for they were too dry even to attract vermin—only little running things, nameless beetles of some kind, that were slowly turning them to dust.

As he walked slowly along shining his light, he became aware that this place was easily half a mile long. Face after face stared out at him, each with its goggled eyesockets and bucked teeth. They were stacked twenty high.

Here was where lay the *real* dead of Paris, the anonymous, the disappeared, the forgotten. Ironic that this other, more terrible ossuary would lie deep beneath the Denfert-Rochereau, almost as if its human builders had known by some kind of race memory, or the whispered intelligence of the dead, that somewhere beneath their feet, there lay an even greater grave.

How many of these people had left weeping lovers behind, people who never knew whether to mourn them for dying or despise them for running away?

Such an anger filled Paul now that he trod steadily, uncaring of his own life, forgetful even of the vital importance of the book he had with him, marching like a soldier bent only on victory, going step by step toward his next kill.

In all this time, there had not been one more turning, not one place to hide. So all the vampires in this place must be ahead of him.

He had two shots left in his clip. He pulled it out, reached back and dropped it into the rucksack, grabbing a fresh one and jamming it in. If it came down to it, he would use the two shots left in that clip to blast the damn book to bits and then kill himself. He might not get it out of here, but they damned well wouldn't get it back, either.

The idea of being sucked dry like these poor people made a taste rise in his throat so vile that he had to choke back his own vomit. He would never, ever die like that, with the lips of a vampire pressed against his neck.

He had to get out of here. The air was sickening. The place was claustrophobic. The bodies were twisted in a hundred postures of struggle and suffering, the faces still radiating horror, agony, and surprise.

Eventually, he saw a door ahead. He hurried to it, looked for a knob. There was a silver ring. When he pulled it, the door slid smoothly back on perfect hinges.

There had never been any place like this in Asia. At least, they had never uncovered such a place. But they had been on a killing spree, hadn't they, compared to the subtle, expert French? He was good at dealing death, not at the cat-and-mouse game that Bocage was playing with these very much more dangerous vampires of his.

His light played on the walls—and he saw a human face staring at him. He gasped, momentarily disoriented by the eyes that looked back at him . . . from the incredibly distant past. No human being had ever before looked upon what this must be, a vividly lifelike portrait of a Neanderthal, appearing as if it had been painted yesterday.

The picture was painted on what looked like a slab of highly polished stone, maybe using some sort of wax process. But when he looked closer, he realized that this was not a painting at all but an incredibly fine mosaic. It was constructed of bits and slivers of stone so tiny that to his wondering fingers the surface appeared absolutely smooth.

What a very fine hand had made this, and so long, long ago. Beside it there was another mosaic, this one of something he thought must be some sort of genetic map—incredibly intricate, incredibly detailed.

Was he was looking at a Neanderthal with its genetic map beside it? If so, then what was this room? What had been done here? All around the walls were more such images, some of even more ancient creatures, in which the shadow of man was dominated by the staring savagery of the ape. If you looked from first to last, there was a logical succession from a small ape with frightened eyes all the way to modern people.

There were at least fifty of the pictures. They went on until they ended with a woman so beautiful that she seemed to have been born of the angels.

This looked like some sort of record of the evolution of man . . . or our creation. Quite frankly, it looked like a record of creation, the way one form followed another in close succession, each with its genetic plan beside it. For years, humankind had been sifting the dirt of Africa and searching the caves of France for its past. But we had never been able to find ourselves, had we? Never quite.

He went to the last figure. Even her green eyes were rendered to the tiniest nuance. Her face was so alive that she might as well have talked to him. She was a girl, maybe twenty, with dusty blond hair and an expression on her face of a sort of delight . . . as if she were beholding everything new. Maybe, he thought, he should call her Eve.

The vampires must be very much older than he had imagined. If this place was what it looked like, then they were also very much more important to us. In which case, we had not evolved through the accidents and ideas of God, but rather had been maneuvered out of the apes by another and terrible hand.

He was not a man who often felt like crying. He'd done a lifetime's worth of crying when he'd lost his dad. But tears came now, rolling down his hard, silent face.

Why had they done it? Why not leave us as we must have been—helpless, two-legged cattle? One day, the secrets of the vampires would all be known. Only then, he suspected, would mankind truly come to understand itself.

He had the chilling thought that maybe they were our creators. He'd known that they lived a long time, but this was totally unexpected.

He went on, deeper into this cave of secrets. Now the chambers he found were rough, and here also the hidden past disclosed a story. This was human work, full of gouge marks. In some incredibly distant time, human beings had dug to this very room, to the center of the secret. Had they died here, in some forgotten effort to throw off our slavery?

There were no records of other vampire hunters in history. He and his team had read volumes of old histories, attempting to see if organizations like the Knights Templar or the Egyptian priesthoods might have known something. But they didn't.

He moved through the rubble of the human tunnel—and, very suddenly, he found a lot of vampires. They were moving quickly, just disappearing around a corner ahead of him when he saw them.

They were running. He'd never seen that before. But there were a lot of things about the Paris vampires that were new to him. He sped up, jumped into the corridor they had gone down and fired. He ran, fired again, waited. Scuffling ahead. He fired. Sounds—gabbling, gasping noises. And then a vampire loomed out of the dust. Its chest was open like a cabinet. It came for him, but buckled, its lips working, its mouth sucking air. Another was behind it, and another. He fired. He fired again.

There was one bullet in the clip. He had to reload. He backed up—and tripped, falling onto the one he had just killed. He fell hard, and heard the clips clatter off behind him. As he was scrambling up, a hand grabbed his flashlight . . . and crushed it. The dying vampire's last act had left him completely helpless.

He scrambled to his feet, then kicked into the dark, kicked at the softness of the creature's wrecked body. He heard hissing and bubbling. The damn thing wasn't dead, despite its wounds. He backed away, lest it regain its strength and attack him. Then he squatted, sweeping the floor for his lost clips, finding nothing. And then he heard before him:

"Come here, child."

Was there another of their kids here? He backed up again, trying to get a wall behind him, to gain some kind of defensive advantage.

"Your end has come, child."

He would have turned his last bullet on himself, but that would leave the book. He'd have to destroy it and just suffer the damn sucking death he loathed.

The one that had spoken was coming closer; he could hear it. Should he shoot it? Was it the monster, the queen? Was this her lair? No, he thought not. That voice had been low and musical, but male, very definitely.

He'd lost his gamble, then. He held the book before him and pressed the barrel of the gun up against it.

But before he could shoot, light burst out around him. He saw a crowd of vampires, all watching him with their grave, strangely empty eyes. He saw them in jeans, in tattered clothes from olden times, in dresses and the shorts of tourists. Their faces, though, were filled with hate, and they were not human faces. Down here, they didn't need to bother with makeup and disguise. All the lips were narrow; all the eyes were deep; all the expressions were the same: calm, intractable hate.

Becky was suddenly beside him, her gun flaring. He fired, too, his last bullet.

As he reached around for another clip, a flaming pain shot through his left side. The arm that held the book went limp, and the book thudded to the floor. He saw why—the handle of a knife was protruding from his shoulder.

From the crowd of vampires there came shots. These had some guns—another surprise for Paul. He heard a grunt behind him, saw Des Roches crumple. He and Bocage had come up behind Becky.

The guns fired again, from both sides. Becky moved to protect him with her own body. "Fall back," she snapped as she shot again and again.

Then there was silence. She said, in a quavering, incredibly tender voice, "You're hurt."

That was a lover's tone, and it touched his heart unexpectedly deeply. "I'll be okay."

Her finger quivered along the protruding handle of the knife. "Oh, Paul, oh, God." She kissed his cheek, and his heart seemed to turn over within him. Thrumming through his pain, he felt a kind of contentment. He could see her rich eyes in the dark, full of tender concern. And he had to admit, it felt damn, damn good.

The beam of Bocage's flashlight played across the room. In the smoke and the haze of blood, there were easily a dozen dead or damaged vampires, all heaped against the far wall. "It's good," Bocage muttered. Then he went down to his man. Des Roches was pale, his face frozen. He was in agony and trying hard to suppress it. Paul was in exactly the same situation.

The question wasn't whether they could go out and regroup, then do what needed to be done, which was to get back down here to spray these creatures with acid. The question was whether anybody was going to live long enough to get out in the first place.

"Bocage, are we all hurt?"

He shrugged. "I'll live." His right leg was sheeted with blood.

"Becky?"

"I'm good."

"We must get out," Bocage said. "Des Roches is going into shock."

Becky was playing her light across the broken mass of vampires. "Eight," she said. "That's a total of seventeen in this action."

"We killed a conclave," Paul said. "Half of Europe, maybe."

"The Germans are doing the same in Berlin," Bocage said.

"The Germans! Why don't we Americans get told anything anymore?" Paul asked.

"You have Echelon," Bocage replied. "It's supposed to put the rest of us in a fishbowl."

"Apparently it doesn't."

Bocage smiled a careful smile. "No, it doesn't."

Paul was beginning to feel the shuddering cold that came with shock. He took deep breaths, trying to stave it off.

Becky went over to the vampires. "Bocage," she said, "we need to blow their heads off. In case we can't come back and sterilize."

They rounded up his lost clips, and Bocage and Becky went among them, blasting first one and then the next. Paul wondered what it would be like with a woman who could do that.

The knife was beginning to hurt a great deal. A wound that penetrated a bone into its marrow, which this one certainly did, was exceptionally painful. On his side he had the fact that he was an exceptionally fast healer. But that came later. Now, there was only the pain and danger of the wound.

"We've gotta get moving," he said.

The little band of them ascended slowly, everybody trying to keep their suffering from everybody else.

Despite the waves of searing pain that swept his whole

body every time he took a step, Paul felt like laughing. The damn queen of the vampires, or the traveler, or whatever she was—was somewhere in that pile of broken bodies. No more perfumed innocence walking the streets.

Between this and what the Germans were doing, Europe was likely to be free of the pest. And the book under his arm would soon free the Americas—if they acted fast enough.

He coughed long and hard, experiencing such great agony as he did so that Becky had to hold him up. "There's blood aspirating into the lung," he said as she helped him to the car.

All the way to the hospital, she held him tight to her, so that the bumps would cause him as little pain as possible. It was still a lot. But he didn't mind all that much. This was not a bad place to be, not at all.

ELEVEN

Queen of the Night

I n the hours since she had first looked into the haunted eyes of Miriam Blaylock, Sarah Roberts had become more and more afraid. Now she held Miriam's hand; Miriam lay against her friend's shoulder.

Sarah had never seen her like this and so far had not been able to find out what was wrong.

Incredibly, they were using the Concorde, a plane Miriam had vowed she'd never fly again. Groaning and thudding came from under the floor where the four engines lay embedded in the wings close to the fuselage. For the first ten minutes of the flight, the cabin smelled of jet fuel. They'd taken this plane for years, believing it to be safe. Then had come the crash and a morbidly careful period of evaluation on Miriam's part. She'd gone over every detail a thousand times, imagined herself in the cabin of a plane she took often, looking out the window at the fire, hearing the awful roaring, feeling the vibration and then the sickening moment of free fall.

For the human beings in it, death would have been instantaneous. Miriam would have lost consciousness only slowly, as she was inch by inch consumed by the flames.

She'd had Sarah get every document there was about the

refit. Despite all that had been done, she was still in a fright over flying on it. But she had insisted, absolutely.

Sarah thought perhaps the other Keepers had assaulted her. If so, it would be an anecdote for the book she'd been secretly writing about the Keepers for these twenty years of her captivity.

Sarah could tell that Miriam was awake. She was always awake unless she'd fed or done opium in extraordinary quantities. Miriam's hand was soft and cool. Sarah lifted it to her lips, enjoying the heft of it, the taste of the skin, the softness against her lips. She inhaled the sweet smell of her friend's skin. Miriam sighed and laid her lips upon Sarah's neck, sucking until it almost hurt.

Sarah closed her eyes, listening to the howl of the engines, feeling the great soul beside her, loving her deeply and dearly . . . and feeling the evil of her at the same time.

Sarah told herself that a wolf might kill a deer, but never would it be murder. She told herself that. As a doctor, though, she was committed to human welfare, and that certainly did not include killing. The creature beside her had eaten children and fathers and mothers—had *eaten* them. As had she herself . . . in the shame of her secret life.

And yet, this was the agony of it: nature uses predators to ensure balance. One reason that human overpopulation was destroying the world was that the Keepers had failed in their natural mission. There were not enough of them to make a difference.

Miriam called herself part of the justice of the earth. And Sarah could not deny that. She had looked into the teary eyes of victims, seen them fade as she did her own clumsy sucking. She had known what it was to be engorged with human blood. Afterward, you felt as light as air. Any small imperfection disappeared. You became supple. Your skin regained a girl's flush and milk. And your heart—it beat with a happiness that seemed founded in something that was deeply right. You had dared the abyss, to do the bidding of nature. What an addiction it was, the addiction to death.

Sarah knew that she was using her strange new relationship to the laws of nature to justify herself. But she had not been given a choice. Miriam had fallen in love with her and had infused her own blood into Sarah's veins without her permission, putting her to sleep to do it. Sarah had awakened exhausted, aching in every bone, not knowing what had happened.

There had begun an awful struggle. She had tried to live on blood bought from commercial blood banks. She had tried to live on animal blood. Then she had refused to live at all. She had actually died and been put in a coffin and slid in among Miriam's other expended lovers in her attic.

But Miriam had used Sarah's own research to bring her back. Sarah had eaten, then. She had not been strong enough to return to the terror of the coffin. Because, when Keeper blood flowed in human veins, you could live for centuries, but you could never really die.

Sarah had experienced the silent, trapped sensation of being unable to move, to breathe, to so much as flutter an eyelid in that coffin. She had been aware of the dark around her, of the lid above her, of the rustle of insects along her skin and the murmur of street traffic outside.

She'd heard Miriam playing her viola, had heard jets passing overhead, had heard the lapping mutinies of the East River and the hiss of the FDR Drive. She gone mad a hundred times, mad in the locked-up remains of her body. All around her, there had been other such coffins, some of them thousands of years old, that contained other trapped souls.

Then she had heard the tap of heels on the wide attic boards, and light had swept in, and her vague eyes had seen a smooth shadow, and life, *life*, had come marching up her arm like a grand orchestra pounding a grand tarantella.

Miriam had read Sarah's studies and her papers, and devised an experiment that had worked. For the first time in two thousand years of trying, she'd brought a lover back. She'd tried with the others, too, but it had been too late even for the most recent one, John Blaylock.

Alive again, Sarah had wandered the streets of a new world. She could be entranced by the play of sunlight on the edge of a spoon. A child's rude singing sounded the carillons of heaven. Each breath that swept her freshened lungs felt like the caress of an angel. She had learned to live in the cathedral of the moment, for the supple touch of fine leather and the sweet of morning air, for the fluttering of a bird in the birdbath or the drip of water in the kitchen sink. She had given away her doubts and her fears with her lost past (where there had even been a lover and a little apartment and a spreading career). She had given away her terror of the coffins upstairs, to the extent that she would sometimes go and lie in her own and draw the lid down and stay there until the rigors of asphyxiation thrilled her throbbing sex and made her frantic. It was sick, she knew that. Miriam's love had transformed her from a healthy young physician into a decadent, murdering libertine with a sick and sorrowing soul. But it was so beautiful ... or it had been, until this awful thing happened, whatever it was.

When, just after being resurrected, Sarah had looked upon her savior for the first time, she had spontaneously dropped to her knees. She was Lazarus, was Dr. Sarah Roberts, enslaved by gratitude to she who had returned her to life. To try and find some sense in the servility that she now felt, she had read long and carefully in the literature of sexual enslavement and finally into the lore of zombies. She worked hard to free herself, even going to Haiti to interview a man who had been killed in a zombie ritual and brought back by a witch doctor. He, also, was mysteriously bound to the man who had dug him up and resurrected him by rubbing him with a foam made from the blood of rats. The moment this man's teary, passive eyes had met her own, she had known that they were kin.

Miriam drew back from her, whispered to her, "I ought to really punish you, you devil."

Sarah turned to her, looked into her amazing eyes, with their child's fresh intensity. You would think she was just a girl, to look at those eyes. There was not the slightest trace that this was an ancient being. If you were observant, you would see that the lipstick was painted on a strangely narrow mouth, and you might suspect that some inner thing had been done to fill out the cheeks. But that would take a very acute observer. To most people, Miriam appeared to be a ravishing, wonderfully dressed, wonderfully affluent young woman, still dewy from girlhood.

Miriam sighed, her breath's heavy sourness filling Sarah's nostrils. "Bring me vodka," she said.

Sarah got up from her seat, moved down the aisle toward the steward, who was serving meals in the second cabin. "Oui, mademoiselle?"

"Madame in Seven-A wishes vodka, very cold, served without ice."

"Oui, mademoiselle, a moment."

"Immediately, please."

The steward understood her tone and poured the drink, a

large one. Sarah took it to Miriam, who emptied it in an instant.

It was clear that Miriam had been through absolute hell over these past days. Sarah had suspected that her odyssey to the conclaves would be a disappointment, but whatever had happened was far worse than that.

"Another?"

"Perhaps in a few minutes."

"I know how you hate this thing."

"I just wonder if the repairs are satisfactory."

"We have to hope."

"Another vodka. Bring the bottle."

Sarah went back to the steward. "She wants the bottle."

"A service of caviar, perhaps?"

"No, only the vodka."

"Mademoiselle, is madame afraid? Would she like the pilot to come and speak to her?"

"That I cannot ask her."

"I understand," the steward said. He had concluded that Sarah was a personal servant, and that madame would be taking all her service from her, and gave her the vodka on a small tray. "Will you want me to call you for her meal?"

"Madame will not be taking a meal."

"Very well." He returned to his passengers. The service in the three cabins of the Concorde was exactly the same, but by tradition the third cabin was for tourists, the second for business people, and the first for personages. Air France might not know just how distinguished this particular passenger was, but Sarah had made sure, as always, that Miriam was treated with the greatest respect.

The fact that Sarah was not privately reconciled to Miriam's way of life and even doubted her right to her prey did not mean that she did not respect her. Miriam was a creature of God, also, and a triumph of nature. To a scientist, which Sarah most certainly was, her blood was one of nature's truly remarkable organs. It had six different cell types, including one that Sarah had watched under the electron microscope trapping and destroying virus particles, transforming them back into the chemicals out of which they were constructed.

The blood sometimes seemed almost intelligent, the way it laid traps for bacteria. And the cells were remarkable, too. Unlike human cells, they did not scavenge for free radicals with mechanisms that grew stiff and unresponsive with age. Instead, the blood converted them into nutrient components, actually changing their atomic structure.

Sarah had allowed herself to imagine that Miriam *was* her blood, that the body was only a receptacle for this brilliant organ.

She had watched it as it worked in her own veins, how after a period of acclimatization, it had adapted itself to her needs, preserving those parts of her own blood that were essential to her life and adding most of its strengths as well.

It could not change the structure of her cells, though, which continued to try to destroy free radicals. What Miriam's blood did in Sarah's veins was to destroy so many of them that little more was necessary. Still, Sarah aged. Just very, very slowly.

Sometimes, she would go to the attic and whisper to the others, "John, I'm coming, Lollia, I will be here soon." She would tell them of Miriam's doings. She would tell them of her own work, trying to find a way to bring them back to life. How it must be in those coffins, she could scarcely imagine. To have been like that for even a few days had been so extremely awful that she still had nightmares about it. But Lollie had been there for three hundred years. And there were others who were little more than teeth and long strings of hair, who had worshiped at Miriam's feet when she was pharaoh's daughter.

The selfishness of Miriam's making herself gifts of these "lovers" had crossed Sarah's mind. This was an unambiguous evil, and for a time she'd believed that she could find in herself moral ground to sabotage Miriam, on this basis.

But the nights in that bed of theirs, the *nights* . . . and living Miriam's exquisite life with her, playing their violas together and going to the club, and seeing the world through a Keeper's eyes, as if everything were always new-washed with rain—she did not have the strength to say no.

She wanted Miriam right now. To lie naked in her steel-strong arms, to taste of the kisses of a mouth that killed—for her it was an ecstasy more appealing, she suspected, than that of being lifted in the arms of God.

The truth was that she revered this creature, whom she ought to hate. She had not the moral strength to hate the pleasures of being Miriam's possession. Had she been the maid of Hera or Proserpine's sotted girl, it would not have been different. A human being had fallen in love with a terrible god.

When Miriam traveled, Sarah made all the arrangements. Normally, she stayed beside her lady, making certain that everything was perfect, that all was as she desired and deserved. It filled her heart with a deliciously awful joy to serve Miriam. She understood her history and her significance to mankind. Miriam's family had invented Egyptian civilization. Her own father had moved the Israelites into Canaan. As far as he was concerned, he was only expanding his holdings, but the significance to human history was, of course, remarkable. Miriam herself had created and nurtured dozens of different aspects of western civilization. Her image haunted our literature. She was the Shulamite maiden, she was Beatrice, she was Abelard's Heloise and Don Quixote's Dulcinea—or more accurately, she had once sung a song for a hopelessly smitten Miguel de Cervantes, and become the model for his character.

She wasn't Shakespeare's Dark Lady, but she had known the girl. The story of her mother, Lamia, had inspired Greek mythology. It had emerged in the seventeenth-century *Anatomy of Melancholy* and the whispered legends of Lamia had inspired John Keats's *Lamia and Other Poems* in 1820.

There were many Keepers, but Miriam and her parents had been more influential in human affairs than any of the others.

And now she was the friend and lover of a humble doctor from Queens, whose highest ambition should probably be to make her happy and keep her safe. Instead, Sarah was caught in an eerie web, unable to believe that Miriam had the right to kill, but also unable to do anything but serve her.

In a year, a Keeper took perhaps twenty lives. Sarah herself took ten . . . and each squirming, weeping victim consumed part of her heart. After a murder, she would weep for days. She would resolve to quit. She would renew her efforts to find a way of feeding on blood-bank blood.

Sarah returned with the vodka and served Miriam a second drink. "I wish I could comfort you," she murmured. "I know something's wrong, something more than just the flight. Please tell me what it is."

Miriam knocked back the drink. "Five thousand dollars a seat and still I cannot smoke."

"You can in the car." She glanced up at the map that was set into the bulkhead. They were traveling at Mach 2, just passing over the Irish coast. "Just two more hours, madame."

"Why are you calling me that?"

"Because you seem so regal today."

Miriam took her chin and turned her head until they were sitting like two intimate girls, face-to-face, their noses almost touching. "I have been through unbelievable hell. And I am angry, Sarah. I am angry at you."

"I know you are." She'd gone to spend a few days in the Berkshires, away from the club, away from Miriam's demands. She had not taken her cell phone.

"Love, if I can't count on you, who can I count on?"

Sarah felt her cheeks grow hot, as they had in the hotel room when she'd been bathing Miriam and had seen the rough areas and angry blushing of her skin. That was healing trauma. Because Sarah knew the power of Keeper blood to overcome injury, she was aware that Miriam had suffered fearsome damage.

"Tell me what happened, love."

Miriam turned her face to the window.

Sarah touched the black silk arm of her blouse, but Miriam said nothing more.

Very well. Sarah had learned to accept Miriam's moods. "You look so extraordinary in those clothes," she offered, gently flattering her, hoping to win a more full response. There was none.

Whatever had happened in Paris, at least it had brought those archaic Chanels to an end. They had gone to Maria Luisa and gotten some delicious Eric Bergère designs. Miriam had been extremely compliant at the shop, spending twenty thousand dollars without complaint, and revealing truly won-

derful taste and an extraordinary awareness of what might
flatter her the most.

Sarah gazed at her. She was so splendid that you never got
tired of looking at her, and in that fabulous black blouse of
sheer silk with a bloodred satin body shirt beneath—well, the
effect was almost perfect. The way it held her breasts high and
suggested her curves was marvelous. This ensemble had been
created by a hand that loved and understood the female form.

"I was nearly killed."

Sarah leaned close to her, kissed her cold cheek, laid her
lips there a long time, until she felt her body tickling within
itself, lusting for the quick finger, the deep tongue. "Don't say
that if it isn't true."

Miriam bridled at the statement. "How dare you!"

"I'm sorry! I—just—please forgive me."

Miriam leaned back, closed her eyes. "Is the passport going to
be all right?"

"Perfect."

"Why so?"

She had asked this about the passport ten times. It was a
perfect passport because it belonged to a real person. "Leonore
is a master of disguise," Sarah said.

"Leonore," she said. "Do you think she would be a good
meal?"

"Miriam, you know I don't find that sort of thing funny."

"Maybe she'll replace you, then, and you'll be the meal."
She smiled that slight, fetching smile that looked so innocent
and concealed such danger. "That might be best."

She was truly a mistress of verbal torture. "I would open
my own veins for you," Sarah said.

"I suppose so." Miriam's voice was leached of emotion.
"You're certain of the passport?"

"Look at it. It's you."

The instant Sarah had understood that Miriam was without a passport, she'd gone down to the Veils, where Leonore was supervising the cleaning crew, and gotten her to make herself up to resemble Miriam. A slightly fuzzy passport photo had been taken to an expediter with a two-hundred-dollar fee and a thousand-dollar bribe. Miriam's new passport—in the name of Leonore Patton—was in Sarah's hand by five that afternoon. The next morning, Sarah had come over on the Concorde to rescue their distressed lady. That was yesterday.

Word had passed through the upper echelons of New York society that something untoward had happened to Miriam in Paris.

The whole club was in vigil, CEOs, aristocrats, celebrities, the brilliant and the beautiful. There would be a hundred of the most fashionable people in New York waiting to greet the queen when her plane landed.

"Please tell me what happened."

Miriam's eyes met hers. Sarah forced herself not to look away, but Miriam was certainly furious. "In good time," she said.

"I wish you could be at peace."

"I cannot be at peace."

Miriam's hand came into hers. Her eyes became like penetrating needles. "You remember I have spoken of Martin Soule," she said slowly, evaluating Sarah, trying to look into her mind.

"He inspired Baroness Orczy. He was the real Scarlet Pimpernel."

Quick as a flash, Miriam's iron fingers were crushing Sarah's wrist. "You're not sad," she snarled.

"I'm scared! What's happening?"

"I ought to put you back in the attic with the others, you ungrateful *bitch!*"

"Miriam?"

Miriam released her wrist, tossing it away from her with a contemptuous gesture.

"Miriam, please tell me what's wrong!"

"My French has become archaic," she snapped. "I want a teacher standing before me at ten tomorrow morning. Ten exactly."

"Yes," Sarah said, aware that her voice was shaking badly, "a teacher at ten."

There was a silence, during which the jet shuddered slightly. "I needed you, Sarah, and you weren't there for me."

Sarah closed her eyes. Tears swam out beneath the lids.

"You weep for me?"

Sarah nodded. "You're the love of my life."

"And yet you ignore the emergency number. You love me, but you want me dead, Sarah. That's the truth of it."

"I don't want you dead."

"You've hated me ever since I gave you my blood." Her lips curled. "The gift of eternal life!"

"You ought to have asked me."

"You're an idiot, Sarah." Then, unexpectedly, she smiled. "But I do enjoy you. You're such a scientist!"

"You're a murderer, Miriam."

"Don't be ridiculous."

"And I love you, too."

Miriam said, "The vodka's warm."

Sarah got up like a robot and moved down the aisle. The faces of the other passengers seemed vividly alive, their cheeks rich with blood. Sarah knew that this was an early sign of her own hunger. In a week, she would need to feed again. She'd try to stave it off, as she always did, with the blood she bought from the little blood bank on Thirtieth Street.

"I need a colder bottle," she said to the steward.

"Of course, mademoiselle." He drew a new one out of the refrigeration unit in his cart, put the old one in.

She took it back to their seats and poured Miriam another drink, then sat down. "I want to help you," she said.

"You're dangerously incompetent."

"I'm the best you've got!"

"For the while," Miriam said, her voice almost indifferent, as if the subject was no more than dull.

A shock passed through Sarah. "If you'd tell me what I've done—"

"I called you and called you."

"You've told me that fifty times! But you have to tell me what happened. Why did you need me? Why are we running like this? Miriam, for the love of God, what's happening?"

The pitch of the engines changed, followed by the angle of approach. "Finally," Miriam said, "you agree that you've proved yourself hopelessly incompetent."

Sarah nodded.

"So you agree that I can't take the risk of relying on you."

Sarah nodded again, and this time tears sprayed her breast. "Miriam, no matter what you decide—"

"It's decided."

"At a time like this, you need me. Whatever it is, I can help. I can correct my mistakes and do better."

"Yes, indeed."

"You're being chased. We've got to get you out of the house. Hide you."

"Do we?"

The plane roared, made a steep turn into its final approach. "It's all right," Sarah said automatically, "everything's fine."

The steward reminded them to place their seat backs upright and fasten their seat belts. He came past and collected the vodka. "Will Madame be wanting a wheelchair?" he asked.

"Mademoiselle will not," Miriam said.

A short time later, the plane was drawing up to the gate. The moment it stopped, Sarah stepped into the aisle in order to prevent any passengers behind them from pushing past Miriam or impeding her way.

As far as the world knew, two resplendently beautiful young women stepped off the plane, one discreetly attentive to her companion, who walked with her cool gray eyes fixed to the middle distance, emeralds and gold glowing around her neck, a wide-brimmed Philippe Model hat on her head. The other girl might have been a friend, slightly less wealthy, or even an indulged secretary or servant. Indulged, because she was so well kept herself, with her superbly tailored green *peau de soie* suit and her fashionably tousled hair.

They passed through customs with the easy indifference of people so powerful that such things did not matter to them. The officers were quick, discreet. "Welcome home, Dr. Roberts; welcome back, Miss Patton."

When they appeared in the Concorde Lounge, there was a discreet spatter of applause. Miriam slowed, then stopped, then turned. She raised a gloved hand, smiled. Nobody who did not know the truth could possibly have imagined, not for an instant, that she was anything but a girl—a girl with wise eyes, but still a girl.

She stepped forward into the richly dressed crowd.

They surrounded her, kissing her cheeks, touching her as children do a mother they have not seen in a very long time. In each pair of eyes was the same regard, the same awe. Sarah watched this with the dispassion of a captive. Most of them probably thought of her only as the sparkling mistress of the most exclusive club in all of the Americas, a secret, exquisite club, a place where the most powerful of people could express their true selves without shame or restraint, where there were no restrictions . . . once you had passed the door. Some few knew part of the truth, the whispered reality of Miriam.

Only Leonore Patton was entirely certain of the truth. Leonore was being brought along. She was being educated. Sarah knew that Miriam planned to infuse Leo with her blood. Now she wondered if she herself would be killed or set adrift on her own?

People murmured around them, expressing happiness to see Miriam—some familiar faces, others less so—while Sarah anguished inside over what was taking place.

Some were staring with the mixture of fascination and horror that the true insiders shared, the ones who knew to be thrilled but also terrified when she swept them into some dark corner of the Veils, and kissed their necks in a moment of tipsy excess.

Miriam went to a young Latino—a kid she had marked as an upcoming star—and kissed him, brushing his cheek with the rough tip of her tongue. Miriam was never wrong about such things as stars. Carlos Rivera would certainly become one. So, for that matter, would Kirsten Miller who stood beside him, her careful, beautiful face radiating intelligence.

Then Miriam was finished with them, speeding out with Sarah behind her. Luis, their driver, came up to take the bags that others had conducted through customs. Inner New York, secret New York, had been waiting for nothing but her return. Now the delicious terror could continue. Was she going to feed? Would it be some forgotten soul, ready for death? Or someone who deserved it—one she had judged in her correct and careful way? If so, would it be one they knew, perhaps some garish magnate who had tried to lie his way past the Veils? If it was, then who must they carefully fail to notice was missing, who next?

"One of my shorts paid off," Sarah said after Luis had pulled into traffic and Miriam had settled back with a cigarette.

"How much?"

"It was BMC Software. We made thirty-three percent."

"On what?"

"Six hundred thousand."

Miriam smoked, gazed out the window. Sarah had heard the little grunt of approval that the awareness that she had made nearly two hundred thousand dollars had drawn from her.

Suddenly she snatched off the big hat, which she had been wearing since Paris. Then she said, "My head is warm." She inclined it toward Sarah, who set about removing the wig. Even when Sarah had bathed her in the enormous tub at the Crillon, she had not allowed this wig to be taken off.

"Are you ready for this, Luis," Miriam called, her voice tart with angry irony.

The silky blond strands of hair that had waved in the wind like fronds in the sea were gone. The effect was so disturbing that Sarah drew back. Miriam smiled, her face looking utterly false and improbably small on her strange, long head. In Egypt, they had concealed their heads beneath tall headdresses. Raise the crown from Nefertiti, and you would see Miriam's mother with the same long head. She was called Lamia only among her own kind, and in myth. In the nations she had ruled, she had been many queens.

Miriam's eyes were wet. The baldness embarrassed her, even before Sarah, who knew every intimate stroke of her being.

"Oh, my love! My love, what—what—"

"They tried to burn me to death," she said.

"The other Keepers? My dear God!"

Miriam's eyes bored into Sarah's. In that moment, she seemed more profoundly alien than ever before. They were the eyes of a goddess . . . or a predatory insect. Glassy, cruel, and way too quick, the way they flickered about.

Sarah's heart broke for her. Lamia had died by fire, and Miriam had spent many a Sleep with her head in Sarah's lap, crying out as she helplessly relived the horror of that day.

Sarah threw her arms around Miriam. "Miri," she whispered, "Miri, I will never let that happen to you, *never!*"

"We're in terrible trouble, child."

"I know it, oh, God, I know it."

Miriam came close to her, took her hand. They remained like that—both silent, Sarah weeping—on the long, traffic-choked drive home.

TWELVE

Sourball Express

Paul watched Justin Turk fool with his pipe. You weren't supposed to light up inside the building. Langley was a nonsmoking facility. Justin lit up. "You know," he said, "you're a good ten grades away from the use of exclusive air transport."

"What the hell are you talking about?"

"You requisitioned a Falcon Jet assigned to General Ham Ratling and took it from Bangkok to Paris on a noncontracted run. Meaning that we got a forty-eight-thousand-dollar bill from the Air Force, plus a letter from Secretary Leisenring. A very pissed-off letter. The general and his wife and kids all ended up in first class on Thai Airways, and we got a bill for that, too."

"It was a hot pursuit, Justin. For Chrissakes."

"A hot pursuit." He pulled a yellow pad out of his desk. "So how do I write this up? Give me words, buddy."

"Agents were in hot pursuit of a female vampire—"

Justin held up his hand. "Say something else."

"Terrorist."

"A terrorist contact incident has to be written up on one of those—lemme see here—Candy!"

Candy Terrell, his assistant, came in.

"I need a TCI form," he told her.

"What the hell is a TCI form?"

"Terrorist Contact Incident. Every field op who thinks he's encountered a terrorist, whether known or unknown, has to fill one out and file it within six hours. It's been days in this case, of course. But nobody expects less from our boy."

Candy left the room.

"We'll return to the plane issue later. I thought you were injured."

"It healed."

"In two days? The police report said you had a knife wound in your left shoulder that took eighteen stitches. Why isn't your arm in a sling?"

"I heal fast. Always have."

Justin cleared his throat and shuffled some papers. Paul was perplexed. He had healed fast—incredibly fast. He should have been in a sling. He should have had a cast.

Why wasn't Justin curious about that? Paul sure as hell was.

"You also have a body coming back. Was it on the transport with you?"

"The French flew it from Villacoublay to Ramstein. It oughta be in Santa Clara tomorrow. It's being delivered directly to the family."

"You've written a letter?"

Paul had not written a letter. He couldn't do that, as Justin well knew. "It has to come out of the pool." Next of kin were handled out of a central office when agents died or were injured in the course of secret operations.

"You do it. Let the pool send it."

"Okay."

"Because I want you to feel it."

Paul sucked in breath. He really did not want to deck Justin Turk, his only ally at Langley, but Paul's tendency was to go physical when he felt threatened, and an insult like that was damned threatening. He was sitting here, and getting this. "I took a hit, too," he said. "We had a terrible time in there. Just awful."

"You couldn't have stayed out of harm's way? I mean, given the French presence on French soil?"

"We couldn't." What else was there to say? Just let it go. The desks never understood operational issues, never had, never would.

Justin was watching him carefully. Paul realized that the needle had been inserted on purpose. Justin was probably trying to make him feel vulnerable, to throw him off-balance.

This meant only one thing: this was not a conversation. It was not a report. It was an interrogation and he was in trouble. The question was, what the hell kind?

"Well, Paul?"

"Justin, I don't know what to say. I don't like your drift. 'Want me to feel it'—what the hell is that supposed to mean?"

"You lose agents!"

"I'm fighting a war!"

"You and Don Quixote. We're not sure about your war."

"The White House is bothering the director, and you're taking heat. Is that it?"

Justin did not reply, confirming the accuracy of Paul's diagnosis.

"Tell 'em they have no need to know. Like the alien business."

"The alien business! We don't exactly have a directive from

another world enforcing the secrecy in this particular case, Paul. All we have is you."

"Thing is, how did the White House find out in the first place?"

"The French have a program. The Germans have a program. For all I know, everybody has a program. This is a secret that's about to come out. And they are scared, because when that press conference has to be called, they will have to explain you and your killing spree, and they don't know how to do that."

"I've done my job. The French have done theirs. No doubt the others have, too. We've been effective. End of story."

"Yeah, the French have a casualty rate of seventy percent. You've lost four out of eleven people in two years. That's very effective, but not in the way we want, Paulie Paul."

"Everybody loses personnel. I saw the French clean out dozens of vampires when I was there."

"We prefer to call them differently blooded persons. DBPs."

He did not like the drift of that. "Who decided this?"

"The Human Rights Directorate." Justin shuffled more paper. "I printed out their memo for you."

"I didn't know we had a Human Rights Directorate."

"It's attached to the Office of the General Counsel. It was mandated under PD 1482 a year ago."

Presidential Directive 1482 had established humane practices guidelines for the Directorate of Operations. Since Paul was not dealing with human beings, humane practices, he had assumed, were not relevant to his work.

Justin held the paper out to him. "We've been instructed to use these guidelines as the basis for a policy recommendation. We're assembling facts for the Directorate of Intelligence now."

Paul took the sheet of paper. "Who wrote this?"
Justin did not answer directly. "Read it."

We must determine if these alleged vampires are human. These are the questions that should be asked in making this determination: Do they have language? Do they plan? Do they experience emotion? Have they enough basic intelligence to perform human activities? If all of these things, or most of them, are true, then it must be assumed that they are human or humanlike creatures, and should be afforded all the protection of the law.

Further, if indeed they must consume human flesh as a natural condition of their lives, then it is not clear that they can be identified as murderers or terrorists, any more than any predator species can be considered the murderer of its prey.

At the same time, there is nothing that prevents us from warning our citizenry about them and providing, for example, survival guidelines. The right of the prey to attempt to thwart the predator would seem to be as fundamental as the right of the predator to kill. However, their status as conscious creatures would preclude simply destroying them to relieve the threat.

Additionally, their relative rarity may identify them as an endangered species and, on that basis, mandate a level of protection of their habitats and limits on killing them.

In summary, the existence of these creatures should be made public, along with guidelines about how to avoid capture by them. Their lives would be protected under the International Human Rights Convention and possibly by endangered species acts in vari-

ous countries. Their right to kill to eat must not be interfered with, except insofar as to aid legitimate attempts to avoid them.

Paul continued to stare at the document, not because he was still reading it, but because he was literally paralyzed with amazement. Had all of his blood descended into his feet? Is that why he felt this sense of having totally lost contact with reality? Or was it the piece of paper in his hand?

"Justin, could you tell me something? Could you tell me if Franz Kafka is still alive?"

"He's dead. What's the point?"

"Oh, I just thought he might have written this—you know—as a sort of kafkaesque joke."

"Paul, I'm required to inform you that an investigation of your activities has been instituted. As there is a possibility that criminal charges could be levied against you, it is our official recommendation to you that you retain counsel. If you don't have a lawyer of your own—"

"I haven't got a damn lawyer!"

"Then you can apply to the Office of General Counsel for a referral to a legal representative who has an appropriate clearance match with you, so that you can discuss your situation with him freely. If you cannot afford to pay your lawyer, you can be referred to a legal aid lawyer with a clearance."

Paul thought, *Just sit, keep breathing, don't turn white, don't turn red, don't hit anybody or break anything.*

"Paul?"

"Just a minute. I'm trying to decide if I should laugh or cry. What's your thought? Tears?"

"I didn't write it, Paul."

"Damnit, Justin, don't you see what this is?"

"It's an attempt to recognize the human rights of an alien species."

"It's a license for the vampires to hunt and kill human beings. Jesus Christ, I lost my father to these things! A little boy waits, and a wife, she waits and waits, and Dad just never comes home. You go on for years wondering, 'Did he die or get killed, or did he walk out on us?' It eats away at your heart and makes you hard, and gradually, it kills your heart. In my case, I found my dad. Most people never find a damn thing."

"The government has decided that the differently blooded are part of nature."

"Justin, pardon my stupidity, but aren't we out there trying to protect people? I mean, isn't that the fundamental promise of government? If a rancher gets his cattle killed by coyotes, you know what happens? He goes out and he damn well shoots the buggers or traps 'em. Nature made the coyote to eat cattle. But that doesn't mean the rancher's just gonna let it happen."

"You're under investigation for suborning your orders, Paul."

Suborning was an ugly word. It meant misusing your orders or intentionally misinterpreting them. It was the kind of word you heard in trials. "That's the criminal route."

"I told you to get a lawyer. This is a serious situation, buddy. You could be looking at a count of murder for every single creature you've killed."

"Justin, for the love of God, help me!"

Justin stared at him like he was something in a damn zoo.

"This is coming from the White House."

"A bunch of college kids with no experience of life. Look, this is about people being killed. You know—mothers and sons, fathers and daughters."

Justin worked at his pipe. "I'm only the messenger."

"Why don't you tell Mr. President something for me—for this stupid grunt nobody who just happens to value human life above all things. A couple of days ago in Paris, I was in a room—deep underground—where I saw maybe half a million dead people stacked in rows . . . long, long rows. Every one of them was a tragedy. Every one of them was a broken family, or a broken heart, or at least a life stolen from somebody to whom it was precious."

"People will have the right to defend themselves."

"From something that can move so fast you can't see it, that's four times as strong as you are and twice as smart? I don't think so."

"The state will protect them."

"Only one way to do that. Kill the vampires."

"Paul, a stupid rancher does the environmentally unsound thing when he traps and poisons the coyotes on his place. A smart one plans so that his herd is never in jeopardy. The state's simply gonna be the smart rancher."

"But they'll get through. They'll find ways!"

"Some people will be killed. But it's been like that for all of history, hasn't it?"

"Let me pose you a hypothetical. You wake up some night, and one of these things is drilling into your neck. What do you do—I mean, personally?"

"This isn't going to happen to me."

"Hypothetically. Do you call Nine-one-one? Come on, be real, here! Christ!"

"The good rancher uses various appropriate and effective

means to chase off the coyotes. We'll be proactive in the same way."

Paul got to his feet. "I'm in the middle of a mopping up operation in Paris. Gotta get back."

"We are not going to continue with this barbaric exercise of yours. It's over, Paul. Totally and completely *over!* Okay? And there are some people you need to meet."

Danger always tapped on Paul's shoulder before most people realized that it had entered the picture. Something about Justin's tone of voice suggested that these people were going to give him a whole lot of trouble.

The U.S. had secret prisons for people who had broken the law in the course of classified activities. The law in those facilities was a strange, surrealistic version of the law on the outside. You had rights—just not the right to leave. Administrative prisons, that was what they called them.

Well, he still had the right to leave at the moment, or at least the ability, so he damn well walked out the door. He went through the outer office and into the corridor. There were two men coming toward the office. He went the other way.

Behind him, he heard their footsteps get quicker and louder. Goddamn, he didn't want this. He'd been part of this organization all of his adult life. He had stood before the Memorial Wall and wept a tear for fallen comrades. He had loved CIA and stood by CIA and been absolutely loyal to CIA, no matter how dumb he thought the latest director was or how misguided the latest policy.

He got the hell out of the building, hurrying out the new entrance to the west lot where he'd parked. As he got into the pretty little Saab that had been waiting in his garage for the past two years, he wondered if he would be fast enough to pass the gate or if Justin had already called them and told them to detain him.

He pulled up to the guardhouse, showed his ID card, waited. The guard looked at it, made a notation, and opened the barrier. He drove out and was soon headed for the freeway. It was a sunny summer afternoon, and once he was out of Reston, the world came to appear innocent again, even sweet. He loved the people in the cars, felt their hopes and loves with the special empathy that only a person who has killed in the line of duty can ever know. There is something about the taking of human life that makes human life seem incredibly precious. Even if killing somebody is necessary, the fact is that your dead remain with you all the rest of your days. Not your dead vampires, though. Only the people.

What if people knew that they were liable to be hunted down and killed, and it wasn't against the law? The very notion was absurd.

On this deceptively peaceful afternoon, he knew that he had to act with the utmost professionalism and speed, or he was going to be hunted down himself. Right this minute, there was an urgent meeting taking place somewhere in the building—probably in Justin's office—covering the issue of Paul Ward. He'd become what was known as a "runner," an agent who, when his actions were challenged, had immediately taken off. To CIA, this response was *prima facie* evidence of guilt. The Company was very skilled at hunting such people down.

What he needed to do was clear: he needed to kill as many vampires as he possibly could between now and the time they did manage to catch up with him.

He took 495 to 95, thinking that he'd go to Baltimore, park the car somewhere, and take mass transit to the Amtrak station.

According to what little he knew about the vampire in America, he needed to go first to New York. The reporter Ellen Wunderling had disappeared there researching the gothic subculture. In Paul's opinion, it was possible that she had stumbled across a real vampire, discovered too much, and been eaten.

So he'd go back to the plan of looking for her. She had disappeared in New York, so that would be his first destination.

He was a man who carried a lot of cash, always, so he'd be able to put some space between himself and his pursuers.

What a hell of a thing that he'd sacrificed lives for the French Book of Names and now he couldn't use it. He couldn't read a word of it himself, and he certainly couldn't stop by NSA and ask them to help him with the translation.

When he reached the exit for Route 32, he decided to make it interesting for whoever would be coming after him. He took 32 up to Columbia, which was a big enough town to have both a bus system and a taxi company.

He went to the Columbia Mall and parked in the covered parking, where his car would be harder to spot. He turned on his cell phone and strolled into the mall. It was so nice, so damn American. He went into the Sears, strolling easily, looking at the washing machines, the clothes. He bought a couple of shirts, a pair of pants, a blue blazer and some black sneakers. When he came out of the men's room, he looked like the same guy in different clothes. He knew that you weren't going to be able to disguise Paul Ward, but every little bit helped.

He dropped his phone in a lady's shopping bag. They'd follow that, for sure, probably track it down in about an hour. There was going to be some excitement in her sweet life.

He went outside and hailed a cab, which he took to the campus of St. John's College in Annapolis. A thousand years ago, he'd been a St. Johnnie for a couple of semesters. The school followed a great-books curriculum, starting with Homer and ending with Freud and Einstein. He'd read the *Iliad* and the *Odyssey* under Professor Klein, who'd had his fingers broken by the Nazis for playing the piano better than an Aryan. Still, as much as it hurt, he had played of an evening, Debussy and Chopin and Satie . . . He hadn't weaned young Paul away from doo-wop, but the playing had been awesome.

Paul had been the only kid in the whole school who'd favored the war in Vietnam, and also been dumb enough to put a statement up on the bulletin board about it. As a result, he'd soon found himself being recruited by CIA, and thus had begun the rest of his life. Old George Hauser, of blessed memory, had sat with him on that bench right over there under the great oak and spoken to him of what it meant to be an operations officer, how hard it really was, and just how disappointing it could be . . . and how much it mattered.

He went up the brick walk toward McDowell Hall, the administration building and meeting hall, where the choir had met. The young voices returned, calling to him from the quiet that he entered when he entered the building. Downstairs was the coffee shop, and there also was the bulletin board where his current life had begun.

There were people here and there, but the campus was quiet in midsummer. He went through the basement of McDowell and out into the little quad. There was Randall Hall, where he had lived—given a single room even though he was only a freshman, largely because they could not imagine anybody who had written an entrance essay like his successfully living in close proximity to another person. He'd written on Saint Thomas Aquinas, the *Summa Theologica*. In those days, he had been a fiercely ardent Catholic. How long ago that was, the days of the skinny kid with the close-cropped hair and the delicate wire glasses.

He wondered why he had come here. Was it because he was dying, and the inner man knew it? He'd seen many an operational death that started with just this kind of official abandonment. *I will not go to prison,* he told himself as his eyes counted windows to his old room. How small Randall Hall looked now. He remembered it as a grand place. But look at it, you could almost jump over the damn thing. A vampire probably could, or come close.

He'd gotten to this place on the back of a hell of a scholarship, the Stephens Piper Award for Scholastic Diligence. Full tuition to the college of his choice.

He thought to himself, *How do I kill vampires, now that I am alone? Dare I assemble my people? No, they'd all be stopped at their ports of entry.*

He'd signal Becky not to come back—stop at the college library, see if they had a public computer. He'd send her an e-mail, using the team's own emergency code. She could share it with the ones still in Kuala. He went over to the library, which was wide open and, typical of St. John's rather tangential approach to organization, totally unmanned.

He booted up the computer behind the librarian's counter. No password needed, of course. St. John's was still St. John's. It wasn't that they were especially trusting. It was details—they avoided them. Was it the best college in the United States? Not by all standards, but by any standard at all, it was the most intellectually healthy.

His opinion. He opened up Outlook Express and logged

onto their server. One code he'd never expected to use was "sourball express." It meant the unthinkable, that CIA had turned against the operation and everybody needed to go to ground immediately, wherever they happened to be.

When she saw it, she would go into meltdown, but she would do her duty. He typed the words. Then he added, "Go to B." There was a guaranteed job, given his recent casualties. Bocage understood American intelligence very well. He'd give her a good home.

He sighed. It was likely that he would never see Becky again, never hear from her, never know how her life played itself out. Well, hell, that was the nature of this game. You worked in total darkness. Sometimes there were other figures beside you, sometimes you were alone. He could have loved that kid, though. He could have loved her.

He sent the e-letter from the name of the person who used the computer, then immediately shut it down. There was no point in encrypting it. All of their encryption was backdoored to CIA. The point was not to write anything that would make an Echelon search possible. He hadn't done that, he was quite sure. Pretty sure. Somewhat sure.

He went out, hurrying down toward the playing field and the bridge with its bus stop. There was the tree under which he had kissed Connie Bell. Even all these years later, he remembered just how sweet she had tasted, Connie Bell. She was the loveliest woman he had ever known, even to this day.

He recognized, abstractly, that he was crying. At least, his eyes were wet. What a damn asshole he could be. Fortunate that he was alone. He was crying for his lost career, for his despised honor, but more for Connie Bell and lost youth . . . and for Becky Driver, whom he had never gotten an opportunity to kiss.

He crossed the playing fields and came to the bridge and the bus stop. He'd take the bus into Baltimore, to Penn Station.

His pursuers would spend their time looking for cell phone usage and credit card usage and ATM usage. Nobody would take to the streets, nobody would try to think as he thought, try to follow him in the old-fashioned way, by following his mind.

He did not intend to stop killing vampires simply because he'd lost his backing. To hell with the CIA; he was going to do this thing. Maybe he'd rid the United States of the creatures before his employers caught him, who knew? Let Justin stuff that in his damn pipe. Endangered species, hell. If he rendered the damn things extinct before they could be protected, what would those White House pantywaists do—apologize to the world for allowing such a terrible thing to happen?

They were totally out of touch with the situation. If the vampires were free to hunt openly—if they had rights and legal status—oh, God, how awful that would be. Inside of a decade, they would rule the world again.

The bus came, and he paid his fare and took a seat. He leaned back, closed his eyes. "Should've graduated from St. John's, asshole," he told himself. He could've become a professor of classical languages, a doctor of philosophy. He could have led a quiet life, tasted of love and marriage. Except if you went through a childhood like his you were—well, you were scarred. He was a strong man. Tough guy.

But why? What motivated him to get so good with a gun, to learn the art of killing, to live in the shadows?

He knew. Hell yes, he did. This particular mystery man had himself figured out. When his dad disappeared, the world changed for him. It became a place where anything could happen and nobody was safe. He was as he was for a very simple reason: he lived in deep inner terror, and it never, ever went away.

What if his kids disappeared? Or his wife, or him? He was too insecure to be able to enjoy real love.

In his lifetime, he'd killed at least fifty men, some of them with his bare hands. He'd tortured people, done it sadly and methodically, but with the same determination that drove him now. He could see beyond the immediate tragedy to the greater reward. He had wired up the gonads of Cambodian kids to get information that would save American lives. Would the mothers and wives whose lovers and sons he'd sent home alive tell him he'd done wrong?

He transferred to another bus line and rode this one to the station. He went to the newsstand and picked up some magazines, then bought a club ticket for the 4:35 Metroliner.

There was always the possibility that the station was being watched, so he went to the men's room and sat in one of the stalls reading. Guys came and went, toilets flushed around him. He read about elk hunting, then paged through the classifieds. *Field and Stream* always reminded him of the last time he had hunted, which had been with his dad. They gone up along the Chattaminimi Ridge, and just at sunrise had seen a buck to stop your heart. That had been about two weeks before Dad was killed. The vampire would have been watching him by then, for sure. It was probably only a few feet away during that walk, pacing them, waiting, doing its research on its victim. "What's that smell?" young Paul had asked. "Bats," Dad had said. "There's a lotta bat caves up this way." It had not been bats.

He waited until four-thirty-two, then left the john and hurried across the station. This would cause a sudden redeployment of officers, if there was anybody there. He knew how to flush a tail.

There was no tail, and he also nearly missed the damn train. But he did not miss it. He got in the club car and found his seat, dropped down and opened another magazine, *Newsweek*. He stared at it, while actually evaluating his surroundings and all the other passengers. There was a woman with two little girls, some businessmen, a couple of tourists, maybe from eastern Europe. Any of these people could be tails preset on the train. He was especially interested in the mom. That'd be a clever twist, the kind of thing they might use when a pro was the target.

Still, he didn't think they were on him, or anywhere near him. He thought he'd have a good week before they decided to put him on wanted posters. Probably call him a serial child killer or something. Be sure to get police attention all over the damn country that way.

He gazed out the window. This was his America he was passing through, this America of rolling hills and tidy suburbs, and rusty old factories clinging to the rail line. He remembered a very long time ago when this was still the New York Central Railroad, and the cars had been painted olive drab. He'd made his first trip to New York on this line, emerging in Penn Station with saucer eyes and fifteen wadded up dollar bills in his pocket. He'd stayed at the Taft Hotel on Seventh Avenue, with three other guys from the college.

It was on that trip that he had seen his first truly great painting, Van Gogh's *Starry Night* in the Museum of Modern Art. It was also on that trip that he had gone to his first opera, *Turandot*, about a cruel princess in a moonlit palace of long ago.

He had been a person, then—a young person, just awakening to the world around him. Fresh as the dew, drinking his first drink, smoking his first cigarette, lying in bed at night with Connie Bell on his mind.

He was a killing machine now, was Paul Ward. He'd lost his ability to love women. He could still have sex, and he did that whenever it was convenient, either with whores or causal pickups. But love? No. That part of his heart had gone out like a spent old coal.

It did not seem as though two and a half hours had passed, but they were entering the Pennsy Tunnel, sure enough.

New York. It probably wouldn't be where matters ended, because he intended to follow this path to the last vampire in the country. He probably should have started here. But nobody they were aware of had ever even seen a vampire in those days, so Tokyo looked like found money. Too bad the Europeans had kept their programs to themselves.

He left the train last, walked up the platform alone. Nobody was watching him. He crossed Penn Station. Nobody here, either. He went out, up the stairs to Eighth Avenue.

Cabs roared past, people swarmed the sidewalks. He was tired, bone tired, and he wanted a major drink. A whole lot of 'em. He'd really love to have found some bar fighters, but he was too deep in cover for that now. First chance he got, he planned to spend some time smashing his fists into a goddamn wall.

You burned down your house, fella. Just jumped up and ran out of there. What the hell did you know? Maybe those two guys were gonna give you a decoration.

He stuffed his hands in his pockets and started up the avenue. He wasn't going anywhere in particular—just away from here. He needed a place to crash, for sure. The flight from Paris to Dulles had been lousy—a middle seat, a kid with massive quantities of popcorn on one side of him, the King of Sweat on the other. Then touchdown and straight to Langley, and the shit spitting through the fan.

He was so fucking tired; he didn't think he'd ever been this tired. Tired or not, though, he was a man obsessed, and his obsession kept him going. He was here to find and kill the parasites that had taken his dad away from him, and he was going to do it. He slogged off down the street—and soon found himself passing the Theater at Madison Square Garden. Lou Reed was giving a concert tonight, which might actually make him feel a little less miserable. Also, dipping into a crowd never hurt. He'd use it to strip tails, then find a room later. He turned the corner and went up to the ticket booth, asked for one on the aisle anywhere in the auditorium.

"Sold out."

"What're they scalping for?"

"Eight hundred up. Guy on the corner, black jacket, he's got a few."

The hell with that. He couldn't afford anything nice, never had been able to. Intelligence work was not a comfortable life, especially not in the field. James Bond was a cruel fantasy.

He decided to hunt up a fleabag that would sell him a few hours sleep for cash. Then he would start his investigation, and he would find the parasites in their holes, and kill them all.

THIRTEEN

All Through the Night

Across the sour reaches of an uneasy day, Sarah had waited and Miriam had remained silent. At the last moment, Miriam decided not to go to Lou's concert, saying that she was too tired. But that wasn't it. Miriam was never tired. The truth was obvious to Sarah: she was too scared.

Whoever she was running from was obviously extremely dangerous. But who could be dangerous to her? The other Keepers might not like her, but they weren't going to terrorize her. Could it be a human being? That seemed impossible.

Miriam's world had gathered her in, shielding her behind its walls of money and power. Only a few of her admirers *really* knew—or, if they had been told, actually believed—how she sustained her life. They preferred to view the *frisson* of danger that clung to her as part of her extraordinary personal style—an intoxicating mixture of sin and savagery and high culture. Had they known for certain that the whispers were true, most of them would have abandoned her to the police. Or so they told themselves.

During the watchful, uneasy night, Sarah's hunger had increased. Miriam did not offer Sarah the comfort and support she was used to getting from her. Instead, Leo was given the responsibility of attending to Sarah's suffering, giving her aspirin, then preparing a pipe for her. Leo's presence, since they had returned from England, had obviously become more important to Miriam, and Sarah found this disturbing. She did not like Leo. She did not want her in their lives.

Sarah smoked in the library while Miriam paced and consulted an old Keeper tome. She seemed to be looking for something in her books, paging carefully through their heavily illuminated pages. Sarah had been unable to crack the incredibly intricate hieroglyphics, and when she asked to be taught the language, Miriam had said, "Your species isn't intelligent enough to learn it. I might possibly be able to teach you to read a list, but who wants to do that?"

Of course, all of the important information about the Keepers was recorded in long lists in the Books of Names. If Sarah was ever to complete her own book, she needed to know that language. But she would need professional linguists and cryptographers to help her, if Miriam would not.

Miriam was now wearing one of her many wigs, a darling bobbed affair, pert and blond, that made her seem even younger. In it, she appeared her usual resplendent self. But she had been *burned*. Who would have done that? Even if it had been Keepers, why was she still afraid? Keepers didn't hunt each other down. They argued and fought, on occasion, but their battles were never to the death.

Could it have been a human being? If so, then what manner of human could have managed it?

Near dawn, Sarah had awakened from a sleep made gaudy by opium. She felt awful, her stomach full of acid, her body aching, her heart hammering. She knew the symptoms perfectly well: Miriam's blood—that strange otherness within her—was literally devouring her in its hunger.

The symptoms were not unlike those of a severe bacterial

infection, as her immune system fought the part of her that was turning against her own flesh. Soon, she would be feverish. Then later, she would grow delirious. In the end would come death. Sarah had to feed. She had to do it now.

She was surprised to hear more than two voices coming from the direction of the kitchen. At this hour—about six in the morning—it was most unusual for there to be a stranger in the house.

Sarah hurried toward the kitchen. She found Miriam and Leo attending to the needs of a shabby, heavy woman who wore a tattered coat and scarf and smelled of ammonia and sweat. Sarah the doctor saw immediately that she ate badly and drank—was, in fact, somewhat drunk right now—had untreated skin cancer, and, from the droopy look of her right eye, an undiagnosed stroke.

Beneath her feet Sarah could feel the rumble of the big furnace, which was used to incinerate remnants.

She continued to look upon her—perhaps sixty, obviously a street person, eating a piece of Leo's rhubarb pie. Leo could bake. She could make fried chicken. Now, her sleeves were rolled up. There were handcuffs in the hip pocket of her jeans.

Sarah was appalled. Leo was being allowed to participate in this. Leo! Had Miriam lost her mind? This sort of business was for the Keepers and the blooded only. Never should Leo have been involved.

"Hi," Leo said brightly. "I got you what you need."

Sarah looked at Miriam, who leaned against the drainboard, watching with those crystal eyes of hers. She murmured, "Do it now."

Leo said to the woman, "More milk?"

She replied, "Sure, lady."

"Miri," Sarah said. She nodded toward Leo. You didn't feed in front of one of those. No way!

Leo went behind her as if to go to the refrigerator. As she pulled open the door, she also drew a sock stuffed with ball bearings out of her tight jeans pocket. She positioned herself behind the busily eating woman.

Miriam had obviously instructed her. She had *instructed* an ordinary human in this terrible secret. What if Leo went to the police, tried blackmail—there would be no way to stop her unless she was imprisoned like Sarah, in the bondage of Keeper blood.

Leo hit the woman. It was a gingerly, inexpert blow. She barked with surprise, pie flying out of her mouth.

"Again," Miriam said. She was completely at her ease.

The woman started to her feet, her eyes bulging with surprise. Leo struck her again, but she was in motion now and the blow was even less effective. She stumbled forward against the table. She said something, perhaps in Russian.

Miriam answered her in a harsh voice, in the same language. The woman shoved the table aside, began to run toward Sarah and the doorway behind her.

"Keep after her, Leo," Miriam barked.

This blow came down right on top of the cranium—not well placed, but there was plenty of travel in it and the woman went down like a bag of lard. Her forehead hit the granite tile floor with a jarring crack.

"Now," Miriam said, "Sarah will prepare her with a little bleeding knife, won't you, Sarah? Get your kit to show Leo."

Sarah looked at the body, the slow rise and fall of the chest, the strange repose on the face.

"It's in my office," she said.

"Then get it. But be quick."

She went up to the bedroom, through it, and up the narrow stairs to the tiny space that was her own. Its window looked out on a wall, but it had a lovely skylight. On fine days, she would sometimes lean back in her chair and let her thoughts wander in the sky that unfolded overhead.

Her desk was stacked with papers, and a frame from a statistical analysis program she'd been using glowed on her computer screen. She had been analyzing the effect of a new plasma solution made from Miriam's blood on the decayed cells of her former lovers' bodies. So far, the results were ambiguous at best.

She knew she shouldn't, but she sat down. Her hunger was calling to her, screaming to her. But she still sat down; she still looked at her figures, thought a little about the deliverance she was working on.

A life was about to be wasted, and this was comfort, because somewhere in these statistics and the cellular structures they reflected, there was a way to eject Miriam's blood from your body . . . maybe even a way to rescue those who had faltered while it still flowed in their veins. Faltered, but not died . . .

She clicked her mouse a few times, and a photo appeared on the screen of somebody who had most certainly died. This picture had been strictly forbidden by Miriam, not allowed anywhere in the house.

She gazed into it, into the smiling face of her beloved Tom. She and Tom Haver had discovered Miriam together. It had been a heady time for them at Riverside Hospital, uncovering together the fact that this was a new species of intelligent creature, sharing the earth with mankind.

In the picture, Tom was smiling. It had been their last

carefree moment together. In fact, the last carefree moment of Sarah Roberts's life.

Behind him was the South Street Seaport Maritime Museum, in the days before all the new restaurants and attractions. They'd just come down off one of the old sailing ships. It had been a sunny autumn afternoon. He was wearing a windbreaker.

She knew every detail of how he had been when she had snapped that picture, remembered even his aftershave. It had been something called Jade East. They had walked hand in hand up South Street, bought some oysters at the Fulton Fish Market, gone home and eaten them on the tiny deck of their apartment. They were so in love.

Eleven days later she had killed him. She had killed Tom, and now his soul rested within her. She never spoke of him, hardly dared think of him because sometimes it seemed as if Miri could read thoughts. But he was part of her, and it was to him she would go, if ever her soul was released from the prison of this life.

Working quickly, she returned the picture to its hidden file. Miriam never touched the computer. But she might, and she was certainly smart enough to understand it. Sarah could not imagine what would happen if she discovered the picture.

If Miriam understood the depth of Sarah's rebellion, she might be returned to the attic.

She looked toward the small door in the side wall. It led up.

She knew that she should get her fleam from the desk drawer and take it down immediately, that she was already overdue, but instead she gazed at that door.

It did her soul good to go up there. But it was hard to do

it, to see them . . . and to see the other thing that was there.

She laid her hand on the knob, twisted it. The dark stairs rose steeply. She mounted them, hesitated, then walked quickly up.

Before her was a room dimly lit by small oval windows. There was something almost noble about the wide space with its sweep of gray floor. The attic ran the length of this large house, and thus was its largest room.

Bats roosted in the upper timbers. Ancient brass lanterns hung from crossbeams. This room had never been electrified.

Here were the coffins and boxes that represented her mistress's incredible greed, her invincible belief in her own rights over the rights of others. Here, also, was a humble coffin made of gray steel, still looking quite new.

Sarah went to it. She drew it open. It was here that Miriam had laid her after she had attempted to destroy herself. She ran her fingers along the white satin facing, touched the little pillow where her head had rested.

Here she had passed through death and here been brought back. This coffin, she felt, was her true home. This was the center of her reality and her being. It was where she must one day return. And she did return, when Miri was deep in the dead sleep that followed her feedings or—as now—otherwise occupied. Sarah would get in and draw down the lid, remaining until the air ran out and she finally had to open it to breathe.

There was a deep, profound satisfaction involved in doing this. When she pulled that lid down, it was as if fresh water was soothing her burning, tortured soul.

She wanted to right now—especially now—so very badly. But she had to get back. She had to take the fleam. Her victim was waiting to be robbed of her life.

Through tearing eyes, she looked along the far wall, to the coffin that Miri so frequently came to see. This was John Blaylock. What Miri did not know was that Sarah would sometimes open this coffin . . . as she was going to do now.

She went to it, unlocked it, raised the lid. A familiar dry, spicy scent came out—the potpourri that Miriam kept there. The corpse was narrow, dressed in a tail suit with a wing collar. The neck had grown thin, and the face was distorted by the profound necrosis of a body dead and from drying out for twenty years.

The lips had slid back from the teeth, and the cartilage in the nose had dried out. The corpse was grimacing. But there was something about the grimace—some, strange living essence that made it hard to look upon for long. For this was no ordinary corpse. This was a living corpse.

She laid her hand lightly in the corpse's delicate hand. Then she leaned into the coffin and touched her lips to the dry, rotted cheek. She whispered, "I'm making progress, John. A little at a time. But it's there, John. It's there."

With the slowness of an hour hand, the fingers of the corpse were closing. If she had an hour or two or three, John Blaylock would gradually grip her hand with an appalling grip. His fingers would feel like corded steel. His nails would dig as if seeking to break through to her blood.

But now, there was only the subtlest of changes—a slight tickling of a bony finger in a soft palm, the sighing pressure of a long, hard nail upon the tender inner edge of one of her fingers.

She drew away from him. In his eyes, she could see fire. See it—but was it there? Then she heard the sound of the corpse—for it made a sound when she came. It was moving—dry muscles, dead skin, every part of it. This created a rustle no more than the whisper of falling leaves, but it was unmistakably a sound of life.

In her clear, gentle voice, as soft as the tender airs of the night, she sang to him a song that was familiar to all of Miriam's people:

> *"Sleep my child and peace attend thee,*
> *All through the night. . . ."*

With that she left him. Miriam would not be pleased with this delay. But Sarah had a relationship with John and the others. One day, she would either bring them back to life or give them the release of true death. One day.

Her research had proceeded much farther than she had told Miriam. In fact, she was probably farther along in understanding the physics of the soul than anybody else in the world. This was because science rejected its existence. But she had *been* a soul, one trapped in its own corpse. So she knew that the soul existed. She had discovered that this rich electromagnetic being was accessible to technology, for it was part of the physical world, not some strange supernatural essence. The soul was a living plasma composed of trillions of electrons, each one cast with a slightly different spin, and each spin expressing a tiny part of the harmony and memory of the whole incredibly detailed being.

There must even be a medicine of the soul, she felt, for it could be sick and it could suffer. Oh, yes, it could suffer.

As she crossed the attic, the rustling grew faint, fading on an unmistakable note of dejection.

She drew her spotless sliver fleam out of its case of human leather and hurried downstairs.

They had cuffed the victim, who was laid out on the white enamel kitchen table.

"Pull up a chair," Miriam said to Leo. "It's quite a spectacle." She glared at Sarah, but made no other comment on her slowness.

Sarah tried to control her shaking hand as she felt the pulse. With her doctor's precise knowledge, she could determine exactly which neck artery would offer the best flow.

"What is that instrument?"

Sarah looked at Leo, who was sitting with her chin in her hands, watching from two feet away. She was going to watch an innocent human being die, and all she could bring to it was this ugly fascination. Sarah went from disliking Leo to despising her. She was actually tempted to go after her with the damned fleam.

When she did not answer Leo's question, Miriam said, "It's an antique surgical instrument, from when they used to let blood. That hooked end nicks into the vein, then the blade opens it. It's very neat."

"You don't use one, though."

With a dry sound, Miriam opened her mouth. Leo gasped at the funneled cavern with the pointed, black tongue at its center. "I don't need one," Miriam said, chuckling.

"Fleams were used by vets to bleed horses," Sarah said. "It's a brutal tool."

"It looks beautiful."

"That's because she keeps her instruments so clean. She's a doctor, remember."

"How does this make you feel?"

"How does it make me *feel?*"

"Hurry up, Sarah," Miriam said quickly.

Her throat was closing, her eyes tearing. But she tried to

be proud, to do well what she must do to survive. She was weak; she should let herself die. But she couldn't stay in that coffin of hers, no more than you can kill yourself by holding your breath.

"Aren't you going to wake her up for it?" Leo asked.

Miriam burst out laughing. "She likes them out cold! She has no taste!"

What Miriam meant was that the blood of a suffering victim tasted better. The adrenaline gave it a delectable piquancy.

Sarah hooked the fleam into the carotid on the right side. Leo came around the table so she could see the sucking process up close. Sarah's cheeks were hot with embarrassment; her soul was wretched with shame. But the blood that dripped out—oh, God, oh, it smelled *so damn good!*

There was a small struggle. The woman shifted on the table, moaning dryly.

"Do I hit her again?" Leo asked Miri.

"Please," Sarah gasped.

Leo hesitated, looking at Miriam.

The woman stirred again.

"Leo, *please!*"

Miriam stayed Leo's hand.

The victim's eyes opened. Sarah glared at Miriam. "Miri!"

"Leo, don't you move!"

The woman said, "What the heck?" She started to sit up. Sarah pushed her down, nicked again with the fleam and locked her lips to the dirt-ringed neck. The woman said, "The *fuck!*" Then she rattled along in her own language, obviously cursing. She squirmed; she tried to free her hands.

Sarah forced every iota of air out of her lungs. She distended her belly. She locked her lips tight to the neck, making the best seal she could. The woman flounced and struggled, but Miri held her head and made Leo lie across her midriff. The woman made rasping sounds—desperate attempts to scream.

Sarah sucked. The artery wall resisted, then gave way, spurting a flood of fresh, hot, salty blood straight down Sarah's gullet. The effect was a thousand times more powerful than a hit of the purest heroin ever made. From her toes to her head, her skin rippled and shivered. An orgasm came, spreading through her until her whole body was a single, pulsing, vibrating dynamo of sexual genius. Somewhere far away, she could hear Leo laughing and crying at the same time, and Miri's voice comforting her, saying soft things that she did not mean.

She sucked and she sucked, and the old voice went down to a growling babble. She sucked and the old heart came to a stop. And then the body went slack, and the flow went down.

Sarah drew back. Blood, very black, dribbled onto the table.

Leo was standing at the far end of the room, her eyes round, her face covered with tears. Miriam said, "Come here to me."

Leo shook her head.

Miri went to her and drew her by the wrist. "*Watch!*"

With one huge drag, Miriam did what no human being could ever do, no matter how evolved their technique. She emptied the woman of every trace of fluid that was in her. The skin sank back against the skull, drew tight, crackling as it turned to dry parchment. The eyeballs withered, the clothes went slack around the body. And then Miriam came up, the corpse still popping and crackling as cartilage snapped and muscles twisted themselves into hard, narrow ropes.

Leo put her hands to her cheeks and screamed. Her eyes wild, she turned to run out the door.

Miriam was on her in an instant. She grabbed her collar, gave her a slap that snapped her head aside. "Shut up! You *watch!*" She glared toward Sarah, who was feeling the gorgeous postprandial levitation that came when you fed really well. Moral guilt had its limits. Now all was right with the world. Like an addict who has ridden the horse and lost, she was content with herself, made so by the charm of the drug that had seduced her.

"Sarah," Miri said, "take Leo down and show her how to do a proper burn. And I expect to see no ash, do you hear me?"

"Yes, Miri."

"I'm sorry, Miri!" Leo babbled, rubbing her cheek. "I panicked." Leo went to the remnant, touched the skin that tented the face. "This is incredible!"

"It's a small penalty to pay for eternal life, my dear. An occasional hobo goes to the Big Rock Candy Mountain."

Leo frowned. "The what?"

"Gets released from the toils of a miserable life," Sarah explained. Slang tended to enter Miriam's vocabulary with a fifty to hundred year lag time.

Leo would not touch the remnant, so Sarah threw it over her shoulder and took it down. In the basement, Sarah said, "Having fun?"

"That's not appropriate," Leo said officiously. "A woman had to give her life."

"For me? Maybe I ought to kill myself."

"No, you have a right! Nature made you this way."

"Miriam Blaylock made me this way. And she's going to do it to you, too."

"Miriam Blaylock *is* nature. And if she bloods me, it's going to be the biggest privilege of my life."

They burned the remnant in a fire kept blue by Sarah's careful attendance at the controls.

As they were starting to ascend the stairs, Miriam said, "Come into the infirmary, please."

Sarah turned, surprised to find her down here. She was even more shocked when she saw that she was naked and all trace of makeup was removed. Her hair was coming back, a blond fuzz on her otherwise bald head.

Leo gasped. Sarah took her hand. "Don't be afraid," she said.

"But she's—"

"She's not a human being, Leo." Sarah was stirred by the long, lean body, the deep, dark eyes. This was a being she loved, who had covered her with wild kisses, who had expressed every shading of passion upon her quivering, delighted body. No matter how much Sarah hated Miriam, she also loved her, and loved the fact that Miriam took pleasure in her. "You're my beautiful one," she would say, and kiss every part of her body, her lips, her eyes, her moist pudenda. "You pretty little angel, you dear, soft baby."

Leo made a terrified sound in her throat as the tall creature with the bright red eyes and wire-thin lips strode into the light. She took Leo's hand. Sarah knew that Leo was now trapped. Nothing the girl could do—no matter how hard she struggled and fought—would release her from that seemingly gentle grasp.

Sarah was horrified at what was happening—at how swiftly Miriam was acting, so that the girl had no time to consider her situation. But she was also fascinated because she had wondered about the scientific issues involved in the transfer process. She welcomed a chance to observe it clinically.

Miriam drew Leo into the infirmary, a superbly equipped laboratory designed by Sarah, who followed obediently along.

She was already being buoyed by the effects of her feeding. In an hour or so, the Sleep would come and she would take to bed, and Miri, as was traditional between them, would sing her a lullaby. The Sleep would take her, and as it did, she would deliver herself body and soul into the protective custody of her beloved and despised mistress.

Miriam had tamed Sarah, after a fashion. But so also, Sarah had tamed Miriam . . . after a fashion. Thus does a love affair between species proceed—wild creatures finding what is universal between them, sensual delight and what abides in the heart, that love can cross any boundary and flourish anywhere.

The blooding instrument—a black hose fitted with a small hand pump and two large silver needles—was already dangling from Miriam's arm, one enormous needle a gray shadow in the flesh above the crook of her elbow.

Leo was staring at it, her eyes practically popping out of her head. Stumbling, she followed Miriam into the small hospital room. Miriam patted the examination table. Leo sat.

"Get the ice packs," Miriam said.

"What ice packs?" Leo asked.

"We use ice packs in the procedure," Miriam said. "Now strip." She clapped her hands. "Chop chop!"

Leo threw off her clothes. She lay down on the table, arms rigidly at her sides. Miriam looked at Leo's arms. "Set it," she said to Sarah.

"I don't like needles," Leo said as Sarah stroked up a vein. How Sarah hated her now, the poor, scared little cow with her drippy nose and her big brown eyes.

Now this kid would get what she wanted. Later today, Sarah would take her to the attic, let her listen to the rustling, introduce her to who lay there.

"You will now be delivered of the blood of your eternal Keepers," she said. "You will become part of me and I of you. Do you understand this?"

Leo said in a tiny voice, "I think so."

"You will be given eternal life."

"Miri!"

Miriam cast a glance at Sarah so terrible that her jaw snapped shut.

"Eternal life! But you will be bonded to me by an unbreakable bond. You will be expected to serve me in every way, without question. There will never be an end to it. Do you understand this?"

Leo turned her tear-streaked face to Sarah, and Sarah saw there a call for rescue from the very depth of this human creature. A soul was being lost, and it knew that it was being lost. But she said nothing.

"Set the needle."

"N-no," Sarah said. "No!"

"You do it!"

"Leo, this is wrong!"

She tried to meet Leo's eyes, but Leo would not look at her. Miriam grabbed the needle and jammed it into Leo's arm. Leo cried out.

Sarah reset it properly, secured it with tape.

"You are free to go, Leo," Miriam said. "I haven't started yet."

"It hurts!"

"Again I say to you, you are free to go."

Leo began to cry.

Sarah was awed at what she was seeing. She had a sudden, electrifying insight into who the Keepers were, into what Miriam was. They were indeed a force of nature, and she thought that they might be killed, but they would never die. No matter who hunted the Keepers, the Keepers would always in one way or another wander the world, seeking the ruin of souls.

Miriam grasped the pump in her long, narrow fingers and crushed the bulb smartly. Leo flounced on the table, giving a loud cry. Again, Miriam pumped, and again. Leo's upper arm turned fiery red. She began to sweat.

"How does it feel?" Sarah asked.

"My arm's on fire!"

"Do you feel faint? Woozy?"

"I see an ancient city!"

Hallucinations. Interesting.

Sarah touched the skin of the neck. Pulse very rapid. She laid her hand on the forehead. Hot, dry. She got the ice packs and laid them along Leo's sides. Leo began to shiver.

Miriam pumped, waited, pumped again. Leo's eyes fluttered back into her head.

"Slow down," Sarah said, "she's seizing."

Leo's bowels let go.

"Clean it up," Miriam snapped, and Sarah went to work with towel, sponges, and bedpan.

Leo cried and moaned. Sarah had to hold her arms so that she wouldn't tear the needle out. She arched her back and writhed; she shook her head from side to side.

Sweat, blushed pink, began to bead on her upper lip and forehead. Her epidermal capillaries were hemorrhaging.

Sarah took her blood pressure—270 over 140. Pulse rate 132. Temperature 106 degrees. She had perhaps half an hour to live, fifteen minutes before brain damage or a stroke. Sarah got more ice, put a pack behind her neck, another between her legs. The temperature dropped to 104 degrees.

Over ten slow minutes, Miriam pumped five more times. Leo came to and looked from one of them to the other out of agonized eyes.

"How do you feel?" Sarah asked.

"Water, please . . ."

Miriam withdrew the needles. Sarah took alcohol and iodine and cleaned Leo's wound and stopped the leakage of blood with a small pressure bandage. She didn't need to do anything for Miriam. Her wound healed itself inside of a minute.

"How did you know when to stop?"

"Her skin told me."

Miriam's people could diagnose practically anything in human beings by merely observing their skin tone. It was quite remarkable.

"What would have happened if you'd kept on?"

"I would have wasted blood. She would have died."

Miriam took Leo in her arms and went out with her, saying nothing to Sarah. She was more alien right now, less human, than Sarah had ever seen her. She realized that Miriam's whole personality was a sort of act. Seeing her like this, you realized that she was light years away from being human.

Sarah followed Miriam up to their bedroom. Miriam laid the girl, whose whole body was now flaming red, in the center of their bed. The Sleep was coming heavily onto Sarah, and she longed to lie down, too. But Miriam went to bed with Leo, enclosing her in her arms.

Sarah was left to the daybed. As she drifted into the dreams she would share with the victim whose life flowed yet within her, she heard her Miri singing to her new captive,

"Sleep my child and peace attend thee,
All through the night.
Guardian angels God will send thee,
All through the night. . . ."

She cried herself to sleep, Sarah did, but when sleep came, it took her into a golden ship that sailed a windswept sea. In the purest blue sky she had ever seen, white seagulls wheeled and dove and cried. They came down and flew among the sails of her ship, and called to her with their harsh, haunting voices.

She knew that they were the birds of God's careless and unquenchable love, calling to her and to Leo, and even to Miri, as indeed they do to all.

FOURTEEN

The Veils

Sarah awoke when the afternoon sun, glaring in the tall bedroom windows, turned the inside of her eyelids bloodred. Leo was there instantly, kissing her, embracing her. "Oh, Sarah, I'm so glad you're awake! I've been missing you like crazy!"

"You—you're not sick?" She should have been hanging between life and death.

"Oh, I was," Leo said. "I was *so sick*."

"You slept for two days," Miriam said. She came down out of the light like a descending angel. She was dressed in bright white silk. Her hair was nearly grown back, and flowing golden blond across her milky shoulders. She was perfectly made up, looking absolutely ravishing. Her eyes were their usual ashy gray.

"We're going to play this afternoon," she said. "You'll want to call your musical friends."

Sarah took Leo's hands. "Leonore, do you know what's happened to you? Do you understand anything about this at all?"

"Look at my skin!"

How well Sarah remembered that miraculous discovery. A woman loves a pure skin, more than most realize—until she suddenly has something she never dreamed possible.

Leo shook her head. "And my hair!"

It was as pretty as Sarah's, almost as pretty as Miri's.

Perfection had transformed a pretty girl into a shockingly beautiful one. Leo smiled down at her. "I threw up all yesterday, but I'm better."

"I used up all the antinausea stuff," Miriam said. "She took to it more easily than you."

"But now I feel—" Leo shivered her shoulders. "I feel *fabulous!*"

As Sarah went about the duties of her life, showering and washing her hair, Leo chattered away about herself. When should she feed? Should they hunt together or was that wise? On and on. It was utterly grotesque.

"Leo," she finally said when she was dressing, "I usually take this time in my office."

It was a lie and Leo knew it. But she understood and withdrew at last.

When Sarah arrived downstairs, Leo was sitting crosslegged on the floor of the library looking at Keeper books she'd never been allowed to so much as touch. She tossed one of the ancient volumes aside and rushed up to kiss Sarah, chattering about yet more sensations and symptoms.

Sarah picked up the book and replaced it in its box. "These are very fragile," she said.

"Yeah, they're in Egyptian! Are they from Egypt?"

"They aren't in Egyptian. They're in the Keeper language, which is called Prime. The book you were paging through is thirty thousand years old. It is made entirely of human parchment and is also the finest illustrated medical text on the planet. If it had a value, Leo, it would be, very simply, the most costly artifact in the world."

Leo had the hangdog expression of a surprised hound. But then she tossed her coltish hair and asked, "What are the first signs of hunger? I don't actually know."

"You feel cold. Your skin starts to get cold. Then you become a bit less energetic. That's how it begins."

"Should I get my own fleam?"

She sounded very like a bride planning her trousseau, or a pregnant girl deciding the furnishings of the nursery.

"Use a fishhook."

"A *fishhook!*"

"A shark hook works quite well. I used one for years. The fleam be-longed to my predecessor. Miriam just gave it to me recently."

"Your . . . what do you mean, 'predecessor'?"

"Oh, didn't Miri tell you? We last about two hundred years. Unless there's an accident, of course."

"We die?"

"Oh, no. That we cannot do. We end up in the attic." She smiled. "Like cast-off overcoats."

Leo glanced toward the stairs.

"Miri didn't tell you?"

"No, she didn't."

She took Leo's hand and led her upstairs.

Miriam was at the head of the stairs. "I thought you were going to make an arrangement, Sarah."

"An arrangement?"

"Flowers. For our guests."

"I—yes. I was."

"Miri, do we die?"

"You do not die."

"But she said—"

"The contents of the attic are my affair. As are those

books. You girls do not *ever* touch Keeper things without my permission!"

"I thought—"

"You thought you had the run of my house just because you're blooded? You go downstairs and get things ready, both of you. And, Sarah?"

"Yes, Miri?"

"Be careful. Be very careful."

As Sarah was arranging the flowers that would stand on the piano during the musicale, Leo chattered away about the kinds of people she preferred to "do."

Finally Sarah snarled at her, "You've become a serial killer."

Leo went silent.

Sarah turned on her. "You have! During the hundreds of years you now have before you, you'll take thousands of lives! Men, women, children, every one of them wanting life and deserving life, and you will take their lives—steal their lives—because you're a greedy, self-involved little monster!"

"Sa-*rah!*"

"You're not worth the warts on one of their fingers! Not one! But in your arrogance, you think you've gained some natural right to kill them! Miriam has such a right—maybe! But you certainly do not."

"Then neither do you!"

"I had this done to me. I didn't ask for it. You did, Leo. You knew what it meant and yet you asked for it!"

Miriam strode in. "Miri," Leo wailed, "she's—"

"I can hear," Miriam growled. She looked from one to the other. "Two canaries in the same cage," she said. "You'd better learn to get along, because you won't be let out. I'm in trouble and I need you, both of you. Hell, I need ten of you! Fifty!

But I do *not* need any bickering or moralizing or bitching. You'll work together as a team or suffer the consequences." She glared at Sarah. "Severe consequences." She looked at the flowers. "That's quite nice," she said. Then, to Leo, "You are not her equal. You will learn from her and take her advice and, in my absence, her orders. Is that understood?"

"Yes, Miri."

"Miriam to you, child." She went out.

"Wow," Leo said.

As the sun slanted across the floor, Sarah got out their violas da gamba, and she and Leo set the chairs. Among musical circles in New York, Miriam's talent was well known. Far more had heard descriptions of her playing than had actually been privileged to listen, however, for she never gave public concerts. In fact, she didn't perform at all. This would be, as far as she was concerned, merely an hour's casual entertainment.

Leo greeted the guests, watching to see if they noticed how beautiful she looked. They noticed, all right—especially the women, who were always more aware than men of the details of beauty, the grace of the hands, the taper of the neck.

Sarah and Miriam had been working together on LeSieur de Malchy's splendid "Fifth Suite for Two Violas da Gamba" for a few weeks before Miriam went to Thailand.

Maria Sturdevandt came and said hello to Sarah and Miriam. She would sing Madama Butterfly tonight at the Metropolitan Opera. With her was her companion Charlie Gorman. Bootsie Ferguson, the wife of Henry Ferguson, CEO of Goldman, Sachs was there.

Miriam could play most instruments simply by picking them up, but she had practiced on the piano, the viola, and the flute, and on these she was masterful. Sarah had not been much involved in music before meeting her. But her own viola was now one of the loves of her life.

As she played, she gazed from one member of their small audience to another. She watched Falstaff Rosenkrantz, editor of *Vanity Fair*, searching his pockets for what turned out to be a Chap Stick. His powerful shoulders and narrow waist suggested good-sucking veins. She imagined how he would taste, all salt and wine.

As she watched Miriam's long, splendid hands manipulate her bow with the lightness of a breeze, she drew her own notes as best she could.

Sarah felt rotten about feeding and about Leo, and Miriam was distracted by her crisis, but the listeners, by their expressions, obviously felt as if they were in the presence not simply of musicians, but of masters of music. The suite proceeded from its dancing allemande to the saraband and finally the subtle, generous minuet. They sat side by side, Miriam in a summer dress of the lightest blue silk, Sarah in jeans and a black turtleneck.

Standing open on the piano was a bottle of claret, a Latour nearly a hundred years old. There were glasses about and another, identical bottle beside it. A half-filled crystal carafe, shaped for use in ice, stood on an extraordinary little table. This wine was a white, but its color—a pale, rich gold—suggested that it, also, must be very fine. In fact, it was a freezing cold, exquisitely sweet Yquem, just now, at forty years, coming into its maturity. When guests sipped these wines, they would close their eyes.

The furnishings, also, were extraordinary. The chairs upon which the guests sat were Directoire pieces, some of them. It is to be remembered, though, that the designs of that period were inspired by classical models, and some of the other chairs were originals, carried from hearth to hearth in Miriam's baggage for millennia. Their wood, having been lovingly cared for by Sarah and all of her predecessors, was as rich as when it had been cut in the now-vanished forests of Greece and Italy and the Levant.

Miriam remembered when this piece had first been played. It fit the moment so well because it had been composed out of pain, and this was a time of pain.

LeSieur de Malchy had fallen in love with Lamia, and Lamia had amused herself by leading him on, letting him kiss her alabaster limbs and gaze into her proud and laughing eyes. She had drawn him into deep, true love, as she was so very expert at doing, with the intention of then abandoning him to his music. She didn't want a man. She wanted a composition.

Out of his anguish had emerged music fit to satisfy the ancient heart of the Keeper. Among humans, it had never been all that popular, but when Keepers joined to play, LeSieur was inevitably among the choices.

The instruments that Miriam and Sarah used had belonged to LeSieur, made by Barak Norman, of London, for him.

Miriam, as she played, well recalled LeSieur and her mother playing the piece together.

The room had been small and close with candle smoke, but finished in gold, with scenes of forest walks painted on its walls. The music, Miriam remembered, had captured, as if in a living amber, the passion that this man felt for the woman who sat with him in her tall wig and splendid white gown.

Only Miriam had been their audience, as she was audience to every moment of her adored mother's life. As Sarah served her now, she had once served Lamia.

The music came to its end. There was no applause. They had learned long ago, her friends, that such displays were not wanted. She poured herself some wine. It was the least refined alcohol she could tolerate, wine. But the soul of the grape, captured, gave her spirit enough pleasure that she had collected wine through the years. She'd drunk Falernian in Rome, for she had been intimately involved with the lives of the old emperors.

Most of these men had not died by assassination as history recorded, but as vestal sacrifices. Rome had been secretly ruled by a concealed religion. The emperors were only seasonal kings, doomed to serve the state until the priestesses of Vesta decreed that it was time for them to die. They learned of this little condition only after they achieved the purple. It was no wonder that so many of them went mad.

Some had been throat-slit or smothered or strangled, but others had been delivered to certain dark villas, rich, strange places whose graceful inhabitants spoke a tongue like thunder. The Vestas were a conclave of Keepers.

She put the glass down and walked out, never thinking to excuse herself from her guests. This house was run according to very ancient principles. It was an extremely exclusive place but, like an ancient palace, wide open to all who had the right to enter.

Whatever happened in here, they were free to come and watch . . . or at least, so it was meant to appear. They did so, full of nervous excitement over their attendance at what they perceived as extremely private moments—Miriam at her toilette, Miriam making love.

This was the way the aristocrats of history had conducted their lives. Their privacy consisted of being surrounded by their people, and Miriam could be comfortable no other way.

Or so it seemed. Miriam's ancient life was, of course, far more complex than it appeared. There were secrets within secrets. For, as Sarah and now Leo knew, this splendid house was also a place of murder, where innocent blood was guzzled like cheap champagne.

Paul was pushing a cockroach to the edge of the shower stall with his toe when he noticed something very odd about his feet.

He squatted, then got out of the shower and looked more closely.

It was the vampire blood that had made his skin so pale and smooth. Back in the ossuary, his shoes had been flooded with it. He rubbed his shoulder. Had it also sped his healing even more than usual?

He went back into the shower and washed and washed, using the cheap sliver of soap that had come with this cheap sliver of a hotel room. He stood in the small oblivion of the drumming water, watching the suds go down the drain.

It felt as if he were washing off a whole lot of his past in this lousy shower. Down the drain went his loyalty to his agency. Down the drain went his expectations about his own future: the successful end to his career, the honored retirement. He'd been a priest of death, and down the drain went this celibate life. Freud had said that all men want the same things: honor, riches, power, fame, and the love of women.

Well, he'd lost it all, hadn't he?—except maybe the love of a woman. But what woman would want a burned-out guy who couldn't even tell her what his life had been?

Becky, damnit, was the only woman he really wanted to talk to, and he hadn't realized it until too late. Probably all she'd ever felt for him anyway was a little compassion, maybe. Women didn't fall in love with him. They sensed all the damn violence, was his theory. He scared them. Or maybe it was all the traveling, the lack of time in one place.

He'd taken care of sex almost clinically, using whores like toys . . . or machines. Soon he wouldn't even be able to afford to do that.

Lying on the bed in his tiny room, he concentrated on his immediate course of action. He had eight grand. That would last a couple of months. But he didn't intend to spend anything like that much time here.

He lay paging through his well-thumbed copy of *New York by Night*, looking for the names of clubs, then calling information and asking for the numbers. Things in the world of Goths and Vampyres changed fast, and what had been au courant six months ago was way past its time now. None of the clubs mentioned had numbers. Probably they were all closed or transformed into more trendy incarnations.

So maybe the thing to do was to go downtown and just walk the streets. He'd pass the locations of the old clubs. Who knew what he'd find.

On the other hand, maybe this approach was total bullshit, just an excuse for a bar crawl. In his heart of hearts, what he wanted to do was to get seriously fucked up, then find some whore to suck him off. That would put a decent end, at least, to a real bad few of days. He'd arrived in the Big Apple almost hallucinatory with lack of sleep and jet lag and the spiritual exhaustion that comes after you've been doing a lot of killing. And he'd arrived on the run. He'd holed up here, phoning a sandwich shop for food and newspapers. The room had no TV, so he'd slept a lot. At least one thing: the shoulder was doing lots better. Still hurt, but hell, by all rights he probably ought to still be in the hospital.

He had to get a gun. If he was going to blow the shit out of vampires, he sure as hell was going to need one. Too bad he couldn't get hold of one of those fancy French jobs. Now, that had been a weapon. Hadn't that baby *worked!* He'd settle for a good old .357, though. It had done good service for him in Asia, and it'd work fine here. You got close, aimed at the head. It was effective. Blew their noggins into meat and ketchup.

Problem was, where did you get a gun in Nueva York without triggering some stoolie network? Guys in the illegal gun trade made money two ways—off their customers and off the cops they tipped. Of course, they wouldn't tip on a real customer, but some jerk coming off the street, he'd get fingered for sure. His full description would arrive at the nearest precinct in ten minutes tops. Gun raps were a good collar in this town. Looked nice in a cop's paper.

First things first. Locate the vampires. If the club scene didn't do it, then go to public records, work the pattern-of-disappearances angle. What worried him about that was that a whole lot of people evaporated in this town. It wasn't like Beijing or Singapore or Tokyo, where a disappearance was news. Hell, most missing persons didn't even make the back pages in this wild old burg. So okay, he'd work the club angle to death.

They were on their way to the club, the Bentley rolling down Fifty-seventh Street toward Fifth Avenue. Miriam and Sarah sat side by side. Leo was on one of the tiny jump seats facing them.

Miriam said, "A man may show up tonight asking after Ellen Wunderling. It's about time for him to find us. I want to be informed the moment it happens."

The bottom dropped out of Sarah's gut.

Leo asked, "Who's Ellen Wunderling?"

"One of our dear princess's little follies," Miriam said, playfully kissing Sarah's cheek.

Ellen Wunderling had been Sarah's worst mistake until the Paris emergency debacle. But why would anybody still be investigating that case? The police had closed it.

Sarah wasn't like a Keeper. She would not be able to escape from prison. If she went, she would die there, horribly, of hunger. What would happen to somebody like her, buried in a prison graveyard?

"What man?" she asked carefully, worried that Miriam would say no more. Since Paris, Miriam had obviously lost a great deal of trust in her.

Miriam reached up and opened the car's sunroof. They were now speeding down Fifth Avenue. The spires of St. Patrick's Cathedral swept past one side of the Bentley, Rockefeller Center the other.

Sarah curled up to her. "Miri, I'm so sorry I did her!"

"Don't start apologizing again. We're past that. Anyway, it turns out to be useful." She stroked Sarah's head. "Ellen is our little tar baby." She smiled softly.

Sarah didn't quite understand. She knew, however, that questioning would do no good.

"I hope Rudi's there early," Leo said. "I want to do all kinds of stuff tonight! I want to see how it feels now. Does it feel different, Sarah?"

"No crashes, no hangovers," Sarah said. She gave her a false smile. "But the only drug that really matters—" She glanced toward the intercom button. It was off. "—is blood."

"You're hungry, dear," Miriam said to Leo. "You just don't realize it. We'll need to find you a victim."

Leo kissed Miriam's neck. "Give me more of your blood. I want to be more like you."

"You're as much like me as you'll ever be."

"You're a fool, Leo," Sarah said.

Miriam gave her a shy sort of a smile. "Twenty years of love, and that's all the loyalty you can offer."

Sarah smiled right back. " 'Into whatever houses I enter, I will go into them for the benefit of the sick, and will abstain from every voluntary act of mischief and corruption.' I violate my Hippocratic Oath by the very nature of my life."

"Take off your clothes," Miriam said.

"*What?*"

They were crossing Thirty-fourth Street. The Empire State Building swept past above, visible through the open sunroof.

"Do it."

Sarah didn't want to, not here, not in front of Leo.

Leo said, "I'll help you."

"Sarah." There was a clear warning in the tone.

A few contortions between her and Leo, and Sarah was naked. She felt herself blushing. She covered her breasts with her arm.

Pushing her arm aside, Miriam took one of her nipples between her fingers and pinched it, watching Sarah's face. At first, Sarah tried to conceal her agony, but she finally cried out; she couldn't help it, the pain was so intense.

Leo watched, her eyes going nervously from Sarah's contorted face to Miriam's impassive one. "What's going on? Why are you hurting her?"

Miriam turned on the intercom. "Luis, take us on a tour. Fourteenth, down Broadway, give us half an hour." She released Sarah, who clutched her agonized breast.

Miriam took Sarah's face in her hands, gazed into her eyes. After a moment, she kissed her, pressing her tongue against Sarah's lips until she opened her mouth.

No matter how often they kissed, Sarah was always shocked by the sensation of those narrow teeth and that rough tiger's tongue. Miriam's mouth had a faint, meaty sourness that was at once sickening and delicious. Then Miriam broke away, spread Sarah's legs, and slipped to the floor.

Sarah could not have been more amazed. She looked at Leo and shook her head, to communicate her total confusion.

While Manhattan slid by above them and the Broadway crowds shuffled up and down outside the tinted windows, Miriam buried her face in Sarah's lap.

Never had Miriam taken such a posture. This was Sarah's place with Miri, not the other way around.

But—oh, my. Oh, *my!* Sarah thrust herself at Miri's face, her hands moving to guide her head, to press her mouth more tightly against her.

Miriam knew how to restore the bondage of a rebellious slave; she had done it thousands of times over the eons. She injected her tongue deep into Sarah's vagina. The powerful organ stretched the membranes as tight as drumskins. When there was resistance, Miriam pressed harder. Sarah writhed. Miriam moved her head back and forth, but slowly, pumping carefully. Sarah held Miriam's temples with shaking hands and glared down at her, crying and laughing, then threw her head back and grimaced through a fusillade of explosive climaxes. When they finally stopped, Miriam slowly withdrew, dragging her roughness along Sarah's clitoris. When she raised herself, Sarah embraced her, clung to her, kissing her face and neck, then knelt on the floor of the limousine and kissed her hands and feet.

Sarah lay at Miriam's feet, her head in her lap, weeping softly. *And so,* Miriam thought, *the little creature has come back to me.*

"Hey," Luis said over the intercom, "you're drivin' me crazy up here. I'm gonna come in my pants."

"Leonore'll do you at the club," Miriam said to him as she lit a cigarette. She drew Sarah up beside her, took her head down to her shoulder. "You're my girl?" she said, her tone kindly.

"Yes."

She looked at Leo. "Hot?"

"Oh, my."

"Take it out on Luis."

"I don't want to make love to Luis."

"I'll expect him to report that you were sensational. Incidentally, you're going to feed tonight, so what do you want?"

Leo barely whispered the words. "A man like my father."

"Ah. And your father was?"

"Powerful."

Miriam smiled slightly, parting her lips just a little.

"When you do that," Sarah said, "you look ten and ten thousand at the same time."

Miriam burst out laughing. "It's one of my *best* smiles!" The laughter was brittle and harsh, and Sarah was glad when it ended. "Stand up," Miriam said suddenly. They had never closed the sunroof.

"I'm naked!"

Miriam gave her a familiar look out of the corner of her eye. Immed-iately, Sarah rose to her feet.

Miriam thought, *Good. She does not think, she obeys. She's come back at last.*

The slipstream roared in her face, sending her hair flying

back. They were going down Houston Street toward the Hudson. Crowds on both sides of the street started cheering and applauding.

Sarah threw back her head and raised her arms high and screamed and screamed and screamed.

New York wasn't exactly the most dangerous city in the world, but the screams that Paul was hearing made him think that a woman was being killed. He looked up West Broadway toward the sound—and saw a black Bentley pass, going west on Houston Street. Some idiot girl was standing up in the open sunroof bellowing her head off, that was all.

She'd scared the hell out of him, damned rich bitch. He'd've liked to have given her a piece of his mind. Probably some damn tripper, that was why the screams were so blood-curdling.

New York was one giant drugstore. Everybody was young, everybody had money, and every damn thing was definitely for sale. Ecstasy, crystal meth, crack, coke, hash, grass, horse, even old-fashioned shit like his beloved opium. God knew, you could probably buy laudanum somewhere. You could get ten percent absinthe, for sure, *hecho en Mexico*. He liked getting drunk on absinthe. There was a poet in him, and the wormwood brought him out. Last time he'd done a bottle of good absinthe, it had been on the terrace at Las Brisas in Acapulco, one of the most beautiful places in the world to do serious drinking. The mountains, the city lights below, the sun setting over the Pacific—the view was unequalled. He'd gone back to his room afterward and written a thirty-page epic poem about the death of Nebuchadnezzar. Next morning, he'd had to go on the Internet to find out who the hell Nebuchanezzar was. Some ancient king.

A couple came toward him, dressed all in black. The girl's long, loose dress suggested possible gothic overtones. "Excuse me, I'm looking for a club called Shadowcat. Is there a place called Shadowcat around here?"

The couple stopped. The girl was a heartbreaker, round face, merry brown eyes, and one of those smiles that says *I know what you want*. She had a cute rack, too, a couple of sweet little apples. She said, "The things you're staring at are called breasts," and the two of them walked off laughing.

Was he losing his touch, or what? Then he saw a bookstore. Maybe they had some kind of SoHo guide that was more up-to-date than his copy of *New York by Night*.

He loved to read, and he hadn't been in an English language bookstore this big in years. Hundreds of titles, everything very colorful and appealing, all sorts of stuff. A dozen SoHo guidebooks, all brand-new. He opened one, *SoHo Unbound*. Under the heading, "Deep Dark Deadly," was a list of spots with appropriately strange names—The Marrow Room, Bottomley Topps, Dragged to Death.

He sure as hell felt dragged to death, but he decided to try The Marrow Room instead, because it had a more vampirish sort of a ring to it. Actually, none of them sounded much like they had anything to do with gothic play-acting. But one could always hope.

The Marrow Room turned out to be a lavish nightclub full of what looked to him like little kids. There was music blasting, strobes and lasers flashing. Wonderful little bubblegum girls kept dancing up to him and waving their mermaid locks. He smiled and nodded, forcing himself not to so much as glance down. It wouldn't have mattered, anyway—the whole damn place was full of jailbait.

He went to the bar. "Stoli on the rocks," he said.

The bartender looked at him. "Parents room in the back, mister. But it's BYOB."

He didn't really know what the hell kind of place he'd blundered into, but there was no damn point in finding out, that was for sure. When had rock clubs for children come in?

He left. A clutch of what looked like eight-year-olds clustered under a nearby stoop smoking and muttering together. This was different from Asia? How?

Then he saw a storefront with a black cat discreetly painted in one corner as the only indication that it wasn't altogether abandoned. A black cat was promising. He pushed the door open.

There were skulls. His stomach gave a turn. He never wanted to be in an ossuary again. But the skulls contained candles. There was music, very bad rock of some indeterminate kind, and here and there a few people in vaguely gothic costume sitting at tables. A couple danced mechanically under purple light on a small dance floor. The place smelled like cigarettes and sour beer. The bar had a rack on it with bags of potato chips.

"Stoli on the rocks," Paul said.

The bartender, a listless woman of about sixty wearing a black dress, poured something clear out of a bottle with no label into a glass with a whole lot of ice. She brought it over. Her face was painted white, her lips dark, dark red. She was wearing plastic teeth.

"I'm looking for Ellen Wunderling," Paul said.

"You a cop?"

"Not."

"Wanna bj? Fifteen bucks."

Paul was beginning to think of a whole lot of reasons to throw up. He was homesick. He wanted to go to one of those

Bangkok barbershops where a cloud of comely maidens massaged you, cut your hair, did your nails, *and* gave you a blow job for fifteen damn bucks.

"I'm doing research on Ellen Wunderling."

"Never came in here." She turned away, busied herself pulling a beer—for whom it wasn't clear.

"Any other place I could go? I'm new here, and I don't know the scene."

"Well, the first thing to do is not dress like a bus driver trying to pawn himself off as another bus driver. That horror show isn't gonna get you in anywhere."

"These are new clothes."

"Go over to Shambles on Prince Street. You can get all kinds of stuff there. Get a hat, some blacks, some fingernails." She cackled. "Get pierced, officer, then we'll all just *love* you!"

"I'll pierce you," a voice called.

"Oh, shit," another voice murmured.

Paul went over to the table. He wasn't absolutely sure if he was talking to a man and a woman, two women, or two men. But he sat down anyway. He wasn't planning to get in bed with them. Or get pierced. "I'm looking for Ellen Wunderling," he said.

"Mistah Wunderling, he dead," the most likely to be male said. His mouth was full of potato chips.

"Miss Wunderling."

"You gotta go deep into the jungle, man—real deep. Try Hexion or the Hellfire Club—"

The girl—and Paul was now sure she was a for-real female and that underneath all that Vampirella makeup, she was your basic Queens chick—shook her head. "Hexion is a cannibal place," the girl said. "They serve brain soup."

"It's not *real* brains."

"What's the Hellfire Club?"

"A Catholic hangout. Run by former nuns."

"Any Ellen Wunderling connection?"

"He should go to the Veils."

"Him and the Count of Monte Cristo."

"What's the Veils?"

"Just the most exclusive club in Manhattan."

"The world."

"Same difference. But it was the last place Ellen was seen alive."

FIFTEEN

Scorpion Dance

Normally Leo was not much interested in the lesbian stuff that went on between Miriam and Sarah, but watching them this close, with Sarah going wild like that right in her face, was thrilling. When Miriam had kissed her before, she'd been polite about it and pretended, but it hadn't really been a turn-on. This had been the most amazingly intimate, beautiful thing.

She'd been a lonely little rich girl before she came to the Veils, her main claim to fame being that she was the daughter of, like, the second cousin once removed of General Patton. She had a co-op loft in SoHo in an artist building that was full of lawyers. She had a Maserati and a little pocket yacht called the *Y'All Come,* but Y'all generally didn't.

At, like, four o'clock one morning when she was so fabulously wasted, Miriam had said to her, "Come and follow me." They'd laughed. But she'd been totally in wonder because she was not exactly the kind of super cool person who'd be invited into Miriam's *house.*

Next thing she knew, she'd been given a little bedroom with cute curtains and a high brass bed. She'd had pretty much the run of this, like, amazing house. Gradually, she'd realized what Miriam did, Miriam and Sarah. They were lovers, but they also—well, wow, she was one of them now.

She squeezed her toes in her shoes. It was totally incredible to suddenly have this ultimate power. She'd never had any power at all. But now she sure did. She could point to somebody and say, "I want that one," and that person would undergo the most important experience of his or her life.

She wanted to feed for the first time. Even if she didn't have all that much hunger. She wanted this to happen.

It was unimaginable that she would live a really long time. But Miriam had stuff that was, like, Egyptian that was still in use. They had some three-thousand-year-old chairs in there. Leo had researched it. She'd priced it. A chair like the one Miriam had been sitting on during their viola drag would go on at Sotheby's easily for one million bucks.

She was going to see, like, the future. Spaceships. Aliens. Whatever the hell. Unless the world ended. Global warming, was that for real? Miriam said, "What happens happens." That was the way to approach it.

They were coming up to the club. Great. She was already high. She'd been awful sick at first, but since this morning, she'd started to feel better and better and better, and now she felt completely damn wonderful. She didn't have any aches or pains at all.

The Bentley stopped. "Okay," Leo said, popping the door.

But Sarah grabbed Miriam's wrist. "Don't do this!"

"It's safe enough."

"You can't be certain."

Leo watched them bicker. They'd both been real scared lately. For sure; Leo was no fool—she could see it. This guy was bad news.

Miriam started to get out again.

"The front of the club's too public. Go in the back."

Miriam stroked Sarah's head. "There's going to be a confrontation, child. And the club is where it's going to happen."

Leo watched her go in. Then she helped Sarah dress. "That was so cool. I feel like I really know you now, Sarah." Nervously, she kissed her cheek. Maybe Sarah would do something sexy with her. She'd love to find out how it felt. Or Miriam—but that was too, too awesome.

"You know me," Sarah said. She followed Miriam, and Leo hurried after her. As usual, the club was dark, entirely invisible from the street. There was never a crowd outside the Veils. Ordinary people couldn't find the place. They weren't supposed to—only those who knew. And now Leo was, like, at the top of the food chain. She knew the truth behind all the rumors about Miriam Blaylock and Sarah Roberts. Sarah'd had a lover whom Miriam had killed, that was the main rumor. Another doctor. *That* they never talked about.

Miriam intended to capture the monster that was tracking her and feed off him, maybe even feed him to Leo; she wasn't sure. That depended on Leo. She was a tiresome little thing, truth to tell, but pleasant to have around and very eager.

Sarah, by contrast, was that most dangerous of slaves— one who did not understand the real meaning of servitude. An evil old Roman emperor, Septimius Severus, had once asked Lamia, "As all the world is my slave, why is it that only I am not free?"

Contained in those words was the ironic essence of the relationship between slaves and masters. Sarah was a poor slave because she thought of herself as a captive. Leo would be a good one because she would always look upon her accession to the blood as an achievement, not an imposition. This was why Miriam had been so careful to let her make a clear choice.

As Luis opened the door to the club, Miriam gave a tweak to the little rod in his pants. "Leonore," she said, "will go to you in the Pump Room."

"Yes, ma'am."

"I really gotta do him?" Leo whispered.

"Leo, I've serviced Luis dozens of times myself. You'll enjoy it."

"But I'm not a whore, Miriam. I'm . . . one of you."

"And we are objective about sex. It's a commodity just like booze and drugs. Sex is part of this business. Leave your emotions out of it, and your ego. Sex isn't the sort of Blue Broadway that the average Jill imagines, my dear."

Sarah laughed. Miriam wondered what she found funny, let it go. She strode across the glittering bar that was the club's first and most public room, calling out, "The front's to be open tonight, Bill."

"You want the sign up, ma'am?"

"I want the sign."

Sarah came hurrying along behind her. It was only ten, so there were few people here. "That's a bad idea," she hissed.

Miriam stopped, turned to her, put her hands on her shoulders. She had not understood the notion of the tar baby. "He's going to find us. But he must do it on his own, and the sooner the better."

She went to Bill, who was digging behind the bar for the small brass sign that said on it only, "Veils." This sign was placed on the door. Beyond that, they never went. "William, love, there's a good chance that a man will come in looking for Ellen Wunderling."

"That again! Don't they ever give up?"

"He's not a cop. I want him drugged a little. Offer him a drink. Lace it with—I don't know—something that'll relax him, make him a little hallucinatory, perhaps. Ask Rudi. But be careful with him."

"Oh, yeah, you bet."

"What's the crash so far?"

"Nobody upstairs. Dungeon's active, though. Seth's on the horse, and that bishop is back. Upstairs is gonna get jammed later. We got DJ Bones tonight."

"Make him a regular." His sound had incredible drive, but there was an elegance to it that fit this club very well.

"Twenty thousand dollars a night."

"Do it."

So that her early guests would see her and be able to tell the later ones that she was indeed here, she went to her customary table at the rear of the bar. Also, she was most interested in watching who might come in that door. He'd had three days to find the place, and he was far from stupid. He'd be here.

At first glance, this room appeared to be the extent of the Veils. But the point of the name of the club was that there were many levels, many layers to pass through. Beyond this room, there were eight others, but many more than eight different ways to sin.

Rudi came up to her. "I got great meth," he said, "plus them new Hi-Los and some dig hash. The hash was cheap."

"Push it hard," she said, looking past him. "I'm probably going to do a pipe later with a friend." She had a room in the basement that was locked using Keeper techniques. Not even Sarah could enter it unless invited. Sometimes, when the club was crowded and some target was available, Miriam might take it down there. Hidden in the room's floor was an entrance to a short tunnel that led into the boiler room of an adjacent building. The boiler there had a very good firebox, where Miriam could dispose of remnants quite easily. She would crush them to jagged bits, and they'd burn with a sparkle and a hiss when she threw them in. If the tunnel was ever found, it would appear to be nothing but an old, disused drainage line.

Miriam liked her room. She enjoyed the absolute privacy, the absolute secrecy. Being that it was entirely hidden, she had done some extremely wicked things there, so wicked that not even Sarah could know.

She intended to be very, very wicked to the hunter, more wicked than she'd been to any human being in hundreds of years. If he brought his little gang of helpers, so much the better. She would take them all, gorging herself in the fashion of old, tormenting them so terribly that the ones who had to watch would be sick all over themselves before their turns came.

"Cigarette me," she said to Leo, who was hovering.

The girl lit a cigarette, handed it to her. "Um, can I go down with Seth after I do Luis? They've got that Presbyterian bishop in the cage."

"Play your heart out, baby."

Sarah leaned close to her, whispered. "Thank you so much for what you did. I'm still singing inside."

Miriam smiled up at her, then watched her carefully as she disappeared into the back of the club. She was watching the way the shoulders were held, and the head. A slave's posture was very subtly different from that of a free man. Not that they were bowed, but there was in the way they moved the aimlessness of somebody who has not planned their own actions. Sarah walked with decision.

Miriam sighed. Sarah was perhaps too much in love to be a good slave. A lover sought constantly to remake the beloved in the image of her dream. A slave accepted mastery.

"Sarah," she said.

Sarah turned back. Miriam noticed that there were tears in the edges of her eyes. "Yes, Miri?"

"Turn on the veils, dear!"

"God, I forgot!"

Sarah turned the doorway on, causing the back of the club to disappear behind what appeared to be a dark mirror.

Doug Henning had designed the doorways for her, using his unique skills with light and mirrors. People seemed to disappear into a shimmering black haze when they left one room of the club, and come into view just as uncannily in the next. Thus the Veils.

She sat smoking and waiting. Miriam could wait well. She could wait for days, weeks.

She wondered if the hunter had as yet done any of his evil work in the United States. At the last conclave, held in January of 1900, there had been nine Keepers in America. Perhaps a few more had come over the past century, but probably not. They were not a migratory people. They had divided the corners of the world when they first arrived here, and nobody had wanted the Americas—there had been no indigenous population to work with there.

Two American Keepers had been killed in the airplane collision at Tenerife Airport in 1977. It was thus possible that there were only seven Americans left, including herself. It was also possible, if the murderers had already been here, that she was alone.

Even alone in all the world. That was possible, too.

She was contemplating this eerie thought when she heard a male voice, pleasantly strong, say, "I wonder if you've ever heard of Ellen Wunderling?"

He stood at the bar, a tall man with penetrating eyes, smiling at Bill with a detective's careful eyes.

Miriam's heart never beat with excitement. At least, it hadn't in so many years that she could not remember the last time. It was humming now.

"That's him," Leo hissed excitedly, "that's *him!*"

"Have you done Luis?"

"Miriam, do I *have* to?"

"Go! Now!"

The girl left. Miriam could now concentrate on the hunter. Look at those eyes, that face, the rippling power of the muscles beneath the cheap clothes. He was damned beautiful, this one. She felt herself getting wet for him . . . which was quite odd, but not entirely surprising. Humans could amuse her, but they did not cause spontaneous sexual arousal. Even as her sex came trembling to life, her mouth filled, for another part of her was threatened and preparing to fight.

Look at him there, in his rumpled clothes, with that fearsome face of his. Did anybody else find him so ferocious looking? They had no idea what he was. They had no idea where he had been or what he had done.

Look at the cast of his jaw, the line of his nose, his darkly glowing skin. And his eyes, look at the way they flicked here and there, like the eyes of a nervous fox.

Almost, it was not a human face. Almost, it was the face of some sort of exotic animal.

The outline of his suit told her that he was carrying, and the gun was big—a magnum, maybe worse.

She was well back in the shadows, but she wondered now if it had been wise to get even so close as this. If he recognized her—but that was absurd. He was, after all, only human. But look at his movements, the grace, the precision—*was* he only human?

Well, of course he was. She was losing her grip, actually panicking. And yet . . . it wasn't panic. It was desire, damnit, real, live desire. She wanted to be with this man.

What had she done to herself, playing around with human beings? This *was* perverse, to want to lie beneath a human male. She'd had a little of this with John Blaylock, which was why she'd switched back to females after he faltered. The females could give you real pleasure, and they were also better servants. Sarah, with all her conflicts, was fun. Interesting. Leo was going to be a hungry little animal. Miriam had all sorts of delicious wickedness planned for that one . . . beginning with Mr. Hunter, here, who was to be her first human meal. The warrior was going to die a lingering, humiliated death at the hands of a rather stupid girl. That would be most fitting.

She watched him sipping a vodka on the rocks. He'd ordered Stoli, then asked Bill a question that she had not heard. Bill had said very little to him, but she knew what it had been: "That's the owner over there. Ask her."

So he was fortifying himself. She watched him throw the drink back. He turned toward her.

This was the moment. If he recognized her, she was going to be blown apart.

He met her eyes and came toward her.

"You're a Stoli man," she said as he approached. "You ought to try Charodei."

Paul was so stunned when he looked at her that he almost lost his balance. In all his nearly fifty years on this earth, he had never beheld a woman who affected him more powerfully. She was a vision, just a damn vision. He loved noses, and she had one of those graceful, sweet noses with a tip that begged to be kissed. He loved complexion, and her skin was like frozen cream, a rich, deep white, perfectly smooth. He loved lips, and hers were exquisite, and they had in them the kind of small, amused smile that suggested a good personality. And eyes—her eyes were so calm, so gentle, so fresh-looking that he thought she couldn't be a day over twenty. She was wearing dark blue silk that looked as if it cost a few bucks. And she owned this fabulous little place. It was small, but it was class.

"Please," she said in a voice that would put the angels to shame, "have a seat." She glanced away from him. "Bring him a Charodei, Billy."

When she met his eyes, he found himself unable to look away. God, her eyes were frank. God, she was confident. He loved that in a woman.

"I want to see if you like it. It's my little test." Her smile—it was incredibly kind. That was the thing; this was a hell of a sexy woman, with those fabulous, beautifully proportioned breasts and that angelic face—but she was *kind*. You could see it in the gentle ease of the smile, hear it in the melody of the voice. In a place like this, he would have thought "pretty, but hard." He knew special when he saw special, and this lady was *real* special.

But Paul was also a very single-minded human being. He was here to kill vampires, not to fuck-talk some kid into bed. He said, "I'm doing research on Ellen Wunderling," but in his mind he was saying, "If I leave here without your phone number, I'll kill myself."

Her smile turned, he thought, a little sad. "I didn't catch your name, mister."

"Ward, Paul Ward. I'm a journalist."

"May I see your press credentials? I'm sorry to ask, but we're almost a tourist attraction because of that story. It's ironic, because we aren't even involved in the Goth scene."

"No, this looks like a very nice place. I wonder if you could tell me—"

"Sir, I really think you should ask at the precinct. Detective Lieutenant Timothy Kennerly. They questioned every employee in this place at least three times."

"Nothing ever came of it?"

"I saw her. We all did. She came in and got a Coke. She was sweaty; she'd been running or something. She seemed totally at ease. Not a problem. That was it."

Paul realized that he was going to have to leave in a minute, as soon as she demanded the press credentials again. He had no credentials. In his wallet were driver's licenses in five names from three different countries, and half a dozen credit cards, some of which might be good, all of which would flash red lights from Langley to Foggy Bottom the instant they were used.

Miriam saw that he was getting ready to stand up, and realized he was about to go. If he did that, she'd have to have him followed, but there was nobody here capable of doing it except Sarah. She did not want use Sarah that way; it was just too dangerous.

Ward himself was her key. He seemed so straight, though, that she didn't know quite how to seduce him, or even if it was possible. She would do it by acting the young, innocent girl. Given the panting-dog expression presently on his face, it was a type he liked.

"Listen," he said, "I'm working real hard on this. I think it's a huge thing. There's something incredible behind it— what happened to her. Almost certainly. And I'd like to enlist your help. What I want to know is, do I have any chance at all?"

"Try me."

He knocked back the drink. Miriam pointed to his glass, and Bill brought another. At that moment, a crowd came in. Among them she saw Jewel and a rather nervous Ben Stiller. Good faces for the club. It would be a good night.

Paul watched the people disappear one after another into the back wall. It told him that there was a lot more to this place than he'd initially thought. He wondered what would happen if he suddenly got up and went through. This little girl sure wouldn't stop him. When he'd first sat down, he put her at about thirty-two. Now he was wondering if she could even damn well legally drink the liquor she sold. Christ, though, she was lovely.

She also knew a little something about Ellen Wunderling that she hadn't disclosed. A flicker in the edges of the eyes had been his tipoff. He wished that he could interrogate her freely. She was an innocent little thing. You wouldn't even need a rubber hose to get her going. A light slap would set this powder puff to babbling.

He wanted to get in her pants, and it was distracting him. This damn town had to be full of vampires, ripe for the killing, and if this bitch was holding back about Ellen, maybe she was also holding back information that would lead him to them.

"Let me ask you this," he said. "In the *New York Times* story—do you know it?"

"Of course."

"It suggests that there are people who think they're vampires. Who actually drink blood. If I said, maybe such people drank Ellen's blood—how do you react to that?"

"The vampire scene is dead."

"Not for these assholes. They think they're getting something from the blood—besides AIDS, I mean. Some kind of life force. The soul, I guess."

As he spoke, she thought of how he looked behind a gun. She remembered the hate in his eyes, the eager spark as he killed. This creature *loved* his work, damn him. When she let Leo feed on him—and she would certainly do that in the end—she would make her go very, very slowly.

"Soul eaters," she said. "Wow, that's heavy."

"I know it's heavy, but it's true—I mean, in the sense that it's what they believe. Of course, it's all bullshit—"

"Of course."

"But they believe it, that's what's important. You look at the stats. A lot of people disappear without trace, don't they?"

"I don't know."

"In the U.S. in a year, over three hundred thousand."

"You're kidding . . . walking out on their debts, or a spouse they don't like, that'd be most of it, I'd think."

"There's plenty of foul play, Miss—what's your name?"

Beautiful, he was. Gracious, not. "Miriam Blaylock."

"Miss Blaylock." He paused. His eyes were searching hers. How hungry he was. She realized that he was an innocent. Incredibly, his sexual curiosity was that of a boy.

She said, "You look like a soldier."

"Is that good?"

She laughed, raised her eyebrows, delivered a slowly developing smile. "Is it?"

His left hand came into view as he brushed his cheek with the tips of his fingers. *For God's sake,* he thought, *let her see there's no ring.* She was talking to him like a person, here. She was being nice to him. He was beginning to think to himself, maybe he should lay off work for a little while. Lie low here in Manhattan. Let some personal life develop for once. He'd been married to the damn Company for too damn long. He was ready for a little real life.

He tried an opening line. "So, how long have you been in the club game?"

She took out another cigarette, offered him one. She lit them both with a lighter that looked as if it belonged on the *Titanic*. It was tiny, gold, and complicated. He wouldn't have been surprised if it had blown up in her face.

"Lemme see that."

She handed it to him.

"How old is this?"

"I bought it in a shop. I thought it was cute."

"Well, it could be dangerous."

She tried to recall how long she'd had the damn thing. Seventy, eighty years, at least. She'd never had occasion to get a new one. She took the lighter back. "It's fine."

"I'm gonna get you a real lighter."

"It's fine!"

"No, I'd like to. I'd really like to." He'd go to Bloomingdale's, spend fifty bucks. This lady had to be impressed. He could not let her slip through his fingers.

She looked at him out of lowered eyelids. There was even a little hint of Asia in her miraculous face. He loved the way Asian women looked; they were just so damn beautiful. She was more beautiful.

He just plain wanted to kiss her. But how did he get there? Maybe she'd drink with him. He said, "Listen, lemme buy you one a these Cordiers—what are they—hey, this is great vodka. And coming from me, that's high praise."

How pathetic he was. For the moment, his attraction to her was pushing his fanaticism aside. If she kissed him, she wondered, would it draw him closer or scare him away?

"What do you actually do for a living?"

What was this, he wondered. Was she evaluating him? What if he told her he was CIA? Sometimes that was a major turn-on; sometimes they hated it. Usually, they thought you were a complete asshole.

"What I really do is—I'm a—well, I'm not a reporter."

"I know you're not a reporter, and I'm getting kind of pissed off, since you won't show me any kind of credentials and I'm still waiting."

"You're waiting, and I'm gonna—well, this is not kosher at all. This is really against regs—"

"You are a cop. I thought you were."

"No, no." He pulled out his wallet, opened it to his ID card.

Miriam took the wallet, looked at the card. She thought that it appeared entirely legitimate, and it was certainly not a good piece of news. Her opposition was apparently governmental.

She memorized the card, and the information on the driver's license, and the number on the one credit card that was visible.

"Are you offended?"

"I'm curious. I mean, this is—it's so weird. What the hell was Ellen Wunderling really up to, that she rates attention from you people?" She motioned to Bill, who gave him a fresh drink—lots of vodka, less ice. "I mean, this vampire thing seems like something pretty stupid for the CIA to take an interest in."

"What if I told you it wasn't stupid at all?"

"I wouldn't know what to say. But I wouldn't be real interested, either."

Paul found that a very unexpected reaction. He sat back and regarded her. Given the past few minutes of conversation, he decided to revise his opinion about little Merry Blaylock. He'd bet thirty years in clandestine service that this kid did not know a single useful thing about Ellen Wunderling or vampires or anything connected with them. But the way she was looking back at him, with that dee-licious little smile—well, her innocence told him that conversation should go in another direction entirely.

The smile widened a little, played very fetchingly in her eyes. He could practically see her deciding that she thought his being CIA was kind of cool. The damn tag had worked for once. Damned amazing.

"Would you like to see my club?"

"They say it's the most exclusive club in New York."

She reached over, touched the back of his hand with the tips of her fingers. Then she laughed, a deliciously suggestive little bell-note, one of her favorites. "Oh, it is. Very, very exclusive. But if I like you, then you can come in. Welcome to the Veils."

SIXTEEN

Demon Lovers

I t looks like a wall—I mean, *just* like a wall." Paul extended a large hand toward the entrance.

"Doug Henning was a master."

"Isn't he the one who died? Kinda young, wasn't he?"

"Yes, he was." He'd been a delicious young man.

She took his hand and stepped through with him.

Techno music hit him like an avalanche—one made of pure sound. The space was dark, milky with smoke. Lasers played in time with the very fast music, revealing random slices of a whole lot of dancers. On a small stage, its floor glistening like a mirror, was a shadow capering behind the most complex set of control panels and turntables he'd ever seen in a club. The dj was faceless, even his head was covered. He appeared to be as thin as his bones, but that was probably some sort of an illusion.

The intensity of the music was completely beyond anything in Paul's experience. For a few seconds, he was virtually unconscious, reeling through a fog of reefer and crack and crys so thick he felt himself getting high on his second gasp for air. The next thing he knew, the music swept him up, seeming to yank his soul right out of his body and levitate him across the floor. He cried out, he knew it, he could feel it. But the music was so loud, the beat so intoxicating, the rhythm so danceable that his consciousness lost control of the primitive parts of the brain and his body began to move of its own accord. He thought voodoo, the shaking of priests, the trance of the gods.

He was dancing, and he could not do anything but dance. He was helpless to stop himself. The lasers showed sweating faces all around him, beautiful faces, goddesses, gods, and he thought he'd gone to some Olympian mountain. He thought he had risen above the ocean of life into the air of life. He was so happy, his heart was exploding with happiness, and it rushed through him as if fire had replaced the blood in his veins.

It was sorcery, he thought, it was magic. Satan's hooves were trampling him, but Satan's soft hands were also stroking him. He saw the girl—Miriam—standing there beside the stage with two other young women—both lovelies as well. Then a guy came out and began racing around the room like he was in some kind of a major seizure. He was wearing a magician's coat, black with red sequins and green sequins in the shape of a pentacle on it, and he ran in a jerky, unnatural way, striking dancers with a sparking wand and making them cry out.

Then Paul saw that most of the dancers were stark naked and there was a girl shooting a huge syringe straight into a guy's mouth, the needle penetrating under his tongue, and his eyes were flickering like a dying sign. There was sweat in the air with the smoke. There were pills rolling on the floor. The drugs were more plentiful here than anything he had seen in Paris or Bangkok.

It was hell, it was heaven, he was happy, he was scared to death, and he felt as if Satan were right there in this god-for-damned room and he was being butt-fucked by that NVR interrogator again in Muang Sing. Jesus wept, why had they done shit like that to him? The music got louder still and tighter still, driving, driving, crushing through his heart, burning through his brain, and then the magus struck him with the wand and the blow felt like an incoming mortar round.

The lights changed from lasers to white slits, and huge shadows swept over the dancers. When he looked up, he saw into a tremendous sky full of cloud towers and in them there was the Hindenburg exploding and burning, and from its belly there fell sparks that were people.

His whole self was torn away and torn out of him—his name went, his sense of being, the presence of and pain over his father, his place where his mom lived in him and said, "You're a good boy, a good boy"—all of his innermost self was torn out of him and swept away in the sea of smoke and the goddamnest best, most exciting, genius-level rock and roll he had ever heard in his life.

Then there was a girl there, one of the lovelies who'd been with Miss Blaylock. She had dark bangs and the kind of shape you wanted to put your hands around. She came dancing up to him and started undressing him, dancing with him and pulling off his clothes. He thought, *You know what I'm doing?—I am letting this happen, because this is the most fun I have ever had or known about.* He helped this exquisite girl with the light brown brush get every stitch of his clothes off and toss them down on the floor.

Nobody gave a shit, nobody stopped, he was dancing in a wonderful ocean of vibrating pricks and sailing boobs, and all the faces of all the gods and goddesses of the dance were smiling on him.

He yelled out, "I'm blown away! I am just plain *blown away!*" Then he remembered that he'd been carrying. The gun—had it been in his pocket or where did it go? Well, it wasn't his lookout anymore, and anyway, who gave a damn? He was not hunting vampires now.

This was not like any kind of damn club he'd ever heard of before. This was some kind of magic shamanic demon hole, this was.

Cool!

The room changed again, and this time he screamed bloody murder because he could not help it, he could not even think about stopping it; he screamed and he stumbled forward because the floor had disappeared and he was standing a thousand feet *above* Manhattan, and down there the traffic was racing as fast as the music, and little puff clouds were shooting past beneath his feet. The illusion was so perfect—man, it was so perfect!—you did not believe that you were standing on anything. That music, that wonderful, driving, animal-perfect, jungle machine music just totally blew out his nerve endings, so he was not a body with weight and age but an eternal light-being flying over the city.

Somebody knelt in front of him and started blowing him, and for the first time in his life, he just enjoyed it without worrying about who was there. He didn't care if it was a girl or a guy or a damn gorilla; he just loved; he loved with all his blood and his hammering, crashing heart, and the little light in the middle that was him.

Then he did look down and he saw the naked woman from the limo on Houston Street. She was giving him a hard-sucking blow job in the middle of the goddamn dance floor, and it was the best damn blow job he'd ever had.

The pleasure was so intense that he could not stand, his knees started to give way. Somebody held him up, somebody strong as shit, so he just let himself go limp. The hands were long and thin and cold against his skin, but the arms were as steady as steel rods. No way was he gonna get dropped. The pleasure swept up and down him, crashing like great waves from the top of his head to the singing tips of his toes.

He closed his eyes, and in his mind he saw not the woman blowing him, but Miriam Blaylock. How could she be that beautiful? How was it possible? With this club, she was some kind of magician, some kind of demon, but God love her, she was so beautiful.

Then he noticed that he wasn't being blown anymore. Hell, that was tough, that was intense to leave him with his gob half down the chute. "Shit!" he yelled aloud.

The music snatched him up like a wave. His balls were aching from him being hard too long with nothing happening but the *music;* the music just did not stop, did it? He was dancing again, they were all dancing again. When he looked over at the stage, he saw six women and six men dancing in front of the consoles, and behind them the dj had his hood off. Paul noticed that his eyes were yellow.

Miriam Blaylock was dancing, too; he saw her. She saw him and her eyes sparkled; then she saw he was naked and she cocked her head and gave him a mock-angry look and wagged her finger at him. Oh, she was just the cutest little girl he had ever seen. God love her for letting him into this wonderful place where he was dancing with the beautiful. She must actually like him. She must be impressed. Actually. He'd tell her he was the damn CIA director, if he had to. He never wanted to leave this place as long as he lived.

Then it was total dark, total silence. He stumbled, almost fell again, but nobody else moved. Everybody else just stayed still. He couldn't hear a damn thing, not after that music.

The lights came on, and all of a sudden the magical

beings were just people. They were boys and girls in their teens, mostly. Some older ones. There were famous faces here and there, not people whose names he knew, but the kind of faces you recognized from TV or the movies but you didn't know exactly who. He'd never been in the same room with famous people before.

A guy came onto the stage. The dj. There was a faint sound like rustling leaves, and Paul applauded, too. Had the music fucked up his hearing or what? He'd listened to plenty of loud rock in his life, but this had been something more. This had been music that blew you so far out of yourself that he now felt as though some sort of internal reset button had been pushed. He felt blank, a deprogrammed soul.

In the light he could see people were getting dressed, and they were still doing drugs, right out in the middle of everything. Some of them were even still making love. Guys were still hard, thinking nothing of it. Some of these kids were not even teens. They were, like, teenyboppers. There were friggin' children in this place, drinking and doing drugs, naked with naked adults. It was total, amazing, awful sin.

"Hell," he said to two of them standing nearby, "this place almost got Bangkok beat!"

Waiters came through two big doors and started laying out food and wine. They brought it in on huge gold trays, in golden bowls and crystal bowls, and the utensils and the plates were all gold, too.

"Christ," he said to another couple, "those pots must be worth a million bucks!"

He hadn't noticed that he was the only one making any noise until a guy held his finger over his lips.

"Be quiet?"

The kid nodded.

Hell, he didn't want to be quiet. He wanted to talk dirty to some frail. He wanted to get finished getting blown. But, hell, he was okay with it; this was what they wanted to do. He was the damn newbie, looked like.

Sarah watched Leo pull Miriam away from the dj's stage and heard her say, "Miri, that *man!* He's utterly dreadful!"

Very quietly, Miriam said, "He's also utterly alone."

Leo seemed not to comprehend. "Well, just get him out of here, please. He's pissing everybody off."

Sarah marched over to her and said, "We don't talk to Miriam like that."

"What? About him? She was an idiot to bring him in. He even had a gun!"

Quickly, Sarah took Leonore out of the room. The hard lights of the kitchen were a better setting for this discussion. "Listen, Leo. Do not *ever* make demands of her. What's been done to you doesn't give you the right. In fact, it does the opposite. Before, you were her friend. Now, you're her possession."

"You know something, Sarah? You're a complete asshole." Leo flounced off through the doors.

Sarah was amazed at how angry she felt, watching those doors swing behind that arrogant little ass. It was a calm, dispassionate sort of anger, a deep anger. The idea that she would have to live years and years with Leo interfering between her and Miri was just plain awful.

Before Leo, she had not been loyal enough. She had been unable to shake the scruples she'd brought from her old life. Miri had stolen her from herself. But because she was not a volunteer but a captive, something else was also true. Miri was responsible for her. Miri, also, belonged to her. She had

(

rights in this relationship. She had her place, and did not intend to be disloged.

She went down to the office and stood at the one-way mirror, where she could see the dance floor. Everybody was eating, gobbling away at the braces of honey-dipped sparrows and other exotic foods that Vincent had prepared at Miriam's instruction. Miriam had little interest in human food, but it wasn't as if she didn't know about it. Her recipes spanned three thousand years. Honey-dipped sparrows had been the hot dogs of Elizabethan England.

Sarah watched the man. He was, in a way, beautiful—huge, muscular, his eyes extremely intelligent. She'd gone out on the floor and sucked him for a little while. She imagined that his ample organ would feel really nice inside her.

"You're drooling," Miri said as she came in. "And get your clothes on, you're the only one still naked except for that big slab of ham you're drooling over. Want to eat him?"

"What's the deal with him?"

Miriam sat down behind her desk. She tossed a small suitcase on it, clapped her hands. "Chop chop."

"The count, already? It's only two, Miri."

"Rudi's bag got too full. You'll have two counts tonight."

"I thought it was gonna be good."

"You want to know what the deal is with him?"

"Yeah." Sarah was sorting, preparing the pile for the count. It was over a hundred grand, though; she could already tell that. Money came to Miriam like metal shavings to a magnet. Ancient Keeper magic, Sarah thought. "So, what is it?"

"I don't know if I should tell you."

"Please trust me, Miri. It's agony for me when you don't."

"It's agony for me when you forget your place, child."

Sarah sorted bills into neat stacks of fifties, hundreds, a few twenties.

"I've been thinking about that. I want to ask your forgiveness. I want you to know that you've got my absolute loyalty."

"Now that there's a replacement threatening, yes. I wish you'd come to me before I blooded her."

"Why did you? We've got to endure her now forever and ever! And she's—oh, Miri, she's tacky and she's quite stupid."

Miriam shrugged. "You want to do pipe later, child?"

"I thought you were mad at me."

"I'm not mad now. In fact, I'm going to do celebration pipe. The two-hundred-year-old opium."

"What possible occasion could there be now?"

"I'm going to take that man downstairs with you and me and Leo, and we are going to spend a very long time with him. We're to feed Leo with him. Her first pabulum. Do you think she can handle it, Doctor?"

She was instantly excited, instantly appalled. A "very long time" would mean hell for the poor man. "Miri, I hate for them to suffer."

"What if I told you that he's the one who assaulted me?"

She stopped counting. In fact, lost the count. "You mean—"

Miri smiled slow. "I snared him, Sarah, in my very fine net. Anticipated his moves correctly. He is, at present, our prisoner."

"He's the one from Paris?"

"Yes."

Sarah looked at him again. "If we kill him, is that it? You're out of danger?"

"They'll be set back, because that man out there is a very powerful weapon. That man is the reason they win."

"Who, Miri?"

"There are people killing the Keepers, Sarah. Making carnage of us all over the world."

"*People?*"

"And that man is their leader."

Sarah found a chair. "And we're going to feed him to Leo?"

"She needs to eat, dear, just like us. She has a right to her food, too."

Paul wanted his clothes. Everybody else was already dressed. This was becoming not fun. "Excuse me," he said again, "I think that's my—" But it wasn't his. Nothing was his. "Look, hey, I'm missing a wallet, here." He really didn't need to lose *that,* for Chrissakes. There was six hundred bucks in there. The rest was safe enough inside the springs of the bed at the Terminal Hotel, except for the three c's he'd spent on the also-gone magnum.

"Hey, ladies!" he called out to no one in particular. "I got no clothes, here! Is there somebody in charge?"

They were purposely ignoring him, all of them. That was obvious. It was some kind of joke, apparently. He was now the only person naked. The lights were so bright they might as well be on a beach. Goddamnit, this was like one of those dreams—you're naked in a department store or something.

He spotted some guy giving him the eye and flopped his dick at him. "Like to look at it, doncha?"

"It's pretty."

Oh, Jesus, and he'd been having so damn much fun. Normally, he had very little fun. Getting blown and then sick drunk in whorehouses was not fun; it was a job, servicing your urges.

The management was undoubtedly back there watching

the New York sophisticates having their vicious fun at his expense. *Lemme put one of you turds in a vampire lair sometime,* he thought, *see if you find that fun.* He glared around him. Female laughter bubbled up from somewhere in the crowd, was instantly extinguished.

He went over to the food table. Little dead eyes stared at him. But there was also caviar, and his guess was that this was the most expensive thing on the menu. So he cupped his hands and got a great big glob of it, causing all the cognoscenti to gasp. Then he threw the caviar at the damn one-way mirror.

"Gimme my damn clothes," he said quietly. "Or I'm gonna tear this place apart." He spoke with the kind of gentle intensity that suggested that immediate compliance was essential.

Leo, who had had enough of this jerk for this evening and the rest of what might be a very long life if things went her way, said, "I'll get your clothes."

"Wise girl."

The delay was because Miriam had decided that she didn't want him to get back into his rags. She wanted him properly dressed, so she had sent Luis up to the house to get some of John's clothes. He had just reappeared with a black silk Donna Karan suit and a bloodred shirt, also of silk. Miriam would not allow John's things to be put into storage, not even yet. Maybe Sarah would come up with some new process someday, that would work for him. His body was still fairly intact, after all. So his things waited for him.

"It's crazy to have this guy here," Leo said.

Sarah, who was counting again and could not interrupt herself, did no more than glare. Now that she shared a secret with Miri that the bitch wasn't party to, she felt better, less threatened.

Miriam put Paul's wallet in the breast pocket of the

superb jacket. The magnum, which was on her desk under some piles of money, stayed there.

"You're to bring him to my room," Miriam told Leo.

Leo knew that people who went in there did not come out. "Am I invited?"

"You are indeed," Sarah said.

A chair hit the one-way mirror, bouncing off with a distant thud. He was getting physical about his nudity.

Miriam shook her head. "My, my."

"He's out there naked in a fully dressed crowd," Sarah said. "I'd be pissed off, too."

Miriam chuckled. "Show him the club, Leo. Let him play with you a little. But don't you dare fuck him dry. Is that a promise?"

Leo came around behind the desk and kissed Miriam's cheek. Sarah couldn't watch it. She stared down at the magnum. She picked it up and pointed it at Leo. "Remember this," she said. "He's dangerous."

Another chair thudded into the window.

"Arrange to be at the door to my room with him in half an hour," Miriam said as Leo hurried out. Then she turned to Sarah, "Don't point guns at her."

"She's rude to you."

"She's as she is. Accept her."

"You want her instead of me!"

Miriam went close to Sarah, cradled her face in her hands. "Control yourself," she said, pressing harder, compressing the jaw and cheeks until the eyes almost popped out of the head. "Will you?"

Sarah nodded. She could not speak.

Miriam could crush a human skull. She pressed harder. "Are you certain?"

Sarah nodded again. Mucus began dribbling from her nose. Her feet stomped and scuffled, her hands came up and fluttered along Miriam's arms.

Miriam let her go. Sarah gagged, sucked air, pitched forward out of her chair. Then she came to her feet. Her cheeks were flaming.

"No jealousy," Miriam said.

Tears pouring from her eyes, Sarah threw herself against Miriam. "Please don't abandon me!"

Miriam had heard that cry from every one of them, and it went straight to her heart. They were tragic beings, her humans. She was ashamed of them. But she enjoyed them a great deal, and that, ultimately, was what mattered to her. Keepers caused human suffering. That was simply the nature of nature.

She kissed Sarah. "Better?"

"I'm sorry, Miri. It's just that you're so precious to me. I can't live without you."

"My love, I have a task of great importance that I need you to do." She held out a brass key. "This is the key to his hotel room." She tossed it onto the desk, told Sarah the address. "Go up there, take Bill or somebody with you. Go through the room, take every trace of him out with you. And especially, if you find a small, black book, very old—"

"He has a Book of Names?"

"If we're lucky."

Sarah was shocked. "What use would it be to him?"

"They can read Prime. Some of it."

Sarah was truly amazed. She had counted a hundred and eighty different symbols in a single glyph. It was the most complex written language by a factor of a thousand. Who could possibly manage to crack a code like that?

"You're sure of this?"

"I imagine they used National Security Agency cryptographers."

Sarah felt a coldness within her, as if her heart had been pierced with a knife of ice. "Your name is there. Your holdings. Oh, Miri!"

The Keepers were in terrible trouble if these people were able to read such records. "Where would he get a Book of Names? How?"

"When you get the book—if you do—bring it straight here."

"And if I don't?"

"Then we'll just have to get him to tell us where it is, won't we, dear?"

Sarah managed a smile. Sometimes Miri made them scream, which Sarah normally hated. She would not hate it if this man screamed.

"We'll make him tell us," she said. She put her arms around Miri. "Thank you for trusting me again."

"Now go, child. Go like the wind."

Paul pulled on the pants, got them sort of closed. "This guy must be thin as a rail," he said. He managed to get into the shoes, too, which were of leather so soft it made his skin crawl. Could these people have somehow gotten something from a vampire? From what he'd seen in Paris, the vampires were much more capable of mixing with humans than he'd believed. His sense of it was that the Asians were more ancient than the Europeans and far less able to be seen on the streets. Maybe the Americans were younger and more humanlike still. Hell, maybe they would even fit into a hip crowd like this.

He looked more carefully at the shoe. Gucci sure as hell didn't make them out of human skin, so that theory was out.

The clothes actually fit pretty well, although they seemed decades out of date. The jacket had a wide collar, and the trousers were subtly flared. They belonged to a man with big shoulders like Paul's, a tall man and a strong man. But a slimmer one.

He regarded himself in the mirror. "Jesus," he said, "I look like a million bucks."

Leo decided that she utterly loathed him. "You look just fabulous," she lied.

"Whose clothes are these, anyway?"

"A friend of ours. Listen, I've got an idea. The next set doesn't come up until after dinner. Want to see the rest of the club?"

A guided tour from this babe? "You better believe it."

She walked through another wall. Expecting to be blasted by music again, he followed her. But he was not blasted. In fact, he wasn't in a room at all. He was in a Japanese garden, outside— at least it seemed like outside. The sky was velvet swarming with stars, a sickle moon just turning yellow as it slid toward the horizon. Bamboo chimes made restful sounds; water hurried over stones. Crickets chirped; a bat whispered past his face. Here and there in the dark, he could see pale bodies. There were at least a dozen people here, all covered by black cloaks, lounging on benches or on the grass. A guy with glasses and an old-fashioned doctor's kit went among them like a waiter, discussing in quiet tones, then ministering to them out of his case.

Paul smelled opium . . . real good opium. He was already contact high and passive-smoke high, and maybe high on something he'd ingested in the food or those damn drinks he'd been given a million years ago. But he really loved opium, and it was one hard drug to come by these days. It took him back to quiet times in the Cambodian jungle, those magical times when they were more-or-less safe, and they could sweetly indulge.

They weren't outside, of course, not really. They were under a deep country "sky," and this was the middle of Manhattan. Leo took his hand, led him around the edge of the garden.

"Hey, wait, I could do some pipe."

"Um, if you stay in here, it's a thousand dollars an hour."

You could probably drop ten grand on this place in a single goddamn night. "Let's see the rest of it."

"This next room is rather unusual. But please remember, our credo is no limits and no restrictions."

"Sounds like fun." Paul followed her through another veil and into a completely mirrored foyer. There was a tunnel entrance. He hesitated. "Where does that go?"

"Just downstairs. And it only looks like a tunnel. There's a stairway when you get past the veil."

It was not easy to walk into what looked exactly like one of the Paris tunnels, but he followed her. He found himself in a stairway, dimly lit with recessed bulbs, its walls and ceiling black. The rubber treads on the steps gave it an institutional feel. He thought that it must be like this in certain prisons.

There was a thick iron door here. "What is this place?"

"We call it Foggy Bottom," she said with a laugh. "It's full of politicians." She drew the door open.

The first thing he saw was a red butt. Leonore went in, giving it a spank as she passed. "Thank you," a male voice said.

Paul followed her. "Should I? A guy?"

"He doesn't care."

Paul gave him a whack, and not a light one.

"Thank you, sir!"

Paul looked down, trying to see the face of the guy who was trussed up there.

"No, honey, we don't pry. Not in here."

But he had seen, and he knew the face. "Um, are these people all from Washington?"

"Washington, the Kremlin, Downing Street, the Vatican. You name it."

Not all the whipees were men. There was a woman hanging naked from the ceiling, with what looked like heavy chains hooked to her nipples. "Ouch!" Paul said to Leonore, who kept walking. Another woman was encased in spectacular bondage, tied up like some kind of a ball, with what looked like a pair of underpants stuffed in her mouth.

"My God, who's that?"

"A publishing executive on a guilt trip."

There was a guy tied to a pole being whipped by two other guys with thick, black paddles.

"More publishers?"

"Two congressmen kissing a senator's ass. They'll be taking their turns on the post later."

"You ever get a president in here?"

"What country?"

"U.S."

"Which one?"

"Well, how about Bush?"

"Which one?"

Okay, that question was answered. "How much for this room?"

"Oh, you can do this room on my nickel. I'll top you."

"In your dreams, sweetie. Not my *schtick*."

She shrugged. "You'd be surprised what it's like, getting topped really well. Your ego is, like, imploded. This whole club is about blowing the ego away. Every room does it, but differently."

"The Japanese garden?"

"The right kind of high, and you'll feel very close to heaven there."

"High is high."

"No way. Our dealer is an MD who not only deals, he designs. He's given all our customers physicals, he knows exactly what makes them tick. He's doing blood tests, prescribing, adjusting, all during the course of the evening. They are being taken so high they're gonna forget even their damn names."

"And then the music blows you wide open."

"You can get very close to God in here, mister. This place is sacred."

Hell called *sacred*—that was something he never thought he'd hear. "Can we go somewhere else?" This was not the part of the club for him. He wanted to do some pipe, or at least get another drink. There wasn't much second-hand smoke down here, and he was crashing.

This time they went up in an elevator so small that they were touching. He sprang up instantly. When the doors opened, he stayed like that, because this was a ballroom full of beautiful beds, and there were people openly making love on them.

A pair of singers, a lovely, tall girl and a young man who was even taller, stood together singing in voices so filled with gentleness that they might have been saints. He recognized "All Through the Night."

"O'er thy spirit gently stealing,
Visions of delight revealing,
Breathes a pure and holy feeling . . ."

There was a solemnity to this place that seemed at odds with what appeared to be an orgy in progress. Paul was a smart man, and he was well able to see the careful thought that had been put into all this. This room, for example, was about disconnecting sex from sin. No more need to hide.

Once in a while, he'd hit a house in Vientiane or Phnom Penh with a bunch of guys, and it would develop into pretty much of an orgy. It was fun but it was ugly, and you felt dirty afterward. In this room the lack of shame brought with it a sense of purity. Thirty or forty human beings were enjoying one another in all kinds of intimate ways, doing everything you could imagine with each other. Their faces glowed with lust, they sweated. But it was all so joyous.

Maybe Leo was right, maybe there was something kind of sacred here.

Seeing all these bodies entwined, he was starting to look at Leo real hard. But she probably outclassed him like everybody else in this place . . . except for the morons in the dungeon. They were pols, and that was sorta his world. But he could not relate to getting whipped. He got punished plenty without any assistance. The knife wound was still healing good, for example, but he sure as hell knew it was there if he tried to raise the arm too high.

Leo was terrific looking—clean as a whistle and sexy as hell. He could get into her in a second, *way* into her. His equipment had been considered pretty sensational by some. Maybe she'd like a little taste.

He decided to give it a try. "Look, I'd like—" She rested her eyes on him, which instantly shut him up. "Let's go downstairs," he said, his voice husky with embarrassment. He couldn't proposition her in here, for Chrissakes. He was no damn angel; he needed his privacy.

She strolled out into the foyer. He wasn't quite sure where she was coming from, and he didn't want to insult anybody. But he had to get it on somehow. He was human. He couldn't just be left to Sally Five himself in his hotel room, not after all he'd seen and felt here tonight. He wanted to be loved, too. But since that didn't seem likely to happen to him, maybe she'd just give him a break, here.

"I think you're really—I mean, I could sure as hell give you a nice time. If you need a tip—if that's the drill—"

"I want to show you a very special space now," she said. She took his hand.

How anything could possibly top what he had seen so far, he could not imagine. This wasn't just a place of pleasure. It was a whole new approach to pleasure, as something that did not need to be hidden and wasn't a sin. Even the ones in the dungeon were learning that lesson, in their own peculiar way.

The people who could come here were immensely privileged. All of his life, he had thought that the social barriers by which we live were a tragedy. Miriam Blaylock, whom he viewed now as something of a young genius, was challenging those barriers here, and he was beginning to decide that she was succeeding.

They went down a back stairway, steel stairs in a fluorescent-lit well. There were doors with Exit signs all over the place and a hose station on every landing. He'd also noticed that the place was sprinklered and smoke-alarmed. "I've never seen so much safety equipment."

"We're very careful. You don't want the least feeling of danger."

"I've never felt so safe in my life."

She squeezed his hand.

"Look," he said, "I'm sorry if I embarrassed you. Or insulted. I just—I find you, you know, really, really attractive."

"I'm flattered."

They came to the bottom of the stairs, where there was a door with a breakaway bar that looked as if it must lead into an alley. A horrible thought crossed his mind. "I'm not getting the boot, here, I hope?"

She opened the door. There was a tiny chamber entirely made of mirrors. When he went in, there were Pauls staring at him from every direction, all of them disappearing into an infinity of repetitions. It was a sort of visual echo. "Hey, this is—"

"Have a fabulous time." She slammed the door, and he found himself alone in the small space. He turned around immediately, but saw only more mirrors and could not find the door.

Above all things, he hated confinement. But this was a place of pleasure. He was getting the ride of a lifetime for a poor bastard like him. He was not going to ruin it by freaking out.

So he wouldn't freak out, but the guy looking back at him out of all these mirrors, he looked like he would. Look at the eyes, look at all that pain. Then he thought he saw another face. He saw—Jesus God, he'd been a fool to come here! It was one of them, watching him through the damn mirror. He went for the gun that wasn't there, then lashed out. His fist smashed into the mirror. The room shook, he felt a blast of pain up his hurt arm . . . but the mirror did not crack.

There was a voice then, very soft, "Turn right and walk toward me."

He turned right. There was nobody to walk toward but his own reflection.

"Come on."

He took a step, feeling ahead—and felt air. This mirror was another one of the veils.

Was he walking into whatever had swallowed Ellen Wunderling? Some kind of damn superexclusive vampire lair? Oh, hell, if he was, he'd at least take a few with him.

He stepped into the most palatial bedroom he had ever seen. On the bed sat Miriam. She was playing the flute, and doing it with exquisite skill. He gaped at her, at the tall bed she was in, at the phenomenal tapestries on the walls.

There was a window, and outside he could see smiling green fields with people working in them, men with brown tunics and caps. A horseman rode along a path, a man dressed in the fabulous clothes of the distant past.

She stopped playing long enough to say, "It's a TV screen."

But it was very well done. The image was so clear that it looked more like a window than a window.

There was a chair across from the bed, big, carved, almost a throne. He sat in it. He watched Miriam Blaylock play, watched and listened. This was one talented lady. What the Veils was about was limitless wealth and the power of human genius. If you had the cash, the Veils could rebuild your soul.

Or if you were a damn dogface on a lucky streak, like yours truly.

Miriam was wearing a white nightgown cinched just under her breasts with a pink ribbon. He thought, *I have never been in such a wonderful place with such a wonderful person before, and I think I'm about to get laid.*

Christ almighty. Now, he had to prepare himself. When she was finished with that sweet prelude, she was going to raise her eyes, and he was going to see once again her angelic and spectacularly sexy face. He was already as hard as iron. The issue was, how did he do it, if indeed he was to be afforded that privilege, without wadding her on stroke two?

The music came to an end. She put down the flute.

When he applauded softly, she laughed. "I was just fooling around."

"You fooled around with the *Prelude to the Afternoon of a Faun* better than anybody I've ever heard. Better than Galway."

"I adore James."

"You know him?"

"We've played together."

"Okay."

Silence fell. He didn't know what to do next, what to say. He was way out of his class; that was the truth of it. He looked up at the ceiling, which was painted with a night sky, dark blue with gold-leaf stars and a moon that looked more like it had a snake in it than a man. The constellations were strangely off, too.

"That's an antique ceiling. Do you like it?"

"Oh, yeah. How old is it?"

She got off the bed and came over and sat on the arm of the chair. "It's from Atlantis."

"Okay," he said again, and instantly felt like a total jerk. What was he, a stroke victim, here? Couldn't he come up with something a little funny at least, in response to a funny remark from her?

"Okay what?"

"Sorry, I'm just—well—I gotta be honest. I'm just totally overwhelmed, here. Your club—I mean, Jesus. I admit to feeling just a little outclassed."

She leaned down and grasped him through the silk pants.

There was no underwear involved in this outfit, so it was a pretty intimate contact. The pleasure was intense.

"You need to cool down a little," she said.

"I need to cool down," he repeated.

She got up and went over to a big chest. It was made of dark wood, carved with writhing snakes. She opened it and he was amazed to see her bring out an opium rig with two of the most magnificent ivory pipes he'd ever seen. "You said you'd like a pipe. I think it'll help a lot." She stopped, though, then cocked her head, as if considering something that was a little new to her. "We're not against drugs, are we, Mr. CIA man?"

"Nah, the Company's a big importer. Anyway, I been doin' shit since 'Nam. I'm in an extreme business. You can't handle it without extreme relaxation. You gotta compensate."

She gave him a pipe, started to prepare it for him.

"There's that antique lighter again. Lady, you gotta ditch that thing; you're gonna burn up."

She glanced at him in a way that kind of shook him up. Was it a cold glance? Or hate? Jesus, if—

But then she smiled, and it was just so sweet that he could not believe that she was anything except very charmed by him.

He took a long pull and in a second was rewarded with good vapor. It seeped through him like blood in a sponge. It was very good vapor.

She lit her own pipe, then went to the bed and lay back, cradling it. He did the same, lying face-to-face with her. As he smoked, he felt his erection calming down. That was good. The opium would make the evening last.

She kissed him on the neck, just a peck, then giggled. He kissed her back, right on the mouth, hard and long.

After that she didn't giggle again.

SEVENTEEN

Blood Child

Miriam was careful with his kiss. She was not sure how much Keeper anatomy he knew, and until she was, she would take no chances touching his tongue with her own. Afterward, he gazed at her with what she thought were the saddest eyes she had ever seen.

Now, they were smoking together. She was handling the pipes.

He was still devouring her with his eyes, and there was in the back of her mind the thought that he might have some level of recognition.

She gave him a smile calculated to seem shy, a little surprised.

He sighed, smoked, closed his eyes.

She removed the pipes after a few more minutes. She wanted him calm, but not in a stupor. Two pipes of this opium would put a human being in one, no matter how strong he was.

"Nobody's interested in opium anymore," he said, lounging back on the bed. "I mean, I picked up on it in the jungles of Cambodia. Primitive place."

"My opium is grown on a Crown estate in Myanmar, processed in a facility built for the CIA in 1952. Some say it's the very best pipe on earth. Did you know Maurice McClellan? He was in charge of that operation for CIA."

"I knew Maurice."

Then he was suddenly watching her with eyes as hard and cold as black diamonds. She was surprised—stunned, in fact—to realize that she'd just now made a mistake. If she were really in her early twenties, Maurice would have died when she was just a child.

"He was a friend of my father's," she said, rolling over on her back and putting her hands behind her head to telegraph how complete was her ease. "He introduced him to Prince Philip."

"Yeah, that'd be Maurice. He traveled in pretty rarefied circles."

"You know what we should do?" she said.

"What?"

"We should get you more comfortable."

"This is a boss suit. I like the way it feels."

"It's club wear. When somebody comes in—"

"Dressed like a bum, like me."

"You were confusing my guests. They thought you were some kind of a cop."

"Do you get cops around here?"

"Sure. The precinct's just around the corner."

"I noticed."

"It's not a problem." Not when fifty thousand dollars a week was being sent over there and half the powerful people in the city were making sure that this particular block just plain was not patrolled.

She slid her hands under his shirt. He blinked his eyes. He got so hard so fast that there was a hissing sound as his organ slid against the silk of his trousers. As she unbuttoned the shirt, she wondered how much blood he could lose without dying. He was very strong. He'd probably last and last.

Once he was well trussed up, her plan was to remove all her makeup, to let him know that he had been captured by a Keeper. Then she would prick a tiny hole in his neck and use him as a teaching tool, letting Leo take him by small sips.

She ran her hands along his shoulders, pushed back the shirt. "You're *so strong*," she breathed.

"I work out."

"What do you press?"

"Oh, two hundred. Two-twenty if I'm healthy."

"You're unhealthy?"

"I tend to get wasted." He nodded toward the pipes. "That, booze, girls. I've lived in Asia too long, done too much—too much work."

"What is your work?"

"Classified."

She laid her head against his chest, drew herself, catlike, close to him. "That's exciting."

"What do you think I do? What's your guess?"

"You—let me see—you're *very* strong. But you're also smart." She whispered. "You're a government assassin."

He chuckled. "You kept my gun."

"You can't bring a gun in here. It's against the law."

"I thought the law didn't apply to you."

"My law."

"How did you get so rich?"

"My great-great-great-great—let's see, five greats—one more—great-grandfather was Lord Baltimore. He owned Maryland."

"That'll do it. But I still want my gun back."

"When you leave."

For a moment, he looked, she thought, kind of like a wild animal. He was hair-trigger; she knew that. Up close like this, he seemed even more dangerous.

She stretched, lying half in his lap and half on the bed. When she stopped, the edge of her hand was lying against his erection. She said, "Uh-oh." Then, "Can I be a bad girl?"

"Be a bad girl."

Very lightly, she touched it. Then she snatched her hand away. "Oh, it's *huge!*"

He swallowed. He was trembling a little.

She felt more intimately. "It can't be as big as it feels."

"Have a look," he whispered.

"Shall I?"

He was too big around the waist for the pants, so they were only three-quarters zipped. She opened them. He came out, bobbing, the glans gleaming in the soft light.

He *was* huge. She pressed into the tender glans with a fingernail, then held the enormous thing in both of her hands. She drew off the pants. He shuffled out of the shirt.

She had not seen a male so beautiful in years. His muscles were fabulous, his skin lustrous. His face was purest masculine poetry, chiseled and hard, but with the complex, haunted eyes of somebody who had led a dangerous and uncertain life.

Whatever, he was a lovely specimen and he was going to make a sumptuous meal. She was actually a little jealous of Leo. What a great first supper!

A few minutes before he was brought in, she had gone down and checked the furnace next door. All was in order. Under the bed was the black overnight case that she would carry his remnant in.

But all that was for later. Until Sarah returned, she would continue to play with him. She needed that book. If Sarah did not find it, then this creature would discover that Foggy Bottom could be used for more than just games. There were some very serious implements there, and she knew just exactly how to apply them.

She stroked his chest, made a ring around one of his nipples with her finger. She touched the puckered wound on his shoulder. "This hurt?"

"A little. It's healing."

She remembered how good it had felt, seeing that knife dig in. If there had been a little more room for her backhand, she would have sliced the arm off.

"What happened?"

"A client became upset."

"Very upset."

"Very."

She kissed the corner of his mouth, but drew aside when he tried to kiss her back.

"You know, Miriam, I have to be honest with you. This is the nicest night of my life." He looked her up and down. She was still wearing her sheer nightgown. "You are—oh, gosh— so much more than you seem. I mean, please don't take this wrong, but you're just a kid, and this place is really deep, here. That girl that took me around—she said it was sacred and I thought she was a complete moron at first. But I started realizing what you were doing. And I want you to know this—I agree with it."

"Thank you."

"You came up with the whole concept?"

"Yes." She took his hands to her bodice, put the ribbons in his fingers. Then she drew his hands slowly apart. As she did so, the ribbon came away and the gown fell down her shoulders like drifting smoke.

"Oh, my," he said. Her breasts were gracefully full, curved just right to fit the cup of the hand. He raised his hands. But he dared not touch. They were like some kind of perfect art, a porcelain dream.

She took his hands to them. When they lay in his rough palms, the nipples became erect. Gooseflesh dusted the pink areolas.

"Oh, Lord," he said, watching this. He bent to her, laid his lips on that sweet skin of hers. Up close it had the texture of a child's, absolutely smooth, as if life had not yet touched it.

Christ, he ought to ask for her driver's license. But he wouldn't, because if this was a minor, then God had made this kid to boogie and he was sorry, but she was gonna boogie tonight.

Her lips hung slack in a way that said she was real interested and real ready. He kissed her, which was awful nice. But he was careful, because he had a thing about him that had not always gone down with women, although the whores pretended to love it, of course. His tongue was kind of—well, rough. No other way to put it. He had a cat tongue. He went deeper, though. Couldn't help it. The kiss itself was luring him, so sweet was her mouth. He just loved kissing this woman. Oh, wasn't she a *woman?* Nice!

He wanted to touch his tongue to hers, but she didn't seem to have one. It was way back in there. 'Course it was. She was probably scared to death.

But then he did, and when he did, she arched her back and cried out so loud it broke the kiss.

"Sorry!"

She threw her arms around him and latched onto him with her legs. She kissed him and kissed him, and he thrust his tongue into her mouth and her groaning and crying made him wild for her. She loved it; she loved the way he was.

She was haunted by how much he reminded her of Eumenes, who had been not only her husband, but her only Keeper lover. Power like this was something she had not tasted in eons. He was like the roaring oceans of the world, the flames of the stars, a tornado, a typhoon.

She locked her lips to his and opened her mouth to him, and he thrust in and rested in the kiss. Even though he had not yet entered her, she came to climax, came again and again beneath his sweating, eager body.

She looked at him, drinking him with her eyes. Never had there been a man so beautiful, never so filled with raging sexuality, never so—so—there were no words to describe it. No words.

They rolled and he was under her. The opium had done perfectly: he was ready, but he wasn't going to explode.

He let her sit on him, felt her take his penis in her two hands. Her cheeks flushed as she stroked it, loved it, kissed it, and licked it. It wasn't human, it couldn't be—because it was going to fit her and they did not fit her. They were wasted, small creatures in their sex, not like a real man, a Keeper man.

He was—but this was impossible. They didn't interbreed. She put that stupid idea right out of her head. He was a lucky accident, is what he was and that was *all* he was.

She wanted to taste of him. She wanted to know his every intimate truth. He excited her, truly, despite the hate that flapped in her heart.

"Hey," he said, lifting his head and kissing her hard. "You've got a tongue like mine. We're two cats."

It was true, and this was getting very strange very fast. "We're made for each other," she said carefully.

He slid to come from beneath her. She knew what he wanted and responded instantly, with delight. She was *never* on the bottom, but with him yes. Yes. She belonged under him. It felt meant to be. She shifted her weight.

His huge form dominated her. Gazing into his eyes, she spread her legs.

"Okay, baby," he said, "this one belongs to *me*." On that word he pushed into her.

The world turned black. Then a dam burst. Thunder rumbled in her head. Thrusting at him, she screamed out his name, "*Paul, Paul, Paul!*" as he pumped deep and withdrew, pumped deeper and harder, lingered then drew back, thrust and pumped, thrust and pumped.

It was as if she had become a single, blazing point of pure pleasure that was racing out through the universe at a million times the speed of light.

Then he rested upon her, and the feel of his surprisingly great weight on her body was the most wonderfully natural feeling in the world. He felt so much like Eumenes it almost broke her heart.

His loins surged, and the pleasure became a fiery comet that went straight through her. He slid himself almost all the way out, then plunged in again. He held her down, and she enjoyed the illusion of being helpless—oh, for the first time in years and years and years—and it was just so damned awfully wonderful. It wasn't scary—or it was, but that was part of the enjoyment. He was slow with her, and precise with her, sliding in and out, in and out while she shook her head from side to side and arched her back and yammered his lovely name.

It was *just* like being under Eumenes, having all her power stripped away by his greater power, and being free in bondage to him at last.

While he thrust, Paul drank her with his eyes. Not only did she look wonderful and taste fabulous and feel great to touch and hold, she had a very special instrument down there. This lady could use those muscles, yes, she could, to kiss the shaft and compress the tip in ways that not even the most skilled whores of Bangkok or Seoul or H.K. could even dream about.

Oh, my stars and bars, thank God for that pipe, he thought, *or I would've come and been done in the middle of stroke one.*

As it was, he went slow and careful while she kissed his chest and bit his hairs and licked his nipples. She cried out, she trembled like a branch in a storm, she pumped while he pumped, faster now, yelling, grasping his buttocks, pulling and pushing him. He was riding this filly, for sure; he was bigger than he'd ever been, and it felt better than it ever had.

Miriam was screaming, her eyes frantic and amazed.

She shrieked; she bellowed.

This was a damned thing, a very damned, damned thing! Because she was feeling a fire blazing inside her, and she knew what that fire was.

No Keeper woman who had felt it ever forgot it, the alarming, painful, delicious heat that told her she was about to conceive. But her egg wouldn't drop for a human! And it mustn't!

No, no that must not—not—

But the process went on, and she went helpless with it, a speck of a woman lost in a restless, living ocean. He was the storms above; he was the lightning striking her tortured waves.

The lightning, it seemed to her, was alive. And if so, then—well, then he was fertile!

Oh, stars, what was happening?

She had never dreamed that any human male would trigger this response in her body. It was her egg, her last egg, and it was moving within her, she could feel the searing delight of its journey.

She had not had a Keeper man in millennia, but she had wanted one always, and now suddenly this enormous body surging above her—that dear, powerful face, those driven eyes—this was a Keeper!

Paul was pouring with sweat, his thighs working, his every muscle singing with the amazing pleasure of this long, long session. Every thrust touched the shivery edge of climax; then as he pulled back, she loosened her muscles and they started again.

He'd never been in a state of pleasure this intense for this long, and things were happening to him that had never happened before. His heart was thundering harder than he could ever remember. Even his skin was tingling with pleasure, especially where it was in contact with her. Electricity—real, humming juice—seemed to be passing between them.

Again he thrust into her. Then he paused, drinking in her perfect flower of a face, her lustrous, joyous eyes.

She screamed. She had screamed a lot for Paul, but she *really* screamed now. She could feel the egg. Definitely. It hung in her, touching the mother lode of nerve endings, and where that egg touched that womb, a million dancing needles of sheer, tickling, joy sent their prickles marching out through her every sizzling nerve.

Paul was on fire with the sweet fire of the angels. Look at her pure, dear face—she *was* an angel! Oh, look at those eyes, those gray pools of innocence—she was the maid of Solomon's fancy. He pressed himself hard against her, thrust harder, and then as if molten gold were speeding in his shaft, he came roaring and yelling and laughing; he came as he had never come before or thought you ever could come. He came in pleasure and in love, in dear *love*, which had caught his soul afire.

She felt his semen speeding into her like a great flaming fire, a sweet sun—and she knew that it washed the egg, and it went screaming through the wall of the egg and sped down to the center, where slept the waiting shadow.

She threw her pelvis forward and arched her back, and they hammered at each other, squeezing the last demanded juice of the pomegranate, the last starry flower.

A burning wave snatched Miriam up and away, filling her with wonderful fire, shocking her more than she had been shocked since the pyramids reflected the sun, since she had opened her eyes to the eyes of her Eumenes and managed to murmur to him, "It feels like a boy."

Paul collapsed onto her chest, and they both burst into tears like two scared schoolkids.

Miriam Blaylock and Paul Ward had just conceived.

She was crying for the little baby that lay now within her, its cells already waking up. She was crying for she had no idea what that baby would *be*—Keeper, human, alive, dead, deformed—only that it was her second and it was her last.

"I love you," he said, "oh, my God in heaven, I love you!"

She looked scared, and he touched her dear eyes to wipe away the tears.

"Miriam," he said. He suddenly felt awful. "Please never make me leave you."

She gazed at him, her eyes slow and contented. "I adore you," she said, and there was such reverence in her tone that he wanted to cry. Maybe somebody would want a broke-down old CIA officer after all. And maybe that somebody would be this wonderful, special girl.

Miriam slid out from under him and drew his head down

into her lap. With loving eyes, she gazed at him. Then she bent closer, kissing the tip of his nose and then his lips, and then the pulsing vein in the curve of his neck. She lay her mouth there for a moment, then withdrew.

Paul felt her sucking his skin a little. It was a nice sensation.

Suddenly he jumped away from her.

There, across the room, stood the woman from the limo, the woman who had blown him on the dance floor.

Miriam got up, went to her, and took her hands. Sarah nodded her head, and Miriam burst out laughing. Her laughter pealed out again and again, and it was so pretty and so full of fun that he started laughing, too.

"How long have you been in here?" Paul asked her.

"Since you started."

"You sure got an eyeful."

Sarah shrugged.

"May I know your name?"

"Sarah." She nodded toward Miriam. "I do her books."

"You let your accountant in here when you're—" He chuckled. "To each his own, I guess."

"It was lovely," Sarah said. "You're a very lovely man."

The look in her eyes, though, did not suggest that she was pleased with what she had seen. In fact, there was something real on edge about this lady.

Then another one came in through the wall.

"Oh, hey," Paul said as the girl who'd shown him the club appeared. He got his pants on. Not that one more naked male would matter to this crew.

Then he saw that she was blushing like a tomato. She had a funny little silver thing in her hand. A strange knife.

"What's that?"

It disappeared into her jeans. "Sorry, Miriam!"

Miriam went to her. "This is Leo. The three of us run this club together. Leo's the granddaughter of General Patton."

"He was my mother's cousin."

He threw on the shirt, started buttoning it. "General Patton, Lord Baltimore, Morrie McClellan, and Prince Philip. Not to mention Ben Stiller, who was in your place earlier. Lotta names to drop."

"Lord who?" Sarah asked.

Miriam smiled at her in a way that told Paul she was being made to shut up. Which meant that Miriam's story about Lord Baltimore was a lie. Which meant that she felt a need to conceal the origin of her wealth. Interesting.

"We're going home," Miriam said, her voice rippling.

"We are?" Leo's eyes flickered toward Paul.

"I'm in love," Miriam shouted. She raced back to the bed, threw herself at Paul, kissed him hard, then flounced back on the bed, pulling him with her. She said, "He's the best lover in the world." Then she was convulsed with laughter, peeking out from beside his big chest at Sarah and Leo. "Am I being naughty?" she chirped.

"Naughty is not the word," Sarah purred.

"What do I do?" Leo asked.

Paul said, "I think we fell in love."

Sarah suddenly smiled. "I'm so glad." Then she said to Miriam, "Miri, it's four. Can I let the staff go?"

"Is the house clear?"

"Ready for the nighthawks."

Miriam lay back in his lap, her hands folded behind her head. "Leo, tell Luis to get the car ready." She gazed up at Paul. "I'm bringin' my baby back home."

The two women went out without a word.

"They seem kind of upset."

"Pets don't like surprises."

"Am I a pet?"

"You, my dear, are a great big beautiful *man!*"

They got dressed and went out of the little room, then through the kitchen to the rear of the club. The Bentley limousine he'd seen on Houston Street stood there gleaming in the predawn glow.

He got in, settling into the plush cushions.

"Want a drink?" Miriam asked brightly.

Sarah and Leo came in.

"You know what I'd like? Have you got a good cigar? After lovemaking like that, nothing in the world would be as nice as a really fine cigar."

Leo grunted with barely concealed disgust.

"We have some Cohiba Piramides in the club," Sarah said in a dull voice. "But it's awfully confined for you to smoke a cigar here."

"Luis," Miriam called, "go back in and get my lover some cigars."

Luis brought them out and held open the humidor.

"I was looking for a Macanudo, maybe," Paul said.

"Cohibas are a bit better," Leo replied, unable to conceal a sneer.

"We'll all smoke," Miriam snapped, handing cigars to Sarah and Leo. "Self-defense, Sarah! Let me get my hand grenade—Paul says my lighter is dangerous, did I tell you? Hadn't that ever occurred to you, Sarah?"

"I'm sorry, Miri, it hadn't."

"Well, he's going to get me a new one. He says we wouldn't want my pretty face to get burned, would we?" She cut and lit a cigar and handed it to Paul.

Paul took a drag of a smoke that was hard but incredibly rich, and he knew that it was true, that this cigar was better than a Macanudo. Way better, in fact.

Miriam offered one to Sarah, who waved it away. She pressed it on her.

"Look," Sarah said, "I don't want to!"

"Smoke!"

Paul was fascinated. What kind of accountant took orders like that? Miriam treated Sarah more like some kind of a slave.

Sarah took the cigar. Leo lit up in a hurry. In the front, Luis lit up. Only Miriam didn't smoke. She sat glaring at Sarah. Whatever was going on between those two, Paul thought, they were absolutely furious with each other.

There was some cognac in the car, and Paul had a snifter with his cigar. It was as soft as a pillow, this brandy, but full of flavor. He didn't bother to ask how old it was. Probably came straight out of Napoleon's hip flask.

He allowed himself to imagine that what had come between him and Miriam might be serious.

"Where is home, by the way?"

"I have a beautiful home. You're going to just love it. And if you *don't*, then we are going to change it so you do. Isn't that right, girls?"

"Yes, Miri," Sarah said, tears in the corners of her eyes. Paul felt sorry for her. Knowing Miriam, she'd been bedding this sweet little thing. They could have been serious lovers. And then all of a sudden, here comes this guy, and bang, Sarah's strictly backseat.

Paul wanted to kiss Miriam again. He wanted to be in her again, to go in there and just live in there. That was his damn wheelhouse from now on, that fabulous twat of hers. What a creature. What a damn night.

It got quiet in the car. Leo and Sarah were staring daggers at Miriam. They looked as if they wanted to beat her up, as a matter of fact.

Well, let 'em try, Paul thought. She was his girl now and nothing anybody could say, nothing they could do, could change that. Except—he was aware that it was a little dangerous to say you'd fallen in love forever because of a single great roll in the hay.

But, hey, there was something *there,* something damned wonderful and serious. It had happened. It damn well *had.*

He watched Sarah puff a little on her cigar, then closed his eyes and sipped some more cognac.

This was the life, despite the fact that all the exercise had made his shoulder start to sing. He'd like a couple of naproxen or something. No more opium. He'd done his share of drugs for the night.

He thought of his seven grand at the Terminal Hotel. If he didn't show up sometime tomorrow, they'd be sure to toss the room. Probably they already had. That would mean the Book of Names was gone. Also the seven grand. Everybody knew to toss the bedsprings if you were tossing a room.

So, what did that mean to him, now that he was on the lam? Loss of the seven grand would be tragic. As for the Book of Names, he wasn't sure if he was going to continue in that line. Maybe he'd done enough killing. He could write a pretty decent report, so maybe he'd interview at *The New York Times.* They hired out of CIA all the time . . . but mostly from the analytical divisions, not from the tough guys.

They arrived on no less than Sutton Place and pulled up—guess where—in front of the prettiest house on the whole block.

"Man," Paul said as he got out. This was way far away

from his side of the tracks. He looked up at the imposing façade. It looked damn old, but it was perfectly kept.

Miriam hurried up the steps and threw the door open. Paul joined her. "I oughta pick you up and carry you across the threshold," he said.

"Welcome to my abode. Girls, he wants some breakfast! Caviar and eggs! Champers!"

Sarah and Leonore marched off into the back of the house.

"I don't think they like me too much."

"They'll get used to you. In fact, I have a prediction. Sarah is going to totally change her opinion of you."

Paul had big plans for bedtime, which came after a breakfast where Miriam picked and drank champagne, and he thought he must have consumed sixteen eggs at least. Sarah served table, and Leonore cooked. Sarah was awful pretty when she was mad.

Paul smoked another of the cigars in the big library. He saw all kinds of amazing books. There were also locked bookcases with really ancient looking black books in them, their spines unmarked. There were even scroll boxes, smelling of beeswax. He drew a scroll partly out, but it was real old and he was afraid to unroll it for fear he'd crack the parchment and cost her a cool million or something.

He would not have been surprised to find a Gutenberg Bible in here. What he did discover was to him equally amazing—a portfolio containing an original collection of opera libretti. These were not simply early printed copies. They were the manuscript scores.

Here was *Rigoletto* in what was apparently Verdi's own hurried scrawl. Reverently, he drew the score out. Miriam came up behind him so quietly that he was startled.

She laid a delicate hand on his shoulder. "You take an interest in opera?"

"A great interest."

She took the score and walked through to another wonderful room. The wide parquet floor was covered with a Persian rug—the real thing, undoubtedly. But Paul's attention was taken by the Steinway, a concert grand set in an alcove all its own. The windows that framed it appeared to be Tiffany stained-glass.

The sun was rising, spreading golden light across the rich mahogany top of the piano. On it stood a vase that was probably an ancient Greek original. Sarah was quietly filling it with flowers from a garden that could be seen beyond the windows, just beginning to glow with the light of morning.

Miriam opened the piano. She toyed with the keys for a moment, then riffled in the score. "Sarah," she said, "would you?"

Sarah sat down at the piano. Suddenly she looked up at Paul. She held out her hands. "These belong to a surgeon," she said.

What was she getting at?

She trilled up and down the scales, shaking her head in the shafts of sunlight, so that her locks shot red-brown sparks.

Miriam set the score before her, and Sarah began to play, and quite well. It took Paul a moment to recognize "Caro Nome," and then Miriam was singing it, one of the greatest homages to the female soul that had ever been written. That she was singing it directly from the hand of its author made the experience all the more haunting.

Leo came in and listened, wiping her hands on her apron and blowing a curl out of her eyes.

When the song came to an end, Paul wanted to hold

Miriam, to let her know again how he felt. They had just had profound sex together, and he was in profound love. It sounded stupid, he knew that, and he couldn't actually *say* it. He'd only known her for a few hours, for the love of Christ.

She threw back her head and sang at the top of her lungs, "I'm in love, I'm in love, I'm in love with a wonderful guy!" She danced him round and round the room.

At noon she was still showing him her collections, her poetry—she had the original folio manuscript of John Keats's "Lamia," and Tennyson's "Tithonus," among many other wonders.

Paul struggled to show interest, but he had been asleep in the chair where he sat for at least a full minute when she shook his shoulder.

"Come on," she whispered in his ear, "you need a cuddle."

She took him upstairs, then, and they stripped in the sumptuous bedroom. She dropped her clothes to the floor for Leo to run around picking up. He was afraid to do the same, and put his on the edge of a little daybed.

Sarah drew them a bath in a huge onyx tub that must have, in itself, cost a million dollars. In fact, it was the damnedest tub he'd ever seen—beautiful, glowing stone embedded with gold nymphs and satyrs and sea creatures.

It reminded him of something you might find in a palace. It had an ancient Roman look to it. The only place he had ever seen anything carved with such perfection, however, was in the King's Chamber of the Great Pyramid. The sarcophagus there looked a little like this tub.

Sarah wore a green dress with a maid's cap and a white apron. Between her soft good looks and Miriam's wondrous, long-legged nudity, Paul was damn well ready to go again. Sarah gave him a playful tweak as he stepped into the tub.

"Don't misfire his cannon." Miriam laughed as she joined him. Sarah washed their hair and their backs with fragrant soap. She washed his face, which was an incredibly intimate experience. Being naked with Miriam would mean being naked with her friends, apparently. Hell, the more the merrier.

Here in this bathtub with these amazing people around him, he definitely decided that his past was no longer his problem. He told himself that this decision was now and forever. The world had survived a long time with vampires hiding in its shadows.

From this moment on, he had a new job: getting Miriam to marry him.

He lounged back, eyes closed, as Sarah's fingers delicately massaged his cheeks and softly caressed his forehead. Miriam's toes appeared between his legs, pressing and touching.

Yeah, it was heaven. The crusty old tough guy had found one hell of a pasture, looked like. He thought—hoped—that he was presently feeling the tiredness and disappointment of a lifetime, and maybe even its many, many sins, slipping away into the past and welcome forgetfulness, being cleansed away by the ministry of angels.

Then he noticed Leo. She had come in quietly. She sat on the john with her legs crossed, smoking and watching him. He saw the strange little knife again. It was outlined in the pocket of her very tight jeans.

Their eyes met. She smiled.

EIGHTEEN

Careless Love

Miriam and Sarah stood hand in hand looking at the magnificent human specimen lying asleep on the bed.

"He's in hog heaven," Sarah said.

"He is."

Leo took out the fleam. She moved toward the bed, then looked to Miriam, her face questioning.

"Leo, we're not going to do him."

"But I feel—" She shuddered. "We have to."

"She's right, Miri. Think what he's seen. Think who he is!"

Paul stirred, throwing a large hand out from under the covers. "Miri . . ."

Miriam went to the bedside and knelt and kissed the hand. "I'm here, my love."

The hand reached out, stroked her cheek. "Mmm . . ."

She slid in beside him.

When Sarah saw the tenderness in Miriam's eyes, she was horrified. What had happened to her? Had she gone insane? This was the most foolhardy thing she had ever done.

"Leo," Sarah said, "do it."

Leo looked at the fleam. "H-how?"

Miriam's head came out of the covers. She raised herself

up. She whispered, her mouth close to Sarah's ear. "I think I'm pregnant."

Sarah stepped back, for a moment too surprised even to respond. She was a scientist and doctor who'd had twenty years to study every aspect of Miri's body. A limitless budget had made the lab in the basement a wonder of science, equipped with every conceivable instrument, including many that Sarah had designed herself and had built by the finest medical engineering establishments in the world.

Sarah knew, therefore, that this "pregnancy" was a tragic fantasy. It must mean—could only mean—that Miri's last egg had dropped. She was not pregnant; she just wanted to be. She could not become pregnant by a human being. All that had really happened was that Miriam Blaylock had lost her last chance to bear a child.

Sarah rushed into her and Miri's sunroom, where they had their private little place together. Miri sewed for a hobby, using the intricate stitches taught her by her mother, producing the exquisite leatherwork of the Keepers. On the floor where Sarah had laid it, beside a couple of ancient half-opened scrolls, was the Book of Names that so much blood, human and Keeper, had been shed over in Paris.

Sarah threw herself down on her daybed and let the bitterness and the sorrow that had built up over the last terrible hours flood out of her in the form of huge, gasping sobs. Sometimes Sarah hated Miri, but mostly she loved her, and especially when she was suffering and vulnerable, as she most certainly was now.

It would fall to Sarah to examine her in the stirrups, as she had done so often, and to give her the news that would break her heart. In the end, Miri would come back to her, turning as always to Sarah's enfolding arms for comfort. Sarah would give her what comfort she could, but how can you relieve the sorrow of a woman who has just learned that she has lost her last chance for a baby?

And worse, by so doing she had exposed herself and her household to mortal danger. She was in there alone with that evil creature—how could she *be* so heedless?

There were tender sounds coming from the bedroom, sounds of lovemaking. Sarah went to the door and signaled Leo, who was standing by helplessly and self-consciously.

"Sarah, I feel dreadful!"

"I know, dear." As much as she detested this foolish girl, she could only sympathize with her now. She had lived this suffering.

"I've got to have blood." She gave Sarah a desperate glance. "I tried to eat some of the omelet I made him, but it was revolting, it tasted like wet paper." She threw her arms around Sarah. "He smells good. He smells like—like—"

"Food."

"What have I done, Sarah, what have I done to myself?"

Sarah could not answer her. There were no words to describe the ruin of a soul. But she held her, she kissed her soft hair. "We'll hunt you up a meal. Like that old woman. A nice meal."

Leo looked at her out of awful, stricken eyes. "I don't want to kill anybody."

"You made a choice."

"I don't want to!"

Sarah moved quickly to close the bedroom door. He mustn't overhear this.

"Leo, I'm going to tell you something about that man in there. I don't want you to be frightened. It's all going to come right. I hope it is."

She went across to the graceful New Kingdom table that stood beneath the wide window. Paul's magnum pistol lay there. The table had been a gift to Miri from Thutmose IV, "in exchange," as she put it, "for some girlish indiscretions that he found very enjoyable."

"This is going to come as a surprise, I know. That man in there is a killer of the Keepers. A professional."

Leo's eyes went to the closed door. "I didn't think anybody knew about them."

"There are people who know. He's one of them. He's murdered hundreds of them." She said nothing of how that made her feel—the combination of relief and cold terror.

"Oh, my God. But why is she—"

"Leo, something happened tonight that I still don't fully understand. She apparently enjoyed that man immoderately. She thinks, for whatever reason, that he fertilized her egg."

"Only another Keeper can. Isn't that true?"

Sarah nodded. "It's a fantasy, nothing more. A tragic fantasy."

"She can make a mistake like that?"

"Miriam—a Keeper woman—has only four eggs in her lifetime. This is her last one."

"Does she have any children?"

"No. Apparently she's lost her last egg, and—well, she seems to have had a bit of a breakdown."

"Can't you give her anything? I mean, you're a doctor and all."

"What we need to do is to give her a pregnancy test. When it comes up negative, my hope is that she'll come to her senses."

"And I'll get—I'll get to . . ." She lowered her eyes. Her face burned with shame. "I hate this!"

"You bought it," Sarah said. "Wear it."

"I don't want to do any more killing! Not ever, Sarah."

"Join the club."

"But I have to, don't I?"

"Join the club."

Leo began to weep. The hopelessness in the small, defeated sobs was familiar from Sarah's own private moments. Sarah embraced her, and Leo held on tight. "It hurts, Sarah. It hurts terribly!"

"Blood will fix that."

Leo grew pale. "I'll kill myself," she said.

Sarah was silent. Leo hadn't yet seen the attic. Better to put that off for a few days.

"What do I do, Sarah?"

"Leo, that man in there is a monster. He's killed hundreds of Keepers, and he'll kill Miri the instant he discovers what she is."

"She won't let him."

"In bed together for hours, exploring each other naked, and him being familiar with Keepers and how they look—it could happen at any moment." She gestured toward the magnum. "That thing is loaded with explosive bullets. They'll blow your brains right out of your head, your heart out of your chest. The only thing that Miriam's body can't survive is the failure of blood flow. Given an intact circulatory system, she'll heal. Always. He knows this. He knows exactly how to kill a Keeper."

"I had a nice life. I had my loft and my little boat and my friends—a few friends—and I was collecting cool artists like the Starn brothers and John Currin . . . but I spent most of my nights at home, or going to clubs by myself, trying to look like the group I wanted to be part of. But nobody wanted me. I was a washout . . . until all of a sudden *Miriam Blaylock* starts taking an interest. In me! I was totally impressed, Sarah." She choked back a sob.

To her credit, she did not break down, which is what Sarah had thought was going to happen. She raised her head, stuck out her chin, and said, "What we have to do is pretty damn simple."

"It is indeed."

She took out the fleam, handed it to Sarah. "You know how to use this; I don't."

Sarah opened it. "You hook the end in behind the vessel, then jerk it toward you. The blood'll come out in a stream. You get your mouth over it and just keep swallowing as fast as you can."

"What if I throw up?"

"You won't. You're carrying around a pint of Miri's blood in your veins. It'll be like taking the most intense drug you've ever known. It makes the most powerful horse ever sold seem like aspirin."

"He'll go nuts when he gets stuck. I mean, he's gonna feel it, Sarah."

"I'll do the incision. All you have to do is cover the wound with your mouth and suck as hard as you possibly can."

"He'll fight."

"It's not like that if you're fast. They lose consciousness in a couple of seconds."

"You better do it."

"You need to eat! If you don't, her blood's going to start destroying yours. You'll go into shock."

"I'll die?" She actually sounded hopeful, as if she thought it might be a welcome release. Sarah thought of what was in the attic.

"Feeding draws the blood right out of the brain. He won't even get a chance to yell."

Leo looked to her with the gaze of a little sister, and Sarah realized that her feelings toward this kid were changing. She squeezed Leo's hand, trying to reassure her. "You're going to be perfect. The hard part is the incision, and I'm doing that."

"It's quiet," Leo said, looking toward the closed door of Miriam's bedroom.

"He's sleeping."

"But she isn't?"

"No."

Miri only slept after she fed. Since she hadn't, she would be completely conscious the whole time.

"You stay at the door, Leo. Come in at my signal."

Sarah went into the bedroom, her fleam concealed in her blouse. Paul was as comatose as a mouse-stuffed snake. Miri was cuddled up to him like a schoolgirl with her first lover.

She looked so happy, eyes closed, face blissful. She was nuzzling his chest hair.

When Miri saw Sarah, she gave her a secret, delighted smile. Sarah went to her and stroked her hair, which was twice as full as it had been even a few hours ago. The Keeper body was astonishing in its ability to regenerate and restore itself. Sarah had been fascinated to find out how it all worked. Some nature somewhere had evolved this wonderfully regenerative organism, but it had not been earthly nature. Miriam had never told Sarah where they had come from, only that it was the stars. Why they had appeared here, as colonists or refugees, or—as Sarah suspected—on some far more exotic mission involving the evolution of species, she would not discuss, and perhaps did not know.

Sarah went around the far side of the bed from Miri. She hated so to hurt her, but this had to be done, and there was no time to waste. Poor Miri could be foolish in love. It was her one failing. Sarah had been the victim of some of that foolishness, but also the beneficiary of its indulgence, for which she was profoundly grateful. Miri's love also lasted. In the past twenty years, she had probably spent ten million dollars on Sarah's scientific efforts, even indulging her struggle to see if she could remove the Keeper blood that Miri herself had put in her veins.

Sarah slipped into the bed. Paul's back was to her, his form concealing her from Miri's vision. She stretched out against him.

"Isn't he wonderful?" Miri whispered.

"He's certainly big."

Sarah brought out the fleam, then drew the narrow silver blade with the hooked end out of its ivory sheath. Using the delicate tips of her surgeon's fingers, she found his jugular.

The pulse was excellent. He was going to be an extraordinary first meal for Leo. In fact, there'd be plenty for Sarah, too. She could top off that weak old woman and maybe get a month more time before she needed to feed again.

This was one kill that she wasn't going to mind. How strange her heart was, to want to kill an enemy of Miri's who had literally stolen her from herself. But she loved Miri at least as much as she hated her. She didn't think of herself as a lesbian—she had no interest in Leo, for example—but what Miri had done for her in the car on the way to the club had been wonderful beyond words, so fulfilling that it seemed to literally feed the soul. Not even with Tom had it been like it was with Miri.

This love across the border of species was deeply awful, yes, but somehow also deeply sacred. For all of her anger and all of her striving to escape her fate, Sarah knew that she would always be here, always in the end choosing her Miri over freedom, over death, over everything.

She rose into a sitting position. Now she could see Miri, whose eyes were closed, whose lips reflected deep happiness—deep and pitiful.

She motioned to Leo, who came quickly to her side. Sarah gestured toward the sleeping man, then toward Leo's mouth. Leo nodded. On her face was a child's expression of fascination.

With the quickness of long practice, Sarah slit the vein. Blood spurted, and she pressed Leo's head against the wound.

She did surprisingly well, sucking with ferocious energy.

"He's out," Sarah said, as Paul's body sagged.

But then a shock like an explosion went through the huge body. Sarah heard air rush into the lungs. Leo was sucking hard, but he was most certainly not out.

On the contrary, he roared out his pain and surprise. Miri screamed, too, and leaped back away from them.

Still roaring, with Leo stuck to him like a stubborn leech, Paul lumbered up off the bed and started pulling at her, trying to rip her off him. She was not going to be pulled off, though. She sucked, he screamed, he staggered, Miri screamed.

Obviously, this man was not like ordinary men. Somehow, this man had remained conscious through a sudden and total loss of intercranial blood pressure. Somehow, this rather easy kill had become a disaster.

He lurched across the room, trying to peel Leo off. Her eyes were wide and she remained stuck tight. It was the blood, Sarah knew, the incredible effect of the blood. Her first taste had driven her almost mad with pleasure, and she would fight off the devil before she would stop sucking it out of him.

Sarah also knew that this monster was not going to be killed. She raced out of the bedroom.

Leo was hardly even aware of what was happening. This blood—it was a miracle, it tasted like sunlight, like heaven. Every gulp of it went gushing into her starved cells, filling her with energy and power and buzzing thrills.

Then strong arms—really strong arms—came around her and yanked her off. Paul dropped to his knees, his neck spurting. He was gasping, he was swaying—and then he reached out and grabbed Leo's wrist and drew her down to him. He tried to speak but nothing came out. But the look of hatred on his face was something phenomenal, something unnatural. He was like some kind of hell creature, this man.

Miri grabbed her away from him and screamed directly in her face, a banshee wail. "He's of my kind," she shrieked. "Of *my* kind!"

A high-voltage shock of total surprise flashed through Sarah, who had returned to the bedside. She was saying that this man . . . was a Keeper? *This* man?

He rose up, his eyes blazing. He tore a newel post off the bed and swung it. It whistled past Leo, nearly hitting her. Then he swung it at Miri, who ducked easily. It shattered instead against the wall with such force that the whole house shook.

He leaped on Miri. His hands tightened like a vise around her neck. Leo grabbed his arms, but he could not be dislodged. No matter the blood he had lost and was still losing, he was as strong as iron.

"He's killing her," she screamed. She beat on his back. Miri's eyes came bulging out of her head. Leo screamed, she cried, she hauled at the iron arms. Miri's face was disintegrating, her mouth returning to its natural shape, the prosthetics that altered her appearance popping out. Then the compression of her throat forced her tongue between her lips. It appeared, black and pointed, gorged with blood. His own blood was still spraying out of his neck, spattering her with a red shower.

Leo hit him and hit him, but he was totally fixed on this; he was like a robot programmed to kill.

Suddenly there was a terrific, blinding blast and he dropped like a stone. Leo threw herself between him and Miri, who went to her feet coughing and rubbing her neck.

Sarah stood quietly, the magnum in her hands.

Miri staggered. Then she threw herself on him; she turned him over, tried to stop his bleeding. "Help us," she screamed.

"Miri, let her feed! Let her take him!"

"You're a doctor! Help us!"

"Miri, he's dangerous! He's got to be killed, come on!"

"Save him, Sarah! *Please!*"

"Miri, no! Leo, take him!"

Miriam leaped up, and before Sarah could stop her, she had tossed Leo across the room like a rag doll. Then she yanked the magnum out of Sarah's hands.

Sarah prepared to die.

But Miriam stuck the gun in her own mouth. She screwed her eyes shut.

This would not kill her, but it would leave her too damaged to recover. In the end, Sarah would have to stop her heart.

"Miri, *no!*"

"Then help him."

Sarah knelt to the unconscious form, stemmed the bleeding from his jugular with a finger. His eyes were fully rolled back, and he was seizing from blood loss and shock. He had probably five minutes, maybe less.

"We've got to get him downstairs," Miri said. She tossed the gun aside.

Miriam carried his shoulders, Sarah his feet. They took him to the lift in the front hall, squeezed in with him while Leo raced ahead on the stairs. She had the examination table dressed with a sheet by the time they reached the surgery.

He was in deep shock now. "This is going to be a problem," Sarah said. She slapped a pressure bandage on his neck. The flow had dropped by two-thirds. His blood pressure must be almost nothing. "I'm losing him."

Miriam burst into tears, threw herself on him.

"Get her off," Sarah said to Leo.

But when Leo touched her, she threw back her head and howled with an agony beyond anything Sarah had heard from her or anybody ever. She'd never seen her like this, crazy with grief, her emotions like an exploding volcano.

"Leo, have you ever assisted in a surgery?"

"God no."

Sarah took Miri's shoulders. "Miri, can you hear me? Miri!"

Slowly, by what looked like tormented inches, a more sane expression returned to her face. "You did not have the right to take him." Her eyes flashed with a ruler's pride. "*You did not have the right!*"

"Please forgive me," Sarah said.

"Then save him! Save him!"

Sarah stabilized the neck wound, then got them to turn him over on his stomach. The entry point of the bullet was below the heart. If the artery was intact, he might have a chance. She couldn't type his blood, there was no time, so she had to go with O+. She told Leo, "Get me six pints of blood from the fridge. Miri, set him up." While they worked, she went to the cupboard and took out her instruments. She had a complete surgery here, even an extractor for bullets. She had once promised Miri, "If I can get you here, I can fix it, no matter what may befall you."

There was an X-ray machine, but there was no way they could move him to the table now. There was no time. "Scalpel," Sarah said as she swabbed the entry wound with Betadine. A glance told her that Miri had set the blood properly.

If he was really a Keeper of some unknown kind, she was flying almost totally blind. In Sarah's own veins, Miriam's blood functioned like a separate organ. It flowed with Sarah's natural blood, but did not mix with it. It could not. Sarah could not even begin to guess what was going on in this man.

She dissected around the entry wound, opening it wider and wider, snapping orders. "Spreaders!" she called when she reached the rib cage. "Clamp!" she said when she found torn blood vessels.

She could not entirely save the lung, but she managed to isolate the bleeding enough to resect. Time disappeared for her. She concentrated totally, remembering her training and her work experience from so many years ago. Her fingers worked sometimes almost by magic, but for the most part it was her careful training that saw her through this terribly challenging procedure without—she hoped—a serious error.

When she could at last close him up, his blood pressure had risen to 80 over 50 and his pulse was 160. A temperature of just 99 suggested that he was tolerating the transfused blood well. She put him on an electrolyte drip, then got her prescription pad. She wrote for some time, then handed it to Leo. "They'll have all this in the drugstore at Riverside Hospital."

"What's the situation?" Miriam asked. Her blood-spattered robe still hung off her naked body. Her face was hollow, her skin gray.

"He's hanging on."

Miriam's face twisted, and she threw herself sobbing into Sarah's arms.

"Oh, baby," Sarah said, "baby, I'm so sorry. I didn't understand. I didn't know . . ."

"There was an attempt to cross the species, recorded in the Books ten conclaves ago. Keepers trying to escape from the need to eat human blood. The result wasn't good. We'd created human beings with the speed and power of Keepers. So we destroyed all the family lines, except one. We found a last survivor about forty years ago. He was destroyed. Apparently he had a son."

"I don't think this is true, Miri. There's no way we could interbreed. We're as different as tigers and cattle, except on the surface."

"You have no idea what our science was capable of—when we had a science."

"What happened to your science?"

Miriam regarded her. She laughed a little, and Sarah sensed a whole hidden history in that laughter, a history of secrets that would never be told. "It was so good to be with him; it was like going back to the one time in all my life that I was truly and deeply happy. Oh, Sarah, I love him so!"

Sarah found herself hoping that the pregnancy was real. Because if this was true, and it was a healthy fetus, then maybe the great hope of Miriam's life was being realized.

But still Sarah saw Paul to be mortal danger, and Leo was stationed to watch his monitors.

"How about your hunger?" Miriam asked her.

"I got some blood," she said. But Leo's hollow expression told them both that it had not been enough.

Sarah took Miriam back upstairs, to their private room. They turned on the video system so she could watch the infirmary every moment.

She lay back on the little sofa where she so often read and worked. Sarah knelt beside it. "Please forgive me, Miri."

Miriam gazed at her. "I forgive you, child," she said. "But you must help me with this."

"Miri, he hates you. And he's a killing machine."

"He has a heart, Sarah, a huge heart. I want my chance to try to reach his heart."

"When he wakes up, Miri, God knows what'll happen."

"I want you to help me. Both of you."

"Of course we will. That goes without saying."

Miriam went over and picked up the encaustic painting of her lost Eumenes. "I left my happiness in another world."

"We have happiness."

She smiled a little. "I'm the last of my kind, you know—the last Keeper."

"There are others."

Miriam looked at her. "Living in holes? That's not being a Keeper—a true ruler of mankind." She gazed at the portrait of the handsome young man in his white toga. "I'm lost in time." She put it down and came back to Sarah. "But I have a baby. I have hope."

Sarah did not know what Miriam had in her belly, and she wasn't sure she wanted to find out. If this much-shattered heart took another blow, it was even possible that Miriam would join her peers in the shadows, living like an animal and waiting—no doubt hoping—to die.

"I want a pregnancy test."

Sarah played for time. "As soon as Paul recovers."

"No, no," Miriam said. "You'll do it immediately."

"I need the resources of the infirmary for him."

Miriam came to her. "You can do the test and we both know it."

Sarah took her in her arms.

"I have to know," Miriam whispered.

Sarah hugged her tight.

They stayed like that, in the declining light of the afternoon.

Leo paced to the wall and back to the door, and she remembered chocolate icebox pie and blinis and blintzes and beluga. She went to the back windows and wiped off her sweat and remembered Mommy's chicken fricasee and Aunt Madeline's molasses cookies. She slapped the wall and hugged herself and sweated rivers and remembered rib eyes at Sparks and smoked salmon at Petrossian.

But all that really mattered was the raw, delicious taste in her mouth and the smell in her nose of blood, blood, blood.

When she'd drunk his blood, she'd drunk his soul, and she was drunk on it and she had to have more of it.

Her jeans were soaked with pee, her underarms and hair were awash, and she felt as if she couldn't breathe and couldn't think because she needed more, she wasn't finished—she wanted a lovely bowl of cherry cobbler, but she needed blood.

She went to the black front door, put her hand on the gleaming brass handle, and she pushed out into the flaring evening.

The city was its ordinary self, humming its indifferent hum, traveling down its million uncaring roads.

She was a hunter now, off to the hills. She ranged down the turning street and to the secret steps that led down to FDR Drive.

A car screamed past three feet away, then another and another. Leo darted out into the roadway. Two more cars came speeding toward her. She leaped forward just as one almost grazed her back. Then she was on the far side of FDR Drive, climbing the iron railing and going along the narrow promenade.

A full moon hung over the surging East River, its glow touching the black, uneasy waves.

She was absolutely frantic; she'd never felt anything remotely like this. By light-years, this clawing, flaming inner agony was the most intense sensation she had ever felt in her life. She ached the way people ache when they can't get enough air.

She dashed along, searching for a derelict like a pig snuffling for truffles. She was strung worse than she'd ever known anybody to be strung. This made you wild; it made you want to run and never stop; it seethed like ants under your skin; it pumped pure desperation straight into your brain.

As she ran, she thought of home, the imposing house in Greenwich, her taffeta-and-lace bedroom, her daddy probably right now watching Monday night football, her mom reading.

Home was lost to her, home and all she had known of the peace of life. Her feet throbbed; her heart raced; her skin felt as if it were being sandpapered. The taste of Paul's blood lingered in her mouth, its scent in her nostrils. All she could think about was blood, the way it tasted, the way it felt going down, the way it had cooled the fire that was consuming her from within.

Then she saw a clump of shadow on a moonlit bench. She went up to it. Just a mass of rags. Good. Man or woman? Man—not so good, they were stronger.

She sat on the end of the bench nearest the head. Her hands almost shook too much, but she managed to get a cigarette lit. She'd quit two months ago, but that was before she met Miriam. Miriam smoked all the time. She didn't care. Why should she? Keepers were immune to cancer.

She dragged hard, wishing that the smoke was stronger. You could get a nice hit smoking horse in a cigarette, but she didn't have any horse. She had to calm down on her own.

She had the fleam and she had the victim. All she needed now was the guts. She looked down at a shock of dark, oily, lice-ridden hair. She knew he was dirty and that he probably stank to high heaven, but all she could smell was the blood, which was so good that she kept sucking in air and leaning closer.

She took the fleam out, fumbled the blade open—giving herself a nasty little nick in the process. Before she had even sucked it, the wound closed.

A damn miracle.

Stealthily, she shuffled the rags aside. There was the neck. Not an old neck. She knew she was supposed to take them back to the house, burn the remnant in the furnace and all. But how could she get some drunk back across FDR Drive and up the narrow steps that led to their property? The business with the lady, whom she'd found on Fifty-fifth Street and First Avenue, had been difficult enough.

She held the fleam close to the neck. She couldn't see any

veins. She dared not touch the guy. She tightened her grip on the instrument. Then she plunged it down. There was resistance; then it went sliding in—way deeper than it should. In fact, she almost plunged it all the way in.

She was snatching for it as he rose screaming through clenched teeth out of his pile of newspapers and rags. He was face-to-face with her, his teeth bared.

He was a kid. Maybe younger than she was. He had long eyelashes, and the moonlight shone in his dark eyes. His hands went to his neck, his head cocked—and a flood of blood came out of his mouth.

Instinct made Leo go for it, but it was all over the ground already, splattering and splashing like spilled milk on the kitchen floor. He went to his feet, still screaming behind his clenched teeth, and began jerking and staggering, his bloody fingers slipping on the bloody hilt of the fleam.

And then, incredibly, she recognized him. Not from the club, not from her present life at all. She recognized him from prep school, from Andover. It was Benno Jones. He'd been a performance artist. His family was wealthy but very conservative. Obviously, there'd been an estrangement.

She was confused. But also now, desperate. She lunged at him; she got her fingers around the fleam and yanked it as hard as she could. It came partially out, dragging red gristle, followed by a gurgling black flow of blood.

She latched on like a starving jungle leech. The blood seemed to flow into her almost automatically, pouring down her throat into her belly. Benno staggered along, his back bent, his hands made into fists, his barely-remembered acquaintance inexplicably sucking the life out of him.

He went down like a staggered bull, to his knees. She pushed him over and dragged his head into her lap, bending the neck to give herself the best possible angle. Then she put her lips around the bubbling gouge and sucked as hard as it was possible for her to suck. She got lots more blood, and from his lips a gentle question, "Leo?"

She did it again and it worked again. A third time and it worked, but less well. The fourth time, it hardly worked at all.

But he wasn't getting any thinner or lighter. He was still normal looking, except he was very dead. She tried again, sucking with all her might.

Nothing happened. She sat back on her haunches. Only Miriam could dry them out. He was way too heavy to carry. He felt like a sack of lead.

Then she saw, some distance down the promenade, a man walking about ten dogs. They were coming toward her and the dogs were going completely berserk. You couldn't hear the man, but you could see him yelling at them. Their voices were a riot of barking and howling, and they were struggling so furiously to reach the kill that their paws were digging dust up off the pavement. They looked as if they had exhaust.

She managed to get Benno to the railing and, with a massive, grunting effort, to roll him over and into the East River. Then she ran like hell, and as she ran, she began also to feel wonderful.

Behind her, the dogs quickly consumed any small trace of Benno that she had left behind. She could hear the dog walker now, still screaming himself hoarse.

Her body seemed almost ready to lift off. She could run and run without even getting tired. Incredibly, it felt as if there were somebody inside her, a living presence that was not her but was friendly to her and part of her. It was a grand way to feel as if you had your own angel in you.

She did not see the solitary figure on the high cliff that separated Miriam's neighborhood from the Drive, who had been watching her from the beginning. She did not see it put a small instrument away, perhaps a set of binoculars, perhaps a camera.

She did not see it as it got into a car, nor did she see the car drive swiftly away.

NINETEEN

Trapped

Miriam raced through the house screaming for Leo, her voice shrill and shattering. Sarah was terrified. She'd never seen her like this. She was crazed with fury; there was no other way to describe her. Then those awful, inhuman eyes were suddenly glaring at Sarah.

"Miri, calm down. Please, Miri!"

Miriam shot across the sitting room and grabbed her and slammed her against the wall. "Where in hell were you?"

"I was with you, Miri!"

"You let her out, goddamn you! You careless, foolish—"

She slapped Sarah so hard she went flying. Then Miriam was on her again, shaking her, screaming and smashing her head again and again into the floor. Sarah saw stars; the world reeled; she screamed, screamed again.

Miriam went to her feet, lithe and quick, glaring down at her. Then she was back again, her eyes glowing, her narrow lips twisted in some expression so alien that Sarah couldn't even begin to interpret it.

She kissed Sarah. Then she lifted her and helped her to a chair. She knelt before her and kissed her hands. "I'm sorry. Sorry. I'm just—" She made a small sound, the snarl of a hurt tiger. "I'm feeling things I've never felt before." She laid her head in Sarah's lap. Now she was weeping. "When I last had a baby in me, I was *so* protected. We owned Egypt! We lived in walled compounds. The wealth, the power—you can't even begin to imagine! But now—I've got my last baby and I need to feel safe and I don't!"

Sarah stroked her hair. She looked down at the lithe, powerful body in the magnificent butterfly robe, a garment made in China six hundred years ago, of thousands of individual bits of silk sewed together with tiny stitches. It was like a cloud of butterflies, this robe. Miri wore it casually, but that did not change the fact that it could easily be the most beautiful garment presently on earth.

Sarah had always been a lonely sort of a soul, but Miriam was *really* alone. Her baby had been her hope—Sarah realized that now—her one hope to relieve the despair that lay concealed behind the elegance and the headlong decadence that filled her time.

When she found out that this baby was a fata morgana, a mirage, she was going to be absolutely devastated.

Paul knew he was alive because of the pain. From his waist to his neck, he was a mass of sheer agony. His breath was coming in light little gulps, but he felt no air hunger, so he knew there was oxygen running.

He inventoried his body, working from training and long experience. He could wiggle his toes and hands, and lift his arms. That was good. He was too weak to lift his legs. That was not good. The left side of his neck ached. That must be a healing wound where that bitch had tried to suck his blood. His chest was gunshot real bad. There was bubbling when he inhaled, which meant that his lung capacity was dangerously low.

He was looking up, at least, into the ceiling of a hospital room. He could hear monitors beeping, and he could see an IV.

How the hell he had ever gotten himself to a hospital, he could not for the life of him imagine, but he damn well had. His self-evaluation told him that he had been shot in the left lung, which had resulted in aspiration pneumonia, caused by blood and debris. There wasn't any fever, so whatever antibiotics were in that drip were clearly doing their job. Also, the pain was diffuse, not concentrating on a certain spot the way it did when you had a bullet in you. Okay, so he'd been operated on. How much of the lung was left in there he had no idea. Maybe none, the way it felt.

Altogether, he had been in worse shape than this and come out of it okay. So, great, he was going to have himself a killing spree as soon as he recuperated . . . unless, of course, his presence in this intensive care ward meant that he was back in the hands of the Company.

After a long five minutes, Miriam came up off Sarah's lap. The red eyes glared up at her. Instinct made Sarah cringe back away from her. Miriam sucked in breath. Sarah realized what was happening: she was hearing something.

"Is it Paul Ward?" But a glance at one of the monitors that had been set up in every room said that he wasn't the issue. He was stirring from the woozy state induced by his Valium drip, but he came in and out of consciousness three or four times a day. His lung capacity was too low to allow him to be fully awake.

Miriam came to her feet, catlike. In an instant, she was at the front door, listening against the thick mahogany. Then she rushed across the foyer into the music room, sat down at the piano, and—of all things—began to play Beethoven's *Moonlight Sonata*. The vision of the cloud of butterflies floating around that narrow, incredibly graceful being was heart-stopping. She played with a touch as soft as a dusting of snow.

Sarah watched the great front door. The lock clicked. The handle moved. Leo's face appeared. From its flush, Sarah knew at once that she had fed. Hearing the music, seeing Sarah sitting with her head back against her chair, Leo's nervous face smoothed. All seemed well to her, all at peace.

Sarah could not imagine the reason for the false tableau. It was as if Miri didn't believe that Leo would come in unless she was lured by an artificial appearance of serenity. Perhaps Miriam overestimated Leo's intelligence, because she was entirely deceived.

She came strolling in, smiling a conspiratorial smile at Sarah. There was blood on her blue T-shirt, more on her jeans.

"Where's the remnant?" Sarah hissed. Leo tried to go around her. Sarah grabbed her collar. "Where is it?"

"Leave me alone!"

"Leo, *where the hell is it?*"

Miriam played on, seemingly oblivious.

"None of your business," Leo sneered.

"Did you leave it on the street—for God's sake, answer me!"

"If you must know, it's in the East River. And so is that stupid toy of yours."

Sarah felt a nervous twinge in her left eye. "What toy?"

"Oh, that thing—that stupid thing went all the way in his neck."

"You left my fleam in your victim?"

"I couldn't get it out!"

"Jesus!"

Leo tried again to go around her.

That damn bunch of vampires had been smart, real smart. They'd played him like a piano. God only knew how many of the parasites infected that filthy club. And the house—this vampire was a rich bitch, wasn't she? She was light-years beyond the others. Kill this one, and you got the queen bee. Just like that really human looking one in Paris. Just like Mrs. Tallman.

Holy Shit—maybe they were one and the same. And maybe, if it was in any way still in his power, he was going to really strike a blow when he destroyed the damn creature. It had fooled him totally. Even making love to it had felt great, better than making love to a real woman. A fucking animal had tricked him into screwing it, and that made him even angrier.

His throat had the metallic taste that you get when you're having electrolytes pumped through your body. He wanted water and food.

"Nurse?" he called.

He listened. Whatever hospital he was in, it was as quiet as a damn tomb. Probably an isolation ward for cases with classified material. He felt around for a call button, found one attached to the headboard.

Thing was, when he pressed it, who was going to come through the door—a sweet little nurse or Justin Turk? His money was on Turk. They'd been on his tail, for sure. Whenever he'd gotten into trouble before, the Company had very kindly rescued him.

So maybe he wouldn't be free to kill the filth. Goddamnit,

maybe he ought to get up and bust out of here before it was too late. Unless it was already too damn late.

He actually started to raise himself, thinking to pull out the IV and take off. He felt pretty strong, except for his breathing. But if he tried this, he'd violate a rule that had kept him alive over his entire career: Never attack into the unknown. If all you knew was who was there, or supposed to be there, that was enough. But if you knew nothing, then you had to wait.

So he'd get the lay of things, build up his strength. Right now, what he wanted was a big rib eye, but a cup of broth would do. He pressed the button again. Nothing happened. Typical, probably meant this was some VA hole. He pressed it again, harder.

Sarah watched the monitor. Faintly, she heard the buzzing as Ward struggled to get some attention. He was more awake now than he'd been since the surgery five days ago. She thought, *He's healing.* She could not help but feel a little professional pride. She'd brought a man back who should be dead.

The music stopped. Miriam got up. She turned and came toward them, the butterfly robe billowing behind her, a cigarette fuming between her narrow lips, her eyes flashing. "Where the hell were you?" she snarled.

"Me?"

Miriam's eyes met Sarah's. "The remnant's exposed," Sarah said. "My fleam was left in the neck."

Miriam went up to Leo. Long fingers grabbed her throat. "This is how you repay me?"

Leo pulled away from her. "I threw the guy in the fucking East River. He's gone."

"A body is never gone unless it's burned," Miriam shouted.

Once or twice, she'd alluded to the fact that she had done away with human companions who hadn't worked out. Sarah thought for a moment that she was going to finish Leo right now, right here on the marble floor of the foyer.

But then Miriam threw back her head and laughed. It was strange laughter, almost silent. "Come with me," she told Leo.

"Come where?"

Miriam grabbed her wrist and dragged her off up the stairs. Sarah got up to follow. Miriam stopped her. "My husband is calling," she said. "Can't you hear him?"

Paul heard a sound beyond the room's closed door. He'd punched the call button about fifty times. He shifted in the bed. "Nurse," he said. The single word ran him out of breath, and he sank back against his pillow sucking oxygen.

When Sarah Roberts's face came into his view, he was so surprised that he delivered a croaking "Oh, shit!"

She was a vision of absolute beauty, her eyes glittering like coals. He tried to lift his arms, to strike out at her, but something stopped him.

He was cuffed to the bed. "Christ!"

"You're healing," Sarah said.

He inventoried his situation. Both wrists were cuffed to a length of chain fastened to the bed, along with both ankles. He had about two feet of travel, which was why he hadn't noticed until he began trying to move.

"Where the hell am I?"

"In my infirmary." She came over to him. He got ready to grab for her. "I'm a doctor, you know."

"Yeah, that's believable."

"You've survived a lung wound from a three-fifty-seven with an exploding tip. I think it oughta be damn believable."

"You kill people for food. How can you be a doctor?"

Sarah came closer to him. "I need to examine the wound," she said. Her tone, which had been carefully neutral, now seemed sullen—or no, sad. It seemed sad.

He prepared to make a grab for her. He didn't know what he'd do next. All he knew was this: he was in the worst situation he'd ever been in, and he had to do whatever he could to get out of it.

She tossed back the sheet, barely glancing at his nakedness. She drew back the dressing that covered the left half of his chest.

As she gazed at the wound, a sound came through the open door. Somebody out there was screaming, and horribly. Even as he lay here, somewhere else in the house, the vampires were killing.

His speed was not up to its usual standard, but he managed to grab Sarah's arm. Bandages flew from her hand as he yanked her to him.

He found himself staring down the barrel of his own damn pistol.

"God damn you," he said.

"God damn you! If it wasn't for her, you'd be dead, you vicious bastard!"

She reached up to his IV, opened the cock. His attention wandered. She seemed to sway, then to float above him like a madonna ascending to heaven.

The screams rose and fell like a terrible wind in a winter tree. Sarah Roberts's eyes bored into him—cold, indifferent, murderous. Despite his pounding, relentless hate, his anguished hunger to rise from the bed, knock that gun aside, and physically rip her head from her body, he sank into sleep. The awful screams wove themselves into a dark and nameless nightmare that the drugs in the IV soon transformed into an empty, aimless void.

Miriam held Leo's wrist and would not let go, not even as the slow, dry hand came and closed around her fingers. Leo felt the strange, dry strength of the corpse; she saw the spark of life in the withered eyes.

She couldn't look at it. She couldn't bear its touch. But she also couldn't understand what this awful place was, and above all, what was the matter here.

"Open your eyes!" Miriam said. "Look at it!"

"I am! But what—why—"

"You stupid little cow—didn't you think there'd be something—some price to pay?"

"Make it let me go! Let me go!"

Miriam dragged her away from John's coffin. His clinging fingers caused the corpse to rise up, then, as its grip failed, to fall back with a dusty thud. Miriam slammed the lid.

"But he's not dead! We have to help him!"

"How compassionate you are." She marched her over to Sarah's coffin. "This is where your friend came from."

"What friend?"

"Sarah. That dreary zombie."

"Zombie?"

"After I blooded her, she cut her own wrists. But she's clever. She left me the knowledge I needed to bring her back." She gazed toward John Blaylock's coffin. "Too bad it was too late for him."

"But they—I don't get it!"

"Now that my blood is in your veins, Leonore, you cannot die. You're not like us. We don't have souls. But you do have one, and my blood has bound it forever to your body." She glanced around the room, tossed her head. "This is your fate."

Leo stood up. She backed away from Miriam. She had to get out of this awful place; she had to find a cure for herself. This was—it was unimaginable. And she had to kill—to stop this from happening to her, she had to kill and kill for the rest of her . . . time.

"Sarah's become servile. She's not an independent soul. She's boring and I hate to be bored. I hate it!"

"Bored?"

"You have no fucking idea! This isn't life, always hiding, creeping in the shadows. I'm a princess, not a damned sneak thief! I want the philosophers, the kings about me, not the sleazy gaggle of decadents I attract now."

Leo had never known a thought this strange, this subtle, but her mind at last grasped the terror of her situation. "You've stolen me from myself," she said. She felt wonder at the evil, the cunning of it. "I'm a slave."

"No! *No!* Not like her, you aren't. When I resurrected her, her will was gone. She knows it, but there's nothing she can do about it. She even went to Haiti, to try to learn about zombies, to understand her predicament." She laughed a little. "By all the stars in heaven, she's *boring!*" She yanked Leo's hand. "You're going to be great. You've got a mind of your own. You went out there and fed, against my specific rule. You did it *your* way. You know how that makes me feel?" She grasped Leo's hand, glanced back toward John's coffin. "Ever since he died, I've been alone. Now I'm not."

"What about Sarah?"

"You are foolish, though. But never mind, you've got excellent basic intelligence. I will educate you. Do you know what you're going to be? Why I've taken you into my home?"

"God that I did."

"You're going to be governess to my son."

"Husband," the vampire said, "you're awake at last. Welcome, welcome back!"

He didn't have any idea how to react to that particular gambit. But you never knew what an animal as smart as these things might come up with.

The vampire took his hand in the same slim fingers that he had kissed. He felt his gut wobbling at the thought that he had ever touched his lips to its skin . . . let alone the other things he had done. It pressed his hand against its belly.

"Do you feel him?"

He looked up at it. It was all aglow, like a real woman asking you to feel a real baby.

"He's kicking, he's *very* strong. And Sarah says he's robust. That's the word she uses—*robust*. We're going to have a son, Paul!"

What bullshit. You couldn't make a baby with a creature that wasn't human. "You're a liar," he said, barely disguising his contempt.

They left, then, all except Leo, who stayed watching him. She had the gun, Paul could see it stuck casually into her belt. This was a tough kid, this Leo. She looked like a cross between a punk rocker and a schoolgirl. She was stationed right in front of the door.

Even if he hadn't been shackled, he was probably too weak to do anything at the moment. But he wasn't real concerned. He'd get his ass out of here soon enough. He looked at Leo, and she looked back at him.

Here was a question: Was this pretty kid, this Leo, a vampire or not? You really could not tell with these creatures.

They were that good. He needed to know because he needed to know what kind of physical abilities he was dealing with. His instinct was that Leo was not a vampire. She was a hanger-on who knew the score. A very sick puppy, this Leo.

Paul tried an indirect approach, an interrogation technique he'd used a thousand times. Let the subject assume you know more than you do.

"So, Leo, what're you in it for? Drugs? Dough?"

Leo looked at him.

"Love."

"Oh, yeah, that. You love the monster. You ever fuck it?"

"Shut up."

"You know, I don't get you people. I mean, you're not a vampire, but you tolerate it. You go along with it."

"Miriam is a beautiful and ancient being. She deserves our support."

"Oh, I *see!* I guess Ellen Wunderling would agree with you. Hell, yes!"

"Sarah took her, not Miriam."

He stopped. He thought about it. Sarah had come after him with some kind of an instrument, not her sucker mouth.

Could it be that she didn't have a sucker mouth, but that she still fed on blood? If so, was there more than one species of vampire? Meaning, more vampires than he thought?

"Ellen wasn't the right kind of food for Miriam's species, or what?"

"We're blooded. Miriam gives us her blood, and—it's a miracle. You stop aging. You get incredibly healthy. You live for—well, a very long time."

Paul stared up at the ceiling. Now it develops that Miriam can make ordinary people into vampires. Jesus *wept!*

Then Paul had another, equally chilling thought. Maybe

this baby bullshit was not bullshit. If this blooding thing was real, maybe the two species were closer than anybody thought. If he'd given a vampire a baby—

He uttered a carefully contrived chuckle. "I can't believe that I knocked her up. Like, I'm human!"

Leo came over to the bed. She had the gun down at her side, hanging there in her hand. One step closer, and he could reach it. "You're not human," she said. "You're a Keeper—or half a Keeper."

It hurt, but he laughed. He really got a good laugh out of it. She was quite a bullshit artist.

"Okay. So, when do I feed on my fellow man? When I'm asleep?"

"You're something that isn't supposed to exist. They were trying to create a line that would live forever like they do, but not have to eat human blood. A better version of themselves."

He remembered them in their lairs, their sneering, contemptuous faces. "They have utter disdain for the human species," he said. "They don't care whether they eat our blood or not."

"They only hate those who kill them!"

"You're a liar."

"They do what they have to, to live. But there's no hate in it. Just hunger."

"You're lying through your teeth! They hate us and they love to kill!"

"You think so? You remember when your dad died? The way he just suddenly disappeared?"

The words seemed to come from a very long way away— echoing, strange words, terrifying words. Because there was no way she could have known about that unless—

Bellowing like a stuck bull, he rose up out of his IVs and his monitoring cuffs and his oxygen line. She backed away, but he lunged at her—and collapsed against the shackles. He was a helpless pile of rags.

She stood over him, the gun expertly braced. Somebody had taught this lady how to make a mag work exactly right.

"Don't you fucking move," she screamed. "Don't you fucking *breathe!*"

He stared up at her. "You lying bitch." But he knew she was not lying. She knew something, all right. He hadn't ever told any of these people about his dad.

"Your father was killed because he was a part of a failed mutant bloodline. We think you must have been overlooked. Unfortunately, because now you've gotten Miri pregnant with God only knows what."

"The baby's okay?"

"The first ultrasound's in two weeks."

During his outburst, she'd obviously tripped a silent alarm, because Miriam and Sarah came blasting in. They all had magnums. This place was hatching guns.

They got him rearranged in the bed.

So, Paul thought, *I guess this is a setback.*

Over the next few days, Dr. Sarah Roberts methodically showed him things about himself that he had never even dreamed. She took his blood and showed it to him under a microscope. He could see the strange cells that had been in the past attributed to a benign deformation. Then she drew blood from Miriam before his eyes and showed him the two samples side by side.

He was not blind, but he still did not want to believe. He clung to the idea—which in his heart he knew to be ridiculous—that this whole thing was a coincidence. Because he could *not*—no damn *way!*—have their blood running in his veins.

Sarah created a chromosomal map and showed him how his own nineteenth chromosome differed from that of a normal human being in the area known as 19a22.1. She showed him smaller differences in sixteen of his twenty-three chromosomes. Then she showed him Miriam's chromosomal map. It was different in every single place that his was different, as well as in three more places.

Those three places represented the need to consume human blood, the great brilliance, and life eternal.

Paul's grandfather had lived to a hundred and eleven. The whole family was like that. Supposedly there had been a Ward back a couple of centuries ago who'd made it to a hundred and nineteen.

She demonstrated to him that, because of the chromosomal differences, he would probably never be able to have a child with a human mother, but that he could indeed fertilize Miriam.

Finally, he had to face it. *He* was one of *them*. He wanted to crawl out of his own skin. If he'd been able, he would have put one of their damn guns in his mouth.

His dreams became nightmares. He hungered for death; he begged God to kill him. But he did not die. Instead, he kept getting stronger and stronger, throwing off the injuries the way he always did. Only now he knew why. It was because of his damned, accursed, evil *blood!*

Often, he would awaken and find Miriam gazing at him. She changed his dressings and cared for his bedpan, brought him his food and asked after his pain. Once in the morning and once at night, Sarah would examine him. Always she was cool and detached. Often, when they were alone, she would threaten him: "If you hurt her, if you break her heart, I will kill you with acid, I will rip your living heart out of your body."

His response was always the same: "Same to you, bitch."

He came to loathe himself. He'd fallen for Miriam because he was *one of them*. As the days passed, he got lots better. He also began to lay precise plans for the destruction of this household. He had to win their trust, first. It would not be easy, but Miriam—dear Miri—was totally smitten by him. That would be his opening.

So when Miriam came to him and sat gazing at him, he started to play little coy games with his eyes.

Miriam would twirl through the house singing "Caro Nome," and laughing, all the while feeling the baby within her. They took a year to gestate, and giving birth was very hard. But the baby—the baby was fine! "No indication of a problem," Sarah kept saying.

She really didn't know. She didn't even know for certain that Miriam was pregnant. She'd given her a urine test, but who knew if chorionic gonadotropin levels in a Keeper would be the same as in a human female. Probably not, in fact. Maybe their placental tissue produced another hormone altogether.

Unspoken in the household was the fact that the date of the first ultrasound was approaching. They would know then for sure, then and only then.

Miriam sang to her baby, she sang to her friends, and when Paul started smiling at her again, she sang to all the world.

Miriam had never before been so happy. Her household

was thriving. Her body was glowing with health. She sensed that the baby was growing beautifully. And her new husband was slowly coming round.

"You know, Paul, I think you need to see it from our viewpoint, morally."

"Try me."

"We didn't make ourselves. Nature made us."

"That's what the CIA says."

She was quite interested in this. He'd never referred to what his employers might think of her before. "How so?"

"You're not murderers; you're predators. You have a right to kill us, and we have a right to defend ourselves. That's the basis of a policy statement they're working on."

"Well, that's exactly my point." She just ached to kiss him, he was so luscious. But he had not so far been willing to do that again.

Tomorrow, she was going to surprise him. He was finished with the infirmary. Her hope was that he would return to the marriage bed. She was going to be as sweet and as tempting as she knew how.

She got Sarah alone and said to her, "It's time to take off his cuffs."

"It'll never be time for that."

"Do it."

"Miri, it's crazy!"

"Do it."

Sarah went to him. She locked the door behind her, then produced her key.

"Hey," he said.

As she unlocked first the ankle cuffs, then the wrists, he watched her. She did not like his eyes, hadn't liked them from the beginning.

"Well," he said as he rubbed his wrists, "that feels a whole lot better."

She backed away from him as she would from a spreading cobra, with care and sick fear.

He smiled.

She had been made what she was by Miriam. She was thus weak and vulnerable, the victim of inevitable imperfections. But he had been made by nature, and there was something she did not trust about nature. Perhaps it was because of something she had seen in her scientific work, that nature did not appear to be blind. The wildness of nature, the ruthlessness, was the outcome of thought.

Because of this, no matter how tame he seemed, how compliant, how much at ease, she would fear him and hate him. She knew a secret about nature, and she sensed that Paul Ward was an outcome of this secret. Nature, she knew, had a great and terrible mind.

TWENTY

The Love Child

The vampire was partial to him, so he would use that. Every hour that passed, he was closer to the moment when he could kill them all.

She loved him, but they were damn careful anyway. They watched him on video cameras, every move he made, and they kept the infirmary locked. His approach was to go along with it. He didn't even try to get out. He sat up in his bed reading *War and Peace* and listening to endless opera CDs.

He ate lots of rare steak, which had always been his comfort food. Sometimes he asked for Thai cuisine. Everything he was given was beautifully cooked. He wondered if it was also drugged. With the steaks would routinely come bottles of wine worth thousands of dollars. Château Lafite-Rothschild 1945, Château Latour 1936.

He smiled at his captors. He was affable. When Miriam came in, shining and beautiful, he let her kiss him, as much as he could bear. When she put his hand on her belly, which she imagined even now to be a little distended, he would smile at her.

*   *   *

"As much as he hates the Keepers," Sarah said to Miriam, "when he found out what he was, you'd think there would have been more of a reaction."

"Sarah, the man is in love. He's realized that he's one of us. He sees the moral situation. Even his agency sees it. His hate is dying. That's why he's so quiet. It's a very thoughtful time in his life."

"I just think you need to be very damn cautious when you let him out of there."

"Oh, come on. You're too careful."

"I thought you were the one who was too careful, Miri."

"He's my husband and I want him in my bed. I want to have him in me again, Sarah."

"That's unwise. This whole thing is unwise."

"What do you think, Leo?"

"I think he's a really cool looking guy."

On the afternoon of the release, they came down with a cake. They made a party of it with a thirty-year-old Yquem and the Lane cake, made after a sumptuous eighteenth-century recipe, with macerated fruits and cognac. Miriam joked by carrying a cherry to Paul in her mouth. He took it with his teeth and chewed it sensuously.

Miriam gave him the run of the house, all except the attic.

Sarah waited and watched. She tried to enlist Leo, but Leo was little more concerned than Miriam. Leo was a young fool, in Sarah's opinion. Sarah noticed a subtle change in her own personality. A certain realization came upon Sarah that was similar, she thought, to the kind of assumption that comes to dominate a man's mind in a terrible battle. It was the assumption that there would be no escape, that what

Miriam was doing was so foolish that it could not lead to anything but destruction.

How could it be, though, that somebody who had clawed their way through so much life and so much danger to have a baby would, upon becoming pregnant, put at risk both her own life and that of the child?

Miri was a dear and familiar friend. Sarah knew her every mood, the meaning of every expression that flickered in her eyes, had lived with her in deepest intimacy for two decades and more. She knew Miri's fears and her joys, had drawn her to extremes of sexual intensity and observed her with a lover's fascinated dispassion as she lost herself in pleasures. She provided friendship and love and loyalty. But Sarah thought now that they had come to an extreme edge, a strange country of the Keeper mind into which her understanding could not penetrate.

There was only one conclusion to be drawn from her actions: Deeply, profoundly, Miriam wanted to be destroyed as much as the rest of her race did. They had a death wish, otherwise why would beings so brilliant and wise be so easy to kill? The Keepers might not know human science, but they knew the human soul, and that was the key knowledge, what was required to defend yourself.

That they did not defend themselves was, as far as Sarah was concerned, an act of willful self-immolation. They must have recognized this in themselves eons ago, probably as soon as man became intelligent. This was when they began to experiment with melding the two species. They had been trying to escape from their own nature.

Miriam looked forward to feeding, though. She relished her kills, especially the ones that put up an interesting fight.

Every time Miriam stood close to Paul, Sarah waited, her

insides cringing, for the end to come. Didn't she see what he was—a loaded gun, a trap ready to spring?

Eventually, Sarah and Miriam had to feed, and nothing she said could convince Miriam to make her meal of Paul Ward.

So they did it at the Veils. There must be absolutely no chance that Paul would see. At least Miriam agreed to that. So far she had not allowed him back to the club. That, also, meant that she had not yet become a complete fool.

They left Leo with him. Privately, Sarah instructed her to carry the gun, and to never get closer than twenty-five feet to him. If she saw the least sign of his trying to leave the house, or if he tried to come too close to her, or even to use the telephone, she was to blow his brains out.

Sarah hoped that it would happen. They would deal with Miriam's fury. But Miriam threatened Leo—if you kill him, I will kill you. Wound him if you must, but do not kill.

When they came back after taking two Korean businessmen, they had to sleep their deep and helpless sleep.

Sarah told Leo, "If he makes the slightest move toward our bedroom, kill him. No matter what she says."

"But—"

"I'll deal with her! You'll be in no danger."

"Sarah, can you think of any reason *not* to kill him?"

"No."

"What about the fact that Miri loves him?"

"She doesn't know her own mind right now—and her name is Miriam, not Miri."

"You call her Miri."

"And you don't."

Despite the many tensions, life in the household had

returned to something approaching its normal pattern, at least on the surface.

Sarah and Leo managed the Veils. Miriam went occasionally. Paul kept asking to go, and every time he did, Miri was a little more tempted, and Sarah trusted him even less.

She and Miri played their music. Miri began teaching Leo piano, then took her on as a student in a way Sarah had always wanted but had never gotten.

Leo began to receive a classical Keeper education. It began with the Ennead of Ra, the first tier of the Egyptian pantheon of Gods. She started to learn spoken Prime. Sarah doubted Leo's ability to learn the written language, but Miriam was optimistic.

Sarah was surprised that Leo was such a good student. If Miri had wanted a tabula rasa who did not need reeducation because she had nothing to unlearn, she had chosen well. What was amazing to Sarah was that Leo turned out to be a very quick learner. She was actually quite brilliant.

Miriam had picked her out one night at the club with a mere glance. They had been looking for somebody else to blood. They needed more personnel to keep ahead of the burgeoning of their business affairs. Sarah had assumed that they would take a man. But then, almost as an afterthought, Miriam said, "That one." Leo had been in the Japanese garden with some friends, calling on Rudi's skills to get them really, really high.

Slowly, Leo had left her old life behind. Now, all that remained of it was an occasional nervous visit to her parents, and soon even that would end.

Sarah knew that she was being prepared for something, and she came to think that it probably involved her own eventual removal from grace.

So Sarah was waiting for the coming of Leo. She was also waiting for Paul Ward to take whatever action he was planning. She was waiting, in other words, for the end of her world.

When she had been with Eumenes, Miriam had been too young to understand the rarity of happiness. She treasured it now. The overriding reality was that she had a baby in her, her very own baby after all these long years. The trouble was, her husband was turned against himself—a Keeper who had come to hate his own kind. True, he didn't have life eternal and he didn't feed on blood, but he was still a Keeper, and she was still working on him. She longed to draw him into the magic ring of her joy, and she thought that she could. What she was planning was a seduction. Back in the old days, Keeper men had found her hard to resist. She had lost none of her ability to seduce.

But that was all for later. First, there was a door she had to pass through, an essential door. As the days had passed, she had grown steadily more uneasy about it. She'd wanted to roll back the days, to prevent them from dawning. But they did dawn, one and then another, and her baby grew.

Now, Sarah told her, the baby would be sufficiently developed to see. In the way of Keeper mothers, she already knew that she had a son. But what was his condition? It could be that he was deformed. Nobody could be sure what would happen when a Keeper was fertilized by one of these exotics like Paul.

At noon on the appointed day, Sarah came to her. She was in the library teaching Leo. Sarah said, "It's ready." She smiled down at her. These days Sarah was very warm and very grave. There was about her a sadness that Miriam found distressing to be near. Sarah thought that their life together had come to its burnt-out end.

She thought wrong, of course. She must midwife, then become a pediatrician and gynecologist for another species. Sarah thought that Leo was replacing her. She could not understand that Miriam's needs were expanding.

The group of them went down to the infirmary together.

Sarah had bought the very finest new ultrasound machine, so the baby would appear almost as clear as a photograph.

Miriam got up on the examination table. Sarah started the machine, which made a high, whining sound.

"Is it radioactive?" Miriam asked nervously.

"Not at all. It sends out sound waves, then reads the reflections. It's entirely benign, but just to be safe, we'll only use it for a couple of minutes."

Miriam lay waiting, her eyes closed, her body trembling. If it was bad news, she did not think that she had the emotional reserves to bear it. She did not think she could live past the loss of this child, but she didn't know how to die.

She felt the cool instrument sliding on her stomach, which was ever so slightly larger now . . . or was that her imagination?

She put her hand out and Paul took it. They had kissed a few times recently, but he was still being very cool. He wasn't dangerous to her, though, not since he'd understood that he was partly a Keeper. At least, this was her opinion.

"Miri, look."

There on the screen was a ghost. It had a small mouth and tiny, still-unformed hands.

She opened her eyes. She stared at the image on the screen. She always had trouble decoding pictures generated by machines, and at first all she saw were red smears.

"There are the hands," Sarah said, pointing to a slightly less smeary part of the screen.

"Oh, hey," Paul said, "that's my boy."

Miriam still didn't see . . . and then she did. A tiny face swam into focus. "He's—oh, he's *beautiful.*"

Paul asked, "Does he have teeth?"

"His mouth is human," Sarah said.

Miriam felt a tingle of concern. "How will he feed, Sarah?"

"Not like you do." Sarah had tested the blood of the fetus. He was ninety percent Keeper.

"Won't he starve?"

"Miri, he has what look like normal human organs and something close to pure Keeper blood. He's going to live—well, maybe forever."

"As a predator," Paul said.

"I don't see any evidence of that," Sarah replied. "This child has an entirely human mouth and organs."

"How can you tell? It's a tiny embryo."

"I can tell because I'm trained to tell."

"You're a gynecologist?"

"I'm a gerontologist. But you're talking basic medicine."

Paul's face went white. He sucked his cheeks in, a sign in a human being of great rage. Miriam watched him, her heart on a shivering edge. She wanted so to love him, but if he threatened her baby, well, she would have to do what she had to do.

When he spoke, his words were knives. "It's important to me, Sarah."

"I see a human embryo."

"Damned, damned *important!*"

Miriam tried to conceal her smile. In that instant, she had understood something new about Paul Ward.

Leo, fearing his tone, dragged her ever-present pistol out of her belt. "Okay," she said, her gum cracking. She didn't like Paul any more than Sarah did. She wasn't afraid for Miriam, though, not like Sarah was. Her concern was that Paul was a rival for Miriam's interest and affection.

Paul looked at the gun. "Thank you," he said.

Sarah, who had been examining the embryo, was the first to see an extraordinary phenomenon. For some moments, she watched, her attention captured by what she was seeing. She moved her hand back and forth in front of the monitor. She found it difficult to believe what she was seeing.

Sarah was a scientist. She didn't believe in the supernatural. She only half believed in the human soul that Miri was always talking about. "You have souls, we don't." Uh-huh. "You humans are the true immortals." Okay.

But this was something very extraordinary. This was a genuine miracle, unfolding before her scientist's eyes. "Look," she said, her voice gone soft with awe.

Miriam immediately saw that the tiny, unformed eyes, little more than blanks to which the art of seeing had not yet come, were somehow looking straight out of the monitor. It was as if the fetus were staring at them.

"Can he see us? Is that possible?"

"Miriam, I don't know."

Then the eyes flickered again, and they were looking at Paul.

"It's an optical illusion," he said.

But the eyes did not look away. Paul said, "My God." Then he, also, fell silent beneath their eerie gaze.

Miriam's heart seemed to her to open in her chest like a flower. "Our baby is a miracle, Paul," she said.

He smiled the way he always smiled, and that made her sad. Why wasn't he the beaming father he should be? He had a magnificent son. He should be so proud that he could hardly bear it.

Sarah brought the ultrasound examination to a close. Then she presented Miri with her first picture of her child. "His face is aware," Sarah said laconically. "It's impossible, but there it is."

They all gathered around. The photo was detailed. The soft, half-formed face with its black eyes and its slight smile was just luminous.

Miriam drank in the picture. She felt the presence in her belly. Her heart beat with love, her blood flowed with love. And he wouldn't be like her, he wouldn't have to suffer the curse of being a predator. Her son would be great, but he would also be free.

She was not a weeper, but she wept now. Sarah noticed the tears and laid her arm around her shoulder. Miriam did not respond. She wanted Paul to hold her. She wanted him to embrace her and cry and laugh with her, and ask for a copy of the picture for his wallet, to treasure just as she would treasure hers.

Still, he made appropriate noises of admiration, and maybe that was a beginning.

"Let's go upstairs," Miriam said. She took Paul's hand. "I think I'd like us to be alone together."

"Me, too," Paul agreed.

She led Paul into the music room, closed the door. "Do you like my playing?"

"I love your playing."

"Then I'd like to play for you. You know this piece?"

"You've been working on it for weeks."

"Sarah's working. I've known it for three hundred years."

He laughed a little. "It sounds so strange when you say something like that."

She shrugged. "I'm just me." She got her viola out of its

case. She set her bow, tuned the instrument for a moment, then began to play.

Miriam was not completely surprised when Paul launched himself at her.

To see that *thing* grinning at him over the health of the monster in its belly was more than Paul could handle. He knew as he flew toward it that he had snapped, that this was wrong, that he was making a huge mistake.

He slammed into the creature, certain only that he had to stop it from making a sound or the others would come in and he would die. Even though they were human, the other two wanted to kill him a lot more than the vampire did; he was certain of that. They would blow him to pieces without hesitation.

It was smaller than he was. But for all its grace and beauty, it had even denser bones. So it was the heavier of the two. It staggered with his weight, but absorbed the blow.

He clapped his hand over its mouth. Its steel-strong arm came up and grabbed his wrist. They fought a silent battle, strength against strength.

He locked his elbow, tightened his muscles. The two of them twisted and turned, falling against the piano, then against the chair where it had been sitting. Its viola crunched and twanged beneath their slow dance. Paul caught the instrument with his shoe, purposely driving his heel into its body, making certain that what the creature loved was destroyed.

Its free hand came between his legs. It got a grip on his balls and began crushing them. They compressed harder and harder, until his deep guts were awash in pain. He used breathing techniques he'd learned in the war to try to control the pain. But he could not control the pain; the pain was astounding.

He started to lose the use of his legs, began to buckle.

Then he got his teeth into the flesh of its neck—its own favorite place. Too bad he couldn't suck its blood. He bit, grinding down with all his might, his incisors ripping into the hard muscles.

Check.

They broke away.

He waited for it to call to its people. He waited to die.

It stared at him. He stared back. It did not call anybody. They began to circle, and while they circled, he wondered why not . . . and because he did not know, he began to get scared.

It turned its head to one side, lowered it, and looked at him out of the side of its eyes. He knew that it was made up, that it didn't really have those perfect lips or those beautiful, soft eyes, but he could not help reacting to it as if it were the most wonderful woman he'd ever known.

Why didn't it call out? Was it here to die, or what?

He leaped at it again. He grabbed its throat, preparing to give it the most fearsome uppercut he could manage. He would stun it; then he would take the shattered neck of the viola and rip out its throat with it.

It stopped the uppercut in the palm of an iron hand. Then, very suddenly, his own hands were trapped at his sides. It was riding him, using its knees to pin his arms. It smashed its fists into his chest, using him like a punching bag. He toppled back, his chest wound making him cough hard.

It lay on him full length. He felt its weight, felt its vagina pressing hard against his penis. He fought to free his arms, but he couldn't. This was a death grip.

Its head came up; its lips contacted his neck. He threw himself from side to side, but it was no use. The creature's mouth locked onto his neck.

He could feel the tongue then, probing against his skin. At the same time, its wriggling, squirming body brought him to sexual life. His erection grew until it felt as though it would rip out of his pants. Faster it rubbed back and forth, harder it drove into his neck.

This was the death they gave their victims—an evil sexual charge and then the penetration—and he felt it—the cold, slim needle that was normally enclosed deep inside the tongue—as it came out and pricked delicately against his skin, seeking the vibration of the humming artery.

As it penetrated, the delicate, persistent pain made him gargle miserably. He was as stiff as a steel rod, its haunches were pumping, but he could also feel his blood sliding out of his neck, leaving him breathless and faint.

This was death by vampire, what his father had known.

And then, suddenly, it was on its feet. The lens was gone from one of its eyes, and it glared at him out of one red eye and one ash-gray one. Its face was smeared, the prosthetics gone from one sunken cheek. Along its lips was a foam of blood—his blood.

He was too exhausted to move a muscle. He could only watch as it opened his pants and sat on him. He felt himself being inserted into its vagina, and he struggled to prevent that, but he could not prevent it.

The creature raped him. There was no other way to describe what was done. What was worse—more humiliating, more angering—was that the sensation was not like the dull, empty horror of a true rape. There was something else there, another emotion, one that he did not want but could not deny.

It wasn't only that she was incredibly beautiful, even without her makeup—maybe more so without it. It was that she just *felt so right*. That was the reality of it. In her makeup or out of her makeup, she was the most wonderful woman he had ever been with.

He realized that he had been tricked into making his move. This was no battle to the death. It was a damn seduction!

And, oh, my, but it was a good one—so smart, so deeply knowledgeable of Paul Ward. It made his very soul ache to see her trying so hard to win him and to love him through his hate, to draw him to her side and the side of their son.

She stopped. He realized that he had climaxed, but also that she had taken a lot of blood out of him, so much that he was surprised that he still conscious, let alone capable of coitus. But she knew the human body with incredible precision. The borderland between life and death was where she was most comfortable.

"So," she said as she got off him, "what do we call him? I think it ought to be Paul. Paul Ward, Jr." She smiled the smile of a sultry Venus, the most amazing expression in the most amazing face he had ever seen. "Agreed?"

She lifted him to his shuffling feet and led him through the house in triumph. They had to help him, but he went upstairs. He went into her bedroom—their bedroom—and fell upon their bed.

"It's only a quart," she said. He'd tasted lovely. It had been hard to stop. "You're not *that* weak."

His eyes almost twinkled, and he seemed to revive himself. "Okay," he said, "maybe you're right. So let's finish this in bed."

She was heavy, just like him, and lean and strong . . . but

also soft, soft in wonderful ways that seemed to fit him just about perfectly.

She lay in his arms, gazing at him with such adoration that he almost wanted to laugh from the pleasure it gave him. All the love and tenderness that he had been trying to suppress, that were part of his nature and one with their bonded spirits, now blossomed forth in him.

"I never will leave you," he said.

"I never will leave you."

This, he felt, was their marriage vow. "You're my wife," he said.

"My husband."

Leo and Sarah, who had come with them, now withdrew from the room. "I think she made it," Leo said.

Sarah just shook her head.

When they had been in bed together for a little time, however, she felt it her duty to be sure that they were entirely comfortable . . . and that all was indeed well.

Miriam gave her a very large smile, her lovely face almost buried beneath Paul's big, plunging back.

Sarah laid her hand on Paul's shoulder. Then she went softly out and closed the door.

Paul finished, a second time within just a few minutes and with a lot of blood lost. He sank down upon her, then slid into the softness of the bed.

What had he done? He'd capitulated. Maybe it was the damn blood loss, maybe it was the brilliance of her seduction by violence, maybe it was the staring eyes of the baby—but one thing was certain: He was not going to kill this vampire.

She lay beside him as still as still water, her eyes closed, upon her face a narrow smile. He slipped his hand into hers, and she made a startlingly catlike purring sound.

It was while she was purring that he heard another sound, very soft indeed. Curious as to the origin of this very slight thud, he turned his head and looked toward Sarah's office.

As if by magic, the door came slowly open. First he saw a blond head, then a pale face in the gloom of the curtained bedroom. A small figure came in, moving quickly, almost as catlike as Miriam herself.

What the hell? It looked like Peter Pan. As much as his mind wanted to believe that it was part of a dream, he had to face the fact that it was real. He stared. It came, catlike, closer to the bed.

It was small but it seemed extremely dangerous. Paul's struggling heart started to struggle harder. He did not understand. There was nobody else in the house, and they were incredibly careful about that.

When the figure reached the bedside, he almost leaped out of his skin with surprise. It was Becky. Cocking her head, she gave him a look that said, *Naughty boy,* and the slightest of smiles traveled across her face.

In that instant—seeing her so unexpectedly—Paul came back to himself. It was a homecoming to see her. His very soul rejoiced. She reached out and touched his cheek, and he was so incredibly glad that he would have cried if he hadn't been such a tough sonofabitch.

She smiled, then, more broadly. She pointed a finger at the vampire and mouthed, "Bang bang."

Paul nodded.

Miriam burst out of the bed, leaping almost to the ceiling. She came flying across Paul and tackled Becky, who was sent crashing all the way back into the office, where her rope still hung from the open skylight.

Paul wasn't as fast, but Becky recovered herself. She dragged out a pistol—and it wasn't a damned magnum. It was one of the French babies. Good! This thing was going to be decided at last.

Miriam snarled when she saw it. She snarled, and then she backed away. In two lithe steps, she was beside him. "Shoot us," she said. She knew damn well how it worked. It was meant to clear a room. Becky could not kill Miriam without killing Paul.

"Hey, Beck," Paul said aloud.

"I thought we were a thing, you prick!"

The natural goodness of a love like that was fresh water in a desert that Paul had not even realized was dry. "Becky," he said, "oh, Christ—"

"Men. They're all the same," Miriam said. She had that little smile on her face that was always there when she felt in control of a situation.

"She's an ugly cuss, Paul! Jesus, you must be drugged or something, man!"

"Becky, I thought you were with Bocage. I thought—"

"We're here for you, Paul. All of us that are left."

"What about Justin?"

"Screw him. And screw the Company."

"They take an enlightened approach, it would seem," Miriam said.

Why in hell was she so calm? What did she know? "Be careful, Becky."

"Oh, yeah. Look, Mrs. Blaylock, we've got this place surrounded. We've got video of one of your little helpers committing a murder. And we've got you."

"You won't kill Paul."

Becky's face changed. It grew as hard as stone. Nothing

needed to be said. Miriam took Paul by the arm and began to back out of the room.

Becky stalked forward, bracing the gun. "Shoot, girl," Paul said.

Miriam backed them up another step. Becky came forward. "I love you, Paul," she said.

"Me too, baby." And his heart told him—it's true, it's always been true. He wanted her. He wanted normal human love, and that was what she had to offer. By the God in heaven, he wanted her.

She closed her eyes. He saw tears. He knew that he was about to die at the hands of the only normal human woman who had ever loved him, before he had even damn well kissed her.

So he made a move. Why the hell not? Might as well attempt the impossible. What he did was to leap toward Becky, hoping that Miriam wouldn't expect that.

He was free, falling toward her. Becky danced aside. And suddenly he was behind her.

The two women faced each other. Miriam covered her belly with her hands. Miriam screamed. It was the most terrible, bloodcurdling wail of despair Paul had ever heard.

The bedroom door burst open, and Sarah and Leo piled in behind her, both of them bracing Magnums. Paul recognized a standoff. He also recognized a situation that wasn't going to last more than a few seconds.

"We're gonna get 'em all," he murmured to Becky.

In the same instant that she squeezed the trigger, a desperate Miriam used her great speed to leap into her face. Instinct made her raise the weapon—and the blast went crashing into the trompe l'oeil ceiling, which came crashing down in sky-painted chunks, filling the room with dust.

Becky was hurled all the way back against the far wall of the office. She hit the wall with a resounding slap. But she was Becky, she was no ordinary girl, and she came back immediately.

Paul had the gun. Behind Miriam, Sarah and Leo were getting ready to open fire. He started to squeeze off the shot that would reduce them all to pulp.

Then his finger stopped squeezing. He stood, agonizing. "Pull it," Becky shouted, *"pull the damn trigger!"*

The clock ticked. Sarah Roberts began moving slowly to the left, sliding like a shadow. He saw her plan: she was going to throw herself between them, try to absorb the shot.

"Pull it!"

"Please, Paul," Miriam said.

He stood there like a pillar, and pillars cannot move, they cannot pull triggers. He saw not Miriam, but his baby, the little half-made child who had maybe looked at him.

In all his years of killing, he had never killed a baby, and now he found that this was his limit. This was the one murder he could not commit.

His mind searched for a way to let his heart win. And his mind spoke to him in the voice of his father . . . or maybe it was his father's real spirit there, giving his son the guidance that he needed: "If you kill that child," his father's voice said to him, "my life and my death and all the suffering of our family will have been for nothing."

All those thousands of years of struggle on the earth—the slow evolution of the apes, the coming of the Keepers with their breeding and their feeding and their tremendous acceleration of human evolution—all of it had led to this moment, to the burning, unanswerable moral question of the mother, and to the baby.

"Gimme that gun," Becky said.

He did it. He gave it to her. As he did so, Sarah Roberts came forward. Her face was white, her eyes were huge. She loomed up, pointing her own weapon. With the clarity that comes to men at moments of great extreme, Paul saw a tear come out of her left eye and start down her cheek. And then her magnum roared and Becky's pistol roared, and the room was choked with dust and debris.

Silence followed, and in it the improbable bonging of a distant clock. Before them lay the shattered remains of Sarah Roberts.

Becky looked down, then stepped quickly across the blood-soaked corpse.

The other two were nowhere to be seen. Paul and Becky followed them out and downstairs, saw them as they were disappearing into a pantry.

There was a brick tunnel leading deep. "Know where it goes?"

"Nope."

"Shit. And there's no map?"

"No map."

"Then we've lost it."

"Temporarily. It ain't over till it's over, girl."

She dropped her gun to her side. "That one really got to you," she said.

He looked down the dark tunnel where the monster that carried his son had taken him. "Or ever the silver cord be loosed, or the golden bowl be broken . . . then the dust shall return to the earth as it was."

"Okay."

They were silent together. Paul could feel the cord that linked him to his boy, feel it unwinding into the void.

"That's the last one," Becky said.

"The last vampire? Are you sure?"

"They're cleaned out. All of them."

"Even here in the U.S?"

She nodded. "Bocage is almost as good as you."

He felt her hand in his, her strong, good hand. "Becky?"

"Yeah?"

"How the hell did you get in here?"

"They got a lotta skylights in this dump, boss."

He threw his arms around her. When he kissed her at last, he immediately found what he'd lost hope of ever finding, which was his heart's true happiness. This was where he belonged, in the arms of this wonderful, normal, completely human woman.

They left the house, leaving the maggots or the police to deal with the corpse upstairs. As far as the vampire and its helper were concerned, they would be found. Their time would come.

But not until his son was born, no way. Not until then.

"What's your opinion on kids?"

"Kids're okay."

"You could raise a kid?"

She looked at him. "Married to you I could."

"Married to me."

About the Author

WHITLEY STRIEBER is the #1 bestselling author of the landmark horror novels *The Hunger* and *The Wolfen*, and the million-copy bestsellers *Communion, Transformation*, and *Confirmation*. He is the coauthor, with radio talk-show host Art Bell, of the *New York Times* bestseller *The Coming Global Superstorm*, published by Pocket Books. His newest novel is *Lilith's Dream: A Tale of the Vampire Life*. Visit www.unknowncountry.com.

ATRIA BOOKS
PROUDLY PRESENTS

LILITH'S DREAM

Whitley Strieber

Now available in hardcover
from Atria Books

Turn the page for a preview of
Lilith's Dream. . . .

Lilith's eyes focused, then focused again, until the firmament revealed its wonders to her. The reefs of stars became a jeweled host as she began to perceive each individual strand of light. As the rays entered her eyes, each sent its own message to her heart.

She could not keep from singing, and she raised her voice in the long, rich tones of her kind, a shimmering regiment of notes like the deep songs of the whale and the wind. The jackals laughed and yapped, and when she stopped, she heard them rutting again.

Motionless, she waited for them to return to their task of guiding her. Her stillness was as precise as her movement. Indeed, she was so still that a cruising owl used her as a perch, hooted twice, then swept back into the sky, its wings trembling the silent air. She thought nothing of this, she who had slept upon the desert reaches in the company of lions, and, in her youth, swum the crystal waters off the point now called Aden, singing until the whales rose from the dark ocean.

She walked steadily and precisely, as silently as the jackals, a shadow in the shadows of the night. But for her skin glowing pale beneath the hood and her eyes gleaming with a tiger's shine, she revealed nothing of herself to the world around her.

Long before she came upon a Bedouin camp, she knew that it was there. Ten leagues away, she spread her nostrils and drew in the scent of blood and cooked meat and dates, and the scintillating odor of human skin. She lived as much by scent as sight, and it was one of her favorite smells. They liked to be kissed, which was a matter of indifference to her. But she would kiss them to smell them. She knew the different ways each part of the human body smelled, and enjoyed it all.

Romans bathed and slicked themselves with oil. So these were not Romans. She lengthened her stride. The jackals scampered ahead of her, then stationed themselves on a tall outcropping, their forms dark against the sky glow. She moved directly toward them, knowing that the village or camp of the humans would be in their sight.

She caught the sweet, milky scent of young children, and the odor of men with sweat in their hair. Also, now, the musk of the women, of whom there were three young and two old. She went closer, rising to the point on which the jackals stood.

As she approached, they melted away. She looked down into the top of a canyon. There were three pinpricks of light lost down there in the darkness—cook fires.

Then she noticed something odd. On the far horizon, just where the afterglow of the set sun marked the horizon, there were lights moving back and forth. She listened. Below, she heard expected sounds—soft adult voices and the sharper cries of children, the rattle of flames and the hiss of cookpans—human sounds no different from any others. But the horizon offered a different noise. What was it, though? It was extremely faint, perhaps thirty or forty leagues away. Not growling, not a living creature. What, then? She could not place that noise. Almost, the rumbling of wagon wheels. Almost, the running of a waterfall. Almost, but not quite, either of those things.

She could make a nice meal down in the campsite, but her instinct was not to take even the smallest chance. Far better to do it in a back alley, to some social cull, than to cut out a paterfamilias or a valuable slave, and cause the others to rush from the nest barking and waving torches.

What would they do if a noble came walking out of the dark of the night? They would think her a goddess, no doubt of it. That would be well. She would prevail upon their transport, and they would relate to their grandchildren the story of the deity they had conducted to town.

When she started down the mountainside, the male

jackal yapped three times. She stopped, confused and amazed. Why, in a setting that offered absolutely no threat, would it sound warning? Had she missed something?

She drew in scent. Nothing but the peace of the cook-fire and the fragrance of the bodies. She listened. The voices were as calm as the night.

She continued on. Again, Anubis sounded warning. Again, she stopped, and again detected nothing. The moon rose above the mountains behind her.

Soon, she was close enough to see the creatures moving about. They were all heavily clothed, and so prosperous enough to afford ample cloth. Could they be Sumerian merchants, then? They had far more linen to weave than Egyptian peasants, and wore long robes to announce their wealth. She might take a Sumerian merchant, who had far to go before he could raise an alarm. Or maybe they were travelers from the land of Punt, far to the south.

The women were covered all over, even their faces. Now, this stopped her. It was strange. But no, when she'd gone to examine the Englishmen, she'd seen such. Yes, they must be Egyptians living in this new fashion. The Egyptians were thriving, to have this much cloth. Even the children wore blue leggings and white shirts imprinted with letters and designs.

She came to the edge of their firelight. They were playing on an instrument and singing, watching their fire with sleepy eyes. She could wait until they were in their hutches, then creep in and take one by stealth. Or she could simply rush in and grab one so quickly that the others would be unable to follow. Still, it would be best to do it the safe way.

She walked into the camp. For a moment, they did nothing. Then the one with the musical instrument stopped playing it. The children became quiet. She stood before their fire and said, in Egyptian, "Carry me to Thebes."

One looked to the other. A smooth boy went against its father's hip. She repeated her demand. It was obvious, though, that they did not understand her. She switched to English. "Take me to your city."

Still no reaction. She could speak many human languages from many different times: Prakrit, Ogham, Vitelieu, Akkadian, Egyptian, Greek, Latin, French, Russian, Chinese, Farsi, and Deutsch were just a few. In each, she had a few hundred words and could easily absorb more. She tried the next logical choice, which was Arabic. "Please convey me to your city. God is good."

"We are wanderers, by the mercy of God."

"Then to the Romans. Take me to the Romans."

They glanced at one another, muttering. Finally, the oldest one spoke, a creature with a white twist of beard and a dirty cloth turban. "Do you mean those ruins in the Abu Ma'mmal? Are you a tourist?"

Some of the words passed her by. "I am a traveler," she said. She drew back her hood. The men all gasped. Their eyes opened wide. Behind their veils, the women did the same. The children went into defensive postures, clinging to the adults. Two of the men began backing on their haunches, slipping away from the firelight.

A sour whiff of fear told her that she had only seconds to deal with this unexpected situation. She had bred man not to fear her, but these certainly did. She opened her hands, palms out. "I am in need of your help."

A woman said, "It's a djin. A djin of the night."

The elder man raised his own hand in a gesture of dismissal toward the woman who had spoken. "God willing, would you take some tea?"

She came closer to them, then went down on her own haunches, her superb clothing whispering around her as she dropped. "It would be my pleasure, sir."

It had been a long time since she had done this, but she found herself enjoying the company of her creatures more than she had expected. Really, now that she thought of it, she'd been tucked away in her cave much too long. Here, beside an open fire, beneath the crystal of the moon, surrounded by the jackals and the sailing nightbirds, this was the life.

The old one came close to her, his eyes down, his poor hands trembling so much that he almost spilled the tea. She watched the veins of his neck throb. They were a little caked inside, and would offer a hesitant draw. With this one, she'd go straight to the main artery and with a single heave of her belly dry him to dust.

Laughing easily, she took the tea. "Thank you."

"May God be with you."

As she sipped her tea, the tension among them continue to rise. The children and women had repaired to their tent, and could be heard speaking softly together. A little boy was whispering, "It is a rich djin, look at the gold!" A female replied, "It is an American."

That was a word she did not know. She made a note to discover its meaning.

Taking tea with her were four males. From their eyes, she could see that they found her beauty hypnotic. Her spell was coming down upon them as swiftly as the dew that falls before dawn.

She noticed, however, that they were moving themselves about, maneuvering so that her way was blocked except directly behind her, which would take her into their tent. Within, there was rustling. An ambush? She said, "How may I get to Thebes?"

The old man nodded toward the west. "The road is there. You can get the bus to Cairo. There's tours to Thebes." There was another unknown word for her list, 'bus.' "A few kilometers."

There was no road off in that direction, she knew quite well. If she walked west, she would go many leagues before she reached the Nile, a journey that would kill a human. Perhaps they were trying to trick her to go off into the desert, with the intention of following her and attacking her.

If they did, she would take them all. She'd bloat like a tick, but she wouldn't need to eat again for quite a time. Her tongue was stiffening with eagerness when she heard a distant and very surprising noise: a clanking sound, followed in a moment by clattering that quickly became continuous.

"My cousin comes," the elder said. "He will take you

in his car as far as el Maadi. There you can take an East Delta bus into Cairo. Is your hotel there?"

She had understood some of it. His "cousin" would be a blood relative. But the rest-whatever did he mean? How was it that there were so many new words in the language of Arabic, in just—what—oh, it couldn't have been more than a hundred years or so.

Of a sudden, the clanking sound became louder. There was a rhythm to it, and seemed to be moving faster than was natural.

All the animals that had been lingering about her in the shadows hustled away. To the west, she saw a glow. She had no idea even how to ask a question about it, so she remained silent. In what seemed like just a moment, it became enormous and burst over the edge of a nearby hill. The light was accompanied by a terrific roar and an odor of some sort of bizarre fire.

Forgetting all of her careful poise, Lilith jumped up, cried out, and scrambled into the tent. She tripped over a child and went sprawling, her cloak settling around her as the great light swept across the thin fabric walls.

Then it went out. A moment later, the noise faded, and with it, but more slowly, the odor.

"God be with you," a male cried cheerfully. "You have a lost American! What beautiful good fortune for us, my brothers!"

"She speaks Arabic," one of the young men murmured.

"Well, all the better, may God be pleased! My dear lady, come forth, would it please you."

She stepped from the tent. There was a carriage visible in the light of the fire. It had obviously come far, for it was covered with dust. It was also the source of the odor of fire. There was not the faintest scent of a horse, or sound of one, or sight of one.

Very well. It was a puzzle that would be solved.

"Look, I can take you for twenty pounds. Do you have a cell? Is there somebody to call? What hotel are you in?"

None of the questions were sensible. In fact, only the inflection told her that they *were* questions. "All is well," she said. "May I go now into the carriage?"

"She talks like an old movie," the cousin said. "What kind of Arabic is that?"

"It's her way. But look at that costume. She must be a rich one."

The cousin gave her a long, frank stare. "You are pale," he said, after his appraisal was over.

"I have not been much in the sun, in these past years."

"Hey, Abi, I have to get that line up tonight or the boss'll be on my ass. The fatties don't get their air conditioners at the monastery until I do."

"How many fatties?"

"A bunch. Big busload. First-class extra and a bit."

"Tips if we go to be pictured?"

The cousin nodded. "Borrow that camel from Duli. You'll get nice money. But be late. They'll not be up with the sun." He laughed, then, through gaps in his teeth.

"Lady, we go now."

How interesting this would be, to go in a carriage without a horse. Did he pull it himself? Roman boys played at war, making their slaves pull their baby chariots about in the peristyles of their houses. But a human being was not strong enough to pull a heavy conveyance like this carriage. It had two rows of seats within, and four doors, and seemed at once dirty and beautiful. It also had wide, small wheels that would make it quite impossible in the sand, even for somebody much stronger than a human being.

She got into the thing, seating herself behind a circular rail, placing her hands firmly around it. She detested the bouncing of carriages, and there was always the threat of the ditch.

"She can't drive," the cousin said.

"The American thinks the Arab cannot drive, my cousin. She is afraid of your foolish ways."

She heard this. How dare they consider her a drover. "I'll not drive," she said.

There was a silence from without. The men grouped together at the back of the machine. As low as they whispered, she could hear them with ease.

"I tell you, it's a djin."

"There are no djin, no more than your foolish god who never—"

"No, no, Allah be praised, go with God. Look at her! Look, she looks like some kind of a—what is it? Marble. A woman made of marble. It's horrifying."

"I see money. Twenty pounds for ten kilometers, and she says not a word! I'm going."

"Cousin, I would not go out into the night with that thing."

But he went.

　　　　•　　•　　•

Leonore Patterson looked down at the steak that her servant set on the coffee table before her. She cut into it and watched the blood come out in runnels, then spread in intricate rivers across the bright white china plate. She touched one of them, then brought the tips of her fingers to her lips. Memory.

She wanted to get high and drunk both, anything but feel what she was feeling right now. Compared to this addiction, alcoholism was baby stuff and drug problems were child's play. No, no, this was what you could safely call the big time.

She didn't want to, but she left the room. She left the apartment without eating. There was only one food that would work now, no matter how little she wanted to consume it. But there was no choice, and she went out into the streets, out along the blowing, shadowy side streets and into the broader reaches of Third Avenue.

It was not long before she came to what she expected, a lonely man looking for some kind of love. When she smiled at him, he nodded sharply, telegraphing that he wasn't to be taken for granted. He was a man to be bargained with.

His eyes met hers, flickered away. So he wanted a kink. He was out looking for something odd. Fine, she'd done it all five times over. Guys looking for anonymous sex weren't generally interested in the missionary position. He offered her a weak smile.

"Look, honey, you want a date or not?"

"What're you—uh—"

"It's a date. Whatever you want."

"Uh, I, you know, it's just ordinary."

"C'mere." She put her arms on his shoulders, smiled up at him. "Now nobody can hear us but us." She met his eyes. "Honey, you look like you lost your mommy."

"Maybe that's what happened. I did. You know, what about the, sort of, that I'm—I have a big job. A lot of people work for me. I spend my life giving orders and my wife, she's not—she can't . . . she just can't."

She took his hand. "You just forget it, okay. Okay? 'Cause I know what we're gonna do."

"You do?"

"Baby, don't you worry. You found the right girl. It's lucky. I'm looking for it. I love it. So just—here, come on, don't you pull away now, honey." She took him by the wrist and led him toward the old house, the place where she had found her miracle and lost her humanity. She didn't actually enter it often, not unless she had to.

When he entered, she immediately pushed the door closed. He could not know that there was now no way for him to get out, not through that or any door or any window, not without her keys and her knowledge of these intricate locks. No matter who he was or what he was, a dead man now stood before her.

He smiled, revealing neatly kept teeth. "Well, wow," he said. "Wow."

"It's very old."

"This is—I don't know, you're just a little girl and this place—is this your folks' house? I don't know."

"What's the game, honey? We can't do it if you don't say it."

He remained silent.

She sat down on the bed, drew him down beside her. Then she saw that his face had changed, that he was not a sweating, nervous fool anymore, that there was something acute in his eyes. His hands, which had seemed as soft and loathsome as the rest of this bloated maggot, came around her throat, and proved to be not at all maggoty. No, the pudgy fingers concealed iron.

"Fuckin' cunt," he snarled.

"You're killing me!"

"So. The fuck. What?"

She writhed. He was strong, damnit, real strong. "You're a—"

He smiled, thrust against her. "You're number twenty-one, filth! You goddamn fuckin' piece o' shit, in this nice house, how dare you. How dare you!"

As his fingers jabbed deeper and her windpipe threatened to collapse, her mind registered the truth: she had picked up a serial killer. He was strong, too. He was very strong. He was humping her, not entering her but thrusting against her as he killed her.

Incredibly, she was actually in trouble with this guy.

She lay still, and in his eagerness he shifted just a bit. This gave her the chance to use her hidden strength, and she exploded out from under him. He flew up and back and landed with a thud that shook the house.

The vampire blood made you strong. It made you much stronger than anybody thought you would be.

Snarling with surprise, shaking his head in confusion, he leaped at her. Her hands shot up as quick as the flicker of a falcon's wing and took his wrists in a grip that he would not be able to break.

His eyes bulged with the effort. He growled and shook and struggled until purple veins throbbed in his delicious neck. She watched, waiting until he bent down, preparing to throw himself back away from her. Then her knee came up and connected with his face. Howling, his teeth bared, he flew back ten feet into the wall, which his head hit with a sound like an egg cracking. As he sank down, she took handcuffs out from under the bed and snapped them around his wrists.

She marched the astonished, spent man straight down to the basement and hooked the cuffs to an eye in the wall.

LaVergne, TN USA
28 March 2010
177334LV00001B/2/P